After Anderson

Aftermath of a Tragedy

Jamila Mikhail

Keep Your Good Heart
Ottawa, Canada

Copyright © 2019 Jamila Mikhail

Keep Your Good Heart

Ottawa, Canada

ISBN: 978-1-7753089-2-8

Visit www.jamilamikhail.com for contact information or write to jamilamikhail@email.com for inquires.

This is a work of fiction. Names, characters, businesses, places, events and incidents are either the products of the author's imagination or used in a fictitious manner. Any resemblance to actual persons, living or dead, or actual events is purely coincidental.

To all the Andersons of this world, their victims, and those left behind to pick up the pieces...

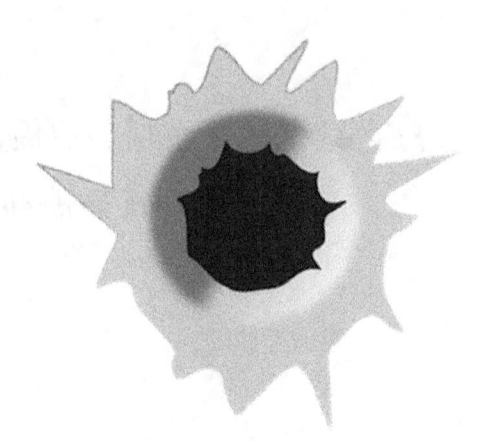

CONTENTS

CONTENT WARNING

This book contains mature content that may be disturbing and offensive to some readers including a graphic scene of a school shooting and mentions of violence, sexual assault and self-mutilation. This work of fiction is solely meant to be a cautionary tale and great care has been taken to be as respectful as possible when dealing with sensitive and controversial topics.

If you or someone you know is dealing with anxiety and depression following a trauma, other mental health issues or suicidal or homicidal thoughts there exists many resources that will allow you to begin to heal and move forward without causing another tragedy.

Log on to https://www.jamilamikhail.com/after-anderson.html for a periodically-updated list of resources to help you take that first step towards reclaiming your life, or stopping someone else from destroying theirs. For immediate help call your local emergency number.

ACKNOWLEDGMENTS

For this project I wish to thank my cats Squeaker and Carling for forgiving me after I ignored them because I was too busy writing, for being my moral support when things got emotional and for overall being a cat lady's dream come true.

Secondly, I owe an endless amount of gratitude to my production team, notably the fabulous ladies who produced my audiobooks, and those who've helped me put things together behind the scenes. You know who you are and I look forward to collaborating again in the future!

I also want to thank Duane, Dave and Katharina, the three greatest friends I've ever had. You have each supported me (and put up with me) no matter what I've chosen to do. This third book of mine wouldn't have been possible without you.

Last but not least, a big thanks is in order to my many loyal fans and readers who make being a writer possible. Since my very first book you have all been there and that means a lot to me considering that you could have picked any other book!

I

DÉJÀ VU

It had been almost two years since I'd last walked down those halls. They were all still the same, nothing had changed. The dark green floor was still the same, just like everything else. I imagined that it was only green instead of another generic colour to imitate green marble, since actual green marble was way too expensive for the school's budget. Black and burgundy covered the walls, just like the last time I'd set foot in that hallway. I had even helped paint the far north hallway on the top floor after class during my freshman year. Nothing in that area had changed.

The east and central hallways on the top floor had been completely renovated though, and the bright white paint and grey tiles made for a stark contrast with the other half of the school. New lockers were neatly lined up along one wall and brand new windows on the other. The new lockers were blue and much wider than the old grey ones still left in other parts of the school. That building had barely been renovated since my mother had attended when she was my age.

Until Anderson.

The principal had a new office and the secretary's office was merged with it in the same room since their old offices had been destroyed. Mr. Pasquale was still the principal but the school had a new secretary since the previous one hadn't been able to return. I had liked

Mrs. Elgin quite a lot and it was shame that she had to be replaced. The new secretary and I share the same name: Alyson.

She was a very short woman, not even five feet tall. She had more than a few extra pounds in her tight plaid dress that I thought was inappropriate for a woman her age but she wore a beautiful smile on her face and politely greeted me when I walked into her office. She wore her chocolate brown hair in a bob and had pale green eyes popping out of her head. She was in her early fifties but still dressed like a preppy teenager in expensive clothes that she probably couldn't afford since she still drove a 1982 Ford truck that had seen better days.

Ms. Alyson handed me my class schedule along with some other paperwork and my locker combination on a little sticky note. I ended up with #347 which was one of those new lockers in the hallway with the new windows. It was a lot nicer than my old #501 that I'd had to put up with at the end of the south hallway for over two years, but I would have given anything just to have everything back the way it was before.

I exited her office and sat down on the side of the window and looked outside for a brief moment at the cars down in the parking lot below before taking out my notebook to write a little bit in an attempt to clear my head since I hadn't expected to react so negatively to my first day back to school.

Dear Anderson,

I want things back to the way they were before. It's so weird to be back here. You'd think that after almost two years things would be different, but they aren't. Well, yeah, they are, in a way I guess. I feel like an alien inside my own body. Is that weird? You wouldn't know anything about that, would you? You're dead. None of his bothers you, does it? Do you have any regrets wherever the hell you are now? You probably don't, because you're dead. I don't know what's wrong with me, but you sure messed things up for me Anderson. I'm sorry I wasted your time.

Alyson

I let my head rest against the cold glass of the window as I thought back to a happier time. I remembered when I first arrived at the largest high school in town from my small elementary school and got lost a few times in the building. On one particular occasion I was walking down the hallway when the fire alarm rang as part of the drills we had to do at the beginning of each semester and I couldn't find the door to the nearest stairwell to go outside so I stood in the window and waved at the students in the street down below.

On another occasion I got lost on my way to the bathroom and a teacher had to come looking for me. For a long time I didn't venture out by myself until the administration finally decided to put up maps of the school at every hallway intersection. The only area of the school I had never been to was the basement. There was just something eerie about that basement.

I got off the side of the window and turned around to see who was behind me. It was Jennifer Lyell, a girl I used to tutor in Spanish class. She was just a year younger than me and was having a hard time and since Spanish was one of my best subjects, I was assigned to tutor her and as a reward, my time with her counted as community service hours that were required to be performed by each student in order to graduate. I had all forty of them, but hadn't graduated. Growing up I'd had this grand vision of my future self but all of that had been taken away.

"I didn't mean to startle you," Jennifer apologized, "is everything alright?"

"Yeah," I muttered in an absent-minded tone of voice, "I was just taking a free trip to the moon there."

We both laughed at once. Jenny and I had become great friends after spending hours with each other, trying to get her to speak Spanish. She was this cute seventeen-year-old with bright red hair and bright green eyes. She somewhat looked like she could have been Ms. Alyson's daughter, only that Jenny wore shape and age-appropriate clothing. I always liked her alternative lifestyle and free spirit. She wasn't rebellious but she didn't let others tell her how things should be.

I greatly admired her for that since I was a victim of cliques and stereotypes. I didn't always have fancy or expensive clothes but I always made sure to dress as nicely as I could and to still by stylish. Jennifer had always thought that I was the pretty one between the two of us while I'd always believed it to be her! I was tall and slim with long caramel hair that went down to my shoulders. I had naturally curly hair but I preferred to wear it straight. I thought it complemented me more.

"I haven't seen you in a long time," Jennifer whispered to me in a concerned tone of voice.

"I know," I softly replied as I hugged her, "I've missed you a lot. How have you been holding up?"

"I still can't speak Spanish, they still call me fat and Josh and I are still together!"

"That's wonderful! I know how much you two love each other and I can tutor you girl, you know that, always."

"Thanks Aly, but I decided to switch to French this semester. I've completely given up on Spanish, but they say that the two languages are similar so we'll see how I like that."

"Oh! I've signed up for French too! We can sit next to each other in class if you want! I've also given up on Spanish because after everything it sort've leaves a bitter taste in my mouth."

"I completely understand Aly, and I would love to sit next to you!"

"Then that's a deal!"

It was going to be awkward for me being an almost nineteen-year-old young woman in class with students that were only sixteen and seventeen. I felt as though they still had their youth and their innocence while I'd matured too much. Sure, there were students even older than me, but that didn't change that inexplicable corruption I felt inside. I felt as though my youth and my carefree spirit were gone forever.

I knew that most of the students I'd be with in class wouldn't be immature, in fact, most of them were probably very mature but that gap between our lives would certainly make things awkward at times. It would be especially awkward for me since I barely knew any of the people at school anymore. All of the people I'd been friends with had either long since graduated, or passed away, to the exception of Jen. I had a few other friends outside of school, but that was the problem, they were *outside* of school. They were far away, out of my reach.

"In French class we can still sit in trios like we did before," Jen told me, "you know on those really long tables with the wheels. They also have new smaller tables where we can sit two by two. It's your call if you want to have someone else sitting with us but if not I'd like to sit next to the Petrov sisters."

I'd never heard of the Petrov sisters but I agreed to Jennifer's proposal. There wasn't much I could do about it in the first place. I didn't know anybody! It would just have to do as the first step to making friends. As the two of us were walking quietly down the renovated hallway, the bell rang and we arrived in class only to hear an announcement from the principal telling everyone to meet up in the auditorium.

I walked in silence down the hallways and made a left turn at the end just before the stairwell. Everything in was still the same in that area of the school. In the auditorium things were a little different though. The carpet had been ripped out from the staircase and replaced with dark red linoleum, ironically the same colour that the carpet had turned right before its removal. There were new windows and new shades covering them as well as new seats from top to bottom.

The place didn't look like it used to at all. My feelings of going back there were mixed but I prayed for a new start, a new beginning. I sat in the very first row and Jenny sat next to me. Two girls then got out of their seats and came to sit next to Jennifer. I figured that they were the Petrov sisters that Jennifer was friends with because the two of them looked exactly alike, *twins* alike. They spoke amongst themselves in a language I did not understand as we all waited for the presentation to begin.

The girl sitting next to Jennifer wore a long gold shirt underneath a jean jacket and black palazzo pants. The gold buckles on her sandals matched the full set of gold teeth in her mouth that almost sparkled underneath the artificial lights as she spoke to her sister. Her hair was covered in a black headscarf that contrasted with her very pale skin. Her twin sister, on the other hand, was far more outrageous.

She wore faded blue years and a baggy dark hoodie that might've been black once upon a time and had carrot orange hair that landed here and there over her head. As she spoke I couldn't help but notice the contrast with her sister in the fact that all of her bottom teeth were missing and the top ones had nearly completely fallen out. They looked like they'd been crushed by something as pieces of them were missing. To some degree it awfully reminded me of a creepy presentation in the seventh grade where the teacher had showed us pictures of what happened to sailors who had scurvy.

"*Zdravo*, I'm Svetlana Petrov," the one in the headscarf exclaimed as she stretched out her hand to shake mine once she noticed I was looking in her direction.

"Alyson Feldman," I replied as I shook her hand, and then her sister's hand.

"I'm Sveta's twin sister Vera," the one with no teeth added.

"It's nice to meet the both of you," I responded, trying to be as friendly as possible.

As the other students filled up the auditorium, I took a good look at the twins underneath the lights that had shifted to shine down directly on them. Vera was very thin, a real walking skeleton in fact, and her sister didn't seem to be a whole lot bigger underneath her baggy clothes that covered everything except her face, hands and feet. Svetlana appeared to be wearing designer clothes while Vera's clothes looked like old rags that had been in the family for centuries.

Neither one of them seemed to be interested in school as they looked around the room for distractions. The two sisters had bright green eyes that seemed to burn with both annoyance and anger as Mr. Pasquale stepped up on stage. He'd never been a very popular principal but since the massacre his approval rating within the student body and the community at large had dropped dramatically.

Vera looked like she hadn't slept in a century as she brushed her hair out of her face with her hand. As she lifted up her arm I noticed that she had many tattoos under her baggy sleeves but I couldn't make out what they were. The sister returned to speaking amongst themselves with defiant edges in her voice just as the last students walked in and finished filling up the seats. Mr. Pasquale then began to speak in his usual overly diplomatic tone of voice with a hint of arrogance.

"Good morning students," he announced proudly in an overly loud microphone, "welcome back to Belden High! I especially want to welcome the students who are coming back for the first time since the incident two years ago."

"*Incident?*" Someone behind me spoke in a hoarse, voice. "What happened was a lot more than just an *incident*."

"There will be counselling available to any student who may need it beginning after this presentation," Mr. Pasquale went on, "we are Belden!"

"Belden," Svetlana grumbled to herself, "what kind of name is that? It sounds like Bergen-Belsen!"

"Bergen-Belden sounds more like it," I grumbled under my breath.

"Mr. Belden was an Austrian philanthropist that came to America centuries ago and people loved him so much that they named a school after him." Jennifer whispered back.

I did my best to zone out of Mr. Pasquale's speech because his high-pitched self-righteous voice reminded me too much of my last up and close encounter with him. I desperately tried to shake the image out of my mind but I couldn't. My breathing dramatically accelerated and my hands began to shake as the memories came rushing in and eventually my whole body shook uncontrollably. I got up as quickly as I could on my weak legs and bolted out the door that was just to my right to catch a breath in the hallway but I came face to face with the memorial plaque set up on the wall.

I hadn't previously known that it was there and I hadn't noticed it upon walking to the auditorium either but it was right there in front of my face with nineteen names engraved on it. Twenty minus one. My stomach tightened and I suddenly felt nauseous upon seeing the plaque so I went down the nearest flight of stairs as fast as I could and flew out the side entrance into the parking lot where I collapsed and vomited. Only bile came out, but it was still vomit.

The cool morning air helped soothe my rising body temperature as well as calm me down. I hadn't expected to react that way. After almost two years I thought I would've been ready to return to Belden but coming back had only made me sick. I sat on the damp concrete sidewalk on the almost deserted street for what seemed like forever before an unknown female teacher came to join me and asked me if I was alright like I was a small child.

I looked up at her in a daze but I couldn't see her face because everything was blurry and all I remembered was that she said she would call my parents to come and pick me up and about fifteen minutes later my mom showed up. My mother took me into her arms and then commented on how pale I looked as we rode back home. I felt lightheaded but the cold of the window pressed up against my forehead helped me come back to my senses.

"I guess that maybe it was too soon to send you back to that school," her gentle voice whispered to me as she squeezed my cold hand into hers.

"Mom," I muttered, "I'm an adult now."

"I know you are sweetheart, but adults also need to be taken care of sometimes."

"I chose out of my own free will to go to school, you don't need to pity me or worry about me."

"I'm your mom, I can't help it."

I knew better than to argue with her because I was well aware of the fact that I couldn't win. Once we arrived home I immediately walked up to my room on the second floor and flopped onto my bed. Lying on my stomach, I looked aimlessly around my room to distract myself but nothing was ever able to stop my mind from wandering into places that it shouldn't.

I looked over at my pictures of Anderson, Elaine and Amanda. I missed the three of them so much, and somehow I wasn't allowed to grieve. I knew that things would never be the same again, but inside I silently begged for some sort of sense of normalcy again. Where I had I been for two years? I wasn't sure. I wasn't sure I wanted to know the answer to that question either. My inner dwellings and contemplations were interrupted by my mother barging in through the door and sitting on my bed next to me.

"Maybe it's better that you don't look at these right now." She spoke softly as she took all three of my pictures and put them facedown on my table so I couldn't see them.

I rolled over onto my back and looked blankly at the ceiling tiles. They were blank and white, probably just as blank as I was. I didn't know what to feel, or even *how* to feel anymore. I was still in denial and I was painfully aware of that but I didn't know what to do about it, as ironic and backwards as that was. Or maybe I didn't want to do anything about it. I wanted my friends back, I wanted my life back, I wanted myself back. I was only a shell of my former self.

My mother looked at me with worry filling her hazel eyes but I wasn't worried. I was too numb inside to be worried about anything. I asked her to give me a few more moments alone in order to collect my thoughts, or try to anyway. She nodded her head and grabbed my picture frames on her way out. I sighed in exasperation. They were the only things I had left other than bittersweet memories.

My eyes darted back and forth from wall to wall, trying to find a distraction. The lilac walls of my room were adorned with picture frames, award certificates and ribbons as well as letters and artwork that my friends had sent to me. I surrounded myself with things and people I loved and while most people thought it was childish to do so, it was really the only way I could cope.

I pulled up my plain white bedsheets over my head and wrapped myself up with my purple and black plaid blanket. I couldn't hide from myself, and especially not from reality. A few seconds later, I got back out from under the covers and sat on the edge of my bed, unsure what to do with myself. I examined the rest of my room to distract myself for a few seconds. The fake parquet wood flooring was scratched but it was still my favourite floor in the house.

My bedroom window was large on the north side and although the sun didn't directly come in through it, the neighbour's window made the sunlight reflect directly into my room. To some people my beige curtains looked like could have previously been a bathroom carpet and my closet doors were the same colour as the floor, a beautiful natural pale wood colour, even though it was fake. Most of my furniture was black which created a contrast with the pale walls and other decor.

My room was large and had enough space to comfortably fit two large dressers, a computer desk, a large bookshelf, a small cabinet, my queen size bed and two night tables without making it look like a game of Tetris gone bad. I could easily rearrange all the furniture and my room was still just as cozy and spacious. It was my own personal sanctuary away from the world.

Dear Anderson,

I just can't cope. Why? WHY? I don't know. I just don't. I don't understand a damn thing anymore! I was convinced that I would be able to walk into that building again today and face whatever demons were left in there but I failed miserably. I even PUKED just to add insult to injury. I think it was really Mr. Pasquale that trigged me. That jerk! I'll never forgive him for what he did, well, what he didn't do at least. I never thought I hated him this much until I saw his ugly face again today.

On the good side I saw Jennifer and that was really nice. She introduced me to the Petrov sisters or whatever their names are. They appear to be Russian or Ukrainian and they seem nice. One of them kind reminded me of you somehow. I still don't know how to really feel about that but my gosh I miss you! My feelings are so messed up and I just don't know what to make of them. I don't know anything anymore! I never thought that things would end up this way.

Are you happy where you are? Because I sure as hell am not happy here! Your presence still lingers around here and sometimes I just wish you'd go away once and for all. I don't know Anderson, I just don't know.

Aly

I eventually went downstairs when I couldn't find any distractions in my room and found my mother still at home, sitting all by herself in the kitchen. She worked part-time with the disabled from eleven to two on weekdays and did freelance photography on her own time and although she should've been at work she didn't look like she was going anywhere. My father worked twelve-hour shifts at a coal mine just on the outskirts of town.

I didn't get to spend too much time with my dad during the day but on the weekends we always got together to spend some quality time. He was my best friend, and had always been, but despite our closeness I also felt a disconnect between the two of us. Nothing had actually changed between the two of us, but *I* had changed inside.

Last but not least, I also had a ten-year-old little brother, ironically named Anderson. I missed him so much even though he hadn't gone anywhere. I was the one who couldn't be around him. There was actually nothing wrong with him, it was me, there was something wrong with *me*. I knew that it deeply saddened him to no longer have his big sister like he used to, but I no longer had the life I used to either.

I sat at the kitchen table across from my mother but neither one of us spoke a word. Basically all of the furniture in the house was made of wood, including the kitchen table and the matching chairs. The kitchen had royal blue floor tiles and plain white walls. All of the cabinets were also made of woods with the countertops made of granite. The appliances were all matching stainless steel, creating a contrast similar to the one in my bedroom.

The kitchen and dining room were merged together, creating one big open space near the staircase to go upstairs. The impressive kitchen was the first things people saw when they walked in through the door. My parents had worked hard for what we had, and I knew that they had financially suffered after putting me in intensive therapy. Once I turned eighteen I'd put a stop to that, in part because I felt guilty that it was so expensive and in part because I felt as though it didn't help anything.

"Aren't you going to work mom?" I asked just to break the silence.

"No," she replied in her usual gentle voice, "I'll be staying with you today."

"I'm eighteen years old mom, you don't need to babysit me anymore. Plus you can just send me back to school for my next class."

"Honey, after your reaction this morning I don't think it's such a good idea. You know, if you're incapable of returning to school we can try homeschooling you Aly."

Homeschool. That was really the only thing I hadn't yet tried. I'd tried virtual school but hadn't been able to last more than two weeks. The general concept of school had sickened me to the core and being away from it entirely was the only way I'd been able to take a few baby steps towards my recovery, a recovery that I wasn't sure was ever possible.

"No mom, I *want* to go to school. I can't stay in here and dwell over my former life for eternities at a time!"

"Why don't you want to go to another school?"

"And travel one hour to get there and one more to come back? I don't think so. Twenty minutes to go and another twenty to come back is enough."

Her and I both knew that it was just a pitiful excuse and a vain attempt at deflecting from the real problem but my mother also knew better than to push the issue on me. My mother nodded in agreement and left to sit in the living room to let me cool off, seemingly holding back tears. I knew that deep down inside she had loved Anderson too even though she had never been willing to admit it.

From the corner of my eye I saw my three picture frames lying facedown on the massive granite counter. I went over to pick them up and brought them back up to my room on the second floor. They were intact, just like they had always been for the past year and a half. I placed them back on my night table in the same position they'd always been so I could look at them while I was laying in bed.

The black frames contrasted perfectly with the lilac backdrop of my wall. In my blank state of mind I didn't feel any sadness because they were dead or any anger towards Anderson because he was beyond dead. Death was something weird. I figured I never really understood the full scope of it because I was alive and I'd only seen *others* die and I had never really come close to death myself. At least not close to me actually *dying* as in *dying* as a verb, not me being *dead* as in a state. I'd been around *the* dying, but that was different.

Dying somewhat weirded me out. I could not comprehend it in my state of mental and emotional blankness. My mentality since the whole ordeal had been one of willful ignorance if one could call it that. That state in which a person convinces themselves they if they just ignore the problem long enough it will go away on its own or someone else will take care of it.

But let me tell you, it doesn't work that way. Any rational person would know that in order to get rid of a problem you have to eliminate it, resolve it somehow and a problem couldn't be resolved the same way it had been created. I knew about the *problem* but not much else. It had come to a point where I'd given up with problems and death and dying and let *life* take its course.

My daydreaming was interrupted again when I heard the phone ring. I picked up the little purple cordless phone from my desk under the window and slouched in the big leather computer chair that accompanied it. It was time for business, time for the real world.

"Hey Jen."

"Hey Alyson! Is everything okay?"

"I'm fine, don't worry about me, I promise."

"Okay Aly, I'm just worried about you. I know it's hard, I feel for you girl! And I'm sorry that I didn't call earlier, I didn't get the chance until now."

"Don't worry about that Jenny, I'll see you again tomorrow."

We said goodbye and I let the phone flop onto my desk. I hadn't spoken to anyone over the phone in months, possibly even years! I didn't want to talk to anyone, and for that reason my parents had come to the conclusion that I was severely depressed, was in shock, and had to deal with grief in the middle of that so they'd sent me to therapy. The day I turned eighteen I'd terminated the sessions and I didn't regret my decision.

I knew that my choice worried my parents because the therapist was the only person I actually *talked* to, but I enjoyed writing letters on good old pen and paper and sending them out to my two penfriends in Malta and Australia. Writing letters was the only way I felt comfortable expressing myself, and that was also the reason why I still wrote letters to Anderson even though he was dead.

My snail mail to both the living and the dead still hadn't solved the problem though. I still felt as empty inside as I always had and I still hated talking on the phone even if it was Jennifer calling out of genuine concern for my wellbeing. It all just reminded me too much of the last words Anderson and I had exchanged over the phone.

"Hello?"

"Don't come to school tomorrow."

Click.

There had been an unusual sharp edge in his voice. That was unlike him. His voice was usually calm, soft and gentle. He had the deep voice of a seventeen-year-old young man but there had always been an element of gentleness to him. What was even worst than his hoarse voice that night what that I'd actually gone to school the following morning and it was the worst decision I'd ever made.

It still made me feel so stupid. Time hadn't erased, or even eased, that lingering feeling of failure and stupidity for doing what I'd done. Anderson had given me a clear warning and I had been too stupid to listen. I showed my face at school the next morning. I'd always made myself believe that I'd gone just because I wanted to see him. Well, that I most certainly had.

"Alyson!" My mother's voice interrupted my dark train of thought.

I was startled by her barging into my room like that again but at the same time I was so grateful for the interruption. I really didn't want my thoughts to wander into that rabbit hole but in moments of isolation, and maybe even madness, the insanity always seemed to find that open door in my mind.

I looked over at my mother in both annoyance and gratitude and waited for her to tell me what was wrong *this time again* as she would say. I just wanted to be left alone but nobody ever seemed to understand that. Apparently it was a symptom of depression, or even worst, insanity. Nobody ever seemed to realize that maybe I *wanted* to be insane just to not have to deal with reality either.

"It's your dad on the phone." My mom whispered in a soft voice and quickly bolted back out the door.

"Hi dad," I answered the phone in a somewhat embarrassed tone of voice because I had been so deep in thought that I hadn't heard it ringing.

"Are you okay sweetie?" His voice was deep and concerned.

"Yes dad, I just barfed in the parking lot, that's all."

"Okay sweetheart, I'm just worried about you. I can't even begin to imagine what it must've been like for you to go back to that place."

"I barfed dad, people barf when they're feeling sick."

"Okay, well I just wanted to make sure. You can call me anytime you need something, even if I'm at work. I'll drop whatever I'm doing and come to your rescue if it comes to that. I love you."

"I love you too dad."

And with that I hung up the phone. I didn't walk to talk on the phone with *anyone*. As much as I loved my dad and I loved speaking to him, *not over the phone please!* Phones just left a bitter taste in my mouth. I turned around in my chair to peek at the digital clock on my night table next to my pictures and was shocked to see that it was already the afternoon! I hadn't noticed all that time go by! Where had it gone? Had I really wasted away all of those hours by dwelling over the past again?

I went back downstairs to the kitchen to grab a flew slices of bread and sat by myself at the island counter that also matched the rest of the room. I wasted away the rest of the day by myself until Anderson arrived from from school on his bus. I dismissed him and my father eventually arrived in his white company truck just over four hours later.

At the dinner table I sat in my usual spot without speaking a word. I stared at my pale spaghetti in my blue plate in awkward silence as the others seemed to be waiting for me to say something. I finally decided to grab my fork and shove the cold pasta down my throat as an excuse for not saying anything. It wasn't good but I ate it anyway. After the dinner the rest of the day was just as bland and so was the night but thankfully, I'd had a peaceful night and a dreamless sleep.

II

DESERVE

My buzzing alarm clock woke me up in a cold sweat. I slammed it with my fist and it stopped. I suddenly felt uneasy at the thought of going back to school. It hadn't bothered me like that the first day, but then again I hadn't known what would have been waiting for me in there. My day obviously hadn't gone as planned.

After I got up I ran to the bathroom and opened the bathtub tap, stuck my head under the cold running way and drank it like a dog. I then sat on the side of the big white tub and let out a big exasperated sign as I looked around the room seeking a distraction. The tiles covering the walls were adorned with little fishies and mermaids and other aquatic-themed decor because it was the only real way that Anderson would actually take a bath. He could pretend to be one of them instead of just sitting in lukewarm water with your parents' soapy hands all over you.

I washed my face in the sink and went back to my room to put on some half-decent clothes to return to school. I picked out a white Lacuna Coil band shirt and the first pair of pants I found in my dresser. They turned out to be designer jeans so I happily put them on and accessorized myself with a golden heart pendant and safely tucked away my stainless steel ring on a chain under my shirt.

I brushed my long, *very* straight hair that I wanted to tint with a hint of red over the weekend and debated for a moment whether or not I should pull it up into a ponytail but I ended up deciding against it. I put on a hint of dark green eyeliner to compliment my golden hazel eyes so I could look as presentable as possible following my previous little puking episode that undoubtedly every student came to find out about in the last twenty-four hours.

My mom drove Anderson to school and then dropped me off in the parking lot of that big white and grey building safely tucked away in a residential neighbourhood. I stepped out of the little burgundy Ford Fusion and stood on the sidewalk for a few moments, just looking at that nasty building. It looked a lot scarier in person than it did on the news. It had two floors unlike most of the other high schools in the area, a big flat roof, cement bricks painted white and big windows all around.

The building seemed to loom over me in some twisted and menacing way that left me with chills running down my spine. I couldn't help but think that it had done the same thing to Anderson, and that it was part of the reason why he'd decided to not let it victimize him anymore. I took a deep breath and barged in through the door much like my mother had barged into my room just a day earlier. I walked down the same hallways I always had and made my way up to the second floor of the place and sat by the window not far from my locker.

"Aly!" Jennifer's gentle mousy voice shouted from the end of the hall.

I turned over to look at her and she and the Petrov twins waved at me and signalled me to join them. I got up and joined the three of them in an adjoining hallway. At the same time I had the chance to take a good look at the twins. Vera had long hair dyed a bright carrot orange that extended down to the middle of her back and Svetlana seemed to have a good bundle of it underneath her hijab as well. The two of them had jade green eyes, perfect oval faces and complimenting small noses centred in the middle. The two of them had dark eyebrows and Vera had a lip piercing on the bottom right side that she always bit.

Svetlana appeared to have the same taste in designer clothes that I did but Vera's clothes were still dingy old rags. They appeared less like rags in the sunlight than they did in the darkness but they were still a stark contrast to her sister's attire. The upper class would definitely have called them something worst than rags but I didn't because I had respect for others, especially after everything that had happened in the halls of the school just two short years prior.

"Hey Tammy!" Vera's voice was apathetic yet soft at the same time.

I turned around in a jolt, just praying that the person I would see wasn't the person I feared seeing. Yep, it was her. Tammy Davidson. I felt my body stiffen at the sight of her standing right in front of me. Her literally square head was covered with greasy bleach-coloured hair and two big round eyes the colour of diarrhea peered at me right in the middle of that ugly disgusting face covered with a mixture of pimples and creases.

She looked like a middle-aged woman going through puberty. She was the ugliest person I'd ever seen in my life. She wasn't ugly because she had pimples, because I had pimples too, but because her soul was ugly. Most people found her disgusting because she had started sleeping with boys in the fifth grade but I thought that she was disgusting for much more than promiscuity.

"Hi Aly," she greeted me in that annoying, high-pitched and self-righteous voice a lot like Pasquale's, "I haven't seen you in a while. I thought you had dropped out."

"You goddamn ugly whore! He should've shot you!" I snapped back apprehensively.

She hadn't been expecting that. Nobody had.

"He should've shot and killed you! He should've served you with what you deserve!"

Her eyes grew big like they were going to explode out of her head before she flipped me the finger and turned around and walked quickly back down the hallways to where she'd come from. Jen and the twins looked at each other in complete astonishment, not having expected that either. I wasn't sure I had expected it of myself. It had just really come out of nowhere.

No, it had come from *somewhere*. She should have been shot! People who only wasted oxygen did not deserve life. I tried to take a deep breath but anxiety restricted my airways so I let out another sigh of exasperation to try to alleviate the stress. I was beginning to sound just like Anderson. I felt like I was suffocating so I turned around to have my back to where she had gone.

Jennifer looked at me with a mixture of both shock and compassion on her face. She knew that I had always been a gentle and soft-spoken person myself, but the twins were completely bewildered. Vera and Svetlana looked at each other, both impressed and taken aback by my bold outburst.

"You knew him didn't you?" Sveta asked me in a gentle tone of voice, seemingly not wanting to provoke me further.

"Yeah, I did," I replied as I tried as best as I could to dismiss the question.

"Well, just know that I have a lot of compassion for that kid," Vera added softly as she put her skeletal hand on my shoulder.

"Let's not talk about this okay?" Jennifer interjected before anybody got the chance to say anything else.

Jen had known him too, and had also been there during the whole thing. We had all known each other since forever, or at least that's what it felt like to me. My forever had been wiped away from me right in front of my eyes and there wasn't a damn thing I could do about it.

"Come on, let's go to class," Jennifer proposed, "I'll catch you up on that stupid junk you missed yesterday."

As it turned out, Jennifer, the twins and I would share all of our classes the entire first semester. That thought comforted me because I felt so alone and out of place in a big building filled with nothing but hate and selfishness. Thankfully, I didn't have any classes with Tammy but I knew that we were bound to run into each other at some point because we had classes in the same hallway in the morning.

In our first class together, I sat in the back row with Jennifer sitting on one side of me and Sveta on the other. Her sister Vera sat on the other side of her, similar to what we had done in the auditorium. Once we'd taken our seats Jen then caught me up on all the crap that Mr. Pasquale had rambled about the previous day.

He had basically just flapped his gums about the free counselling services available on campus as well as brag about the school spirit and all of that stuff about coming out strong after the whole ordeal. I knew that already. In other classes no lessons had been taught or assignments handed out. It was just the usual introductory stuff all schools did on the first day.

The second day of class was much of the same story. I figured they took it extra easy the first week back at school because so many of the students were still so fragile and traumatized. I fell into both of those categories. Jennifer also seemed to be pretty shaken up by the whole thing. How could one not be? Unlike me, she hadn't been out of school for almost two years and she had to deal with being victimized and harassed on a daily basis because of her weight and her social status.

Even after brutal vengeance and retaliation, bullying and harassment was still rampant throughout the halls of the school. The building consisted mostly of multiple short halls put together like a maze and it was impossible for the administration to monitor them completely, but it wasn't like they ever made much of an effort to monitor them in the first place.

At lunch I sat with Jen and the twins in the empty halls of the second floor. The school let us bring food outside of the cafeteria except in the library, the auditorium and the computer room. Apart from that, you were free to eat wherever you wanted as long as you cleaned up after yourself. You weren't free to eat *whatever* you wanted though. The school had this stupid policy that you couldn't bring in food from the *outside*.

Unless you brought your own lunch, and there were restrictions as to what students could eat, you had to eat what was served in the cafeteria or not eat at all. You couldn't go out and buy food during lunch or the morning break and then bring it back. You had to eat it outside of school if you decided to go down that gastronomical route.

"Do they still enforce that stupid rule of no outside food?" I asked the girl.

"Yep," Sveta replied apathetically, "they do."

I grinned to myself at the memories of the better days I'd spent in that school. I was one of the biggest food smugglers in the school, a real kingpin in the business. After all, who would really suspect a good all-American middle class teenage girl who never got in trouble? Not the administration, which made me the perfect candidate for the job. I'd always hated stereotypes, but for once they had served me well.

The school was so afraid of people smuggling in drugs and trafficking them in the middle of a truly horrific boom in the narcotics business and the opioid crisis so they didn't let us bring in food from outside the school during our lunch hour. The polices were overly strict, extreme even, going as far as monitoring the exits during those short fifty minutes. It wasn't even a real lunch hour!

During the morning break I went around collecting the money of students who wanted the sweet treat of *outside food* and marking down their orders. They paid the price of the actual food, plus the taxes, plus the "trafficking" fee since the food trade was as notorious as the drug trade. My car needed gas to get that food, and I took a great risk doing that so I wanted my reward for making their tastebuds happy.

I had an online course during the second period which allowed me extra privileges that included ample opportunities for food trafficking. I still had to be in school but I didn't technically to be in class since all the course material was online and it could be accessed from anywhere. I always did as much work as I could in a single burst and then quietly disappear from the various unmonitored rooms I was allowed to quietly do my work in so I could then go to town and collect all the requested food items.

I came back to school just before the lunch hour began and safely hid the food until my customers came to pick up their orders. Back in the day I drove my mom's car to school and ended up doing the larger part of my online class back home after school once my food smuggling business grew larger and consumed more time. The excuse that it was research for other homework always worked on my parents.

I made a pretty penny in the food smuggling industry and used the money to buy myself all sorts of thingamajigs as well as hide some in my room. I had a sort of stash of cash in a box under my bed that I could just dip into whenever I needed a dollar. It had since run bone dry in nearly two years and my high-end lifestyle had come to a rather abrupt end.

For a moment I thought of getting back into the food smuggling business since Sveta had just told me that the idiotic policies hadn't changed but part of me was afraid of getting caught. Back then I thought I owned the world, but I didn't anymore. I no longer had the energy or the boldness required to do that. The universe probably just dismissed me as an insane and traumatized young woman. I bit my bottom lip as one particularly close call in the food trafficking business came to mind.

I pulled up into the parking lot and parked my car in my usual spot, undetected. I reached into the backseat and dragged the grocery bags onto the front seat. I packed the caramel cakes into the large pockets inside my black oilskin trench coat and filled in the other pockets with candies and soda cans. I had too much food for all the pockets so I simply put the remainder of the food inside my coat and pressed my arms against my stomach so it wouldn't fall out underneath.

I walked in through the front door and greeted the random people loitering in the lobby like I did on any average day and walked down the left hallway passed the first stairwell over to the second one so I could reach the second floor without going down a maze of crowded hallways on the top floor. Once I walked passed the first set of doors the coast was clear so I took the food out of my coat and carried it in my hands. Nobody ever came storming down that hall anyway.

As I was walking down passed the two doors to the guidance counsellor's office, Mr. Jeff came storming out through the first door and bolted in the opposite direction. I literally froze on the spot, I was doomed. Caught redhanded with not only outside food in my hands, but a coat full of it too! Mr. Jeff didn't even notice me or even acknowledge that I existed. Without seeing me, he barged through the set of doors at the other end of the hall and disappeared from sight. I let out of a huge sigh of relief and tiptoed the rest of the way down the hall and up the stairs to where my customers were waiting.

"What's so funny?" Vera interrupted my daydreaming.

"Oh," I lightly giggled, "I was thinking back to when I smuggled food down this very hallway."

"You, smuggling food?!" Svetlana burst out laughing like she couldn't believe it.

"Yep, I did and I made a pretty penny too!"

"Would you be up to doing it again?"

"I'm not sure. You know, after everything I'm not sure I can trust anyone ever again."

The girls understood where I was coming from. At the same time I wasn't sure I could still trust myself. I had learned one hell of a lesson about trust with Anderson. My brain momentarily transported me back to history class and intrusively made me relive a particular lesson about Joseph Stalin. *I trust no one, not even myself,* Stalin had been famously quoted saying. Stalin had always been Anderson's favourite dictator and that had never been a secret.

Stalin's poems were said to have been great but poetry was something I understood nothing about. I'd missed the boat on art in general, though I enjoy it in specific contexts. Intrusive memories, on the other hand, were not part of those contexts in question. No matter what I tried to think about, memories of Anderson always found a way to come crawling back into the most innocent of situations. The guilt that I was burdened with simply wouldn't let me forget.

"And what's the deal with Tammy?" Vera asked in reference to my little outburst earlier.

Ugh, Tammy. I didn't want to think and much less talk about her.

"She's a big ugly hypocrite. One of the worst people I've ever heard of in my entire life."

"What did she do that was so bad that made her deserve to be shot?"

"How about ruining a person's life? Does that count?"

"I suppose, but I don't know. It must've had to be pretty bad."

"Being deceitful, manipulative and taking advantage of vulnerable people doesn't exactly land a person on my nice list."

"Man, I'm sorry about whatever happened that left such a profound impact on you."

"She only pretended to be my friend but she played one hell of a number on Anderson."

"Anderson? You mean the shooter?"

"Because of her he suffered a lot."

"I take it he's the one who had his life ruined in all of this."

"Well, yes and no. It's kinda weird now looking back on it after everything."

Vera didn't say another word on the subject. My face must've given away the intrusive memories creeping into my brain.

"You know there's a free group counselling session right after lunch," Jennifer commented in a little mousy whisper, "and I think I'm going to attend."

It sounded more like a request to join her than merely a comment indicating the reason for her absence from class. The twins both volunteered to accompany her, and since I was going to end up alone I decided that I might as well accompany them too.

"It'll be good for you," Jen tried to reassure me.

She knew full well that I hated therapy. I hated thinking about *it*, and I especially hated talking about *it* with others. *Especially* people I didn't know and *especially* people who weren't even there and knew nothing about the subject. It angered me that only a few months from the two-year anniversary people were still so insensitive.

They all just wanted to be *normal* again and although I wanted to me normal myself most of the time, I knew very well that things would never return to *normal*. I was angry at myself in the middle of that, in part for not doing anything more. Like I wasn't *normal*. I had nothing more to lose so I decided to make my way down the hall for some more meaningless talking to a counsellor who contributed nothing of value.

"Welcome! Come on it!" I was greeted by a female teacher in the doorway of the classroom used for the session.

At a grey metal desk in the corner of the room there was a social worker sitting quietly, looking menacingly at the empty chairs arranged into a circle. She looked menacing to me anyway. I got that bad therapist vide from her sleek black blouse, her matching skirt and even the matching stilettos. Her bleach-coloured hair was neatly tied up into a ponytail and her brown eyes seemed to be glossy but it was probably just the light coming in through the window that created the effect.

The new teacher I had never seen before. I figured that was why she was *new*. Like many Americans, she was overweight but there was a gentle and friendly demeanour to her. She had long sandy hair as well as too much black eyeliner around her perfectly round piercing blue eyes shimmering in the sunlight. She introduced herself to me as Mathilda.

"It's nice to meet you Alyson." Her voice was gentle and calming.

"You too." I bleakly replied.

"For the first week of school we'll be meeting every day at different times to give the most students possible the opportunity to come, and after that our meetings will be held once a week for the rest of the semester. You are more than free to attend whenever you want and don't be shy to also speak to a private counsellor."

"Thank you, I'll keep that in mind."

"If you ever feel sick or otherwise unable to continue don't hesitate to walk out. Someone will come and see you to make sure that you're okay."

Yes, I know, thank you for the information. In case you weren't aware, I'm the one who puked all over the parking lot yesterday. I sat down on one of them cheap blue plastic chairs on the opposite side of the window so I could see outside. Jennifer sat on my left while Svetlana sat on my right with her sister on the other side of her. In my twisted little mind I imagined them doing that so they could restrain me just in case I flipped my lid.

"How long have you been attending this school?" The new fat one asked me as though I looked like I wanted the therapy session to begin with me.

"I was here when it happened." I mumbled in response.

Nobody spoke a word. The silence was interrupted by somebody barging in through the door behind me. It was Theodore Hicks. Although I had never personally known him in the past, I knew who he was because he had the same face as his brother Steven.

"Hi Theo!" Jennifer greeted him.

He gave her a fake smile in turn and sat down as far away from us as he possibly could. The twins both gave him dirty looks like they held some sort of grudge against him but neither spoke. A few more students walked in and distracted me from whatever tension there was between the Petrov sisters and Theodore Hicks. All the chairs were filled up in no time with kids who wanted to talk about metal health, school violence and whatever else was on their hearts that day.

I didn't know any of the other students who came to the meeting, they were all fresh new faces eager to make their voices heard. I knew that I too would have to face my demons someday, but for the time being I really didn't want to talk about *it*. I filled my lungs with air and closed my eyes. I zoned out completely to the exception of dissonant voices in the near distance.

"I feel sorry for him more than anything."

"Me too, you have to hurt a heck of a lot to be able to walk into a school with a gun in hand and kill innocent people."

"It truly saddens me to think of what he must have felt to be pushed to that point."

I couldn't believe what I was hearing.

"He murdered my brother."

I'm well aware, I saw him being shot.

"It makes me angry that even after all this time nothing has changed!"

"I wasn't here when it happened, but this place is a breeding ground for evil. Pure evil!"

"I have both so much anger and so much sympathy for him."

"Maybe it someone had shown him sympathy or compassion when he was alive things would've turned out differently."

For a moment I'd been unaware of it, but that last voice was mine.

Silence.

"Were you there?" One new guy asked me in a shaky, fearful voice.

"Yeah, I was with Steven Hicks, when, uh," I was no longer able to speak.

"It's okay Alyson, take your time," I heard a voice way too familiar tell me.

I looked up and I saw him, Mr. Pasquale.

"It's all your fault!" I shouted so loudly that I thought I was going to rip my lungs wide open.

Just as I had expected, I felt four hands grab my arms and squeeze them too tightly, restraining me. My entire body became rigid and eventually began to shake at the sight of the tall tattooed man standing in the doorway. He looked like the monster he really was. Tall, well over six feet tall, sleeves on both arms, short brown hair and a short goatee under his big square head.

Mr. Pasquale had dark bushy eyebrows that matched his hair and his eyes were just as dark and disgusting. His nose was too big for his face and he was just another one who wore clothes too tight. His suit obviously too small for him made him stand in an awkward and uncomfortable position since it literally suppressed his paunch. He stood abnormally straight and his body seemed more rigid than usual.

Apart from his tattoos, Mr. Pasquale had no actual distinctive features. He could've been anybody. He looked more like a wannabe rockstar than a school principal and he probably would've been a better loathsome musician than principal too.

Silence.

The dead quiet of the room following my outburst was interrupted by the door slamming shut. Pasquale was gone. I exhaled loudly and took a series of deep breaths, slowly calming myself down. I had quit my anxiety medication a few months ago but I still carried benzodiazepines in my bag just in case a panic attack did sweep me off my feet so to speak. I couldn't always remove myself from the situation or practice simple relaxation techniques, but thankfully my trigger had walked out the door.

"Do you wanna talk about it?" The bad therapist asked me in an unusually soft and sensitive voice.

"I hate him!" I snapped back.

"Mr. Pasquale?"

"Yes."

"Tell us why Alyson."

"Ask the girls."

The twins looked at me with puzzled expressions on their faces, not knowing what I was talking about, but Jennifer knew exactly what I was talking about.

"I take it that it's about Anderson Massey," Svetlana spoke in a low voice, "am I right?"

"The way you were looking at him in the auditorium yesterday, I know that you feel the same way about him. I could see it in your eyes."

For a fraction of a second Vera's bright emerald eyes gleamed at me, shining in the sunlight coming through the window. The, out of nowhere, she abruptly got up and stomped her foot on the floor.

"My sister has some serious beef with Pasquale," Sveta whispered to me, "we all do as far as we're concerned but she can be a little explosive."

Vera grumbled something in Russian and walked out. The door slammed loudly behind her and a few seconds later we could all hear her yelling obscenities in the hallway. I didn't understand Russian, but I was intelligent enough to know the difference between profanity and regular speech and Vera wasn't saying anything nice.

I didn't know her reasons to be so angry with him, but it somewhat made me feel better to know that I was not the only person who felt that way. It was almost like an out-of-body experience in some sick way. I didn't even know Vera but hearing her shout at Mr. Pasquale automatically made her my best friend. For a second there she was my hero. After the noise in the hallway quieted down, Fat Mathilda resumed the session by speaking about the shooting and letting the other students say what they had to say.

Dear Anderson,

Why? Why? Why? Why? Why? Why? Why? Why? Why? Why? Why?
Why? Why? Why? Why? Why? Why? Why? Why? Why? Why? Why?
Why? Why? Why? Why? Why? Why? Why? Why? Why? Why? Why?
Why? Why? Why? Why? Why? Why? Why? Why? Why? Why? Why?
Why? Why? Why? Why? Why? Why? Why? Why? Why? Why? Why?
Why? Why? Why? Why? Why? Why? Why? Why? Why? Why? Why?
Why? Why? Why? Why? Why? Why? Why? Why? Why? Why? Why?
Why? Why? Why? Why? Why? Why? Why? Why? Why? Why? Why?
Why? Why? Why? Why? Why? Why? Why? Why? Why? Why? Why?
Why? Why? Why? Why? Why? Why? Why? Why? Why? Why? Why?
Why? Why? Why? Why? Why? Why? Why? Why? Why? Why? Why?
Why? Why? Why? Why? Why? Why? Why? Why? Why? Why? Why?
Why? Why? Why? Why? Why? Why? Why? Why? Why? Why? Why?
Why? Why? Why? Why? Why? Why? Why? Why? Why? WHY???
God only gives us so much precious time.

Alyson

"Sometimes if I listen really closely, I can still hear the sound of his voice." I blurted out.

If anyone said anything else I didn't hear it. I wasn't listening. I couldn't stop thinking about Vera Petrov. Who was she? She occupied my thoughts to the point that I actually got up in the middle of the meeting and walked out, going straight to the newly renovated principal's office Jen and Sveta didn't try to restrain me either.

Too-Tight-Alyson greeted me and I demanded to see Vera. I knew that she was in there, shouting profanity like that at a staff member automatically landed you in his office. I quietly hoped that she'd told him that he deserved to be shot right between the eyes, but he wouldn't've been able to understand a word either way.

When Ms. Alyson saw that I wasn't about to go away she told Mr. Pasquale that I wanted to see Vera and he let me into his office. Vera was sitting on a bright blood red leather couch so I sat next to her and she grinned at me with a severely crooked smile, almost like one of her face was paralyzed, revealing an awful set of damaged teeth.

The first thing I saw on the wall was a memorial plaque, kinda like the one near the auditorium with *nineteen* names engraved on it. Twenty minus one. From the corner of my eye I could see Vera looking in my direction so I met her gaze and she grinned at me again. The both of us then directed our stares at Mr. Pasquale who was sitting right in front of us at his big mahogany wooden desk. He stared blankly at us the same way we both stared blankly at him. Finally, he decided to break the silence.

"Is there something I can do for you Alyson?"

I didn't really know what to say. There was *too much* I wanted to say to him, or was there really? I looked over at Vera who kept on grinning at me, seemingly very happy that I had come to sit by her side. She didn't look like the kind of person who had many friends, at the very least she didn't seem to hang out with anyone other than her sister and Jen. I could only respect and admire that special twin bond the two shared.

When it came to the friendship situation, I was basically in the same boat. I didn't have anyone other than Jennifer and the twins. There were a few people that I'd known before the shooting but things had become too awkward between us. Everyone just wanted to forget about it and part of me wanted to as well, but the bigger part of me wanted to be haunted by it for the rest of my life because twenty people paid with their lives for everyone's collective failure.

"Mr. Pasquale!" A voice shouted from behind the couch.

Vera and I turned around at once and then I saw him, Mario Bartolucci.

I was quietly doing my schoolwork when a code red was announced over the airways. We knew what to do, we had been trained for this. In case of a school shooting or other imminent threat everyone was to crawl under their desks or tables, and the teacher was to lock the door and close the lights. Nobody was to say a word, send a text or even post an update to a social media profile.

Nobody took that crap seriously anymore after practicing it time and time again like it was a morning ritual to hide under your desk from the bad guys in the hallway. My classmates and I were in no hurry to hide our things under the tables and then crawl under ourselves that morning and neither was the teacher in a hurry to shut the door and put out the lights in the computer lab for that matter.

She had been at her desk quietly reading *Fifty Shades of Grey* but all of a sudden an alarmed look covered her face. She abruptly dropped her book onto the desk, got up and went into the hallway, seemingly searching for something. During that time the students, along with myself, crawled under the tables of the computer room and told each other jokes to entertain ourselves during another boring and routine code red drill.

I was crouched under the table, at the very edge of it, so I was able to peer into the hallway during the whole thing. I could hear voices in the distance but couldn't quite make out what they were saying. They seemed to be confused though, by the tone they were speaking in. Mario was crouched next to me and rambling about the slouch code red procedures.

"It would be awesome and so much more realistic if they hired a pretend shooter!" Mario exclaimed, seriously thinking that he was funny.

Less than a fraction of a second later screams echoed in the hallway as loud pops rang out. Everyone looked at each other in confusion, and then it sank in. It was no practice drill. That was the reason the teacher looked alarmed just a few minutes earlier, it was just clicked in her brain that she knew nothing about the drill, because it wasn't a drill!

Just as soon as it all registered in my brain, he walked in. All I could see were his black combat boots covered in dust from walking outside and the tip of a double barrel shotgun. I covered my eyes and ears with my arms and hands but each loud blast sounded like the sky was falling. All I could hear was glass breaking and horrific screams, one probably being my own.

My ears were ringing and my heart was pounding to the point that I thought it was going to explode right out of my chest. His boots stopped right in front of me, I thought I was going to be killed but for some reason he turned around and walked out of the classroom. I couldn't bring myself to look anywhere else other than down through my knees at my own shoes. I had never loved my shoes so much.

"Oh dear!" Vera exclaimed. "Alyson, you're so pale!"

I felt lightheaded and confused. Somebody handed me a cold bottle of water and I gulped down nearly half of it at once. I could hear more voices behind me but couldn't quite make out what they were saying either. Something like *call your parents*. Call my parents!

"No!" I protested.

I was an adult and I didn't want my mother to have to come pick me up from school yet again because I had crossed paths with another survivor. I was a survivor too, weren't I? I couldn't understand why certain things and people brought back the horrific memories but others didn't. Most of the time Vera behaved exactly like the shooter had but it never rubbed me the wrong way.

Maybe it was because she hadn't been *there*. She hadn't actually been there, huddled under a table with some brainless sophomore wishing that there could be a real shooter in the building when one actually walked right through the door and opened fire, killing several people.

"I'm fine I promise!"

It was Ms. Alyson who was next to me holding the remnants of the water bottle that I had mostly spilled on myself, the couch and the floor. Upon realizing what I had done I immediately apologized and offered to help clean up the mess. I sighed as I tried to compose myself now that my little episode was over. I then made the mistake of looking at the wall and catching a glimpse of another memorial plaque.

Elaine Frechette

Frances Mason

Steven Hicks

Tobin Davies

Amanda Andrews

Roger Smith

Katy Henderson

Lynne Taylor

Michael Hazen

Trevor Bradford

Corey Nickels

Eric West

Gary Lewis

Natasha Blackburn

Annie Michelle

Daniel Jonas

Dylan Cardwell

Katherine Price

David Hoban

But not **Anderson Massey.**

III

CORRUPTION

The second week of school started without incident. Until Vera Petrov set foot in French class on Monday afternoon. Nobody liked the French teacher very much. Mrs. Black was this other tall diplomatic woman with a paunch like Mr. Pasquale and short light brown hair puffed up in the back. She was in her mid-forties if not even a little older. Unfortunately for her, she matched all the other people I didn't like in school with her box-shaped head.

Her face was always unusually red like she was constantly running out of air or something, her large glossy brown eyes looked like marbles from the dollar store and her clothes were probably just as old as she was. To say the least, her awful appearance matched her awful personality, or at the very least the awful first impression she gave me. She introduced herself as Meredith Constanza Black. Her name was as weird as everything else.

I hadn't previously met her since I had always been either in group therapy or seeing the school's private counsellor in the afternoon during her class but the other students really seemed to have it against her. Apparently she had made them write an entire short story on their first day of class, but thankfully the students who had been absent due to mental health concerns didn't have to catch up on any of the tasks given during the first week since they weren't graded.

31

Since it was now the first "official" day of class after all the welcome crap, Mrs. Squarehead decided to intimidate us. Svetlana has previously told me that she was a strict one, but I really hadn't been expecting what happened next. I don't think anybody did.

"Girls, if your hair is longer than your shoulders you have to tie it up into a ponytail."

"No I don't!" Vera's harsh apprehensive voice sliced through the air next to me.

"It's class policy Vera."

"Well, it's unethical and I will not conform to it. The Supreme Court says I can wear my hair however the hell I want! It's my human right to refuse to tie it up!"

Vera had since gotten up and stood on the other side of her sister, who was sitting at the desk to my right.

"And don't give me none of that junk about how I can't wear a hat in class or whatever when my sister wears hijab," she went on as she yanked on Sveta's headscarf, "and even covered her face for an entire semester last year! It's called religious freedom or whatever and it's her human right to cover up just as much as it is mine to let my hair down!"

"This is my class and you will have to obey my rules Vera. That's just the way it's going to be." Squarehead retorted unemotionally, not about to budge.

"We'll see about that."

Vera sat back down next to her sister as she rearranged her hijab, seemingly calm, until Squarehead opened her box-shaped mouth again.

"If you don't listen there will be consequences."

"Let me show you how I'm going to listen to your dumb-ass rules, *suka!*"

Vera got up again and stomped her way to the front of the class like a tornado about to take a soul. All eyes were on her as she violently opened a drawer of Squarehead's desk and pulled out a large pair of lime green scissors. With one hand she pulled up her hair onto one side of her head and chopped it right off with the other. She threw a handful of bright orange hair onto the desk and proceeded to cut the other side. She then threw the scissors on top of the orange pile of greasy hair and slammed her first down on the desk, much to the horror of the teacher and everyone else in class.

"*That's* what I think of your *class policies.*"

Everyone in the room was dead silent. I had just befriended a badass! It was obvious from the back of the room where I was sitting that the delighted expressions on some of my fellow students' faces indicated they worshipped Vera. At least they secretly worshipped her, since none of them were brave enough to cheer her on. Deep inside I wanted to, but I didn't want to get in trouble with Squarehead right off the bat just because I admired Vera Petrov.

"Excuse me," Squarehead began in a tone of voice a little too diplomatic but Vera cut her off.

"That's right," Vera grumbled as she turned around and returned to her seat, "excuse *you*."

Some students giggled as Vera proudly showed off the few teeth she had left in a smile that stretched from one ear to the other. She sat down next to her sister like nothing had happened and the two of them grinned at each other. Svetlana and Vera were sitting at the table to my right and Jennifer was sitting just left of me at the same table next to the window. I enjoyed sitting in pairs more than sitting alone, and I silently wished for a table that could sit all four of us girls.

The tabletop was made of cheap black plastic while the overly large legs were made of solid wood. The equally cheap blue molded chairs were the same as they'd always been and so was most of the classroom. The brown floor tiles and white brick walls were still the same. Only the windows were new since they had been shot out from the outside and all classroom doors had been replaced. The building took on a weird U-shape and when Anderson had shot through the windows of the computer room, the bullets had flown all the way into Squarehead's classroom, destroying the windows as they entered.

Squarehead surprisingly let Vera stay in the classroom despite her outburst but I figured that Vera was just one of those kids whom you couldn't control and the most you could do was try to accommodate them and keep the peace. You just had to let them do whatever they wanted and deal with whatever resulted of it. Vera was a stark contrast to her twin sister who had quietly and emotionlessly remained seated the entire time, looking disinterested and downright bored. I knew that the sisters had come to Belden right after the shooting and that they had been in Squarehead's classroom twice before so they were well acquainted with each other. I could only speculate what kind of trouble Vera had landed herself in since then.

After the massacre everyone had become uptight and students who had half-eaten Pop Tarts in shapes loosely resembling guns were suspended for a week. Jennifer had told me about a boy who'd been expelled for bringing a package of bologna manufactured by a company called Natural Selections as though it had been the Columbine gunmen themselves who'd prepared that for him. The only good thing Mr.

Pasquale had really ever done was set up the support groups during the week to *encourage* people to talk about the shooting instead of shoving it under rug, unlike everything else he'd made disappear under that magic carpet of his.

Vera Petrov didn't have a mean or violent demeanour. In fact, from what I was able to observe she didn't take anything seriously. If Jennifer and her boyfriend Josh, both of whom I knew very well, hung out with the Petrov sisters then I knew that they were both good people, albeit extremely different people. There was no making me believe otherwise. I trusted Jennifer and Josh with my life. To some degree the sisters each reminded me of a different aspect of Anderson's personality. *My* Anderson, not the one who walked into the school armed to teeth on February 17th, 2017.

I still loved *my* Anderson even though I was so conflicted about the two of them being the same person. My therapist had always told me that it wasn't wrong to love him in spite of his actions, because they did not invalidate the wonderful friendship and cherished memories we had shared. As much as I swore that I hated him at times, deep down inside I really didn't. I missed him actually. I hated what he'd done of course, but I didn't hate *him*.

Once Squarehead had finished composing her inner diplomat, she went on to intimate us with some more of her class policies. We couldn't have cellphones in class, couldn't slouch on our uncomfortable chairs, certainly couldn't lay our heads down on the tables and everything about us and around us had to be very proper at all times. To pass the time I imagined Squarehead being a military officer turned teacher when she got bored of killing people in Iraq so she came down to New Hampshire where Anderson Massey shoved a gun in her face and made all of the military stuff resurface in her brain. I sighed, it was so much more complicated than my childish daydreams.

Oh yeah, and you weren't allowed to exhale too loudly either because then other students would hear you and become distracted from their mountain of work. I hated school with a passion too. I'd managed to zone out from Squarehead's relentless gum-flapping but my thoughts hadn't exactly gone in the right direction. I thought about how the government wanted to arm teachers in classrooms. What would that have looked like the day Anderson walked into the building? Would it really have stopped him? Or would it just have turned into a Mexican standoff or worst? I didn't want to walk around in a place where teachers were armed. Rogue kids wouldn't even need to find legal loopholes to get guns anymore, they'd just have to show up to school and get one from the teacher.

My thoughts were thankfully interrupted by the bell ringing. The girls and I couldn't get to the bathroom fast enough, I because I legitimately had to pee but I knew that Vera wanted to take a look at her hair. Zigzags of various kinds adorned the tips of her flamboyant hair as she walked ahead of me through the bathroom entrance, Jennifer and Sveta trailing behind talking to each other about the weather.

"Are you gonna help me fix it up when we get home?" Vera asked her sister as she played with her hair.

She was looking at herself in the bathroom mirror as I started blankly at my own reflection. After rearranging it, Vera's makeshift haircut actually wasn't so bad. It was eccentric to say the least, but nothing she couldn't get away with.

"You will not leave me a choice in the matter," Sveta replied without emotion as she pulled out another scarf from her back and arranged it on her sister's head to hide the mess.

"Now you won't have to fight for your human rights in class," I commented in regards to her headwear.

The girls cracked up laughing but I agreed that forcing people to wear their hair a certain way in school was unethical. There was nothing inappropriate or offensive about a girl wearing her hair down. Vera's new haircut was cut just above the chin, sort've making it a hillbilly bob without the bangs. The shade of orange was something to be seen, especially in the sunlight with the darker highlights that made it look like fire, but the hijab Sveta made her covered everything. Part of me was motivated to do something rebellious with my own hair as a defiant act towards the school. Or maybe I'd just wear a headscarf in protest too. That school wouldn't rule over me and what happened in the past wouldn't define me.

"I bet we must be some pretty shady characters if you say you knew Anderson Massey," Vera spoke as though she was able to look right through me.

"Vera!" Sveta chastised her.

"It's okay," I reassured the both of them, "it's okay to talk to me about Anderson. Neither one of you are shady or scary people, and neither was Anderson. At least not until he brought his gun to school."

"Man, I'm sorry you had to go through something like that. I can't imagine what it must've been like to see a guy you knew gun down innocent people."

"He killed the wrong people."

"Yeah, 'cause all the assholes are still here."

I managed to choke out a laugh no matter how inappropriate the subject matter was. It was good to laugh through the pain but all of that also made important issues surface.

"Do you know who Mario Bartolucci is?" I asked the twins.

"Yeah," Svetlana chocked out a giggle too, "rumours are still flying around about how he was flapping his gums about school shootings when Anderson walked in and shot him. And boy you looked pale when you saw him in Pasquale's garbage bin."

"Garbage bin?"

"That place ain't an office, it's a dump where students' souls go to die."

"Shouldn't that be a cemetery?" Jennifer interjected.

"In a way, yeah," Sveta was pensive, "but he looks down on us like we are trash so it's a dump."

And so it was a dump. The old office had been very nice compared to the new one. Anderson had completely obliterated the old one though, in a fury of bullets I couldn't help but wonder if he had intentionally tried to kill Mr. Pasquale even though he had escaped physically unharmed. There was no evidence of Anderson ever having some sort of hate list when he committed the worst school shooting since Columbine but if one existed, I knew without a doubt that Mr. Pasquale was on it.

"It's true that Mario fantasized about a real school shooter immediately before Anderson actually walked in," I blurted out after a long moment of silence on my behalf.

Both the Petrov sisters along with Jennifer looked at me with a mixture of both compassion and curiosity in their faces. Jennifer might've been in the building when the shooting happened but we hadn't crossed paths until much later that day and there were still many things she didn't know.

"I was right next to him when he got shot."

"Damn! I'm so sorry you had to live through something like that!" Vera's heart sank in her chest as she spoke. "Did you—"

"No, I didn't get shot. He didn't physically hurt me."

Maybe he hadn't put a bullet through my brain but he had hurt me on a much deeper level. He had penetrated me on the most intimate emotional level and ripped me apart. There was a part of me that was still so attached to him but I was unwilling to admit it to myself. I didn't know how to feel about him after what he had done. How is a person supposed to forgive their *friend* after something like that? I thought back to what the kids had said in therapy, how they felt sorry for him, and quite frankly I did too but I hated myself for failing him as well.

No, I hated Mr. Pasquale for failing him, but I still hated myself for not doing anything about it. I hadn't done anything more. Was there more I could've done? Anderson had been at the end of his rope and I couldn't have held on to him forever. The bell indicating it was time for our last class of the day interrupted my wandering mind from going into places it shouldn't. It's when I realized that I hadn't done my homework last week for the assignment we had to present in class!

My mind scrambled to somehow find a way to write up the short story we had to present or to have another puking episode to get away and forget about it entirely. The four of us sat next to each other at individual desks at the back of the room for English class, again with me sitting between Jennifer and Svetlana. The classroom was identical to all the other ones. Only the ones on the other side of the "U" had been appropriately renovated to patch up the bullet holes and any other evidence of the kind of carnage that had taken place in there almost two years ago.

"I didn't do my assignment," I whispered nervously to Sveta, "I mean, it's not finished and I'm not ready to present it today."

"Well, you can have mine," she retorted in a reassuring tone of voice as she handed me a paper, "I can just make another one up as I go. Nobody will know the difference and nobody cares anyway."

"You can't do this Sveta!"

"Says who? Anderson Massey? Nobody told him he couldn't do *that*."

I didn't speak. Svetlana's full set of gold teeth let off a warm glow in the sunlight illuminating the entire classroom as she smiled upon seeing her assignment on my desk.

"I'm sorry."

"It's okay Sveta, thank you."

"No, really Aly, I'm sorry. I keep forgetting that you witnessed that horror. All of these punks have been so quick to forget about everything and reminding them from time to time doesn't hurt. I really don't know what it's like go to through that and I hope I never do, but I'm sure as well not a victim of this corrupt establishment."

Was I victim? Did I let the school environment rule over me? Svetlana seemed to hint that it did, or at least that's the impression I got from her comments about those punks. She was right when she said that nobody ever said that you *couldn't* do something and she was definitely right when it came to the fact that nobody could tell her sister what to do. Part of me admired that about the two of them.

Before the shooting I hadn't been that type of person, the kind not to care, the kind of person the Petrov sisters were. I had always considered myself to be upright — apart from the food smuggling of course, but that rule was stupid — and most of all, *honest*. Taking Svetlana's assignment wasn't cheating since I hadn't copied hers and she'd handed it over voluntarily, but it was dishonest.

Sveta's childish golden grin moved me to just shut my mouth and go along with it. Who would know? In reality, I *was* a victim. Maybe not a victim of the social structure inside the school since I had generally been liked and respected but I was a victim of my own ideologies. *Those* ideologies that murdered twenty people. It was like a part of the puzzle had just fallen into place inside my brain. Everything suddenly made more sense, it was those damn ideologies all along! It was no longer so much about my own failure as a person or the fact that it took the police over an hour to enter the school after everyone was dead.

My brain had literally stopped functioning after the massacre. Nothing about my life made sense anymore. Everything had been distorted into shapes I couldn't make out and for almost two years I had been in denial, blaming myself but I hadn't been the one who made Anderson murder innocent people. *It had all been because of the ideology behind it*. It was a small revelation in itself for me to finally understand another small piece of why it happened. It was the collective apathetic ideology plaguing the hallways that had a part in making Anderson think it was okay to bring his gun to school, in making him think that nobody cared. He thought it was the way to get back what belonged to him, what he perceived had been taken from him. Maybe that was the reason why the Petrov sisters' attitudes reminded me of him to some degree, but they weren't victims. Anderson was the forgotten victim.

"I'm gonna kill myself to make everybody pay!" Anderson's words echoed at the back of my mind.

If that was what he intended on doing, he had succeeded.

"I wish I could be good enough just for once! That way I would know that I'm not completely alone."

I was a victim.

"Does anybody want to go first?" Mr. Fish asked the class.

I hadn't even noticed any of the other students come in. Mr. Fish was a tall, way too skinny man. He had said last week that he wasn't looking forward to his fiftieth birthday, that he was married, had two adult children and had been a schoolteacher his entire life. He had a long wrinkly narrow face — not a box-shaped head for once — with a crooked nose and one creepy glass eye. Its shade of blue didn't match his actual eye and it didn't move too well either.

He'd said that he had lost his eye when glass fragments from the windows being shot through damaged it beyond repair. It had to be removed after all and had since been replaced with that creepy thing floating where his eye should've been. He didn't speak about any other physical injury, if any, but the real injuries were the ones nobody wanted to talk about and I perfectly understood why.

"Why don't you get Curvy, Pukey, Scurvy or ISIS back there to go first?" One student told Mr. Fish while he glared at me and my three friends sitting with me in the back row.

That young man was Dominic Gonzalez, some rejected rich kid who had more money than brains. He was small for his age, with him being about as tall as Jennifer who was barely five feet tall. He had a small round face and dark skin, black hair and black eyes. He looked like he could've been a track and field athlete in elementary school but not at Belden High. I didn't even know the boy, but I already hated him for his words about my friends. Jennifer seemed to be very self-conscious and hurt by his remark but Vera showed him whatever was left of her teeth in a big evil grin while Sveta seemed to be accustomed to such remarks.

"I'd love to bite your face off but I can't," she taunted in defiance, "so I'll get my sister and her gold teeth to bite your balls off!"

"That's enough!" Mr. Fish's deep loud voice broke up what I anticipated would turn into a screaming match. "Alyson, would you like to go first?"

No, I did not but I got up from my desk anyway and went up to the front of the room where I quickly read over Svetlana's paper in my head as I cleared my throat for the presentation. The assignment given had been about organ donation where we had to write a short story from the point of view of an organ. I fount it to be completely ludicrous but Svetlana had penned a truly spectacular piece, a lot better than I could ever have done on my own even with an extension due to reasons of puke and insanity. Mr. Fish gave me the okay and I began reading Sveta's paper.

A lot of people regard me as *just another part of the body*. In fact, most people treat me this way. I'm a lung, I'm responsible for one of your most vital functions, breathing. For seventeen years I was in the left side of a girl named Jane's chest with my partner on the right side but now I'm alone in the body of a sixteen-year-old named Britney. She had lung cancer, that's right, at her age. Both her lungs were slowly dying from the inside out and she was hooked up to an oxygen machine 24 hours a day. Even all the machines and the pills and the steroids couldn't sustain her forever though, she really needed some new lungs but the waiting list for a donor was long.

Inside Jane's body I'd say that I did my job pretty well. I could send the much needed oxygen throughout her body to fuel those cells while she was running and jogging and I could hold her breath for minutes at a time underwater. My partner told me that one of Jane's eyeballs told him that Jane became compelled to be an organ donor when she walked in to the doctor's office to get a flu shot (sounds harmless enough huh?) and noticed a lung disease support group going on in another room. The heart told me himself that he though he was sink down all the way to the diaphragm upon hearing the eyeballs' initial report! During that same trip to see the doctor Jane informed herself about organ donation and what she could do to help. That's around the time she decided to give me up along with the right kidney and some blood.

It didn't all happen at once though. Jane had to undergo a lot of tests to see if I was really functioning properly and *in my right mind* as the brain would say. As it turns out I was very healthy and my tissue was of a very close match to a girl named Britney waiting on her deathbed for a transplant. So a few months later I literally went under the knife. Jane was sound asleep under the bizarre effects of something the ears told me was called *anesthesia*. Removing me from Jane's body was fairly easy, I said goodbye to everyone just in time for two big hands to literally scoop me out! Afterwards I was stitched to Britney's blood vessels and airways. It sounds a lot more horrific than it actually was. I didn't feel a thing, and from what I hear the other organs tell me, they didn't either.

In Britney's body I did my regular job like I always did, and for the first few days there we were all hooked up on tubes and machines to drain air, fluids and blood in order to let me fully expand. The other organs were very welcoming to me and the only thing I really miss about Jane were her ears letting me listen to Avicii all day. Gangnam Style isn't really my thing you know? But as it turns out Britney's body responded very well to me and there were thankfully no complications! Thanks to me and Jane's big heart (not literally *the heart*) Britney is now able to do simple things such as walking up the stairs instead of taking the elevator that she couldn't previously do. Can you believe that, she couldn't even walk up the stairs?! And during that time we were all running a marathon!

The other organs tell me that Britney became so compelled after receiving me that she signed her organ donor card too. I guess I might be getting, or losing, neighbours soon!

Everyone, even Dominic, clapped loudly as I returned to my cheap plastic chair of a seat at the back of the room. I wrote a thank you note to Svetlana and slipped it under my desk to her. She just flashed me a golden grin, happy that I had been able to put her story to good use. I wanted to pay her back somehow, and I promised myself that I would find a way to do just that. I wasn't thrilled about having two language classes during a single semester, not to mention two *consecutive* language classes in the afternoon, but if the girls and I helped each other out I reckoned I would survive just fine.

I was able to lay my head down on my desk for the rest of the class and just relax. Mr. Fish didn't say anything about it, and I figured that he sympathized with me because it was my first year coming back after the massacre. As horrific as it had been, I'd gained many special privileges because *I survived Belden* like it was some sort of achievement or something that I had finally accomplished after a lifetime of work. The only reason I had survived Belden was *because Anderson didn't kill me.*

CARL

WANTED FÖR MURDER

1980

IV

THE MUSLIM AND THE MISFIT

After school my mother came to pick me up and we drove to Andy's school to pick him up afterwards. For the past two years my parents Nicole and Johannes had been my best friends, my only actual friends in fact. My mom was a duplicate of me, well, actually I was a duplicate of her and Anderson was the exact duplicate of my father.

My father was a big man, a very muscular fella that worked as a mechanical engineer for a local industry. He had auburn hair and piercing blue eyes, narrow cheekbones and no particularly distinctive features. He had always worn a short beard for as long as I could remember. He also always wore a plaid shirt and blue jeans when he wasn't in his work uniform, *always*. That was truly the only distinctive thing about my dad.

Both my parents were very kind and loving individuals, probably the most loving people I had ever met. My opinions about them were probably biased because they were my parents and parents were supposed to be kind, loving, supportive and all that stuff but so many people came from broken homes. Jennifer came from a broken family, a *very* broken family. She lived with her aunt because her mother was in a mental hospital and her father in prison.

My parents John and Nikki were the best I could have possibly asked for. Without a doubt I'd won the parent lottery and I made sure to show them my appreciation and express my gratitude to them from time to time. I was eighteen, I was supposed to be an adult, independent, off to college or something, but no. My parents still had a little girl to take care of, and they did it extremely well. Like any other parents they could be overly sappy and emotional or completely insensitive but they did the best they could. We fought and we laughed, we were really no different than anybody else, except that their oldest child had survived Belden and that the perpetrator had often ate at their kitchen table.

"How was your day honey?"

"It was okay, thanks mom, didn't puke."

"Your father's going to be home early tonight, there was an accident at work and they closed down the side in order to investigate."

"Oh my goodness! Was he hurt?"

"No, he's fine by the grace of God but we only know that one person was killed at this point in time."

"Mom, that's horrible!"

"Don't tell Andy when he comes in okay?"

My little brother came running into the car and jumped in the backseat with a big smile on his face. He was a little version of my dad, and my father had looked exactly like that when he'd been Anderson's age too. He had a full head of red hair that was getting long but he didn't want to cut it. His hair somewhat reminded me of the haircut Vera had given herself, only Andy's was shorter and curly, and prettier of course.

My little brother had once upon a time been my third best friend, but since the shooting I hadn't been myself and I knew that he suffered because of that too. He didn't let his sadness show when I was around because he was very sensitive to my pain even for his age, but I knew too well that he wanted his sister back, and I wanted my little Anderson back too. Back home my dad was already sitting in our overly big living room waiting for the three of us to come home. When I walked through the door he jumped off the couch and came over to hug me.

My dad's hugs were my favourites, they were tight and loving and I felt comforted more than anything in his strong arms. I was particularly happy to hold him after hearing that a man had been killed at work. He then hugged Anderson the same way he'd hugged me and proceeded to kiss and hug my mom last. The four of us sat in the living room and spent some quality time together. Three brown leather couches surrounded the stone fireplace as well as a large TV mounted on the wall. Both antique and modern furniture complimented the deep green walls. The living room was another spectacular room. It gave an old-fashioned feel to a modern space, it was probably my favourite room of all.

"Why are you home early daddy?" Anderson asked innocently.

"There was a problem at work and they closed down the side so they can fix it," he replied calmly not to scare him, "it's going to be alright little man."

I laid my head on my father's shoulder on the couch and closed my eyes. I was unbelievably thankful that he was unharmed, but most of all that he was *alive*. I was overly sensitive to that kind of stuff because I had seen some of my friends be murdered by my other so-called friend but it still wasn't the same when people you live with escape awful workplace accidents. I silently prayed for the family of the person who got killed on the job and for anybody else who might have been injured, killed or hurt somehow.

There had never been a workplace accident since my father began working there ten years ago in 2008. He was obviously shaken by the tragedy, and it was especially nerve-racking since not many details had been released and nobody really knew what had happened or what was going on. I hung on to my father as he put one arm around me and his big rough hands stroked my shoulder. I appeared to be more shaken about the accident than he was. Nobody knew what would end up of his job either. We needed his income because our family had a lot of debt and without two incomes we risked losing a lot, even if mom were to work full time.

"Do you guys want to go out for supper?" He asked. "You can both bring a friend."

"Can I bring two dad?" I asked, thinking of the Petrov sisters.

"Just one Aly."

"They are twins."

"Well, in that case I can make an exception. If you're going to bring the one you might as well bring the two."

I called up Svetlana and asked her and Vera if they wanted to have supper with my family somewhere in town. It wasn't long before the two of the popped up at the front door, very hungry for both food and a good time. Both of my parents were happy that I had made a new friend at school, two new friends in fact, considering the circumstances up until they actually laid eyes on the twins. Puzzled expressions swept over their faces as they checked out the Muslim and the misfit standing in the doorway.

It was especially the haircut and the flame orange because there was nothing weird or eccentric about a female wearing a headscarf. There weren't many Muslims in the region, in fact Svetlana was probably the only one, but we'd met some before and we knew that they weren't the evil people Donald Trump and other bigots like him made them out to be. The Petrov sisters — especially Vera — were very polite and it only took a few minutes for my parents to warm up to them.

Anderson seemed to be afraid of the sisters as he'd never seen people like them up and close before, yet he was still curious because he didn't run away or make a scene like he sometimes did when he didn't know how to deal with his emotions. He was just a child after all, one couldn't blame him. While the girls and I hung out Anderson called up another little boy and when his parents dropped him off at our door, the boys hopped in with my mom while the twins and I hopped in with my dad and we all headed down the road.

"For English class," I told Sveta as I handed her a twenty dollar bill, "it's not much but I hope you know how grateful I am."

"Nah, supper is even too generous," she dismissed me, "I'm the one who will have to repay you sometime."

"Sveta, you really don't."

"Did it ever occur to you that maybe I want to?"

"I'm not doing this because I want something out of you. I'm very grateful that someone I've known casually for less than a week would just hand me their assignment."

"My religion teaches that I should help people in need whenever I can, and I was able to help you. I treat others the way I want to be treated. Maybe one day I won't be doing so well and I'll need help with my own schoolwork."

I smiled at her to say thank you. As I did so I noticed that my mother's vehicle was next to us in the other lane so we waved at each other and Anderson giggled playfully as he showed us his toys. He was a bit shy and I wasn't particularly outgoing myself. I wasn't one of them gutsy girls per se, but I didn't consider myself to be a shy person either. Yeah, maybe I had been locked inside of myself since the shooting but that still didn't make me shy.

Dad brought us to a jazzy little bistro called Grandma's House in the downtown core of Wintercrest. It was one of my favourite restaurants in the entire state of New Hampshire and I was excited to get to eat there with my family and my two new friends. I hadn't been out to eat in a group setting like that for a long time. Grandma's House was a fifties diner by the side of the road that served the best ice cream in the entire United States if not the whole world. No, the entire *universe*.

"Do I get an old-fashioned bucket of fried chicken for us all?" Dad asked in his usual enthusiastic, optimistic voice.

"We can't eat that," the twins said in unison.

"You are vegetarians?" My dad seemed fearful of having insulted them with meat.

"No, I just can't chew it," Vera replied, "I have no teeth left at the bottom and only seven on top."

"I can't eat it because it's not halal," Sveta added, "but I can chew very well."

The twins giggled but my dad didn't find it so funny. He pitied Vera from his reaction but didn't seem to know what *halal* meant. My father was the kind of guy who loved people from different cultures and backgrounds but he wasn't exactly knowledgeable about them or their way of life. Vera managed to convince him to buy the chicken anyway while the sisters settled for a king-sized platter assorted cheeses, a large order of garlic potatoes and cheesecake on the side.

"We can be part-time vegetarians," Vera muttered with a mouthful of potatoes, "but I definitely look forward to getting a new set of teeth."

"Are gold teeth part of your culture or your religion?" My mom asked.

"I thought they were," Sveta answered, making sure to swallow her food before she opened her mouth, "but it turns out that our culture isn't what we thought it was?"

"Oh?"

"Based on our babushka's stories we thought we had Uzbek and Kyrgyz ancestry, but after taking a DNA test it turns out that we're mostly Bosnian, Scandinavian and English. This came as a complete surprise to us, and I honestly don't know how that even happened. There isn't a single English name in our family tree!"

"Buying only a single DNA test is pretty much the one and only time we've saved money on something!" Vera exclaimed, without food in her mouth. "Being identical twins, everything usually comes in two."

"I saw those tests on TV, I'd be curious to take one," I pondered out loud.

"It also turns out that we have extremely little Russian and Ukrainian blood despite that basically all of our relatives were born there. Most are still there, but several moved to Canada." Vera went on.

"Why couldn't we move to Canada?!" Sveta grumbled with longing in her voice.

She let out a loud sigh before stuffing a big chunk of cheese in between her shiny teeth. The twins ate out of the same plates and drank out of the same cups but the cheesecake was obviously Vera's alone by the way she hovered over it. By the time she was halfway through eating it she had icing even on her forehead! Sveta didn't seem interested in it at all, she was all about the cheese and the ginger ale. The rest of us ate the bucket deal of garlic chicken that was particularly tasty.

"So you three met in school?" My mother asked.

"Yeah, we ended up having all of our classes together." Vera replied, still pigging out in her cake.

I agreed, matter settled. I really didn't want to get into Vera's meltdown earlier or how Sveta had saved my butt because for the first time in my life I hadn't completed an assignment but I did mention that the twins were also good friends with Jennifer. My parents and Anderson loved Jennifer like their own flesh and blood. She was that third child my folks wanted and a fun playmate for my little brother.

"I see you can chew cake pretty well there Vera!" My father joked like he usually did.

"No chewing required Mr. Feldman!" Vera spit back through a mouthful of cake.

"Just John."

"No chewing required Just John!"

Everyone laughed. For the first time in probably the last two years I was able to enjoy myself. For a moment there, as I shoved the chicken down my pie hole and watched Vera put the last piece of cheesecake in her mouth, I was left to believe that I didn't have a single care in the world even if it was just for a fraction of a second. Then Anderson Massey came crawling back into my thoughts from behind that dark door he always had the keys to no matter how many locks I tried to put on it.

Our restaurant had been Wesley's, a little burger joint down by the river across the street from the marina. I hadn't been there in almost four years. I felt nostalgic, I loved Wesley's so much, and I especially loved ordering take-out and eating it by the river on lazy summer days. I had my first kiss on the banks of the Coldbank River. I caught my first fish there. I did my homework here. I fell in love with life itself there. One could say that I'd been born there, and that I'd died within the halls of Belden High.

The following day the twins invited me over to their place so their uncle could serve us supper after school. A girl named Mercedes Hanson drove us to the Petrov house after a particularly boring day at school. I recognized Mercedes from art class in the morning but I had never spoken to her or interacted with her in any way. She was a taller girl with a stocky build and uneven short hair that hung over her sunglasses. Her hair was jet black and contrasted with her pale skin, matching her dark blue eyeliner and blood red lipstick.

Like many other older teens she had many tattoos and piercings, in fact I was probably the only one who didn't. Vera had plenty of tattoos and I saw a few sticking out from underneath Sveta's clothing. Mercedes very fittingly drove some old Mercedes-Benz that was nothing but a piece of junk but it appeared to work fine apart from the atrocious noises that seemed to come out of everywhere. The radio antenna had been ripped out and a cassette tape was jammed in the player so the radio kept making these weird humming noises even though it was turned off. Thirty years ago it probably would've been a nice car, but it wasn't anymore.

Mercedes drove the twins to and from school every day and sometimes Jennifer would hop in too. I felt like *moop*, or matter out of place as my mother would say, as I awkwardly rode shotgun in a dilapidated bucket of bolts surrounded by renegades. I'd never judged such people in my entire life, but it was all a brand new experience for me and those usually tended to be scary after my sense of security had been taken from me.

Mercedes was very nice and sociable. As we rode along she told me about her travels, her taste in movies and her family, among other things. She had a brother named Lincoln, and I figured that her parents were named Chevrolet and Honda. Mercedes made a sharp right turn into this run-down trailer park off a road leading to the interstate. It looked like a swamp, or maybe a dump where teenagers' souls went to die. The trailers looked like they had been there since the early seventies, if not earlier. It was like a trip back in time that matched the old Mercedes. A knot appeared in my stomach as Mercedes made her way almost all the way to the back of the dead end street with a hill behind it. Literally a *mountain* of dirt covered in overgrown grass loomed before me with a giant sign on top that menacingly read **NO TRESPASSING**.

I didn't remember Wintercrest being a nuclear testing site, but that's what the trailer park looked like. The only things that were missing were the mannequins and the guys wearing hazmat suits. Mercedes parked in the driveway of a small lime green trailer that probably had been forest green before the siding faded in the sunlight. It was probably the best looking trailer in the entire park considering that all the others were as dilapidated as Mercedes' jalopy.

I followed the twins inside as Mercedes smoked outside before driving away. Everything suddenly felt eerie in the middle of a radioactive trailer park. The door of the Petrov trailer creaked open and Sveta lead me in to dimly-lit living room.

"Well hello there!" A shadow jumped out at me from the kitchen and spoke in a thick Russian accent. "I'm Dmitry Petrov, Vera and Sveta's uncle. Come on in!"

He tightly hugged the twins like my dad did to me when he came home every night after work and walked over to me and hugged me the same way. It was awkward. The twin's uncle looked like the boogeyman, or at least a version of him. He was about as tall as my own father, mid-fifties, long grey hair tied up in a ponytail, matching stubble on his face, a paunch like Mr. Pasquale and Soviet emblems tattooed on his tanned skin. He had the same bright eyes the twins did and the same set of teeth except that the bad ones had been replaced with silver crowns.

Dmitry Petrov looked like a mean drug-dealing gangster ready to pull a gun out of his dirty bomber jacket and shoot you right in between the eyes at any time, but of course I knew that those were only stereotypes that I'd seen in movies and TV shows. Dmitry hugged like a creeper and looked like one but despite his intimidating appearance, he did not have a menacing demeanour. He was warm and gentle, like a fatherly kind of gentle, even to me.

"Don't be scared now," his voice was hoarse like his throat was clogged up with something, "have a seat."

The four of us awkwardly cuddled each other on a three-seater sofa crammed in the corner of a dirty room. Dmitry sat at one end and I sat in between the sisters like a monkey in the middle. The three of them simply sat there like nothing was wrong and a colossal picture of Joseph Stalin wasn't bullying us with his moustache right above the television. It was one of those old models with the big boxes behind them, like the box somehow contained the movie. I hadn't seen one of those in years and quite frankly did not know that some people still had them.

Soviet propaganda littered the room with everything from old posters to bronze busts of Vladimir Lenin and various little trinkets. The living room was a shrine to the Soviet Union and communism, and although I knew that the Petrovs were Russian I didn't expect people to still be into that. I'd learned all about the Bolshevik Revolution and the Second World War and whatnot in history class but that hadn't included stepping right into a time machine. I was beyond weirded out to put it mildly but everyone else seemed to be oblivious to my discomfort.

"So it's just the three of you here?" I broke the awkward silence.

"Yes, it's just the girls and I," Dmitry replied, "sometimes my son Sergey comes over to spend a night or two but he lives near Norwood with his wife on the other side of town."

Norwood was another trailer park that was somewhat falling apart but still looked much nicer than the former nuclear testing zone I was currently in. Dmitry explained how the twins' parents had been absolutely awful people and how he'd taken them in as his own children after their grandmother had fallen ill could no longer care for them. The twins' mother had died of a drug overdose and their father had been sentenced to perpetuity in one of Russia's toughest prisons when they were both quite young.

Their grandmother, or their *babushka* as they called her in Russian, had raised the girls almost since birth with the support of other family members but had been diagnosed with terminal cancer and Dmitry decided to bring them to America with him. He explained how hard life could be for the disadvantaged in Russia, and not that it was easy for anyone really, but at least in America they'd all have opportunities they never had before. Dmitry also explained how Canada was his first choice, but that coming to America was easier and quicker in the desperate situation they had been faced with.

Dmitry then rambled on endlessly about how he was such a proud father — or father figure at least — to the girls and how he'd been blessed with them during some of the most difficult times in his life. Then he went on an equally long ramble about his son Sergey and how his ex-wife had left him for a rich man in another country and a bunch of other familial drama that in a way made me grateful that I didn't have much of a family at all outside of my parents and my brother. Dmitry was a scary-looking man but not a mean man at all.

It was obvious that he and the twins had a very close relationship as each other were all they really had left to depend on. Sure, they had other family and friends but God only knew that such people weren't always dependable or helpful and sometimes they could be downright toxic. Later on in the ramble the topic of Sergey came up again and Dmitry went on flapping his gums about how the owner of the trailer park, Jihoon Garcia, had assaulted him or something and that Sergey's wife had in turn beat him up and landed herself in jail.

"Jihoon Garcia is the biggest jerk on the planet," Svetlana grumbled angrily, "I mean, what kind of landlord assaults his own tenants?"

I didn't speak. Anxiety about my own housing situation came creeping back in. Although my folks had been in financial trouble for a while following a failed investment we'd never been closer to losing our home and I was painfully aware of Wintercrest's many slum landlords. I didn't want to end up in some trailer park that reminded me of Mercedes' dilapidated car. The only difference was that she didn't live in that old thing.

"At least the place is nice you know," Vera continued, "three nice bedrooms, full basement! Not a lot of trailers have a full basement, or anything beyond a crawlspace, but with one it becomes as big as a double-wide you know, even if it's just a single."

I looked around at Stalin's second home and despite the dirt and the propaganda, the place was cozy. Everything neatly fit together like a good game of Tetris and no space was wasted. I had never been around trailer parks too much but for a small family it seemed like a good option, provided one didn't rent from Jihoon Garcia or lived in the skid row of trailers. I'd be devastated if my parents did have to sell the house, but I could settle for a trailer park as long as my environment radiated the same kind of love Dmitry and the twins shared in their small space.

"The delivery man should arrive soon," Dmitry commented as he got up to go set the table.

"Wanna see my grow operation in the basement in the meantime?" Vera enthusiastically asked me.

Grow operation?! Before I could say no she grabbed me by the arm and dragged me to what looked like a closet at the end of the trailer near the bathroom and opened the door to reveal a spiral staircase heading downstairs to an unfinished basement. Svetlana trailed behind us and as soon as one of them opened the light I saw the mess of plants scattered all over the place. No, they were't marijuana plants. Instead, the Petrovs had plywood boards put together to make makeshift garden boxes that looked like rustic crates all over the floor and filled them in with various kinds of plants and flowers.

I looked around the room and could see columbines in all colours of the rainbow, cosmos candy stripes, yellow sunflowers, red sunflowers, and even a whole patch of buttercup squash just to name a few. The sunlight came in through two small basement windows and fed the plants as well as a dripping extended shower hose hung from the ceiling to periodically make sure the plants were moist since they weren't actually in the ground and the trailer park seemed to be rather dry. Some plants were even growing out of the laundry tub!

"What do you think?" Vera seemed to be so proud of her secret garden.

"Columbines."

"Do you think that's weird? Like Eric and Dylan kinda Columbine weird?"

"No, it's not weird." I mumbled out not wanting to have that conversation.

Belden had been compared to Columbine, Sandy Hook, Thurston and Parkland too many times, like the perpetrators were all some sort of cosmic pact of teenage mass murderers who'd all grown up wanting to kill their classmates. That notion was wrong. Nobody had been born with such vile things inside their hearts and minds. All of them had *become* that way but the reasons why were often elusive, and the political discourse was only about pushing agendas and not about finding solutions.

They even had so-called experts in psychology on TV that rambled on about how there were eighteen letters in *Dylan Bennet Klebold* as well as *Anderson Jack Massey* or twenty characters if the spaces were counted, like that was the answer to everything. Nobody ever thought to ask their friends and family what they were really like as *people* before they went down in infamy. Instead, society was much too busy plastering their faces on news screens and accusing them of being monsters when the wold wanted answers but weren't asking questions.

"Come over here, there's more in the next room."

I followed the twins into another secret garden basement room where miniature trees had almost reached the ceiling. I didn't know what to think upon seeing all the indoor plants.

"Why don't you have any plants outside?" I asked the girls, genuinely curious.

"It's in part because we don't have much of a front yard," Sveta replied, "and there's a pile of scrap metal and other junk in the back so there's no room left for a proper garden."

"And a few years ago there was that weird guy who ate plants right out of people's gardens," Vera added, "a real savage! I don't know what happened to him but he's gone now."

"Food's here!" Dmitry shouted from upstairs, putting an abrupt end to the conversation.

The twins shut off the lights and I then followed them back up the skimpy metal staircase. Two large cats had since appeared upstairs and were flopped over on the kitchen counter.

"Shut the door behind you, I don't want the cats to go eat the plants or pee in the soil."

The four of us sat around a small metal bistro table, the kind that you'd use to decorate the lawn, that kept wobbling from side to side since the floor was crooked. Dmitry and Vera sat in the matching metal chairs while Sveta sat on a stool and I in an old brown recliner that had been dragged into the kitchen so we could all sit together. Both the walls and floor tiles were anthracite in colour like the trailer was some sort of military base or monitoring centre for nuclear tests going on behind the hill.

More Soviet paraphernalia hung from the ceiling fan and I noticed that were a few newspaper clippings of the Belden massacre on the fridge. It made me feel odd to be surrounded by such things and three people who found it absolutely normal but at the same time both the twins and their uncle were very welcoming. I figured that not a whole lot of people were comfortable being in their trailer but there was so much more to the Petrovs than just their taste in decor. Live and let live, simple enough.

Dmitry served us cabbage rolls, rice and a plate of assorted garden vegetables from a local restaurant called The London Cafe. I grabbed some dipping sauce and put my styrofoam plate on my lap so I didn't butt elbows with anyone since the bistro table wasn't big enough to accommodate everyone. The obese calico cats came meowing at the table and Dmitry gave them small pieces of chicken that his meal included. Vera couldn't chew the meat and Sveta wouldn't eat it because it wasn't halal and I didn't want it so that left only Dmitry and his cats.

"Do you pray or say thanks or something else before eating in your household?" Dmitry asked me.

"No, but I have no qualms about adhering to your customs," I replied emotionlessly.

"Only my sister is religious," Vera jumped in, "but she doesn't impose it on anyone. We've had people over in the past who got seriously insulted that we just dug in to our plates before so we figure we ought to ask from now on."

"You don't have to worry about any of that with me. This is your home, you can do whatever you want. I'm a guest here so I'll adhere to your lifestyle while I'm here."

"That's really nice of you Alyson. Common sense and respect aren't common enough anymore."

The food was delicious, spicy and just the right temperature. It tasted like something your grandma would make from scratch, not bad for takeout! The big white calico jumped on the armrest of the chair I was sitting in and seemed to want my vegetables. The somewhat smaller black one left after finishing its piece of meat.

"Bobo likes green beans," Vera gave me the green light to share my meal with the cat.

"It's nice to have someone who's still genuine come over for dinner," Sveta added, "and not just some hypocrites with ulterior motives."

"Oh? I'm sorry that this happened to you in the past." I spoke softly.

"This community isn't very friendly towards immigrants," Sveta continued, "and definitely not towards Muslims. A group of so-called Christians came over a few months ago under the guise of welcoming us despite that we've been here for quite a while, only to then harass us when we rejected their beliefs."

"I'm so sorry that this happened to you. This is never something I've had to deal with before but I know from the news that minorities have been getting it a lot worst since Trump came to power."

"Oh don't talk to me about that crackpot! I know darn well that true Christians don't behave that way and Jesus definitely wouldn't stand for what those hypocrites did to us, but idiots like Trump basically encourage and endorse crap like that!"

After we all finished eating our meal Dmitry served us Oreo ice cream which was a fabulous dessert after a spicy meal. The cats had disappeared back to wherever they'd come from now that they had a full stomach but I was up for more food!

"I still owe you for Mr. Fish's class." I told Svetlana.

"No you don't," she replied like it was nothing, "I'm not like one of those hypocrites with ulterior motives who just want something out of you. I take being a genuinely good person very seriously and please don't think that you owe me because you don't."

"Well, I can do one of your assignments for Squarehead's class."

"Squarehead?!"

The twins cracked up laughing hysterically, and so did Dmitry even though he didn't know who we were talking about. I started laughing too, not immediately realizing that I'd actually said that out loud. I was somewhat embarrassed but I knew that the twins didn't like her either.

"I'm not usually a judgmental person," I began after the hype of laughter had died down, "but her head is actually square."

"That's true," Vera exclaimed as she began to laugh again, "it's like a box!"

"Is that haircut lady?" Dmitry asked.

"Yes, that's her." Sveta replied. "Vera definitely showed her!"

I smiled to myself thinking back to that moment. Vera was my hero for doing that. Schools shouldn't feel like prisons. Schoolteachers shouldn't feel like the supreme authority in the world, and I admired that Vera had escaped those chains.

"I hate that stupid social ideology in that school, that building is what drives people into the ground!" Sveta grumbled, obviously having faced much discrimination in those halls.

"That's why I don't conform to them," Vera finished her sister's sentence, "I am not a mouse! This is a country of wolves ruled by sheep and owned by pigs!"

The twins went back and forth in angry tones as they ranted about how awful that school really was. I knew that none of those rants were directed towards me but I felt like crap since I had been part of the *in* crowd even though I no longer had any friends in it. I wasn't an outcast per se, I had money and I was a pretty athletic girl who didn't get in trouble, but a dark shadow had been cast over me long before Anderson had even fired that first bullet. I had normal people problems but for the vast majority of my schooling had gone without a social hitch. Anderson hadn't been so lucky.

"Did Anderson ever tell you he didn't like school?" Dmitry asked me meekly almost like he could read my thoughts. "It is my understanding that the two of you were friends?"

"Yeah," I replied blankly, "he did."

"I'm sorry you had to live through that."

"I even told Mr. Pasquale that Anderson needed help."

Now I really had their attention.

"Mr. Pasquale will be with you in a minute." Mrs. Phyllis told me as she walked out and closed the door behind her.

I exhaled loudly. I knew Anderson wasn't going to be happy with me. I kept on telling myself that it was the right thing to do, that it was for his safety and wellbeing and everything would be fine afterwards but

I couldn't seem to get myself to believe that last part. He had told me repeatedly to leave it alone, to leave him alone, not think about it and just let him be. But I couldn't. He was my friend, I couldn't just let everything go when it was so obvious that he was suffering and I was the only person who seemed to care. At the very least, I was the only person who paid attention.

"Can I help you?" Mr. Pasquale asked as he sat down behind his desk.

"It's about Anderson Massey," I told him in an urgent tone of voice, "he needs help."

It was apparent in his eyes that he was annoyed and didn't want to hear it from the moment I'd said Anderson's name. Anderson hadn't been the kind of guy to get into any serious trouble. His trips to the principal's office had never been for anything serious, but apparently Mr. Pasquale saw it differently.

"What about him? And why do you even bother to mingle with a loser like him in the first place?"

I was appalled that the *principal* had the audacity to tell me something like that! Who was he to judge?! He was supposed to be in charge of the school, the top person to look out for the welfare of his students! That included Anderson Massey whether he liked him or not.

"Mr. Pasquale!" I urged. "He needs help! He cuts himself, he's suicidal, he needs urgent help and I don't know how to get through to him!"

"Alyson, listen to me," he said in an eerie overly diplomatic voice, "stay away from Anderson. He's a delinquent and will only hurt you, damage your reputation and I don't know what else he's capable of. He's dangerous, keep your distance and leave him alone."

And he got up and walked out.

Just like that.

Mr. Pasquale had later found out the hard way just what Anderson had been capable of.

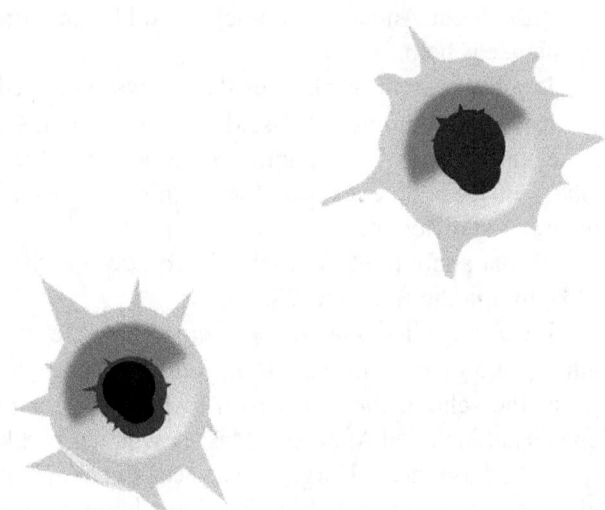

V

GENOCIDE

Svetlana and I managed to give Vera a decent haircut after supper. Dmitry liked it so much that he wanted us to cut his own hair. It was still long enough to tie up in a ponytail, but he looked much better after we'd cleaned up his mane. Sveta then wanted her sister and I to dye her hair but I didn't have enough time before Mercedes came back to pick me up just before seven o'clock. Dmitry and the twins stood in the doorway of the trailer and waved at me as Mercedes pulled out of the driveway and sped off towards the interstate.

"Are you going to run for the hills when I drop you off home Alyson?" Mercedes asked me in a monotone, emotionless voice.

"No," I replied confidently, "I like the twins and Dmitry very much."

A crooked grin appeared on the side of her face but she didn't say anything. I figured that she had brought over a few people to the trailer over the last year and none of them had wanted to return a second time. I grinned too, yeah, the trailer had been quite interesting but I wasn't afraid of the Petrovs. There was nothing to actually be afraid of in that house, that picture of Stalin couldn't hurt me, and I definitely had no reason to fear the people inside. They had been very welcoming and I appreciated that.

I told Mercedes where to drop me off and when she did I gave her five dollars as a way to thank her for the transportation services she provided. It was quite a long drive back and forth between the trailer and my house and gas wasn't cheap. I could almost see her heart sinking in her chest as she told me that it wasn't necessary. Her voice was cracking up like she was about to cry but she smiled at me and waved as I walked towards my house.

"Did you have a good time?" My father asked me as I hugged him upon walking through the front door.

"A *wonderful* time dad!" I happily replied.

"You should invite the girls and their parents over this weekend to have a barbecue with us!"

"I'm sure it will be wonderful, I'll pass along the message but make sure that the food is halal for Svetlana and easy to eat for Vera. By the way, did you hear anything about work?"

"No honey, no word yet. Only one person confirmed dead so far. We should, however, hear something by Friday."

The worst part about the whole situation was not knowing. Despite the fact that my mother made good money, neither of my parents could support a family of four on their own. My father wasn't guaranteed another job if things didn't work out since Wintercrest's economy had been steadily declining over the last few years.

I feared having to end up in a run-down trailer park like the Petrovs if not worst. The Petrov trailer was nasty but the other ones looked even nastier. None of the trailer parks in Wintercrest were particularly nice, but there was quite an abundance of them in the middle of the city's housing crisis.

I sympathized with the people just trying to make it who lived in those disgusting trailers but I didn't want to join them at any costs. I'd always been so privileged, so entitled, so lucky, and most of the time I took it for granted.

I lived as if my dad's money would never run out because he was a highly specialized engineer and the local industries were always going to need him, but that was nothing but a beautiful fantasy in limbo. My eyes had been opened to the cold hard fact that nothing lasted forever, and it wasn't like Belden had failed to make that reality sink in.

I took a deep breath and went up to my room where I took out my notebook and did what I always did when my thoughts were messed up: I wrote a letter to Anderson.

Dear Anderson,

Man, I'm so sorry. I pray for your forgiveness. I'm sorry I didn't do anything more. I am not any different than all the people who hurt you and trampled over you all this time. I didn't attack you but I am just as guilty for not doing anything about it. I really don't know what to say Anderson, the words get lost before they come. I wasn't able to be there for you when you were alive and I sure as hell can't make things right now that you're dead.

I get it though, the ideologies of that place. It's a shame that you never met the Petrov sisters, they would have rocked your world. You rocked mine. And you taught me so many things that sometimes I don't know that I know but I do. I just can't seem to understand that amidst the never-ending storm going around in my brain. It's like I'm this new person that I don't know. I reckon that maybe that's how you felt in the end. AND I DIDN'T HELP YOU.

Alyson

Friday came around, but so did weekend homework. Mr. Fish's class policy was that if you didn't finish your assignment during class, you had to finish it at home. I felt that was fair but it still annoyed me since I had a difficult time concentrating at school and focusing on the class material wasn't any easier. I had already begun English class when Anderson decided to bring his gun to school and the material was nearly identical so it shouldn't have been hard, but it was. Having to read *The Rocking Horse Winner* by D.H. Lawrence a second time particularly got under my skin. I hated that stupid story and I hated the memories that came flooding back because of it.

Anderson Massey never wanted to sit next to me in class. I had managed to convince him to sit at the desk in front but there wasn't a day that went by that I didn't silently pray that he'd change his mind. On my right I had

Elaine's good company, but to the left I had the unfortunate experience of having Trevor Bradford sit next to me. Everybody hated that guy because he was perverted and sexually deranged. He wasn't dangerous, much less predatory, but he was weird. Everything that went through his brain, even the most innocent thing like a sticky note, had something to do with sex and he wasn't ashamed of that.

He touched himself in class every single day and was quite vocal about his enjoyment in the back of the room. Some students were repulsed, others laughed, but none could stop him. When Mr. Fish chastised him he stopped for two minutes and then picked up right where he'd left off. Trevor was particularly aroused by paper. Whether it was a page in a book, the cheap sheets we'd write our class notes on or a poster put up on a wall, he liked to touch it or downright rub himself on it.

He often asked me to write random things on sticky notes and give them to him, which he would in turn rub and vocally enjoy himself. I never wrote anything sexual, I even gave him the answers to many assignment questions but he didn't even look at the actual text, he just wanted to please himself sexually. In a futile attempt to try to distract Trevor from his deranged behaviour and maybe normalize paper so he wouldn't see it sexually, Mr. Fish made him bring the attendance sheet to the main office all the way at the other end of the school one morning. Trevor happily did so, but nearly half and hour had gone by and he hadn't returned.

Since I'd finished my assignment early that day, I'd been given the task of going to look for him. I didn't have to go far, I only opened the door and there he was. Mr. Fish's class had that one odd door that had the hinges on the wrong side so the door opened inward instead of outward like all the other doors in the building and I got quite a surprise when I saw what was on the other side. Trevor hadn't brought the attendance sheet to the office at all, he'd been on the other side of the door, rubbing himself with the yellow sheet of paper and sexually enjoying himself the entire time. I'd caught him in the act, redhanded. I was revolted by what I saw him doing but the rest of the class erupted in laughter.

Mr. Fish, on the other hand, flew into a boiling rage. Trevor ended up being suspended for a week for publicly masturbating in the hallway but the minute he came back he went right back to his old habits. He especially enjoyed himself when we had to read The Rocking Horse Winner because apparently there were several sexual references in the story, including one about masturbation, despite that I'd never been able to find any of them no matter how many times I forced myself to reread that stupid story.

"He died of masturbation!" Trevor exclaimed when Mr. Fish asked the class what the little boy in the story had died of.

The class erupted into laughter again, and even Mr. Fish managed to laugh at him. The little boy had actually died of a fever, but apparently the point of the story had been that a lack of a mother's love had caused him to die. I'd obviously missed the point since I'd missed that part too but I'd still gotten a better grade on that assignment than Trevor did. In all fairness, the study guide that had come with The Rocking Horse Winner did mention a subliminal reference to masturbation but I chose to overlook it since there were already enough sex acts happening at the desk next to me.

"The kid isn't a homosexual like you Anderson." Trevor took his own shot at the only other outcast in class, "By the way, did you find a nice handsome guy to take to the Valentine's Day dance?"

"At least I'm not a papersexual like you, dumb-ass." Anderson snapped back. "My sex life isn't reduced to class material!"

"Stop that right now!" Mr. Fish grumbled. "This is inappropriate and distracts the other students!"

The other students laughed at both of them but I didn't find bullying to be funny. Trevor didn't seemed to fazed by being called a pervert, a rapist in the marking, or whichever other insult was hurled at him at school, but Anderson took it hard whenever he was called a faggot among a long list of other names. He wasn't gay, he very much like girls, but even if he had been gay, what difference did it possibly make? Gay people weren't a threat to society, but bullies were. The week following that comment Anderson put a bullet through Trevor's brain. It happened so fast that he didn't even get the chance to carry out his self-fulfilling prophecy of dying while masturbating with a piece of paper.

"Alyson, will you answer the questions?" Mr. Fish pressed me.

"What? The masturbation?" I mistakenly said out loud, not knowing what had been asked during my flashback.

Reality hit hard as the dreaded familiar laughter echoed around the room. I felt like dying of embarrassment, or at least evaporating. Vera laughed uncontrollably and I noticed that she had more missing teeth than I'd originally thought, but Svetlana wasn't laughing. She seemed to be very uncomfortable and just as embarrassed as I was. Some people simply weren't comfortable with sex, but aside from my experience with Trevor Bradford I didn't see it as anything to frown upon or be ashamed of.

"The question, Alyson, was why do you think the walls of the house kept on whispering?"

"Oh, this highlights the theme of greed in the story."

"Yes, that's correct."

Mr. Fish continued on teaching but I zoned out. I did notice Svetlana growing more and more irritated from the corner of my eye but I didn't bother to think about why. I figured that she was like me and thought that the story was stupid and had zero educational value. It turned out that I was correct.

"I object on grounds of morality and educational value!" She got up and responded authoritatively at something Mr. Fish had asked or said.

"Tell us why you feel this way Svetlana," Mr. Fish seemed to be both open-minded and impressed by Sveta's bold declaration.

"This story has zero moral or educational value. It doesn't teach us anything of value regarding the many instances of immorality in it and holds even less value when it comes to real life issues. There's so much talk within these halls about what we can do in regards to social issues we are facing yet nobody teaches us anything about them in class. At least make us write an essay on a book that presents topics that actually matter to us."

"You make a valid point Svetlana, and what do you suggest that book might be?"

Sveta pulled out a copy of *Death Dealer* by Rudolf Höss and raised it up so the entire class could see it. I knew that Rudolf Höss had been the commandant of Auschwitz from a documentary about the Holocaust we'd watched in history class but I'd never given the man a second thought and did not know what he had to say that might be pertinent to modern social issues.

"Anderson Massey did not tell us why he did what he did, but Rudolf did. Many of the issues that plagued Nazi-era Europe are very much still present within these halls and this society. For example: discrimination, mass murder, hateful political rhetoric, and the indoctrination of average people that subsequently turns them into monsters. Did you know that Rudolf Höss was once a good Catholic boy but ended up turning into the greatest mass murderer in history?"

Svetlana had successfully plead her case and Mr. Fish agreed that Death Dealer was the book we'd have to read and write an essay on. He was probably happy too because teaching the same exact thing and reading over the same exact essays year after year could certainly become repetitive for a man who had taught English class for nearly half his life. Sure, the curriculum was updated every once in a while but that didn't remove repetition from the equation. I didn't know if a Nazi's autobiography would be my cup of tea but I preferred it over The Rocking Horse Winner any day of the week.

Most students were unhappy about having to read a much bigger book, and one that came without a study guide or a downloadable cheat sheet from the internet, but I was satisfied with the decision. Mr. Fish looked admiringly at my friend, happy that someone had finally mustered up the courage to say something. I could already see the parallels between the Holocaust and the Belden Massacre. We'd all been silently complicit in the execution of our fellow humans. We all had blood on our hands. Bergen-Belden wasn't an inappropriate name for the school. Anderson Massey may have well been Josef Kramer and Elaine Frechette easily could've been Anne Frank.

Like I didn't already owe Svetlana for giving me her assignment, she also gave me her copy of the book until the industrial quantity the school board ordered would arrive. She knew that I'd slowed down considerably when it came to school over the years, and I appreciated that she thought of giving me a head start. She assured me that since she'd already read the book she didn't need it, and that Vera wasn't interesting in writing an essay at all irrespective of the book. I put it in my bag and vowed to beginning reading it in the evening after the barbecue.

"Did I make you uncomfortable today?" I asked Svetlana.

"No, you did not make me uncomfortable, but the whole talk of sex is weird for me because I am asexual." Sveta replied, obviously still weirded out.

"Oh, I didn't know, I'm sorry."

"No need to be sorry Aly. It's not anybody's fault that I am asexual. I've always been this way, it's not something I chose but sexuality isn't something I really understand. It's strange for me to live in a hyper-sexual society when I've never experienced such desires. They aren't something I understand but I have nothing against sex."

"I'll make a point to not bring that topic up around you, but you live in the wrong society."

"All societies are ruined by sex and corruption Aly. There's no place in the world free from that. No matter where I go it's always going rule people's lives unless I started an ace colony somewhere. The land of my dreams is Canada, sex and polar bears and Justin Trudeau and all."

Canada was a country that appealed to many Americans, especially those who did not like Donald Trump. Contrary to what his campaign promises had been, he had not helped average families like mine. In fact, he'd only further hurt them and hurt much of the world at large except for the rich white Christian men who were just like him. I dreamed of a man like Justin Trudeau to bring my family and my country back from the brink. Albeit far from perfect, I believed that his heart was in the right place and at the very least he was handsome. Even Dmitry Petrov looked better than the orange orangutang we had in the White House.

"Anderson's anxious to see you again," I told the twins as we walked down the hallway after class.

"Anderson?" Vera seemed confused.

"My little brother Anderson."

"Oh! Oh dear, I'm so sorry Aly, I was gone for a minute there."

"Don't worry about that, do you guys need a ride to come to my barbecue tonight?"

"Nah, it's good thanks. We'll be okay."

After school we each went our own separate ways and in less than twenty minutes after my parents had started preparing the food an old lime green truck pulled into the driveway. The old 1980s Ford F-150 had been spray painted in a shade almost identical to the Petrov trailer and had BIGLEMON written on the license plate. The windshield was broken in two places and one mirror was hang by its side. Atrocious noises came out of the truck, even more atrocious than the sounds that came out of Mercedes' Mercedes.

Both Dmitry and the twins had smiles stretched across their faces as they waved at me through the window. I put on my shoes and headed outside to greet them and invite them in. I prayed that my parents wouldn't be repulsed by them and forbid me to hang out with them but I was eighteen years old, soon going on nineteen. Who were they to dictate my life? I may have been of legal age but my brain had stopped maturing the last day of Anderson's life. I couldn't blame them for still treating me like a child. Part of me probably still needed that. I enjoyed the freedom that came with adulthood though. My life, my choices, only myself to answer to.

"Dmitry Petrov!" My dad exclaimed as he ran down from the backyard and gave Dmitry a man hug.

"John Feldman!" Dmitry exclaimed at his turn, "I didn't know Aly was your daughter."

Looks like they know each other. In Russian culture it was commonplace for two men to be physically affectionate with each other. That wasn't frown upon, but homosexuality was still considered a grave offence. It was interesting to see how two societies could be the complete opposite of each other. It was good for me to see things outside of my privileged American lens.

"Hello Just John," Vera and Sveta greeted my father in perfect sync as he hugged them both.

"Your father Dmitry and I were on the same crew at work in the past," he told them, also happy to have some familiar faces around.

"He's our uncle," Vera corrected him, "but I suppose it makes no difference."

Dmitry hugged me, and then my mom, and eventually Anderson after my father convinced him that Dmitry wasn't the boogeyman. The girls and I looked at each other and laughed. I like the fact that the twins weren't uptight about the fact that that their uncle looked like a gangster straight out of a movie about the Russian Mafia. Vera wasn't concerned at all by her appearance either. Sveta always had to look proper when she was in the company of others, but she never imposed those same standards on others. The entire Petrov clan accepted people as they came, the way things should be.

My dad and Dmitry talked about work and the accident. There was still no word on what had actually happened or what was going to become of the worksite and the people who worked there. Everyone had been kept in the dark and only knew very little information from what they'd seen on the news and that stressed me out but the Petrov twins didn't seem to have a care in the world. The two of them were distracted by the shrubs growing in the neighbour's backyard. I didn't know if it was because they were obsessed with plants or because they'd never seen such a neatly cut tree but they marvelled at the property.

My dad's cellphone rang and everyone looked at him, anticipating it was work calling since nobody other than the boss, the school and the family called his cell. He motioned for Dmitry to continue the barbecue while he went inside through the sliding glass door. It was bad. I knew instinctively because my father never left the room to have a private conversation. He never did except when it was bad, really bad. Dmitry burned the patties as he was anxiously awaiting the fate of his job too. I knew our household would suffer if my dad lost his job, but we'd make it by. The Petrov clan might not be so lucky.

In that moment I probably worried more about them than I worried about my own family since I had been inside their derelict trailer in Jihoon's slum park. The minutes ticked by too slowly until my dad came back out, walking slowly and seemingly gauging our reaction in preparation for whatever he was about to tell us. I swallowed hard, it was bad and it was obvious. Dmitry served the charred patties while my dad sat in a plastic chair by our backyard pool that was primarily just a decoration. Once the food was served my father finally spoke.

"It's bad."

Just the news we all feared.

"Two dead and almost forty injured."

Silence.

"The commission that takes care of workplace safety and work-related injuries ordered the worksite to be shut down permanently, pending further investigation."

"No more job," Dmitry commended.

"No more job," my dad confirmed, "and apparently we were lucky that the place didn't turn into a Deepwater Horizon. Company representatives will be getting in touch with us over the upcoming week to make things official, but that's what the boss had to say."

Everyone looked at each other in disbelief. Was it really happening? Nobody had expected it to be that bad. It was almost like it had come straight out of movie you could watch on the Lifetime channel. My father went on about how the company's head honcho had paid the inspector to fake a good report because he knew the site was unsafe and it would cost too much money to fix the place since their profits had been steadily declining over the last few quarters. My dad also admitted that because of some loophole in the law and company policies neither he nor Dmitry qualified for unemployment.

They had just lost their jobs and neither one would get a single dime. What was worst, two men had lost their lives because of capitalist greed. Apparently the government was investigating the company for corruption and negligence and until that was complete we'd just be left hanging. Upon the initial shock the severity of the situation didn't sink in, but as whatever was left of our party came to an end it all came crashing down on me. I'd have to say goodbye to my lifestyle. It was all over. In that moment it was really all over.

I stayed up late that night, unable to sleep and desperately trying to concentrate on the commandant's book but I kept on being distracted by overhearing my parents frantically trying to come up with a plan to save the day but to no avail. I heard my mother say that the house would have to be put up for sale if we didn't want to lose everything else, and that they'd be looking for more places to stay available quickly in the morning. Just like that, it happened all at once. It was real but wasn't real. I didn't want it to be real, but it was.

I sighed loudly and put the book down. I then flopped over to look at Elaine, Amanda and Anderson. They were all smiling, so happy, at least they looked happy on their school pictures. Happier than I was, that was indisputable. My brother walked into my room and flopped onto my bed right next to me as I was looking at the pictures and put his little arm around my neck. He was so lucky to not be able to understand the full scope of the situation. He only seemed to be vaguely aware that there was something wrong at daddy's work. He didn't have to face surviving your best friend's school shooting and then bankruptcy.

"Why do you have a picture of the killer in your room?" Anderson asked me in his usual cute little boy voice.

"Because he's my friend," I meekly replied, "don't you remember when he played with you in the sandbox and in the pool?"

"But that was before he became a killer."

"Yeah it was, but he's still Big Anderson and you're still Lil Anderson."

I started to cry as I remembered Lil Anderson's final goodbye to Big Anderson's funeral.

"Bye bye Big Anderson."

He had insisted on going and ended up having a fistfight with my dad so he would let him go up to the open casket and say goodbye. I carried him in my arms over to the front where the casket was and Big Anderson's parents took Lil Anderson in their arms as I got my turn to say my final goodbyes. Anderson looked like he always had minus the hair dye.

The funeral home that removed the bright dye and his sandy hair was back to what it had always been. His face was peaceful, serene even. There was no evidence of the gaping head wound where he'd shot himself. Somebody took Anderson's hand and put it in mine. I held it tightly, it was so cold and so *dead*. I kissed his forehead and ran out the door into the dark evening sky.

I collapsed on the stone steps of the funeral home and sobbed and wailed uncontrollably. Anderson's mother came out a few minutes later and sat next to me in silence. She wrapped her arms around me and didn't try to comfort me or tell me that it was okay, instead she cried with me until the service was over. It was probably the best thing she could have done for me at that time.

"Mom!" Anderson yelled out into the hallway. "Aly is having it over Big Anderson again!"

Both my parents dropped whatever they were going and came running up the stairs and barged into my room faster than a bullet from a gun. *Bad comparison.*

"Don't take my pictures!" I chocked out through my tears.

My father held me in his arms while my mother held Anderson who had since gotten upset himself. I felt guilty that my little brother had to suffer because of me, especially when he'd just wanted to spend time with me knowing that I wasn't alright.

"Just so you know," I lied, "I'm not crying over them. It's because of the housing situation."

My parents looked at each other. They knew that I'd overheard them talking downstairs. I held on to my dad and cried out whatever was on my chest because I couldn't be consoled anyway. He nuzzled my hair and held me tightly like he always did until I fell asleep in his arms because the next morning we were both still in the same half-sitting positioned in my bed and he was snoring soundly in his deep sleep. I let him sleep and listened to his heartbeat as it was a comforting sound.

My mom was the only one who'd gotten up because Anderson was also still in my bed, curled up in a ball and sleeping soundly as well. My mother woke the two of them up when she barged into my room and unintentionally let the door slam behind her. My dad awoke from his deep sleep and looked around my room, seemingly having forgotten that he'd slept in it the previous night. Anderson simply stretched and got up to go downstairs, obviously enticed by the sweet smell of pancakes in the kitchen.

"We got a call back from a place we inquired about last night." My mother announced like it was supposed to be good news.

My parents didn't want to sell the house but the cold hard truth is that we'd lose so much more if they tried to keep it. Instead, they figured that we should rent something until the job situation was solved and then see what resulted of it. After that we could always buy a second house, a condo, stay where we were, whatever we wanted. The plan sounded nice on the outside but I knew too well that Wintercrest was an industrial city with more citizens than available housing and getting another job probably wouldn't be easy.

My mom told my dad that this place they had called about was an apartment with three bedrooms, very spacious, storage included, and most of all a low price that my mother would be able to sustain by herself now that she'd be working full time. It was only going to be temporary and the arrangements were flexible, there were no long-term contracts or unbreakable leases to be signed. The apartment building was situated in a middle-class area of town, not dirty trailer park by the interstate. There had been no better offers and the place was available on October first.

That would give us two weeks to pack up everything and put the house up for sale quickly so there would be no additional financial losses. It was more than enough time for us since my dad no longer had anything to do during the day and I had a feeling that Dmitry Petrov would be more than happy to help since he was in the same boat. It sounded like a good plan until I learned that our new landlord would be Jihoon Garcia.

VI

NOW THEY'RE GONNA PAY

The morning of February 17th, 2017 started like any other. Overslept as usual. My dad came pounding on my door telling me I needed to get ready for class. Second semester was in its second week and I had schoolwork to catch up on after the Valentine's Day dance. My dad had taken a week off after my exams when I had a week off too so we could spend some quality time together. We didn't get to do that often anymore but my dad was still the best! I didn't really want to leave him but after a while of nagging he managed to make me get up.

I grabbed the first clothes that weren't too dirty I could find on the floor because I didn't have hours and hours to waste on digging through my closet and trying to create an outfit for myself. Skinny blue years, a Johnny Cash shirt and a purple hoodie would just have to do the trick. I quickly washed my face to take those nasty baggy marks from under my tired milk chocolate eyes but it didn't make much difference. It was officially second semester, I had survived half of another year of school. My mom had already left to take Anderson to school so it was just my dad and I for breakfast that morning.

My father had made me my favourite veggie omelette like only he could make. I blabbed about how I didn't want to go to school and he actually would've been okay with me staying home because it was Friday anyway but then I thought about Jennifer and the project I needed to help Elaine finish. More than anything though, I just wanted to see Anderson. Aside from his cryptic phone call the previous night telling me not to come to school, he'd been ignoring me completely for the last couple of days and my level of anxiety was through the roof when it came to him. I was worried sick and I needed to talk to him as soon as I possibly could. Getting in his face in class seemed to the only option left.

There also were always plenty of activities at that time of the school year, like the Valentine's Day dance that had been quite memorable, and not necessarily in the best way either, but a few things needed to be settled in those halls. A code red was also in the forecast sometime since they did one every semester. No stress there. That meant that Jennifer and I were going to be able to hang out and catch up! Maybe she could even lend Elaine and I a hand with our map project that hadn't made much progress since we much preferred to goof off in class instead of doing what we were supposed to do.

I was also looking forward to some new and interesting things so I could forget about the drama Anderson and I had been inadvertently involved in. He had become quite distant over the months but at the dance it seemed like we had been old friends again. We'd had so much fun but the morning after that the only thing that *hadn't* happened was the sky falling over Wintercrest.

He'd called me last night and told me not to come to school, so I first thought that he'd show up at my house and play hooky with me like we'd done in the past but his tone of voice had been off for that kind of play date. As my dad and I were riding down to Belden I called him to tell him that I'd be at school but there was no answer. I ended up sending him four text messages but he answered none of them. As my dad dropped me off on the sidewalk in the front of the school I dialled Anderson's home number.

"Hi Mrs. Massey, is Anderson there?"

"No, sorry Alyson, he left early this morning and hasn't returned."

"Okay, thanks. He called me last night and told me not to come to school today so I thought that maybe we were going to play hooky but he hasn't been answering."

"At the speed he left this morning it wouldn't surprise me if he forgot to turn on his phone if he even brought it at all!"

"If you see him though, please tell him that I'm at school!"

"I will dear, bye."

She didn't call me back and I didn't see Anderson in class that morning. We had many of our classes together and were both in the advanced academics program at school. Sometimes we ditched school together just to go to the mall and hang out. But lately, he hadn't wanted me around at all but I was hopeful that after the circus died down I was hopeful that our lives and our friendship would return to normal, however. I figured he'd just forgotten that he had called me last night or that he got caught up in something else and had to go to school himself. I shrugged it off, I'd be seeing him at some point during the day anyway.

I texted Jennifer and told her to meet me in the library during our morning break between our first and second classes, and sent Anderson the same text message by chance that he hadn't forgotten his phone so that he could come to our little gathering too. Jennifer had never liked him very much, but she was accepting of him. Not many people were, and that was part of the reason why Anderson didn't want me to be seen around the halls with him. That would've made me a target too, but the library was a little safe space. The bullies were too cool for books and for studying.

"Hey there Aly!" Elaine called out as she caught up to me in the halls.

Elaine had been my best friend since the fifth grade. The two of us were a lot alike in more ways than one. Firstly, we had the same hazel eyes and the same brown hair, but hers was shorter and curly while mine was plain and straight. Her chubby cheeks complemented her long face perfectly along with that touch of vintage makeup. Elaine was always so elegant and beautiful, even on the most boring and mundane of occasions such as an average school day. She wore a long black dress covered in an elegant grey jacket, an outfit that was better than the one I'd worn for the Valentine's Day dance!

I didn't doubt that her beauty intimidated some, but her simple yet elegant style made me feel confident about my own style and identity. She was one of those genuinely good people in the world, the truly energetic remarkable kind that you only crossed once in your lifetime. We had our usual girl talks as we walked upstairs to the computer room where we'd both be taking digital art, and where we'd both try to finish our map project. I had yet to see Amanda, Jennifer or Anderson when the bell rang for our first class. I hadn't realized that I was really *that* late!

If you asked any teenager or young adult in America, they'd all tell you that it's hard to go back to school after writing your final exams for the first semester because the school board gives students nearly a week off afterwards! Belden High was nice enough to do so anyway, many students at other local schools weren't so lucky. Elaine and I ran up the staircase to the second floor where the computer room our class took place in was located. I sat in the very back of the room near the window like I usually did and Elaine sat in the seat right next to me at the computers.

Mrs. Annie then told us to move to the long grey desks in the middle of the room because the school's network was offline, rendering the computers just about useless. Elaine and I sat next to each other in the first row instead. The second bell rang, and class officially started. Mr. Pasquale announced over the airways that there'd be a gathering in the auditorium in about thirty minutes to welcome a group of exchange students who would be joining us for the second semester. Elaine and I grimaced at each other, Mr. Pasquale's presentations were always boring and repetitive kinda like a sermon that dragged on for eternity without an actual purpose.

The door was open so I could see in the hallway but there was never any sign of my three other friends. Eventually, Mrs. Annie's boring plan B presentation was under way but I didn't pay attention. Once she was done and the network was back online she returned to her desk, read some erotic books and didn't pay attention to us. We still had to wait ten minutes for the presentation in the auditorium so Elaine and I decided we had time to kill, doing anything that came to mind just so we wouldn't work on our map project. The teacher didn't seem to care whether we worked or not, and neither did we.

In all fairness, I didn't like Mrs. Annie very much. She was this annoying self-righteous little woman who thought she knew everything and owned the building. She was barely five feet tall with short golden hair and dark brown eyes. She was in her mid-thirties, which wasn't awful, but dressed like a teenager, not a schoolteacher. We weren't allowed to have those taboo erotic books in school but she read them in front of all of us like nothing was wrong. I despised that she could go on about her day with no consideration for anyone except herself. What kind of example was she setting for the young impressionable students in her class?

Mrs. Annie wasn't liked by many students except a few of her teacher's pets in other classes, like the football captain who was related to her somehow. She always put in a good word for him but not for anybody else. In return people began to hate the poor guy for no other reason than the fact that his trampy teacher aunt or whatever gave him unfair advantages. I did not actively hate him per se, but I will admit that I was resentful. I quietly wrote jokes for Elaine on a piece of paper, pretending to be working or taking notes of the presentation or something that would hopefully impress Mrs. Annie to put in a good word for me too when Mrs. Phyllis announced code red over the airways.

It was the standard repeating *code red* three times in rapid succession that we were all so used to after the government made it mandatory to have at least one lockdown practice drill each time a new semester began. I was annoyed. I didn't feel like crawling under a table and laying down on the dirty floor for what could be hours at a time just to be tested. Mrs. Annie was still reading her book like school shooters were just shadows on the wall or ink on a page. Not important. She then looked up at the clock on the wall and her face suddenly became very puzzled, tense.

"It's not supposed to be until eleven tomorrow," she muttered to herself, "it's much too early, unless they changed the date and time and didn't tell me."

She dropped her book and walked into the hallway, which was exactly what you're supposed to *not* do during an active shooter situation. After a few seconds I crawled under long grey table next to some reject kid named Mario Bartolucci that I didn't really know except for the fact that *everybody* knew was immature. He always put on his childish antics like it was some kind of show and we were supposed to applaud him for it. I dismissed him and waited for Mrs. Annie to come back and shut the door like she was supposed to.

I could easily see in the hallway through the open door from where I laying and it was apparent that there were lots of confusion and agitation going on. People had been on their way to the presentation in the auditorium but instead they got a code red. It was a bad way to spend a Friday. I couldn't quite make out what people were talking about in the hallways through the voices of the many people around me but I was sure that I heard *shots fired, auditorium, drill,* and *shooter* in the same sentence.

"It would be awesome and so much more realistic if they hired a pretend shooter!" Mario blabbed on like code red lockdown drills were something we should've been excited about.

"You wanna traumatize the children?" An unknown voice muttered from behind me.

Right at the same time screams filled the air and horrific sounds of wailing came from the hallway. Gunshots were fired through all the yelling and the commotion and people were running everywhere. *Gunshots. Real gunshots.* People ran into the computer room and frantically searched for a hiding place but there weren't many available. I put my hands over my ears and eyes as the shotgun blasts only seemed to get louder until I peered out the door into the hallways from under my table and saw the shooter walk into the room. I didn't know what I felt in that moment, it was like I somehow didn't feel anything.

They say that in a state of shock you feel nothing but calmness and this weird feeling kind of like a voice deep inside yourself, well, it was true for me in that moment. As terrified as I was, I wasn't able to actually feel it. I couldn't feel my body shaking or hear the commotion going on around me. It was all just a big blur. The last thing I was expecting that morning was for a real shooter to walk in. I couldn't see who the shooter was, I could only see up to his knees as he walked through the door and into the classroom and began firing indiscriminately.

He had black leather combat boots and black cargo pants tucked inside them. Suspenders were dangling down from his pants under his long black coat. A black Mossberg pump-action shotgun was pointed in my direction and then I saw him pull the trigger. I screamed in panic, suddenly able to feel again but the bullet didn't hit me. The shooter's bullet hit Mario, precisely the boy who had been bragging about school shooters before a real one walked in. He fired again in rapid succession and all I could hear were dissonant screams and glass breaking immediately after each blast.

My ears were ringing and I couldn't quite make out what was going on around me because I was disoriented but I saw the shooter turn back and walk out of the classroom. Then the reality of the situation really settled in. *Somebody is on a rampage in the school!* For a few seconds afterwards things were oddly quiet until we started hearing some more shots being fired somewhere down the hallway. People were running and screaming but I was stuck under the table, unable to even think. People say that in situations like that your life flashes before your eyes, but it does not.

You don't go into some state of higher awareness or whatever they call that. There's no out-of-body experience like you're floating or divine revelations from God. There is only fear, and nothing but fear. There is no logic, no thinking, just blank fear. I was afraid right down to my bones like nothing I had ever experienced before. I was afraid to breathe because I was scared the shooter might hear my heartbeat resonating through the floor and come back to finish me off. I didn't even have time to be thankful that I hadn't been shot.

"We need to get out of here!" Somebody yelled out.

But I was frozen in place. Mario tapped on my leg and yelled something but his voice was distorted, I couldn't hear it. I looked over at him and saw that he had been shot through the shoulder. There was blood everywhere, including on me. For the first time I felt its warmth. I had to remind myself to breath from time to time because I felt myself becoming lightheaded from a lack of oxygen. People in the classroom around me started running for their lives, some carrying wounded students, while Mario kept on aggressively patting my leg wanting my attention so I finally took a deep agonizing breath and got up.

The oxygen burned my tight airways like I was inhaling sulphur or something even worst, gunpowder. I wanted to either pick up Elaine or Mario but the ravenous desire to just get out of there became overwhelming and my subconscious somehow made my legs move and run for my life. Most people around me had that instinct to just run but I somehow couldn't bring myself to do anything more than just *exist* once I'd made it to the other side of the door.

"Run!" Another voice yelled out. "Just run!"

I did manage to run again after a few seconds too many. Somebody pushed me and my legs were forced to propel me forward. Most people would think that you're in survival mode you'd automatically go running for the nearest exit door, or run for the hills entirely, but in my state of shock and confusion all I could do was follow whoever was in front of me. The crowd in front of me ran downstairs but nobody could run outside because the doors had been deliberately locked with a large metal link chain so nobody could escape. Somebody tried breaking the window but didn't manage to make more than a chip. From inside the school I could see that there was even more chaos and commotions going on outside, and *guns*.

Nobody knew if there were more gunmen roaming the school or the parking lot or if it was a lone wolf attack but the sight of blurry figures holding guns outside was enough for us to not make any further attempts at breaking the windows and escaping that way. It was only later in the library that I found out that the men carrying guns outside were local police officers and state troopers waiting for the SWAT team to arrive. The library was just down the hall from the staircase on the ground floor of the school, adjacent to the reception desk and facing the cafeteria so when the SWAT team did barge into the school they wouldn't have to go far to rescue me.

"There's a shooter!" I yelled out as I entered the library.

The students were all hiding under tables but they didn't seem to take the situation seriously until they heard the shots coming from the hallway for themselves. As soon as I entered the library I crawled under a table near the back of the room where Jennifer joined me and crawled under the table in front of me since there wasn't enough room under a single table for everyone. There was another student next to me, I didn't know her, and there was a freshman that I'd seen around the school a few times but I'd never gotten the chance to talk to her and much less become acquainted with her.

She was obviously just as shaken as I was when the gun blasts got louder as the shooter was coming closer. Panic settled in. People were running everywhere as staff and students who had been shot ran into the library looking for safety and collapsed on the floor, bleeding. Screams ripped through the air in every direction and eventually I realized that I hadn't gotten away from the shooter by hiding in what used to be the safest room in the school, I had only placed myself right in his path.

"He's here!" Somebody screamed as the shooter's shadow appeared on the other side of the library's big stained glass doors.

I couldn't see anything going on from the back of the room but the gunshots never stopped, they only kept on getting closer. Somewhere in the middle of all of that my cellphone started ringing and I freaked out because I didn't want the shooter or shooters — we still didn't know how many there actually were — to hear it and come around to my table and shoot me. I saw that it was my mom calling so I answered anyway, hoping that maybe she could help me or at the very least know that I was still alive for the time being.

I had a hard time hearing what she was telling me because of all the screaming and the gunshots and my ears were ringing and I thought I was going deaf in between all of that! I tried to focus on my mom's voice to momentarily escape reality but I still couldn't quite make out anything more than *school shooting, okay, police* and *I love you* in broken sentences through her sobs and all the commotion going on around me. I wanted to reassure her that I was fine and that I loved her too, but then I saw *him*.

"Mom, it's Anderson."

"Anderson? What's wrong with Anderson? Has he been shot?"

"Mom, *it's Anderson.*"

The young man with a gun who had mercilessly murdered my fellow classmates was one of my best friends, Anderson Massey. I began to wail and sob uncontrollably myself once I saw him. It all made sense at that point why he hadn't wanted me in school. It was no playing hooky, it was because he was on a rampage and he hadn't wanted me to be in the middle of it. Too late. I suddenly recognized his boots, he always wore those boots. I had been too shocked to recognize them upon the initial fright of having a real shooter in the building.

The coat was his usual too, I was the one who'd bought it for him just over a year earlier. Only his pants were different than his usual old blue years from the thrift store a few blocks down from the nearest elementary school. He wore a black shirt with **WASTED** written across it in big white letters along with a spiked belt and studded fingerless gloves. He usually didn't look so brutish and scary, but then again I had never come face to face with a shooter in my own school. Anderson's usually gentle green eyes were filled with something greater than him. It was apparent that whatever anger and hatred that existed inside of him had completely consumed him.

His unruly bleached half-orange hair was all over his face like it usually was, covering part of the narrow cheekbones on his long face as his mane went all the way down to his chin. His little lips were tightly pursed and his body was rigid. Anderson had always a tall slim boy, but that day he looked particularly frail. He looked exhausted frankly, beat up. Whatever was consuming him was obviously stressful to him too. As he swung open his jacket I saw that he had two other rifles apart from his shotgun over his shoulders on slings as well as a handgun tucked safely into a holster attached to his belt. I dropped my phone, my mom still on the line, when he walked towards me and carelessly threw the shotgun on top of my table.

He knelt down right in front of me, looking at me menacingly and taking my cellphone into his hand. My mother was yelling my name on the other end of the line as she had been listening to everything when Anderson hung up on her and handed me my phone. My body trembled in fear as he got closer to me and put his hand on mine. I was dizzy and had a hard time focusing on him. I wanted to be alert and aware for whatever he was going to tell me or be able to plead for my life if he gave me that chance.

"I told you not to come to school today!" Anderson muttered through clenched teeth in a low voice only audible to me.

His voice was sharp, like *he* was in some sort of terrible unspoken pain. I didn't move, I couldn't. Anderson slowly got back up, picked up his gun from the table, reloaded it and kept on shooting. Through the shots I heard some more commotion outside the library, sounding like some more shooting. I couldn't possibly think of anybody else who'd go on a school massacre with Anderson, the boy barely had any friends. The most shocking thing of all though, he never struck me as the type of person who'd do something like that. I knew that he was hurt and angry and frustrated but not like *that*.

Anderson didn't have a mean bone in his body. The only person he had ever wanted to hurt was himself. I could hear him yelling and exchanging words with other frightened students but I couldn't understand. Part of me didn't want to. After what seemed like an infinity of pain, he walked out and went to shoot up another room. My first instinct was to run, jump right through a smashed window and into the arms of police officers. I wasn't the only person who had the idea of running for their lives because a stampede of people went running for the door. Some of them were half-carrying injured students while others were being dragged.

Pools of disgusting thick blood soaked the old beige carpet and bullet shell casings and fragments littered the place. It was impossible not to step in it, the carnage was everywhere. In another rush of panic and adrenaline I ran out the shattered library doors with a herd of other students but I freaked out once I heard the gunshots coming my way again. I didn't know where I was going, I was disoriented and afraid and the hallways all looked the same. I tried to search for some sort of indicator that I was heading in he right direction but there were people running in every direction and *bodies*. I got knocked down by something or someone and fell on the floor flat on my face. I didn't know if I had been shot, I didn't feel any pain but I felt something warm on my body.

It was a pool of blood coming from underneath the door of the classroom I had fallen in front of. The herd of students was long gone as I heard glass breaking and some other commotion somewhere around me but I was too disoriented to be able to know where the sound was coming from. I put my arms over my pounding head and played dead just in case Anderson came back and decided to finish me off because I hadn't stayed home like he told me to. I held on to the belief that if he did come back he'd dismiss me as dead or he would spare me because I was his friend and I had always been nice to him.

"Alyson?" I heard his pained voice from behind me.

I tried to be as still as possible but my body was shaking violently and uncontrollably.

"Alyson!"

Anderson knelt next to me and gently put his hand on the back of my head as I was laying on my stomach in somebody else's blood. He seemed to be crying as he gently placed his other hand on my back.

"Oh no, dear God please don't tell me I shot her!"

I took my hands off of my head and rolled over onto my side so I could see him. His pupils were dilated and he was sobbing just as much as the frightened students. He pushed his hair out of his face and painfully examined my bloody body.

"I'm not shot." I managed to mutter out through tight airways.

"Are you hurt?" Anderson's voice was broken.

"No, I'm just scared."

"Oh Aly, I'm so sorry! Dear God what have I done!"

Anderson helped me up as I was too distraught to stand up by myself and gingerly held me up against the wall, half-carrying me in his free arm and holding his handgun in the other. The cold white brick walls felt good against my overly warm skin. I closed my eyes and took the time to catch my breath and let the dizziness and confusion fade away. The danger seemed to have escaped my brain, but I still could never be certain of what Anderson would do. He was capable of walking into school armed to the teeth, he was certainly capable of killing me.

I didn't know how long it took for my sense of reality to come back to me but Anderson had been there holding me the entire time. For a moment there it felt like were two old friends saying goodbye for the last time before the shooter came back, except that *he* was the shooter. He dropped his handgun and took me into a tight hold as my legs gave out and I collapsed into his arms. My head rested on his chest and I could feel his erratic heartbeat, it was almost like it was going to explode right out of his chest.

"Oh God," he sighed, "if I had known you'd be in school today I never would've done this! I would've just shot shot myself in my room so the world could forget about me and I could forget the pain."

I didn't speak. I thought I was about to puke.

"I'm so sorry Alyson, I am *so sorry*. I never meant to hurt you, but I can't take this life anymore. Just know that I love you and that I always have, and that I'm sorry."

He broke down crying again. I couldn't manage to bring myself to console him or do to anything except focus on not passing out or downright dropping dead.

"Is it just you?" I finally managed to ask after several minutes.

"Yeah, it's just me," he whispered in a choked up voice, "it's just me Aly."

Anderson held me tightly for a few short moments before he let go of me. I wasn't sure I'd be able to stand by myself so I pressed my back against the wall and held on to it with my fingers gripped in between the bricks and the bullet holes. Anderson took off his coat and let it drop to the floor, revealing his full arsenal of weapons. He was literally armed to the teeth with a variety of knives tucked into his belt and pockets full of ammunition. He even had pouches full of bullets clipped to his belt since his pockets were so full. The ammo jangled as took a few steps back from me and looked down the hallway in the opposite direction of the doors leading outside to safety. Anderson took a deep breath in exasperation and hugged me one last time.

"Get out of here."

And he walked away. He walked away leaving me right there with his coat and his handgun as he walked down the hallways with an AR-15 in hand. Everything was quiet, like the moments after a murder. The eerie calm made me feel sick and I puked up a bunch of acid and bile as I collapsed onto that pool of blood coming from under the door that had only gotten bigger. I then heard gunshots seemingly coming from every direction again so I dragged myself on my stomach back in the library that was just across the hallway. The doors were open and it was the only place I had enough energy left to go into, so that's where I went.

I made myself believe that Anderson had already shot up that room so he wouldn't come back, I made myself believe that I'd be safe in there more than in any other room in the school. The library wasn't very big so I managed to easily crawl to my previous hiding place without too much trouble. Jennifer and the freshman girl were both still there. It had been a wise thing to stay put because many students had been killed or injured in the hallways as they had attempted to run outside to safety, not knowing that Anderson had taken the time to lock all the doors with heavy chains.

As I crawled under the table and sat up against the back leg, I noticed that the freshman girl had been shot. She had a bloody ankle and she was holding her left arm. Blood was dripping to the floor from an open wound but there wasn't a whole lot I could do about it. Jennifer had been spared, but I didn't know if Anderson had decided to save her or if he simply didn't shoot there. I curled up in a fetal position and waited indefinitely for some sign that the massacre was over and that it was safe to attempt to move around but the gunshots relentlessly kept echoing in other parts of the school. I could also hear more commotion going on outside but I had no idea what law enforcement were doing out there. I knew what they *weren't* doing though, and was that saving helpless students.

VII

LINES ON THE CONCRETE

My ears were still ringing when the fire alarm went off with a piercing cry with more shotgun blasts immediately following. In the middle of that I swore I could hear my phone ringing again so I looked down at it on the carpet right next to me and saw that it was the house calling. I immediately answered but I couldn't understand what the voice at the other end was saying.

"Hello? Dad? Johannes Feldman?"

"Alyson! Yes, it's dad Johannes Feldman! Are you still in the building?"

"Yeah, I'm still in the library. Anderson's not far away, I can hear him."

"Are you injured?"

"No dad, he didn't hurt me. When he saw me he passed me by."

My father let out a massive sign of relief when he heard me say those words but we both knew that I wasn't out of the woods yet. Anderson could change his mind at any point and still put a bullet right through my brain. I didn't know what was going on in his mind but I knew that he was unstable and unpredictable.

"Can you give me an approximate location of the shooter? Your mom told me the SWAT team is about to enter the building and will be checking the school room by room but they want to know where the shooter is to take him on."

"I don't really know dad, I just know he's not far."

"Okay, I'll pass along the message. They should be on their way soon so just stay where you are! I love you Aly!"

I waited for what seemed like an eternity for the SWAT team to barge in through the door but they never did. At the same time I prayed that Anderson would shoot himself before the authorities could get to him. I could not imagine him being taken into custody, have to go to trial, and then have him left to rot in a jail cell or have to watch him be executed. I knew that he wouldn't be able to live with himself if he got caught, and I wasn't sure I'd be able to live with myself if I saw him being taken away by the police.

I had never really believed in anything, but I prayed to God that he'd just shoot himself and that it would be all over. I prayed for his family who were probably watching everything on the news and seeing their son's face plastered across the TV screens, accused of being nothing but a monster. I prayed that he hadn't actually killed anybody and that all the injured students would live. Eventually the library door slammed shut and more glass broke off of it as it slammed shut and my train of thought was interrupted. I peaked under the tables thinking it was the SWAT team coming in to rescue us but it was an exhausted-looking Anderson with one last rifle in his hand.

The dark brown carbine had blood dripping from its muzzle, obviously having shot someone at close range. *That's it, he's coming to finish me.* I braced myself for whatever was ahead and put my head between my knees as he walked closer and closer to where I was hiding. His bloody boots stood right next to me, I would've just had to reach out to touch them. Again I couldn't breathe, my airways were too tight to let the oxygen get to my lungs. Through all the noises and my ears ringing I could hear Anderson reloading the firearm. As odd as it was to have selective hearing when your life is in danger, I clearly heard him manually insert two rounds and load one into the chamber as he took a few steps forward.

That's it, the end. And he pulled the trigger. The gun went off and soon it fell next to the table near me. Anderson's body came crashing down to the floor with his right hand landing on me. I did the only thing I could do: scream. In my panic I pushed it off and it rested next to my foot. I looked over at Anderson's body, and that's when I saw that he wasn't dead. Yes, he had shot himself in the head but he was still breathing. He was gasping for air, making coughing and choking noises.

I broke down sobbing uncontrollably, immediately regretting my prayer that he would shoot himself. I grabbed Anderson's body and rolled him over onto his back so his head could rest on my lap after I half-crawled out from under the table.

There was a horrific gaping wound on the right side of his head gushing out warm blood all over my clothes and the carpet. I squeezed his right hand into mine and gently stroked his forehead with my other hand. I knew from the very start that there was no way I could bring him back or keep him alive but I wanted him to be comforted in his last moments as much as he could be. He tightly squeezed my hand, still able to feel to some degree or another as Jennifer crawled over to us and cradled his other hand. I was unaware of how much time passed by, but it was long enough for Anderson to suffocate by chocking on his own blood. Jennifer and I held him and tried to make him as comfortable as possible until he took his last breath.

"Dear God have mercy on this boy's soul!" I prayed aloud with Jennifer. "Please Lord, help him because we've all failed him!"

Jennifer and I prayed until his hold on our hands was stiff. It was over. He was dead. I still held on to his hand for a long time even after he was dead and even after Jennifer left too. I mourned and grieved for what seemed like hours at a time until I grabbed my phone and called the house.

"Alyson!" My father shouted as he answered.

"It's over." I muttered out through my tears.

"Are you okay?"

"I'm fine dad. Anderson's dead, he's right here."

"Did the SWAT team reach your area yet?"

"They didn't come in here."

"Aly—"

I hung up on him mid-sentence. I composed myself as best as I could despite the fact that I was covered in the blood of my friends and innocent people who had just been murdered by my other friend whose dead body was lying in front of me. I stroked Anderson's forehead one has time before I removed his gloves along with a stainless steel ring on his left hand a metal link bracelet from his wrist. I shoved it all in my bra where nobody would find it if they ever examined me. All I wanted was one last memento, one last little something of Anderson's before walking out of that school, never wanting to return.

I collected myself enough to get up and stumble out of the library into a ravaged hallway that looked nothing like it had when I'd walked into it earlier that same morning. I ran as fast as I could down the hall into the front lobby where I barged out through the large windows that had nearly been completely shot out by gunfire seemingly going both ways. Outside I was met with law enforcement pointing their guns at me so I put my hands over my head and they withdrew their weapons. I ran right passed them and right passed the paramedics who had set up a makeshift triage station down by the street.

There was no looking back once I darted through the parking lot. I ran around aimlessly just looking for someone, *anyone*, that I knew and that could take me out of there. I ran down the street passed the police barricades until I saw my mom's car. She was calling out my name as I ran straight into her arms. She didn't let go of me until I had to sit on the bumper of the car to catch my breath and breathe in the fresh outside air before going home. I looked up at the blue sky above, it had never been so beautiful. It was clear blue with only a few white puffs floating around here and there. I eventually just lied down on the hood of the car and tried to come back to the real world, far away from the horrors I'd just witnessed.

"Alyson?" My mom's tone of voice indicated both concern and sympathy.

"Oh, it's not my blood." I blandly replied as I looked down at myself.

My mother helped me up and sat me in front seat with her where we held hands as she drove us home. The usually short ride took another eternity as the police had set up barricades and road blocks and detours around the heavily populated area. My dad and my little brother were waiting for us at the end of the driveway when we pulled in, both looking worried and horrified beyond belief. Just as mom turned off the engine I jumped into my dad's arms and buried my face in his chest. My little brother grabbed on to my bloody pants and hugged my leg. He was young but he knew that something terrible had happened.

My mom grabbed him and pried him off of me despite that he freaked out and screamed for his sister. My dad had never hugged me quite like that before. His arms were so tight around me that I could barely breathe but I desperately didn't want him to ever let go. He eventually had to carry me into the house and deposited me on the living room couch where my mom brought me a glass of water. I drank all of it but almost instantly puked it all up in the bathroom. Afterwards I looked at myself in the mirror where I saw in horror my blood-soaked pants and my shirt that was equally covered.

So I stripped off my disgusting clothes and made my way up to my room where I put on an oversized shirt and flopped onto my bed wishing that I could fall asleep and never have to wake up again. Or even better, *wake up* and realize that it was nothing but a bad dream and that none of it was real. But it was. I pulled the items I had taken from Anderson's body out of my bra and shoved them all in the drawer of my night table next to my bed. I just wanted to scream but instead I buried my face in my pillow and cried. I was alone for only a few minutes before both my parents came into my room and held me in their arms until I fell asleep. I awoke again a few hours later with only my dad still by my side.

"How are you doing Aly?" He softly asked me.

"I don't really know dad." I replied emotionlessly, still reeling form the whole situation.

"Do you wanna come downstairs and have something to eat?"

"Okay. Can we watch the coverage on the news?"

"Are you sure you want to do that? It might traumatize you all over again."

"Dad, I wanna see it. I lived through it, I think I deserve to know what's going on."

He carried me downstairs where my mom and Anderson were watching the coverage of the shooting on TV. My dad deposited me on the couch next to my mother and Anderson immediately jumped onto my lap and cuddled me like there was no tomorrow.

"Anything to eat honey?" My dad asked me.

"I'll make you something." My mom proposed before I could reply but I knew it was just an excuse to go talk to my dad in another room.

"Are okay Aly?" Anderson asked me in a worried and confused tone of voice.

"I'm fine little man," I replied to reassure him, "I promise."

"Give it to her." I overheard my dad whisper to my mom in the kitchen.

My mom disappeared from sight for a fraction of a second before she came back into the living room and handed me a folded piece of paper. I saw that it was addressed to me so I opened it up.

"This was left in the mailbox for you this morning." She said without emotion as she returned to speak with my dad in the kitchen.

It was a letter from Anderson.

Dear Aly,

You've probably seen it on TV by now. If you haven't just turn it on and it'll be right there for ya. I guess I don't really know where I'm going with this letter, I just wanted to say that I'm sorry. I'm sorry that I couldn't say it to your face. I'm sorry that I couldn't look you in the eye one last time. I'm sorry for my actions and I'm sorry for whatever lies ahead for you because of them. Just know that none of this was your fault. <u>NONE</u>. Don't ever blame yourself for what I've done, there is nothing you could have done. Don't blame yourself for this because you knew nothing, and this has nothing to do with you. It is not about you or because of you. If there was one reason why I wanted to back out of this, it was you.

I know you'll be hurt but I ask that you don't hate me. Well actually it's okay if you do because I hate myself too. I'm sorry. It's gonna be okay Alyson. You're gonna be okay. Your life is going to be so much better without me in it. You might not believe it now as you're probably in shock at what you're seeing but you'll see with time that I'll be just a memory in the back of your mind. Belden will be long gone behind you and the memories of it will be too. So don't blame yourself, don't hate yourself, just go on with the wonderful life I know is ahead of you. That is my one final request from you, live a good life. Don't let me get in the way. I love you Alyson, and I'm so sorry more than words will ever be able to express. There was just no other way.

Like everyone else, you'll be asking yourself why. But don't ask yourself why. Ask THEM why. Ask them why they did what they did to me. That is, of course, assuming that they survive… WHY?! Why did they do that to me? I will never know why. I'll die not knowing why but it doesn't matter anymore. The blame is on them. No one but them.

There are no good answers and no justifications, I know that. I won't try to make excuses but I want you to know that all you ever did for me was positive and that I've always appreciated everything you've ever done for me. But there was no other way. People have treated me like a rat my whole life. They never gave me a chance, and now they're gonna pay. I'm not going to be able to live with myself after this so don't expect to ever see me again. I've had the most awful pitiful life I could have ever imagined. It wasn't no stupid life, it was nothing but an existence. A PITIFUL EXISTENCE.

Wherever the hell I go I know it's gonna be better than here. I know it's gonna be better than this life/existence. Don't worry about me. Don't cry for me. Just be happy and the wonderful person you've always been. I'm sorry for everything. I'm sorry that this letter doesn't say much and is of little value. I just wanted to let you know somehow because I couldn't tell you to your face because I'm just a coward and a bad person. I'm sorry to have put you through all of this. If you don't hate me you can go visit my mom and dad, there is a package for you under the stairs. They don't know it's there so you'll have to point it out but your name is on it. They'll give it to you no problem. I'm sorry about all this crap Aly. Time to die now.

Anderson

I broke down crying which prompted my parents to come running into the room but I pushed them away. I held the letter next to my heart for a while as my little brother hung on to me again. Once I composed myself I took out a pen and paper and wrote a letter myself.

Dear Anderson,

Not that you'll actually read this letter because you shot yourself right in front of my face this morning, but I just need to talk for a while, you know, like we used to by passing along letters back and forth. Well, I guess I should've listened to you when you called me last night. Somewhere in there you were still decent enough to warn me but I didn't listen and I'm really sorry but I can't finish this right now.

Alyson

The following day I went to visit Mr. and Mrs. Massey and told them about the special box Anderson had prepared for me. Right under the staircase in the closet there was that very special box exactly as indicated in the letter. It was lightweight so I figured it contained nothing more than a few small mementos, maybe a more proper explanation as to why he did what he did, but I'd wait until I was in my room alone to open it up. I hugged Anderson's parents and told them how much he'd meant to me in the few short years we'd known each other but nothing more. They were grieving and so was I and nobody was in the mood for anything more after twenty families had been ripped apart.

At home I opened up the box and found a few objects just like I'd thought. Anderson returned to me everything I'd ever given him minus a few pieces of clothing and added a few trinkets that he thought I'd like. Two notebooks containing his journal entries with the letters I'd sent him tucked inside were also in the box along with some random pages with drawings on them. Anderson knew how much I loved his doodles, they were strange yet beautiful. At the very bottom of the box there was a small framed portrait of me that he'd drawn himself. I immediately hung it up on the wall over my bed and clipped some of his letters next to it.

Passing each other letters in school had always been forbidden but the two of us had been masters at our craft. Those letters had been our primary form of communication and were some of the few things I had left of a boy I'd once enjoyed such a great friendship with. In the days after that the authorities released a report detailing all the deaths and it finally sank in that some of my friends were dead and that I'd never see them again. What didn't immediately sink in was the fact that it was another one of my friends who was responsible.

Elaine had been killed in the computer room under the table right next to mine moments after we'd spoken that morning. My other dear friend Amanda had been killed in the auditorium where the shooting began as students has been waiting for Mr. Pasquale's presentation to begin that morning. Steven Hicks, an acquaintance of mine, had been murdered right in front of my eyes during the stampede in the hallway. I had seen him get shot along with a few others but at the time I never could have imagined that he'd later die from that fatal bullet.

Katherine Price, the unknown freshman girl who'd been shot in the library bled to death next to me under the table. I hadn't really known any of the other dead students on a deeply personal level but I grieved for them just as much, even the ones I didn't particularly like. Dozens of injured students were still in the intensive care unit, many with life-threatening injuries. The last thing anyone wanted was for the death toll to rise again. It was especially difficult for me to process my thoughts about Anderson. I never thought he'd had it in him to hurt, and much less murder, my friends when he *knew* that they were my friends. He'd only left me with Jennifer as a friend. In the weeks following the massacre and all that came after, she was always by my side.

During that time I didn't think about the shooting. I only focused on myself. That was all I could really do because there were too many unanswered questions that would never have answers because the only person who could answer them had committed suicide. I loved him yet I hated him. Somehow my good memories of him had become invalid, like I wasn't allowed to cherish the good times we'd shared together or grieve for him. I felt so cheated, so violated in some weird way that I could not understand. I hated myself for missing the signs despite that Anderson had made sure to tell me not to blame myself for his actions in his last letter.

How could I not? He was my friend. Friends are supposed to take care of each other. He always looked out for me, even bent over backwards for me and I paid him back by ignoring potential warning signs and not doing enough? That was unacceptable. I had failed. Wresting with myself brought me no closer to the answers, if any were ever to be found, and I wasn't up to opening his journals out of fear of what they might contain but turning them over to the police was out of the question. Nobody except Anderson and I knew that they existed and I intended to keep it that way. One day I'd conquer them in my own way, on my own time.

Dear Anderson,

I don't know what to think of you, or of myself for that matter. Our friendship meant so much to me Anderson, didn't you know that? Why? Why would you do something like this? Why didn't I see it coming? I should've known. I should've known better and I know it! I was there during your hard times but I guess it just wasn't enough. Just for the record, I know how bad you were hurting up until the last moments of your life but YOU KILLED MY FRIENDS.

Three of my friends are dead. Yes, three friends in the present tense because your friendship meant a lot to me despite what the rest of the world thought of it. What the hell was going on inside your head? Didn't you think I was your friend? That I could help you? That I wanted to help you?! I wish I could've at least said goodbye to you one last time. There's so much I'd want to say to you but I can't. The words get lost before they come.

There's a part of me that wants to grab you by the collar of your shirt and shake you and ask you what the hell you were thinking! But the greater part of me would just want to hold you and tell you that everything is going to be alright and it won't be like this forever. Your life mattered to me! Didn't you know that? You had a good family and people who loved you so what went wrong? It's weird how we can just take life for granted until its gone. I never took you for granted, but I also never thought you'd be gone so soon. Isn't it funny how it's only when you're dead that people actually start listening?

Aly

VIII

ALPHABET SOUP

Rudolf Höss was my only company amidst the cardboard boxes that seemed to be everywhere. Despite the subject matter I actually enjoyed reading the book up until I got to the part where Rudolf gets transferred to Sachsenhausen. Intrusive memories hit me like the apocalypse was coming down when I read the part about some sexually deranged Rumanian dude who easily could've been Trevor Bradford in his past life. I did not believe in reincarnation or multiple lives but the parallels between the two of them were uncanny.

The no name man from the book was turned on by just about everything from the SS officers to the other prisoners to the sun in the sky. His entire life revolved around masturbation, doing it publicly no matter the circumstances were and covering his body with explicit tattoos to the point that it disturbed even the man who would become the greatest mass murderer in history. The deranged man even ended up dying while maturing in the concentration camp, his bed surrounded by SS officers. According to Rudolf Höss, the man's mother had been relieved that he was dead because he'd been nothing but a nuisance to society.

Maybe Trevor hadn't been so crazy after all. Maybe he'd been right about the boy from The Rocking Horse Winner all along. Maybe we'd all been laughing at him when he actually made a valid point. I'd always hated the guy but the commandant of Auschwitz had managed to soften me up. A huge lump in my throat formed as I swallowed hard and threw the book on top of my night table. I turned around in my bed and reached for my phone, immediately dialling Svetlana's number. She answered on the second ring.

"How does one become asexual?" I asked her.

"You don't *become* asexual," she seemed angry, "it's just the way you are. You're straight aren't you?"

"Yes."

"Did you choose to be straight one day?"

"No, I've always been that way."

"Exactly. Being asexual isn't something you choose more than being straight or gay or whatever is a choice."

"I've just had it with sex! I never again want to have anything to do with it!"

"Why don't you convert to Catholicism and join a covent or something? Nuns are supposed to be celibate and suppress their desires."

"I'm not sure that's the right path for me Sveta."

"Or you can join my sister in dating impotent old guys."

"Oh?"

"Horny and hormonal. We can be so alike yet so different, but I'm telling you Aly, you are much better off not having any sexual desires."

Svetlana and I talked for about an hour about a variety of topics. I didn't tell her about the guy from the book but she probably had a good idea of what triggered me since she'd read it before and new students weren't unaware of the sins of former pupils. After my chat with Sveta was over my parents came to check up on me like I was a small child afraid of the monsters in the closet or under the bed. If there was one thing I'd come to learn in my short life it was that monsters were indeed real. They walked around disguised as people. Maybe they weren't in the closet or under the bed but they did exist.

After what were definitely a few hours of staring at the ceiling I managed to drift away into a world of dreams. I was sitting at the kitchen table in an unknown house with a variety of foods in front of me including several different cakes, pastas, breads and soups. There was enough food for half a dozen people and maybe more but I was all alone. Upon closer examination I realized that the kitchen was warped in strange ways and blended my household's actual kitchen with 1940s appliances and other kitsch. A large picture of Heinrich Himmler hung on the wall where last year's family photo should've been and the utensils on the table had swastikas on them. I was in the commandant's house!

I did the same thing I used to do when I was little and that was get rid of the food before anyone else arrived at the table because otherwise I wouldn't be able to leave until I was done my plate. My aunt had never fallen for that clever little girl trick but dreams weren't reality so I grabbed as much food as I could and walked upstairs to the bathroom. The bathroom was a lot like the one my family had in our house but it was warped much like the kitchen was but the toilet was modern so I figured it would swallow toast, cakes and oatmeal just fine.

One by one the plates of food were tossed and flushed with no one in sight. The toilet ate the food beautifully so I went back downstairs and repeated the process until the only thing left was my bowl of alphabet soup. The little letters floated around, almost like they wanted to spell things for me, but I didn't want to hear a word of what they had to say. I emptied the bowl of little letters into the toilet and flushed, relieved that I wouldn't have to endure a dinner with a bunch of Nazis and maybe Anderson Massey and others. Much to my horror though, as soon as the toilet swallowed the alphabet soup, it backed up.

An exponential number of little letters came back up with the rising water and soon they were spilling out onto the floor, into the hallway and everywhere else. A flood of alphabet soup was raging out of the toilet like the wrath of God and were spelling out vile things as they flowed passed me. They insulted me, spilled out all of my secrets for the world to see and there was nothing that I could do to stop it. I could hear jackboots walking in through the front door as the alphabet nightmare began to flow downstairs.

ANDERSON MASSEY IS DEAD BECAUSE OF YOU! YOU LET YOUR BEST FRIEND BLEED TO DEATH RIGHT NEXT TO YOU! HOW DO YOU SLEEP AT NIGHT?

I grabbed as many towels as I could from the spacious bathroom in a futile attempt to stop the demon alphabet from causing even more destruction. I tried both creating a towel barrier in the hallway and stuffing the cloths down the toilet to stop the flow completely but nothing worked. The vicious alphabet washed away the towels into the deluge and kept on coming at me with fury.

THE WHOLE WORLD KNOWS YOUR SECRETS NOW BITCH! YOU'LL NEVER GET AWAY FROM THIS NO MATTER HOW HARD YOU TRY!

My last hope was to race downstairs and bolt out the door and hope and pray that I outran the embarrassment. When I got to the doorway several high-ranking Nazis were blocking my path and laughing hysterically as they read what was in the alphabet soup. Once they saw me they pointed fingers at me and laughed even more. I knew then that there was no way I'd be able to get through that door so I darted through the labyrinth of a house until I made it through the backdoor and flopped down right on my face once I made it outside. It took only a few seconds before the nasty alphabet made it's way to me.

HOW MANY TIMES A WEEK TO YOU MASTURBATE ALYSON? DO YOU THINK ABOUT PAPER WHEN YOU DO? THERE'S NO MORE TIME FOR THAT BECAUSE YOU'RE IN AUSCHWITZ NOW. GOOD LUCK! HAHAHA!

I thought I saw the commandant in the distance so I crawled over to him, not having enough strength left to get up and run. The alphabet trailed behind me as I desperately tried to outrun it. Once I made it to the commandant I could only see his boots. I tapped on them with my hands and begged him to get his toilet under control and make the torture stop. He had no reaction so I kept on pestering him up until I looked up at him. As soon as I did so he morphed into Anderson Massey, blood on his boots and gun in hand. He laughed at me with a demonic voice like he enjoyed watching me suffer.

All I could do was scream.

I screamed and screamed and eventually my father screamed too. He screamed for me to wake up and snap out of it. The bright lights burned my eyes when I opened them and saw my father standing over me telling me that it was okay and that it was just a dream. I could hear my little brother screaming in his own room too, obviously triggered by my own outburst, and my mother trying to console him. If I didn't feel like crap enough as it was, I felt even worst knowing my little brother suffered because of me yet another time. No matter what I did or didn't do, Anderson always paid the price.

"It was just a dream Aly!" My father tried to calm me down. "It's not real, it was just a dream!"

My heart was beating so fast that I thought it was going to detonate. Having a full blown panic attack wasn't how I enjoyed waking up in the middle of the night but it wasn't the first time something like that happened. My dad opened the window and handed me a glass of water. Eventually I managed to calm down and when I looked at the clock it was almost five in the morning. Luckily it was the weekend so nobody would get angry if I slept until noon. My dad rubbed my forehead like a parent would do to a sick child until I fell asleep a second time, not really wanting to after being tortured at the hands of alphabet soup.

My second round of sleep was peaceful and dreamless. When I woke up again around noon I was still tired but I knew that my body wouldn't want to sleep anymore. I'd never been able to sleep in the afternoon no matter what. I envied those who could sleep their troubles away because mine kept me awake. I gathered my courage, took a cold shower and then got dressed. I could smell food being cooked in the kitchen and I was very hungry. I'd need all the energy I could muster to finish packing up the house. I hadn't made much progress on my own and quite frankly I didn't really want to.

It was futile, my brain wasn't ignorant of that, but part of me still wanted to hold on to what was already gone. Maybe, just maybe if I didn't pack I wouldn't have to leave. My house wouldn't be gone. I wouldn't live in some foreign place owned by Jihoon Garcia. I knew it was a losing battle so why did I keep fighting? Was it because I was stubborn? Was I stupid? Was it simply what people did? I sat down in the now quite bleak kitchen and waited to be served some chicken souvlaki. The kitchen had lost its majestic touch. The stainless steel appliances would have to be sold because they wouldn't fit in the new place.

It was only a fridge and fridges weren't objects of sentimental value but I couldn't help but feel like pieces of me were being ripped out one by one. It was probably time that I accepted that Alyson Feldman no longer existed and had stopped existing a long time ago. She was somebody else, somebody I didn't know and somebody I wasn't sure I wanted to know. I'd never taken well to change, even when the change was positive, and that kind of unwanted change was no exception. I dug in to my tender souvlaki while my parents were speaking to each other privately in another room and my little brother was spelling his name with the little letters of his alphabet soup.

ANDERSON

IX

THE BANALITY OF POLITICS

My dad dropped me off at the Petrov trailer on the other side of town. He looked absolutely horrified as he looked at all the run-down trailers in there like the park was some sort of post-apocalyptic little world of its own. I honestly felt like laughing at the lack of seriousness of the whole thing but truth was that it was indeed a very serious matter, because I was going to live in some crummy apartment building that might as well just be as bad as that. Dmitry and my dad might have worked at the same worksite but it was like Dmitry had never been on the payroll considering the kind of life he was living.

"Dmitry's gonna take good care of you." My dad promised, probably more to reassure himself than anybody else.

I got out of the truck and picked up my bags then joined the twins and Dmitry who had politely and patiently been waiting for me outside. The three of them hugged me before we all waved at my dad who sped away from the radioactive trailer park, making the gravel of the driveway fly behind the vehicle. I sat in the living room facing Stalin while the Petrovs were rummaging through the kitchen, having insisted on making me a little snack for my arrival.

My parents thought it would be a good idea for me to stay with the twins and their uncle while they moved because they thought that I was somehow mentally unstable. Somewhere along the way they had picked up on the notion that moving was something too stressful for me on top of my return to school so they decided that me sending to a time machine back to the Stalin-era Soviet Union called the Petrov trailer was a good idea. Svetlana popped out of the kitchen a few minutes later with a plate of falafel, garlic potatoes, crackers and mango juice.

"We hope that you enjoy your stay with us." She said as she handed me the plate.

"Thank you," I muttered, "I'm sure I will."

Both the twins then retrieved their own plates of various foods and flopped down on each side of me while Dmitry was nowhere to be found. The fat cats showed up and meowed for food despite having a full bowl in the corner not far from the television. I threw a piece of the crackers on the floor and the calico swallowed it whole without chewing it. They were very well fed considering their size.

"What's up with all the Soviet propaganda?" I asked out of curiosity.

"Most of the artifacts are from the Second World War," Vera replied, "what's the use of owning it if you can't display it?"

I didn't speak.

"I know you probably think it's creepy," Sveta continued, "and I totally understand that you're probably not used to this but we're not some new breed of radical communists. Yes, we hate capitalism but we're not out to take over the world with some modern Bolshevik conspiracy. We've got all sorts of historical stuff all over the house including American artifacts."

"Our grandfather fought in the Soviet Red Army," Vera had food in her mouth, "and this is our way to honour him. Honestly, with the way things are going now in America I'd prefer just going back to Russia."

"I want to move to Canada."

"You have a crush on Justin Trudeau just admit it already."

"Well, he is very cute." I added.

The twins and I cracked up laughing. Poor Sveta, she was asexual in a hyper-sexual society and her sister was pestering her about the Canadian prime minister's good looks. After that they returned to talking about their grandparents during the war and I listened attentively to their stories. The twins also showed me some of their military tattoos and explained their meaning. Their Soviet pride made more sense now that I knew their reasons why and quite honestly after the financial disaster my family was facing I hated capitalism too.

"You're the first person who didn't go running for the hills after coming in here!" Vera laughed.

"Nobody ever comes back a second time," Sveta also chuckled with food in her mouth, "but come over here, we've got all sorts of other stuff too."

The twins showed me around the other rooms which all featured decorations from different eras and different regions. Sergey's old room was the most beautiful with the Victorian decorations and various antiques. The place had since been turned into a sort of makeshift office or junk storage. A desk and a bunch of books were in there along with cardboard boxes stacked up all the way to the ceiling in one corner. The room was small but very clean compared to the rest of the trailer. Hopefully I'd get to make myself a makeshift bed in there for the rest of the week.

The trailer was a miniature museum that was probably worth quite a bit of money. I knew that neither of the Petrovs wanted to sell their artifacts but I imagined that they'd make a pretty penny if they did. They wouldn't have to sell their house or their fridge if they sold Stalin. I looked at every piece as I literally took a trip back in time. I had learned about most of the stuff on the walls and the places they came from in school but I had never experienced it quite like that before, not even at actual museums. At first I thought it had been rather creepy but now I saw the decor as being beautiful.

Dmitry and the twins were quite proud of their collection and I was proud to have had the chance to see it all and become part of it in a way but not running for the hills as Vera put it. After the tour of the trailer that included another visit to the basement to see the plants the twins and I sat on the bed they both shared in a tiny room that looked more like a pen for small animals. It was another bad game of Tetris but neither of them seemed to be bothered by that. If that was all they'd ever known it was normal for them but I wasn't used to not having my own big *private* room.

I laid down on the bed looking at a big poster of Emir Abdelkader, an Islamic scholar and military leader, mounted on the wall. I remembered him from a trip to Elkader, Iowa a couple of years ago. The town was named after him and I'd learned of his heroic story of rallying different Algerian tribes as well as Christians and Jews in the area and fighting a defensive war against the French in the 1800s during rampant colonialism and imperialism. He eventually managed to establish peace in a hostile region before going to rescue persecuted Christians in Syria. He was known as a fierce defender of human rights, for chivalry and his kindness, even towards his enemies. A Sufi saint, I understood why Svetlana would admire him.

"One day I hope I can be half the person he was." Sveta commented once she saw me staring at the poster.

"He was a truly honourable man," I muttered, reflecting on everything, "dedicating his entire life to what we now call human rights."

"I especially admire how he managed to combine religious and political authority to champion for human rights. That usually ends up being a disaster of epic proportions."

"Our current president is a good example of that."

"And that's why I believe in secularism, but people like Emir Abdelkader give me hope. He reminds me that for some people it's really not about pushing agendas, getting the mosts vote or any other dumb-ass political gimmick, but really about doing what's right for the people, *all* people."

Agendas. Politics. Those were two of the words I hated the most in the entire English language. After the massacre agendas had been the only things being pushed. Politicians didn't actually care about mental health, school safety or anything else. They only wanted to indoctrinate people into an ideology and get a reaction — and a vote — out of those only seeking to understand why. Mental health, gun control, bullying, the role of parents and the community, those were all legitimate issues that pertained to what happened at Belden and so many other schools across the nation but all politicians wanted to do was prove their opponents wrong. They didn't care about us, the students, those who had suffered the most.

The Republicans did something just to piss off the Democrats and the Democrats did something just to get back at the Republicans. When one side screwed up we elected the other and that pattern did nothing but repeat itself without ever coming to any resolution. Neither side ever did anything of value to remedy the problem and that was painfully obvious when one looked at the statistics. School shootings were only becoming more common and more deadly. In all fairness I had no solution either, but at least I was looking for answers instead of pushing ideologies that were just as toxic as the ones that had led Anderson and nineteen other people to their deaths.

"For what it's worth Alyson, no amount of mental health programs or gun laws will stop these tragedies from happening." Sveta added almost like she could read my thoughts. "It's toxic masculinity, it's the sensationalism, it's the mentality that it's your right and not a privilege you have to earn and maintain to walk around armed to the teeth just waiting to pounce. Those are the real culprits."

"Why can't Americans understand that?" I was on the verge of tears.

"I don't have a solid answer to that but it's much easier to understand when you're on the outside looking in. And there are no easy answers, this problem is so deep-rooted that it'll take a lot more than my objectivity to solve it but I can tell you that all social issues plaguing this society need to be looked at and resolved before we'll ever be able to stop any type of senseless violence."

"You are correct about that."

"People don't do something for nothing. Whether a person steals food out of desperation or shoots up a school out of vengeance, there's always a reason. Eliminate the underlying cause and you eliminate the problem."

"Funding mental health programs and strengthening gun laws are legitimate policies because there is a social need for that but taking away the firearms of perfectly sensible people and putting every depressed kid in an institution won't solve the problem."

"Exactly."

Framed photos of Erwin Rommel and Bernard Law Montgomery adorned the walls, as well as various magazine cutouts of Justin Trudeau pinned to a homemade cork board. I knew that was Vera's doing because little hearts had been drawn in red ink next to the cutouts. I couldn't help but notice that the photos were being held in place with recycled bullet shell casings made into pins. The walls were painted — a terrible paint job I must add — a yellowish golden color with an imitation wooden plank floor. Whatever it was really made of, it looked moldy and disgusting despite that the girls had multiple cleaning supplies and harsh chemicals next to their broken bedroom door.

A white painted door, broken and fallen off its hinges was awkwardly arranged in the doorframe with a Breaking Bad poster pinned on the back. The entire room was decorated from top to bottom with vintage military propaganda, pictures of celebrities and people the girls admired, and various wall stickers that I'd seen on my many trips to the dollar store. Most of the decorations hid the hideous wall and a fancy Persian rug covered parts of the floor. The furniture in the room looked like it had been picked out of a dumpster too.

An old desk with a missing leg was crammed next to an industrial spindle used as a night table and finally a bare mattress that the twins shared on a makeshift frame created with recycled pipes. At the other end of the room there was a closet without doors with clothes, boxes and books spilling out onto the floor. A tall, slim dresser with eight drawers was in between the closet and a red metal toolbox. On the ceiling a lone bare bulb illuminated the place with posters pinned all around it.

A small rectangular window was on the north end of the room overlooking the bed but we couldn't exactly see outside since it was near the ceiling. The room was exceptionally unfashionable but it was still very cozy and reflected each of the twins' personalities. It was apparent that their room was their own little sanctuary away from the world, I only hoped that my own room in Jihoon's apartment wouldn't look like that. I bet my father was having second thoughts about leaving me in that trailer park but at the very least I was in good company.

"What's life like in this trailer park?" I asked with a surge of anxiety. "Like, is it quiet or whatever."

"Nobody bothers me," Vera replied, "but one gorgon named Kaye Roberts likes to come here and harass my sister."

"I honestly don't know how people like her can make themselves believe that they are good Christians when they behave like that." Sveta grumbled. "I've read the Bible and I promise you that Jesus would never condone or approve of harassing people of other faiths."

"If it makes you feel any better Sveta, it happened to me too."

"I'm very sorry to hear that."

"But to answer your question Aly, this place is pretty screwed up."

"In what way?"

"The neighbours. The stupid neighbours! And they think *we* are the weird neighbours."

"Everybody's scared of our uncle Dmitry, and one of them even called the police and said that the Russian Mafia had a hideout in our trailer."

"The worst part is dealing with that corrupt ignominious crackpot Jihoon. How about we grab a snack and then I'll show you around?"

I agreed to the proposal and the three of us went into the kitchen and devoured what was left of the snacks that had been prepared earlier in the day. Dmitry was nowhere to be found but I could hear a bunch of people making conversation nearby through an open window so I figured that he was one of them. As the three of us were stuffing our faces an alarmed look swept over Sveta's face when she heard a knock on the door. She swallowed her piece of cheese whole and got up in a flash. She grabbed her styrofoam plate and bolted towards her room, doing her best to arrange the door so it would partly close and disappearing behind it.

"Guess who this is!" Vera announced, faking joy and excitement.

If I had to take a wild guess I'd guess it was Kaye Roberts. I didn't know who she was but I found out quickly that I didn't want to get to know her either once Vera opened the door. The woman on the other side was in her fifties with long grey hair pulled up into a ball on top of her head and a long dingy dress. She had a Bible in her hand and as soon as the door swung open she began yelling and trying to push her way in. All I heard was *terrorist, bitch, go back to your country,* and *lynch* before Vera slammed the door right in her face so hard that it made the trailer shake. Kaye kept on yelling outside and it wasn't long before I heard Dmitry's deep angry voice shouting at her before he came back inside.

"That's Kaye the goody goody Christian girl for you." Vera muttered through her teeth.

I didn't say anything. The two of us went to find Svetlana in her room where she'd prepared a little makeshift bed on the floor in the only little space left in the room using a folded piece of foam, an old but clean sheet, a pillow and a blanket.

"So here's the deal Aly, when we first moved here this woman was very welcoming. She brought us this nosy neighbour pie and all but then her mask fell off. She got creepy and then downright abusive. She invites herself over anytime she likes like she owns the entire trailer park and it's always this same Islamophobic abuse. We usually don't open the door but since you asked what life was like in the trailer park…"

I didn't speak as there was another knock on the door. It must not have been her because Dmitry answered it almost immediately. He spoke briefly with a man before I heard the door closing again.

"The creepiest thing of all Aly is that this old hag knows *everything*. She never said much about herself, it was always about interrogating us. I swear that she knows what I'm thinking and what I dream about at night! I don't know what her deal is or why she doesn't get the message that she's not welcomed here after all this time."

The twins obviously had chips on their shoulders when it came to Kaye Roberts who lived just down the street. Vera seemed to be paranoid of her while Sveta was downright afraid. Considering all the violent hate crimes happening in the country I couldn't blame her. I'd experienced a nightmare neighbour next door when I was younger but they didn't come over and discriminate me because of what was on my head instead of trying to see what was inside my heart.

"I don't know why Kaye even lives here. She has this rich capitalist husband with an insanely high-paying job like an engineer or something in whatever trade is popular around here and they both live in this dirty post-apocalyptic trailer park! Did you see the cars they drive? Get in it and drive the hell away and don't ever come back!"

A huge lump formed in my throat as I swallowed hard. I didn't want to live like the Petrov clan in what might as well have been called an insane asylum at the least. To be fair I didn't know everyone who lived in the trailer park, but the twins didn't belong there. They weren't weird or abusive crackpots who liked to be miserable and make everyone around them miserable too. Yeah, they could be intense and their trailer was reminiscent of a Stalin-era communal apartment but they were the people who made the most sense in my life.

They were both amazingly talented, super smart, awesome writers and they each spoke *four* languages — Russian, French, English and Bosnian. Their lifestyle might've seemed odd to me at times but if there was something I was sure of it was that they did not belong in the trailer park. They deserved better than what they got from Jihoon Garcia, and as low as my self-esteem might have been, I still believed I did too.

"Are you ready for the grand tour?" Vera asked me once the quiet returned.

The weather was nice outside, clear blue sky with just a soft breeze blowing through the trees. The first place the twins took me was the end of the street at the very bottom of the radioactive mountain. Sveta looked over her shoulder the entire time seemingly anticipating an assault from Kaye who lived nearby and probably lurked around in the shadows like a predator looking for prey considering what she'd been like at the front door. Thankfully, Kaye Roberts has been nowhere in sight.

Vera was the first one to climb up the very steep hill and after an exhausting eternity and a few falls Sveta and I reached the top and stood next to the massive **NO TRESPASSING** sign that was probably the biggest sign I'd ever seen. On the other side of the hill there was an industrial wasteland. There were pools and basins the size of the Great Lakes filled with this nasty oil residue or some other thick black gunk. It was absolutely disgusting and repugnant to see. A little further down on the other side of the hill there was a large barbed wire fence with a human health hazard warning sign attached to it. I was appalled to see such a thing in the otherwise beautiful community of Wintercrest and had no previous knowledge that such pollution existed in my part of the world.

"It's called a tar pond," Vera's voice was low, "for decades people thought they only existed in Nova Scotia but little did anybody know, we have some here in New Hampshire too."

I was baffled and did not know how to feel about what was right in front of my eyes.

"Whatever operation went on here, it was really under the radar and closed off from the public eye and not a lot of people know what actually went on there because the government owned the factory. We can only speculate what went on in there by examining what they left behind. It all sounds like a big Area 51 conspiracy thing."

The pools of black gunk stretched our as far as the eye could see with old half-standing structures that looked like they once could have been industrial warehouses in the far distance. It really looked like a post-apocalyptic wasteland. I had imagined the trailer park being part of a secret government affair but I never in a million years expected it to be true!

"Do you know what they did with the tar ponds in Nova Scotia, Aly?" Vera continued. "They *rehabilitated* them by stuffing the toxic basins with cement and other chemical crap and built a park for the children to play on over it!"

"How screwed up is that?" Sveta finished her sister's train of thought. "Poor kids don't know they are playing on top of a wasteland that's freaking dangerous for your health! And they tell you all this scientific stuff about how it's safe and all but I have my doubts. You just don't do something like that!"

"That's some scary stuff," I muttered emotionlessly, "and you say there were conspiracies?"

"Well, nobody really knows for sure, it's just hearsay and I don't believe in that Area 51 weather control stuff but I believe they manufactured some pretty nasty stuff in there for the ponds to look like this."

"Like, stuff *for* alleged conspiracies?"

"Yeah, something like that. And to answer your question Alyson, life in this trailer park is interesting."

As we walked back down the hill I kept on looking behind me at the pools of thick black gunk in disgust. Even more fear came creeping in as I thought about my own upcoming life in Jihoon's apartment building.

"Isn't that stuff hazardous to public health?" I asked the girls. "I mean, shouldn't a trailer park be built far away from that stuff?"

"Apparently it's built far enough," Sveta grumbled in obvious disgust, "but I'm with you on this one."

As we walked down the street of the small trailer park Vera told me the stories behind each and every trailer accompanied by the life stories of the people that lived in them. She was almost as knowledgable as Kaye Roberts.

"This trailer here," she pointed at a trailer with a door that looked like it was painted by a toddler with excessive finger paint, "a French guy named Henri lives in there. He's high on dope all the time and if you think the door is bad, the *entire* trailer is painted like that inside. His brother and our uncle Dmitry worked together briefly before he died of an overdose."

Further down the street we arrived at Kaye's trailer. It didn't seem like anybody was home — much to Svetlana's relief — and next to that trailer there was another trailer that looked like it came right out of a movie about an alien invasion.

"That one right there," Vera said pointed to it, "it looks abandoned but it's not. An old ninety-year-old-guy with too much money lives in there."

"Oh God," I muttered to myself as I looked at the trailer that was about to crumble from the inside out.

"If I tell you a secret, you won't tell anyone will ya?"

"I promise."

"I broke into his house, well I actually just had to climb through the caved in roof, one day this summer and stole his credit card."

I didn't speak. The look on Svetlana's face indicated that it was a surprise to her too.

"I actually still have it," Vera went on, "but I don't know if it's still good."

"Why do people who have money live in this kind of place?" I asked raising my eyebrows. "And no offence to you Vera."

"Nah, no worries there Aly. And I don't know. I honestly have no idea. Heck, if I had as much money as he did I'd be long gone!"

"And more importantly, why'd you rob him of his credit card?"

"I needed to pay an exorbitant phone bill."

I laughed but Sveta seemed to be genuinely shocked. She probably knew something I didn't but I didn't believe the phone bill excuse. Nonetheless, I decided to go along with it just for the hell of it.

"Who in the world did you talk to in order to have to steal a credit card to pay your phone bill?" I giggled.

"Vladimir Nikolayev," Svetlana grumbled looking like a lightbulb had just gone off in her head, "her boyfriend in Russia!"

"Nikolayev the cannibal?" I asked in disbelief.

"No!" Vera exclaimed. "They aren't related, they just happen to have the same name. Where'd you hear about that?"

"I watch National Geographic you know."

"We don't have cable but I buy the magazines at the corner store sometimes."

Sveta had told me that Vera was boy crazy but I hadn't put all the pieces together, and neither had Sveta, but everything was out in the open now. I didn't think less of Vera for stealing a credit card. It wasn't like I hadn't done some shady stuff in my life.

"What the hell Vera!" I exclaimed laughing.

"Do you wanna talk to him?" She laughed too. "I'm gonna call him tonight but he doesn't speak English."

"I think I'll just stick to trying to learn French. You're gonna have to tutor me sometime because as it turns out it's a lot harder than I thought it would be after all this time."

"You could practice with Henri."

X

IN COLOUR

And I'd thought the Petrov trailer was ugly. Henri's trailer was right out of a cheesy horror movie. Whatever colour the walls once were, you couldn't see it anymore. On a table in the corner of the room there were little bottles of acrylic artisan paint that Henri had used to decorate his trailer. The entire walls in *each* room were painted along with the cabinets and the counters in the kitchen. His paintings were weird and looked like they had been made by a toddler coming down from a cocaine high.

My name was written in orange letters on the top of a cabinet with a drawing of the Loch Ness monster below it with a bunch of other weird symbols. Henri seemed to be a big fan of Canada too since maple leaves covered one wall and several paintings honoured the Royal Canadian Mounted Police on another. Even the kitchen ceiling had been painted in a rainbow of colours! Henri was currently working on the ceiling of the living room when the girls and I walked in. The ceiling fan had been ripped out for him to paint around it and was discarded in the corner next to the front door.

The rooms were dimly lit with nothing but the light coming from the TV to illuminate the place. All the windows were covered with tape so not a single particle of light could come into the house from outside. Henri was an overweight man in his mid-fifties with thick black curly hair in an eighties hairstyle. He had a hard time speaking English but I managed with basic French and the twins filled in the blanks for me when I didn't understand. Henri invited us to sit down at the kitchen table while he rummaged through the cupboards to find some snacks.

Eventually he found some molasses cookies in an old dust-covered box and handed the girls and I each a bag. Neither one of us ate them and I didn't even open the bag but Vera did out of curiosity only to find the apparent cookies disintegrated into a million crumbs. Henri went on rambling incoherently about just as many different things in rapid succession and I didn't understand a thing and neither did the girls because they kept on looking at me and at each other from their respective ends of the table. After a few minutes Sveta told Henri that we needed to go help out uncle Dmitry do some yard work just so he'd shut up and let us go.

Before the three of us left he begged us to come again soon. Vera promised him we would although I got the impression that she didn't exactly want to return. Back in the streets of the trailer park the girls finished showing me around the place filled with run-down trailers and telling me the stories of the people who lived in them. One household apparently kept chickens as house pets for their mentally retarded children while anther had eaten a pet rabbit Svetlana had sold him. There was this one old guy the girls called the Blueberry Man and another younger fella they called the Apple Man because they always wanted to sell their fruits when the season came around.

"That old one with his freaking blueberries," Vera grumbled angrily, "he's nothing but a two-faced hypocrite and a weirdo. This one time I asked him how much his blueberries were and and they costed like an arm and a leg and maybe an eye so I told him it was too expensive and he went to sit in his car and cried."

Both the girls and I burst out laughing at once but I quietly hoped that I'd end up in a half-decent place. I didn't want to be harassed, hassled or creeped out. I just wanted a regular quiet life. Was that asking too much? Other trailers were completely vacant or partially fallen to the ground. There were no fire hydrants anywhere and a lot of domestic fire pits in the yards. The girls also rambled about the construction of a new, much nicer trailer park on the other side of the interstate that they wanted to go live in if everything went according to plan and Dmitry's job didn't take them out of town. At the same time they were fantasizing about their dream house I grieved mine. My parents kept on telling me that we'd get another nice house once my dad found another stable job but that didn't change much. My life as I had known it for eighteen years was gone.

"My dad's paying your uncle to let me stay here isn't he?" I asked Svetlana.

"Our uncle Dmitry's not gonna accept any money." She blandly replied without emotion.

"Well, he better because I owe you Sveta!"

"Owe me for what?"

"*This* for starters, and for saving my butt at the beginning of the school year."

"Nah, don't worry about any of that. Aren't you curious to see how the moving process is going though?"

"Yes and no, but both my parents insisted that I should relax, focus on school and stay with you while they worry about all that stuff."

"Well then, let's go have some fun!"

The girls and I hiked through the overgrown grass passed the trailer park near the tar pond mountain until we reached the railroad and an old industrial train station that once served the factory operations. Vera told me that the freight train still passed there around midnight each night but that it just passed straight through instead of stopping like it once did.

"So where exactly are you moving?" Sveta asked me as she played on the rails like a little kid. "Jihoon owns like half of the apartment buildings in town."

"South Spring Drive."

The girls' faces both lit up as soon as they heard those three little words. They seemed to be more excited than me about living in one of Jihoon Garcia's places.

"Dude!" Vera shouted happily. "That's just a few streets down from where our cousin lives!"

"Sergey?" I asked.

"Yeah! Him and his wife Marissa are awesome! Their friends are epic and you'll love them too. Hey, we should go pay them a visit tomorrow and cheer on your parents and their moving!"

"That actually sounds like a great idea!"

My spirit was immediately lifted as the girls spoke about Sergey and his folks with such contagious enthusiasm. Maybe I was overthinking and things wouldn't be so bad after all. At least I'd be in good company and I'd probably see the girls more often since I didn't really have any other friends and Jennifer and I had consistently been growing apart lately. I smiled again for the first time in what seemed like another eternity as we walked back to the trailer just before the sun began to set in the distance over the highway.

Once we got in Dmitry hugged each of us again and asked us if we wanted to go out for a late-night supper or if we wanted something delivered. The four of us agreed on pizza, cake, garlic potatoes and root beer so Dmitry phoned it in and we watched TV while we waited for the delivery boy. The TV had nothing but rabbit ears with only one channel and the reception was awful. I had never watched such horrid TV before and it annoyed the life out of me but it appeared to be normal for the Petrovs.

"Gotta go water the garden, wanna come Aly?"

I followed Vera into the basement where all her plants had grown considerably bigger since I had last seem them in her year-round garden. I also noticed a little patch of new plants that had just sprouted in the corner.

"They are so cute," Vera told herself almost squeaking, "I love it when they stick their little heads out of the earth like that!"

"What do you do with all of these plants once they have matured?" I asked out of curiosity.

"Some friends sell the produce at the farmer's market in the fall and most of the flowers are sold to some flower shops. That's how Sveta and I support our lifestyle."

"That's a good way to make money! And I guess you can eat whatever you grow too which is awesome considering the price of groceries around here."

Vera began to laugh.

"You know Alyson, there was this old man that used to live in this trailer park that would eat the flowers, like the actual blooms!"

"He ate your flowers?"

"Oh he ate more than just the flowers! He was just like a zombie straight out of Plants vs. Zombies, just chomping down indiscriminately on plants."

We both laughed until Vera told me to step back as she was going to water the plants. She opened the water valve and water sprayed down from a punctured shower hose on the ceiling, giving each patch of plants just a little bit of water at a time.

"There we go," Vera commented as she turned off the valve and turned off the lights, "you wouldn't believe how thirsty these things get."

The two of us went back upstairs just in time for the food to be delivered after loafing around a while. Dmitry served our food and drinks in large styrofoam plates and plastic cups. I was hungry so I dug in immediately and didn't leave a single crumb behind.

"Thank you for letting me stay here Dmitry," I told him after we were done eating our midnight meal.

Dmitry told me not to thank him because he was happy to have me around. Afterwards the twins sat on their bed and me on my makeshift bed on the floor as Vera punched in Vladimir Nikolayev's number into her cellphone. I had to refrain from laughing as I thought of Nikolayev the cannibal from the Russian prisons documentary on National Geographic. He giggled as he recounted his story of killing a man, dismembering him and making his friend eat pieces of him, telling them it was kangaroo meat. Vera's boyfriend answered on the second ring and the two of them immediately began flirting in Russian.

"Hey Alyson, say hi to my Vovochka!" Vera told me as she held out the phone.

"Hello!" I said very awkwardly, not really knowing what else to tell a guy as old as my dad with a cannibal's name over the phone.

Vladimir responded with something in Russian and the girls both laughed before Vera returned to having her gibberish conversation with him. I had a mundane talk about nothing and everything with Svetlana in the meantime and at about 12:30 in the morning we heard the midnight train rumbling on the other side of the hill.

"So you like old men?" I joked once Vera hung up.

"Not old," Vera replied giggling, "mature."

"Oh, I see."

"Have you ever dated Alyson?"

"Yeah, a little bit, but not *mature* men."

We both laughed as Sveta put her hand over her face. I then patted her on the back to reassure her that I wouldn't subject her to boy-crazy antics the same way her sister did. It did not seem to make her feel better as her sister carried on with the conversation.

"Well, you should try an older guy just for fun and experience the difference for yourself!"

"I'll keep that in mind."

"You wanna know something crazy Aly?"

"Try me."

"We're both terrified in peeping in our bed."

"What? Out of all the phobias you can have you're scared of peeing in your bed!"

I laughed hysterically and for a while so did Vera but she was serious about her fear of bedwetting. Svetlana now had both hands over her face, completely embarrassed about her irrational fear and I felt bad about bursting into laughter when it was obviously something both the girls were uneasy about.

"I don't know why, but it's been this way since we were little girls," Sveta explained, "and it's never left us despite the fact that neither one of us has ever wet the bed."

"Well, apparently psychos and serial killers all wet their beds as children," Vera whispered like a mouse, "I just don't want to turn into one of them."

"Vera," I told her, now laughing even more, "peeing in your bed doesn't make you a murderer. My cousin is a year younger than me and he still wets his bed. That doesn't automatically make him a serial killer."

The girls didn't speak. Vera's face was red with embarrassment and by the look Sveta was wearing I knew she wanted the conversation to be over with sooner rather than later.

"Anderson Massey didn't wet his bed," I went on, "and he killed almost two dozen people. Regardless of whether you pee in your bed or not, it doesn't change anything. Those killer profiles are nothing but nonsense. *I* knew Anderson Massey, those so-called experts and psychologists didn't. To me he was a person, to them he's just a statistic."

"Man, I'm sorry Alyson."

"You have nothing to be sorry about. And take it easy, you won't turn into him even if you pee in your bed once."

Vera giggled awkwardly at the triviality of it until we simultaneously looked at the digital clock and noticed that it was almost two in the morning. And so we both said goodnight and went to bed. My makeshift bed wasn't very comfortable and the trailer park was noisy at night but I managed to doze off eventually and had a strange dream about Anderson Massey. In my dream I was begging an unknown man to help Anderson, telling him that he was dangerous and to *please* help him somehow, but the man told me that Anderson wasn't important and that I should just move on with my life and forget all about him.

The more I pleaded the less he wanted to hear it and eventually he sent me away. I couldn't see the man's face, I only remembered seeing his tan pants and his black shoes. Then the scene warped and I was transported to a little run-down neighbourhood in Wintercrest where I saw money all over the ground. Everything was pitch black and deserted around me and my only thought was that I needed to get out of there immediately but for some reason I began picking up the money on the ground instead.

I began by picking up silver coins and then as I progressed down the brick sidewalk near the buildings I began to pick up dollar bills of always increasing denominations. The bills were weird, they had all sorts of strange people on them and they came in all colours of the rainbow. One I picked up was purple, another was green, red, and so on. I managed to pick up two fifty dollar bills and a few more hundred dollar bills and at the end of the sidewalk right at the foot of one old building I picked up a red five hundred dollar bill. I had never seen such a thing before, but I was so happy to be able to have so much money again. Maybe I'd be able to return to my old life!

As I turned around, I saw the man's tan pants standing in front of a parking meter but I didn't recall exchanging any words with him before everything warped a second time and I ended up in a concentration camp, still clutching the funny money. All the inmates around me in the barracks were eating alphabet soup in complete silence and staring at me without blinking their eyes like a cat would do. I walked out and found more money on the ground so I followed the trail, picking up the bills that were only getting stranger and stranger along the way. The money trail eventually warped into a trail of pictures of the Belden victims and lead me to the commandant's office where Anderson Massey was sitting in a chair behind the desk

He got up and walked over to me and said something because his lips were moving but no sound came out. He must've been over twenty feet tall because I was minuscule next to him. I immediately woke up in cold sweat and came face to face with a ghost! A faceless mound of white sheets was standing at the edge of my bed just like in those cheesy horror movies! I screamed and as I did so the mound of sheets turned around and I saw that it was Svetlana wearing an Islamic prayer dress and not a ghostly mound of sheets after all.

"Hey, take a chill pill," she urged in a whisper, "it's just me!"

But it was too late, I'd already screamed and woken up Vera who was visibly shaken and confused about what was going on. The three of us each awkwardly looked around the room and then at each other before the twins cracked up laughing.

"So, now you know that Muslim women are actually ghosts!" Vera failed at not laughing.

"What are you doing up at this hour?" I asked Sveta, genuinely curious about what she was doing.

"I'm up for morning prayer."

"You mean middle of the night prayer?"

"Do you wanna come outside with me? You look pretty shaken up and like you could use some air."

"You are correct about that."

I looked around the room, still in a dream-like state and confused. After a few seconds reality came back and I realized that I didn't have all the money I picked up in some strange area of town that I'd never been in before, that concentration camp inmates did not eat alphabet soup and that it didn't matter what Anderson said because it was just a dream and none of that had been real. Nonetheless, my blood boiled with anger because I never got the chance to help Anderson, even if it had been just a dream, but he was dead and nobody even cared anyway. I momentarily let my head flop back on the pillow before grabbing the thick blanket and following Sveta outside.

She was finishing up her prayer on the porch by the time I joined her and sat down on the first step next to her. I huddled up in my blanket because the air was frigid out there. The sun was coming up over the nuclear mountain at the end of the lane so it was later in the morning than I originally thought. Sveta looked at me sympathetically, wondering what was wrong with me and what she could do to help, or at the very least comfort me. Unfortunately for both of us nobody could help me.

"I keep having unbelievable nightmares," I managed to mutter out eventually, "they are weird and warped and screwed up. I don't understand any of them. My only consolation is that none of them are real."

"I'm sorry to burst your bubble there Aly," Sveta began slowly, gauging my reaction, "but in Islam dreams are very much real."

"Say that again?"

"In the Quran sleep is a lot like death. God takes our souls when we sleep and returns them when we wake but during that time our soul can travel to other worlds."

"So you're basically telling me that my soul actually went to those weird and horrible places?"

"It's a legitimate possibility. Look Aly, I'm not God and I can't say for sure where your dreams came from, if they have a legitimate spiritual component or if it's just your body acting up, but I wouldn't be so quick and dismissing them as just dreams. You brain didn't show you something so powerful for nothing."

"I don't know what to say about that."

"Dreams can either be realistic or symbolic and may show you some facts about the past, present or future, regarding yourself or others. The dreams may let you experience certain situations that need to be interpreted. While you sleep you don't just lay there and do nothing, you travel into the world of souls. Different material and spiritual realms, the grave, paradise, hell, you name it."

"Stop for a moment!"

Vomit and acid splashed up into my throat and I felt like being sick. Sveta noticed my discomfort and rubbed my shoulder gently but it didn't help a whole lot. The fact that my dreams might be real and not just my brain going crazy was the worst thing anyone could've told me in that moment.

"Are you telling me that I really met Anderson Massey and Rudolf Höss in another world during my sleep?" I squeaked out through deep breaths.

"It's a possibility," Sveta replied calmly, "but look Aly, I'm not God and I don't know who's being punished and who is free to roam and who goes where and I don't even know the exact details of what you saw, but it's possible. Our souls visit their world and we can come in contact with other souls, good and bad spirits may meet each other, but the specifics aren't something I can comment on. I don't have enough religious knowledge to really go beyond that, but I can tell you that I've had unbelievable dreams that can only come from another world. There's no other explanation."

"I'm listening."

"How do you explain deja vu?"

"It's just a creepy coincidence."

"I don't think so. I believe that the soul travels to other places and sort of takes a vacation there, and that's why there's an unexplainable sense of familiarity with certain people, places and time periods. That's the only explanation I've found to my otherwise inexplicable attraction to Canada. It's like I belong there and I've been there, and I believe that I have, I just need to go back with my physical body this time. But heck, these dreams might just be the devil wanting to make us miserable."

I couldn't help myself, I got up and retched over the railing. The vomitus tasted of falafel and root beer and did not bring the relief I'd been hoping for. Sveta brought me into the kitchen and gave me some club soda and Gravol to make me feel better but the taste nauseated me even more. It wasn't long before the sun rose and so did Dmitry. He might've been out of a job but his brain was still programmed to wake him up for his shift. It had been the same story with my dad and that was just another sore point for me.

"Pray for them." Sveta spoke softly, referring to the people I'd seen in my dream.

Dear Anderson,

I don't know. I just had this really screwed up dream and I don't know. Look, I've never been much of a believer in the afterlife and that kind of stuff but are you okay where you are? Not that you could just respond to this letter like you could do once upon a time, but is that what you're trying to tell me in my dreams? Or something along those lines? I never really believed in anything, it was all just a big "if" before, but now... Now I know even less.

My parents have only grown deeper into their faith since the shooting but that day you robbed me of whatever little faith I had. I just don't see how they do it, you know. I mean, how in the world does you shooting up a school demonstrate God's power? His mercy? Forgiveness? WHAT YOU DID WAS EVIL ANDERSON! IT DOESN'T DEMONSTRATE ANY OF THOSE THINGS!

And about the afterlife, there's gotta be something right? I mean, life can't just be a bitch and then you die and there's nothing. How cheap is that! There's gotta be something more after we're done here, some kind of justice or peace at least! I don't know what exactly, but I've gotta believe that death isn't the end. There's gotta be something. I can't believe that all the people I love are just gone. That belief just doesn't sit well with me. It's just awful.

My whole life I've been going around like I'm never going to die, like I'm going to live forever and that paradise was right at my fingertips the whole time but YOU RIPPED THAT AWAY FROM ME. And afterwards, I just went around aimlessly as I still do. Such a pitiful existence. Was that what it was like for you? The world didn't learn its lesson, and I guess I didn't either. Why is it now that everybody's freaking dead that we all start paying attention? How in the world does this demonstrate the power of God? What the hell is the point of this life?! If only I could feel you right beside me one more time…

Alyson

A few tears escaped from my eyes but I quickly wiped them away before anyone could notice. I was already embarrassed enough that I'd left a pile of puke outside, I didn't want Dmitry or the twins to have to worry about me even more because they were already doing more than they should've. Within a few more moments breakfast was served and the three of them sat around me at the kitchen table. For Vera, that so-called breakfast consisted of Oreo cookies and *whiskey*.

"Whiskey for breakfast?" I asked Vera.

"It's Saturday morning and I had strange dreams." She replied pouring out another drink of Johnnie Walker's twelve-year-old Black Label. "You want some?"

Before I could say no she handed me the mostly empty bottle but I pushed it across the table over to Svetlana without giving a second thought. Since drinking alcohol was forbidden in Islam she passed it over to Dmitry who happily took a sip. My throat and stomach burned for him as I watched him take a gulp. I'd only ever taken one sip of beer in my life and hated the mediocre taste. I knew darn well that the Johnnie Walker was nothing like beer, and not in a good way.

"How do the two of you drink that stuff for breakfast? Alcohol tastes like poison!"

"And where in the world did you taste poison?" Vera asked winking at me.

She was right, I hadn't. The taste of that single sip of beer hadn't been the only thing sour that night but I quickly blocked the intrusive memory. Dmitry handed me a glass of water since I wanted neither Vera's liquor nor Sveta's guava juice. I ate my sausage and eggs in silence while the others conversed in Russian. When Vera was done pigging out in her cookies, ice cream, ginger ale and liquor the girls and I sat outside and soaked up the remnants of the nice weather in Wintercrest while Dmitry went to town.

It was another beautiful warm day outside but I was still bothered by my dream. I couldn't understand what it possibly could've meant but I did know that it bothered me and left a bitter taste in my mouth so I decided to tell the girls about it. Vera was just as puzzled as I was but Sveta seemed to know something we didn't. She got up and went back inside to retrieve something and popped up a few moments later with a handful of colourful dollar bills.

"Is that what you saw in your dream?" Svetlana asked me as I looked at the different bills.

"What the hell is this?" I was completely marvelled.

"From Canada."

"This is exactly what I saw in my dream, except that some colours weren't matched up with the right denominations."

"Brain fart!"

We laughed but I was still mystified at the Canadian currency. I couldn't recall ever seeing dollar bills quite like that before and I was puzzled as to why I would dream of *Canadian* money over the American money my family needed. Maybe Sveta was right about everything and maybe my dreams were actually remnants of another time, another place, maybe another life entirely. Maybe I'd been prosperous in Canada at one point, or maybe it was a sign that we'd all be better off leaving the country.

If there was one thing I was sure of it was that my family finances would've greatly benefited from Canada's universal healthcare. It made me very angry to see those capitalist pigs on TV call countries like Canada communist nations where people are taxed to death and oppressed without knowing it as a futile attempt to justify being the only developed country who leaves its citizens to die in the streets if they can't pay. Canada ranked far higher in just about every area when it came to the quality of life of its citizens. They didn't need to call a taxi when in fact they needed an ambulance.

"Let me tell you about this strange dream I had once." Sveta began. "It was a few years ago actually, I dreamed of a suitcase in an old shed on abandoned industrial land and it was so vivid it's like I was there. When I woke up I went to check it out and you know what? It was all real. The suitcase was really there and I got there the same way I did in my dream, and before I went to sleep that night I had no previous knowledge of this."

"That's amazing," I retorted, "and what was in the suitcase?"

Sveta flashed me the money. She'd actually found some colourful money in real life! I was seriously amazed but still just as puzzled. Did my own dream mean that I'd find money too? What was the significance of the messed up denominations? That I'd find value in another form, another currency so to speak? For a moment there I thought I was really onto something.

"This reminds me of a story in Islamic tradition where two men became brothers and one died. The living one saw his dead brother in a dream where he was told that his sibling owed money to a Jewish man. He asked him to return the money to the man and told him where to find it and sure enough it was really there when he woke up. The exact quantity of money was there and understanding that everything he'd seen in the dream was real, he returned the money to the Jewish man."

I thanked Sveta for her wisdom and her patience with me while her sister called up Mercedes so we could pay my parents a visit and tour my new home. Soon enough Mercedes' old Mercedes-Benz showed up in the driveway with a roar. It sounded more and more like the stereotypical clunker it was with each passing day. I sat in front riding shotgun while Vera sat behind me and Sveta had to climb through the window because the door was jammed shut and there was no way to open it. Once everyone was buckled in Mercedes made the engine roar and we were on our way.

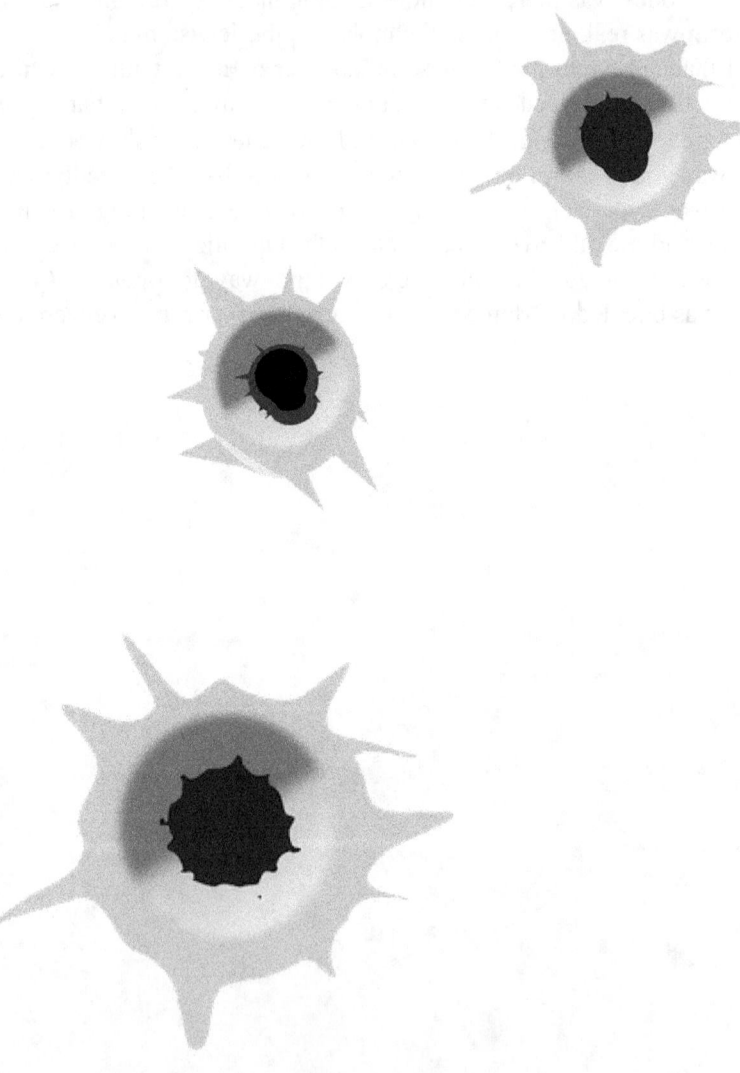

XI

THE WORLD AND ITS SECRETS

There was a traffic jam on the interstate so while we waited for things to get moving I told Mercedes about my dream and what Sveta had later shared with me. Much to my surprise, she had an interesting story of her own to share with us about the universe trying to tell her something in mysterious ways.

"You'll never guess what happened the other day!" Mercedes exclaimed as she turned off the car engine that was making weirder than usual noises.

"What?" Vera asked curiously.

"Somebody left a GPS in my car!"

"A GPS?"

"Yeah! Brand new in its box and everything! I went to the strip mall in the south end for like fifteen minutes and when I came back I found it in my car."

"Any idea who put it there? And more importantly, why?"

"Not a clue! First I figured somebody stole it from the electronics store in the mall and wanted to frame me by putting it in my car so I took it back but it turns out that they don't sell models like that."

"Dude, epic!"

"No kidding! Ain't it strange that people leave stuff in your car instead of taking your stuff?"

"Somebody got ya a gift!"

"Well, it's true that I never lock the doors on this old sloppy jalopy, because, well, you know what happens when I attempt to lock the doors."

"You did get the door open last time this happened, right?"

"After I almost pried the whole thing off, yeah."

The brand new GPS was neatly arranged on the dashboard in front of me with a map of Wintercrest loaded up on the screen. Even the little car on the screen was a black Mercedes just like the actual thing I was sitting in. And yes, it was a *thing* and not a car.

"But why a GPS?" I asked mostly to myself, pondering the significance of it all.

"I think it's because the universe around us just wants to be acknowledged sometimes." Vera responded. "Look, I'm not my sister but I believe that there's more to life than we think exists."

"That's profound."

"No, but seriously! Don't you think that there's some higher state of consciousness to be achieved? You know, like the Buddhists teach? I don't think there's a particular cause and effect reason behind everything that happens, but it still happens so you can gain something from it."

"And what kind of awareness or higher consciousness would Mercedes gain from a GPS?"

"I don't know, but maybe the world is saying hello. *Hi Mercedes! I'm here!* It's all a possibility."

"I guess that's true, that there's more to life than we might realize at any given point. That's something I've really been struggling with since the shooting."

I looked over at Mercedes but she showed no emotion. She was probably in deep contemplation the same way Sveta seemed to be. Maybe it was time I stopped blocking out the world myself.

"They should make pills to be more open-minded," Sveta commented as she came back to the real world.

"You know, that's a great idea," Mercedes added, "it would help us with our *awareness!*"

"Yeah, and our ideologies are limited to what we know; to what we've seen and experienced. As much as I'd like to think that I am open-minded and non-judgmental, I am still limited to my own ideologies."

"I wish the people at school could've take those open-minded heightened self-awareness pills." I added emotionlessly. "Maybe they would not have done to Anderson what they did."

Silence.

"Or maybe the world wants you to take a road trip." I continued blankly.

Mercedes looked at me and smiled. For a moment there I couldn't help but wonder if she'd wanted to take a road trip all along but wanted to find a creative way to ask us.

"We should all go on a road trip!" Mercedes agreed.

"To Lavallette, New Jersey!" Vera exclaimed joyfully.

"What the hell do you want to do in a one-horse town that nobody's ever heard of?"

"Hey! Anybody who has ever watched *Greetings from the Shore* or *Jersey Shore* knows how nice the beaches are at this time of year!"

"What are you hoping to pick up on the beach? A nice sailor? Didn't you complain about the drunken sailors in Russia?"

The two of them looked at me as I burst out laughing in the middle of their argument. I was cool with a New Jersey beach for a couple of days. I wasn't going to say no to having my mind be taken off of what had been wearing me down for the longest time.

"Russian sailors!" I exclaimed laughing. "Vera even has a Russian boyfriend now!"

Mercedes shot a look at Vera who blushed in embarrassment. So it seemed that the Russian boyfriend had been a secret between the sisters and I. Suddenly my laughter evaporated and was replaced with anxiety.

"Is that true?!" Mercedes probed.

"Yes." Vera finally admitted in a mousy voice.

"And you didn't tell me!"

"It's fairly new! And I didn't know if it was going to last!"

"How old is this guy? Please don't tell me you're dating Vladimir Putin!"

Both the sisters and I burst out laughing uncontrollably. No, she wasn't dating a president, she was dating a cannibal! Well, not really, but it was funny for me to think about it that way.

"No!" Vera went on. "His name is Vladimir Nikolayev."

"Oh my God!" Mercedes shouted, almost to the point of jumping out of her seat. "The cannibal!"

"No! He's in his mid-thirties and he has an office job taking care of paperwork for an industrial shipping company. He just happens to have the same name as the cannibal and he has nothing to do with Putin!"

"He's your real life bad boy from the TV fantasy! I knew it!"

"He's not a bad boy, plus I don't even know what he looks like."

"You don't know what your own boyfriend looks like Vera?"

"Mercedes!"

Sveta and I had been laughing through their entire exchange, much to Vera's prolonged embarrassment. I no longer felt bad about having accidentally spilled the beans but I made a mental note to be more careful next time.

"Why don't you invite Vladimir Nikolayev to America and you can visit Lavallette with him!" I proposed as a joke but Vera took it seriously.

"Yes! That's a wonderful idea!" She exclaimed. "I should totally do that!"

"And you could be on that show 90 Day Fiancé!" Mercedes giggled.

"And I would get money from the show to fund our trip to New Jersey!" Vera was almost squeaking with joy. "You girls are seriously amazing. Why didn't I think of this before? I totally wanna be on TV!"

Why couldn't my father have been on some TV show that helped him find a job or something? It was too late for my house and my old life but if Vera could have a better life and something more than what she had now I was happy for her. The girls deserved much more than what they'd been handed by American capitalism. Mercedes fired up the engine again as the traffic jam began to move.

"And how do you know he's not a serial killer?"

"Well, maybe Ted Bundy would be fun!"

"And how in the world did you even find this guy anyway?"

"I dialled my name in the phone."

"What?"

"Well, you know how each number is associated to a trio of letters on the keypad? Well, I tried to dial my name and it didn't really work but some names did!"

"And Vladimir Nikolayev answered on the other end?"

"His secretary did, but yeah, basically."

Mercedes and I cracked up laughing at the same time. She laughed so much that the car began to swerve in the road and I had to grab the wheel and try to steer it in the right direction without making even more strange noises come out of it.

"Like, I mean, what are the chances of this happening!" Mercedes exclaimed, still laughing.

"I know right?" Vera proudly retorted. "It was meant to be!"

"And you know what ladies?" Sveta added. "There's even an entire website dedicated to telling you the various things that your phone number can spell."

I mostly laughed quietly to myself during the ride to South Spring Drive as I dabbled on my phone. My fun ended when it was discovered that my phone number minus the area code actually spelled A-N-D-E-R-S-1, Anderson's nickname that he insisted on being called by everyone except me. I felt like being sick in the rumbling vehicle so I came to the conclusion that simply looking out the window would be the best thing for me. I had never really been to that part of town before, despite living in Wintercrest for a good chunk of my life.

South Spring Drive was tucked away in a little sector on the other side of the river, hidden behind the suspension bridge leading into the farmlands nearby. The area was compromised of both upscale neighbourhoods and borderline slums with the two meeting on, of course, South Spring Drive. I thought that it was odd that they'd build neighbourhoods like that but then again, reality was stranger than fiction. Back on Arbor Ridge Drive we'd been far away from the low-income housing projects but on South Spring Drive the million dollar mansions were right next to Jihoon Garcia's crummy apartment buildings.

It reminded me of some awful movies where the rich took advantage of the poor nearby. It was a situation all too common but who wanted to believe that it happened right in front of their eyes? My family had once been very privileged before my father lost his job, however, we never took advantage of the less fortunate nor were we ever unkind to them. My parents gave money to the homeless on the street whenever they crossed paths, but back then I never could've anticipated that I'd come so close to living just like them. It wasn't impossible and I was also painfully aware of that.

Mercedes pulled into the driveway of a big white building. Big *old* white building, probably twice as old as Vladimir Nikolayev, with a garage that looked like a giant garbage bin in the back parking lot. A bunch of vehicles that looked like Mercedes' jalopy were parked in the back along with my dad's truck hooked up to a trailer to unload stuff and bring it into the apartment. My mother and little brother were nowhere to be found. I only saw my father bringing furniture into the tiny apartment with two other men. Jihoon's block consisted of four apartments, two on the main floor and two on the lower level, with each having three bedrooms and one bathroom.

The entire apartment building was as big as my former house and as I looked at it through the window of the moving car I was absolutely disgusted. My spirit came crashing down since the prospect of a comfortable life had just vanished. My old closet was probably bigger than my new room! Mercedes parked her Mercedes in front of the garbage garage and the four of us got out to take a better look at the place. When my father saw us he immediately stopped what he was doing and came over to see us. The look on his face indicated stress and exhaustion on top of pity for that old Mercedes.

Mercedes' philosophy was that it was still a Mercedes despite turning into a Mercedes that nobody really wanted anymore. I liked that philosophy and for a moment I even thought of adopting it for my new and upcoming lifestyle or something similar to whatever the hell you wanna call the way Dmitry and the twins were living in the radioactive trailer park. My father hugged me tightly and asked me what I was doing at the apartment when I was supposed to be hanging out at the trailer park with the twins.

"I thought I'd surprise you guys by coming over," I replied with disappointment in my voice, "but I see it's just you."

"Your mom and Anderson are with some movers at the downtown storage units," he retorted with an even greater amount of disappointment in his voice, "because things aren't really going according to plan right now but everything's going to be alright, I promise."

A tall man, well over six feet tall, walked up behind my dad and greeted us. He introduced himself as Hans Wagner and he would be our next-door neighbour on the main floor. He was a *mature* man, as the twins would call it, and spoke with a thick German accent. He was in Wintercrest on a work contract to conduct some environmental tests and to apparently rehabilitate the area. Wintercrest was a beautiful city that didn't need any environmental cleanup so I figured that it was some kind of fancy wording meaning that he was around to clean up the tar ponds if it was possible to do such a thing.

Hans Wagner had some bronze eyes, some very short dark hair and a lighter stubble that had just started to grow back. He was muscular and Vera seemed to find him to her liking, and as a matter of fact he was kind of handsome in his own *mature* way. Hans was a very polite man who invited the four of us along with my father to have some food and a cup of tea in his apartment since were all hungry and quite a distance from the nearest restaurant. I quickly but politely declined before anyone could accept for me.

I thanked him for his kind offer though, but insisted that we had to meet the twins' relatives further down the street. I then quickly got back into the car and waited for the engine to roar back to life. Mercedes then drove down a few streets to another ugly apartment complex also owned by Jihoon Garcia where a bunch of teenagers and young people sat on the concrete stairs near the doorstep and happily waved at us. I was in too much of a putrid mood to wave back but that didn't stop them from being happy to see me.

A young man even opened the door for me, seemingly overjoyed about the fact that I was there. He introduced himself as Sergey, Dmitry's son. He was much smaller and much less scary-looking that his father, in fact, the two looked nothing alike. Sergey was thin with long jet black hair neatly combed to one side covering part of his liquid copper eyes. A silver lip ring pierced through the lower right side of his mouth, a tiny detail in the face of his *perfect* set of pearly white teeth. So different than what the twins had in their mouth.

"This is my wife Marissa." Sergey told me as I shook the hand of a skinny little young woman that popped out from behind him.

She had this amazing long flamboyant red hair down to the middle of her back that was as straight as it possibly could be. She had a beautiful oval face and shining blue eyes. She looked like a model, albeit an eerily thin one. Her lips were adorned with plum lipstick and her eyes were covered with dark eyeshadow, contrasting with her pale skin. I smiled when I saw her, she rocked her look and was so beautiful. She wore a black and white vintage dress like only she could get away with along with nothing but socks outside despite the weather getting colder.

The person who really took my breath away was a young man who introduced himself as Bradley Stewart. He had a devastating smile that could knock someone to their knees and honestly light up the whole world. He told me that he had just turned twenty-three and was looking to attend the community college in January. I didn't want to tell him my real age since I was ashamed of being an adult still in high school because my so-called best friend brought his gun to school and destroyed my life so I went on rambling about another subject. Brad didn't appear to notice my avoidant behaviour so I managed to relax.

Brad Stewart's voice was like singing. It was sublime to listen to, not to mention that everything else about him was amazing too. I was infatuated, downright infatuated like a teenage girl. Brad had dark hair with burgundy highlights, *a lot* of hair gel to hold everything together, and some emerald green eyes. I'd never believed in love at first sight prior to meeting him, but he made me a believer. Like much of the alternative crowd around, his arms were decorated with colourful tattoos. None of them seemed to mind that I was more of a jock type and I certainly didn't mind their alternative subculture, I liked it. Sergey then invited us into his apartment where some more young punks were hanging out and having some drinks. They smiled when we walked in, happy to see us. I felt somewhat out of place but they had a certain warmth to them and made me feel part of their group.

"You know, you punks are some of the nicest people I've ever met!" I admitted.

"We may not be society's cup of tea but some of the people sitting in this room truly are the nicest people I've ever met," one of them added, "hands down the best."

"Not to trash jocks or anything because heck, I'm one of them," I went on, "but the majority of them aren't nearly as open-minded and welcoming as you guys have been to me."

"What'd we tell you about pills to heighten your awareness and make you more open-minded?" The twins practically said in unison.

The entire room burst out into laughter but it was the truth. I hadn't felt included in a long time, and looking back, I wasn't sure my so-called friends in my own clique had really ever accepted me for anything more than my brand name clothes, my social status and what I could do for them. And it was certain that after Anderson things didn't improve. Students had never been so divided and hateful.

"Are all jocks nice like you underneath the showing off and the power trips?" Another teen in the room asked me.

"No," I admitted truthfully, "most of them weren't nice to me at all when I sustained a sports injury and had to wheel myself around in a wheelchair for months, or after the Valentine's Day scandal."

"I'm sorry to hear that, but it doesn't surprise me, unfortunately."

"That's okay, the broken bones are not the worst thing that happened to me. A handful of them stood by my side but most of them didn't because I wasn't cool anymore. But once I was able to play sports again they were all my friends like nothing had happened. However, I didn't want that kind of fakery anymore and simply hung out with some different people. True friends don't care what social class you belong to."

"Man, that's really sad. You went to that school where the shooting happened, right?"

"Yeah, I knew him."

I suddenly had everyone's undivided attention.

"Is it true that the jocks bullied him to death? At least that's the rumour still going around."

"It wasn't just the jocks, *nobody* wanted him and I really don't know why because he was such a nice boy. He was *nothing* like the person people think he is now because he brought a gun to school."

Silence.

"I think what really opened my eyes to the reality he was facing," I continued, "was when my own so-called group didn't want me anymore because I was temporarily disabled. That's really when I saw him for who he was. I had seem him around the school in the past but never really knew him because I too had this mentality that I shouldn't associate with people who weren't part of my own clique."

Silence.

"And what hurts me the most is that today people regard him as nothing but scum, like he was never important and that he didn't even die there that day. It's as though the world regards him as having no soul and these so-called experts in the field come up with all of these bogus reasons as to why he did what he did but what nobody does is look at themselves in the mirror and ask why *they* didn't do anything for him. *I* knew him, *I* was there, *I* know."

The faces in the room were like statues. They all stared at me with big eyes, wanting me to continue my story but I wasn't sure if I could. I had never previously explored that area of my mind and I certainly had never dealt with whatever resulted of my emotions after the shooting. I'd merely tried to ignore and forget everything and continuing to speak was defeating the purpose of what I'd tried so hard to do.

"It's all in the ideologies of inferiority and superiority." Mercedes whispered from the back of the room.

Anderson had suffered from that same ideological indoctrination that had turned Rudolf Höss into a monster along with millions of others. They believed that they were superior but Anderson believed the opposite. He also believed that he could only take back what had been taken from him by bringing a gun to school. I suddenly felt sick but I knew I had to keep going because things would never change if I didn't begin contributing to the solution.

"As well as the idea of having a purpose or being worthless." Mercedes continued.

"That's right Mercedes," I muttered, trying not to vomit, "it baffles me how people can just walk around and move on with their lives like nothing ever happened! Like no lessons were learned! Didn't the world learn anything from all these shootings since Columbine? And especially when it happens right here in the town you grew up in!"

"It's that same unwillingness to open our eyes to the lessons of these shootings that pushes these kids to do them in the first place."

"Yes! *Finally* someone understands it! And I completely understand why it's so easy to hate these people that do this, but isn't it exactly that kind of hatred that made them do what they did in the first place?"

Everyone shouted yes in unison. The answers were right in front of our faces, and had always been, but why were they so hard to understand?

"You never know how far a little kindness can go." Marissa's soft voice spoke next to me. "Sometimes the smallest, simplest act of sacrificial love can make a dramatic difference in a person's life."

"To me that means making the choice to extent my hand in love and kindness instead of recoiling it in judgment," someone else spoke in a gentle voice, "because really, it's the small things in life that make it grand."

"Something like this should rip us to pieces inside," I chocked out, trying not to cry, puke or pass out, "and if it doesn't, there's something seriously wrong. It should wake us up, and I don't know what's wrong but apparently no lessons have been learned. No lessons are ever learned apparently."

"It's because of Anderson Massey that I will never turn a blind eye to someone who is suffering again." Brad added in his singing voice.

"And I know why it's so easy to profoundly hate Anderson for what he did," I continued with my voice only being a coarse whisper in the room, "but that kind of anger and hatred are such destructive emotions and in the end they do nothing but cause you greater pain and anguish than what you began with. Look what it did to Anderson."

"Have you forgiven him?" Sergey asked after a moment of silence.

Had I forgiven him? That was a good question because I didn't really know the answer. As much as I liked to make myself believe that I had indeed forgiven Anderson, I didn't really know for sure. I was in denial about the whole thing and that was a realization in itself. As much as I had loved him and still did, what he'd done was unforgivable.

"I don't know."

Or was it really? In some part of me my love for him had never really changed, but in another part of me it had. I'd always been a person who loved strongly and forgave easily, especially when it came to my friends, but how are you supposed to still love someone who murdered innocent people? I didn't have an answer to that question either. Turning into a mass murderer hadn't made him any less my best friend in the last moments we'd shared, yet somehow it seemed to invalidate all the wonderful things we shared together. Somehow those things no longer mattered because he was a *killer*.

"Not that it's any of my business," Brad spoke softly, "but you don't stop loving someone because of something like that. Friendship is sacred. I have many friends in prison and we're still tight."

Like he somehow knew what I was thinking. Anderson and I, we'd known each other for years, shared so many experiences, made so many memories together. That wasn't undone or erased by his actions. It complicated things, screwed things up and confused me, but those good things couldn't be taken from me.

"Somewhere along the way he stopped believing," I whispered, my voice being hoarse, "and I am so sick of people turning these tragedies into all sorts of propaganda when they neglect to actually look at what's going on around them!"

"What are you going to do about it?"

"I don't know."

I was embarrassed to admit that, but was there really something to do? Anderson had brought his *gun* to school and even that didn't seem to shake anyone. People didn't wake from their slumber after that. It traumatized everyone but didn't open anyone's eyes and much less their hearts. I knew that I complained a lot but felt powerless to do anything more. Was that the feeling shared by the rest of the people who simply returned to their regular lives? Was it the only thing they knew how to do? It was hard for me to believe that.

"You know what bothers me," I continued after taking a deep breath, "it's the fact that all these people who turn a blind eye also disregard me and Anderson's other friends and his parents as nothing more than scum because we never stopped loving him."

"And then there are people who have good hearts," Svetlana jumped in, "such as yourself, who know despite the pain and the turmoil that you were a force for good in that young man's life and that although you couldn't've prevented the shooting, you can still contribute something good to the aftermath."

On the verge of tears, I got up and hugged Sveta. I broke down crying over her bony shoulder and ended up snotting on her hijab so I rearranged it to cover up my mess. Multiple pairs of arms and warm bodies then surrounded us and soon there was a giant group hug in Sergey's living room.

"What I really hate is people thinking that because we're also outcasts in society that we're all somehow like him, or that we're dangerous." Sveta continued while fiddling with her headscarf and uncovering the snot.

"Honestly, I think they'd feel better if we really were Columbiners or whatever," Vera added, "but that's a far cry from the truth."

"I know," I muttered, "and I've met some of those kids who elevate Anderson because he outdid Columbine and Parkland or whatever. I guess I kinda understand why some of them would be compelled to do that though, but it's still hurtful."

"Yeah, because these boys are like shepherds to the lost souls out there."

"It's as though Anderson Massey and Kip Kinkel and the one from Virginia Tech somehow validate what they feel inside."

"Like only Eric Harris and Dylan Klebold would really understand what it truly feels like inside."

"And they are the kind of people I hurt for the most because I've seen with my own eyes the suffering they hide deep down."

Despite the powerful and draining emotions, I felt quite relieved to have let everything out into the open for once. I'd never gotten the chance to honestly express how I truly felt in the past. All of my visits with therapists had been bullshit and back then I wasn't ready to talk either. I still didn't know if I was ready to really speak up, but I was content with myself that I'd gotten some of that stuff off my chest. It might've been off my chest but it was never off my mind.

Somewhere deep at the back of my mind it was all there, always there. Anderson Massey never got off the treadmill running around my innermost thoughts all day. What was the most difficult in all of that was that he was no longer around for me to tell him how I felt inside and what was really going on. What hurt on top of that was the fact that he suffered all his life, died suffering and left the rest of us to suffer because of it too.

"Hey, we should throw a party tonight!" Marissa proposed to lighten the mood. "Alyson's one of our own now!"

Before I had the chance to say anything everyone agreed to throw a party. All I could do was smile even though I wasn't really up for a party. The last one I'd gone to had marked the beginning of the end. While Marissa and Sergey were cleaning up the apartment and making sure it was ready for the evening the rest of the misfits there showed me around my new neighbourhood. It wasn't a bad neighbourhood, and it was fairly quiet apart from the constant roaring and humming of engines performing industrial operations nearby.

There was constant traffic but everything else was dead and quiet. There weren't people walking by or children playing and making noise nearby. I kept on glancing over at Brad the whole time and he returned my stare with a smile each time which only made me melt even more. It was probably nothing more than a childish fantasy to lust after him like that but it made me feel better. It made me feel normal, it made me feel like myself. Whoever Alyson Rosemarie Feldman had become anyway.

"I know he's cute and sweet and fun to be around and all," Vera told me, "but don't get hooked on him."

"Why not?" I asked out of curiosity despite that I didn't intend on pursuing anything serious.

"Drug addict."

"Oh…"

"He's still my friend and I still love him but you know how druggies are. They want their fix at all costs. Don't get hooked on someone who's hooked on that stuff."

"Thanks for the heads up, I appreciate it, but I'd still like to get to know these people. Especially him."

"Of course! I encourage you to, he's awesome. And he's a really good singer."

"He sings?"

My voice had been a little too loud when I'd said that because everyone turned to look at me and Brad grinned and winked at me. I blushed and everybody laughed.

"Once upon a time we wanted to start a band called The Nosy Neighbours and release our first album *Songs About Tar Ponds* but things didn't work out even though we already had half the record written."

We all spent the remainder of the afternoon sitting down by the river under the bridge and listening to the cars speeding above our heads, just talking like normal people, and that meant a lot to me. For supper Mercedes, the twins and I swung by the trailer and had some takeout with Dmitry before leaving and returning to Sergey's apartment for the party. I'd thought of a million ways to get out of it but I really didn't want to be disrespectful by not attending after I'd promised considering the kindness and understanding they'd showed me.

The party was already started by the time we got there and Brad was already drunk, laying on the leather couch in a half-dazed, half-awake state. He still had a lit joint sticking out of his mouth and I cringed at seeing that side of him. Only about half of the misfits that had been in the apartment earlier had returned along with a bunch of new faces from all walks of life just wanting to have a good time and free alcohol. I began feeling uncomfortable but the twins didn't seem fazed by what they were seeing.

Cats were running all over the place like they were high themselves while other partygoers, mostly underage kids, had drinks in their hands and were enjoying the evening in the company of their friends. Somebody handed me a bottle of Jack Daniel's while Vera had some of her beloved Black Label. Sveta went around collecting car keys so nobody who had a vehicle could drink and drive and potentially end up in a tragic situation. I wasn't into whiskey but I carried around the bottle under my arm anyway while everybody else started to get wasted.

At one point during the night Vera took Brad's half-smoked joint out of his mouth and smoked it herself. She went ballistic, running around the place and literally climbing the walls, ripping her shirt off and tearing it pieces before yelling something in Russian with her arms up in the air. A grey cat happened to walk by and Vera picked it up and started swinging it up in the air and running around some more. The cat was obviously terrified but there was little it could do. Everybody laughed as they watched the show but it didn't last long because once the cat got free it went running for the hills.

Once all the alcohol had been drunk and all the drugs smoked the night calmed down. Sveta, Sergey and I were really the only ones who weren't intoxicated somehow so we sat down in the only free area of the sectional sofa and decided to have a chat. In the dark of the night we could see police cars going up and down the street but the commotion was long over so all we could do was laugh about it. The three of us were simply talking when a half-awake Brad flopped down on the couch right next to me.

"I guess you don't know what this guy did one night when he got pulled over by the police after a party." Sergey told me laughing.

"I tell me." I retorted.

"He was driving his car without a license and with three drunk underage girls in the backseat with drugs and other stuff he wasn't supposed to have when this female cop pulls him over. She only brought him in to her car and sped off, leaving the girls in a stalled car there on the side of the road with no keys and nowhere to go in the middle of the night. Eventually they managed to push the car home and when Brad came home in the morning do you know what he claimed happened?"

"What?"

"That he had sex with the police officer!"

I cracked up laughing and so did Brad at the story. He must have been high and only imagined that because there was no way that I believed a police officer would do that!

"Seriously?" I pressed, not believing it.

"Apparently it's true," Sergey laughed, "the three girls can testify to the fact that they were left alone in the car when the officer took Brad away. Apparently it was the same officer who busted his birthday party the year prior."

I couldn't stop laughing even though I wasn't drunk. Others joined in the conversation as their stupor wore off little by little and shared their crazy experiences at parties and in life in general. I had been to parties before but I'd never been a wild party girl, especially not when the cops lurked around the way they did. In my freshman year a boy had died of alcohol poisoning and I'd seen the truly dark side of parties on Valentine's Day. I'd never gone out since.

"Are you a virgin?" Brad asked me, drunk.

"No." I lied after hesitating for a while.

I didn't want a lecture about sex or being called a prude if I told him the truth that I was indeed a virgin. If I lied and said no maybe he'd try to hook up with me but telling him no seemed to be less awkward than telling him the truth.

"Who'd you have sex with?"

"The wall, Brad. The wall."

"You humped the wall?"

"Yes, that's right."

"No! It's gotta be a person! Who is it?"

"Nobody!"

"Come on!"

"It was myself. I had sex with myself."

"That's not right, tell me who it is!"

Sergey told him to butt out of my business but Brad insisted on probing the answer out of me. He was drunk and didn't know what he was talking about so I gave him the runaround.

"Did you hump a police officer?" Brad asked laughing.

"No," I laughed, "I've only ever humped my hand."

"Huh? No…"

"Yes."

"That can't be."

Brad rambled on incoherently for a while before formulating his own conclusion about who I'd slept with. It wasn't long before I regretted not telling him the truth about actually being a virgin.

"You humped the shooter!" He spit out in between incoherent musings. "I know it was him! You had sex with the shooter!"

I wasn't given the opportunity to respond before other people began making derogatory and offensive comments. Even the drunk kids seemed to come out of their stupor very quickly upon hearing what Brad had said. For a moment I thought I'd shut them up by going along with their stupid story and flunking it in their faces but I wasn't allowed to do that either. I knew that these people were drunk, but it didn't stop their words from cutting deep into my heart and soul.

"You seriously didn't!" A drunk Mercedes muttered.

"Did you hump his dead body in the library?" A drunk girl taunted. "That guy was a loser!"

I got up without a second thought and stomped out the door leaving everyone behind. Sergey and Sveta tried running after me but I was out out of their sight in the dimly lit streets. Tears streamed down my face as I stumbled on and off the sidewalk in the bitterly cold night. I couldn't go home to my parents on foot and I couldn't go back to the Petrov trailer by myself so there was only one place where I could go: Hans Wagner's apartment.

I made my way to South Spring Drive trying not to freeze to death in nothing but a t-shirt and some skinny jeans. Once I got there all the lights were off in Hans' apartment but I had nothing to lose so I pounded on his door. He answered almost immediately. He was shocked to see me on his doorstep under the circumstances but he invited me inside as soon as he recognized me.

"Are you okay?!" Hans asked me frantically. "Your parents aren't here, but I can call them!"

"No, no please don't! I'm an adult and I'm fine by myself," I pleaded, "I just need somewhere to spend the night."

"Okay, that's fine," he retorted in confusion, "follow me."

He brought me to a spare bedroom in his tiny apartment and shut the door as he walked back out, leaving me alone in the pitch black darkness with nothing but the moonlight illuminating the room through the window. I flopped down over the bed without getting undressed or going under the covers and let the whole day wash away in a sea of tears. After my crying spell I sat up on the bed, turned on the cheap lamp and dug out a pen and piece of paper from the night table and began writing out my thoughts.

Dear Anderson,

How am I ever supposed to put something like this behind me? I get the reasons why Anderson, I get it, but still, nothing can ever be made right. What really baffles me is how insensitive people really are. After a goddamn school shooting nothing changes! What in the world?! If it doesn't affect you somehow then you must be pretty darn disturbed! I am so sick of all these people on TV raving about how you outdid Columbine, for a lack of a better word. And that has to do with...? That's not how it's going to solve the problem of our society. If you did it to prove a point well I'm sorry but you failed. People are are still the same.

And I'm sorry that this is what you thought was the only way out. I wish you were still here so I could tell you myself that it wasn't your fault that you ended up at the very bottom of the social structure. It's not anything you did that landed you there, just like it wasn't anything I ever did to be part of the popular crowd. I don't want to be part of that ideology anymore.

If the next kid at the very bottom ends up doing what you did then I won't have been contributing to his suffering and turning a blind eye to his needs. I know somewhere deep inside that it isn't my fault, that you told me time after time that I was nothing but good to you, but apparently that just wasn't enough.

You're the reasons why things have to change. You're the reason I won't turn a blind eye to another person's pain.

Aly

For the record, I'd indeed shared a bed with Anderson Massey in the past, on Valentine's Day night after the dance, but we'd never been intimate. Nothing that night happened the way people said it did. Anderson never had a girlfriend and had even died a virgin but that wasn't what others believed about him, or about me. Something had indeed happened at the party that night, and I'd been there to witness most of it, but the stories going around in the hallways at school were a far cry from the truth.

A very far cry from the truth.

XII

VALENTINE'S DAY

The black lights made the living room look like a night club. Michael Hazen's house had already turned into a wild rave by the time Anderson and I arrived. I'd been to one of his parties before the previous year but it had been much smaller in size and definitely not as wild. A significant chunk of the school had wound up there after the Valentine's Day dance for what was supposed to be an afterparty of some kind, but it had since turned into a full-blown rave. His parents had separated since the last time I'd set foot in that mansion and since he lived with his father and he was out of town on business, Michael had known just what to do to have a good time.

Michael and I had become acquainted several years earlier when his twin sister and I both played on the same basketball team while he was on the football team. We'd never really been friends per se, but we'd always been on good terms and I was always invited to his periodic parties. I'd only attended a single one but I'd had a great time so I thought why not? Convincing Anderson to attend had been a whole other matter though, but still. I'd managed to drag him to the dance I wasn't about to attend the party all by myself. The night had been going so well up until that point and I didn't want it to end.

Anderson and I had been having the greatest time on the dance floor in the gymnasium of the school when the music stopped and the lights came on. It had felt like a rude awakening on a Sunday morning but I wouldn't have traded the event for anything. I'd bought myself a fancy dress from Nordstrom with my food smuggling money and Anderson had rented himself a nice tuxedo complete with a bowtie for the evening. It might've been Valentine's Day to the world, but I also wanted to celebrate Anderson. He had just begun his very last semester of high school and had a very bright future ahead of him. I no longer cared what the other kids thought of us, it would be all over soon anyway. I still had another year to go but most of them would be gone by the time I graduated either way.

The fruit punch had been a little sour and the music a little sappy at times but those minor annoyances had faded in the distance as I let loose on the dance floor. I had even ended up dancing with the janitor Mr. Igor, who had recently arrived from Ukraine and spoke very little English. Two freshman girls ended up dancing with Anderson who'd been unusually relaxed and stoic but then I found out that he had a flask of vodka that he'd mixed with juice hidden inside his jacket. I even had a swig of it myself before the night was over. After three hours of dancing I was still filled with energy so I went home and changed into more comfortable clothes before hopping in with Anderson and attending Michael Hazen's party.

Anderson had also changed into his regular clothes which were usually made up of a band shirt, jeans and the black trench coat I'd bought him several months prior. I wore my grey jogging pants, a basic pale pink tee and the first light jacket with a fleece lining that I'd found in the closet. The few streetlights out in the outskirts of town gave the road an eerie glow during the twenty minutes it took to get to the party but not a single bad thought could enter my brain. I was happy. Nothing could disturb that.

"You were a rockstar surrounded by jocks out there on the dance floor." I told Anderson as he turned onto Auriga Avenue.

"I'm having the best night of my life thanks to you." He retorted without emotion. "Thank you for taking me out. It felt great to just *be* for once. Be a normal teenager having fun. Blend in with everyone and not have a care in the world."

"And we're in for some more fun, don't worry, this night isn't about to end just yet!"

Anderson didn't seemed to be overly thrilled about going to a jock's party, but I also had the impression that he had a lot more on his mind. I looked over at him as we neared the house but it took a moment for him to speak.

"I love you Alyson. You are the most sublime of God's creations."

A lump formed in my throat and I hoped that it was just the vodka that hadn't completely worn off yet. Thankfully, as he said that he also parked the car on the side of the road in front of the house so I shifted the attention to another topic.

"Are you ready to rock?"

"I've never been readier than this in my life!"

Electronic dance music mixed in with a little bit of industrial rock made the entire house vibrate under the black lights giving off a subtle glow. Anderson was just a shadow in front of me as we danced some more, his long unkempt hair brushing the tip of his shoulders as his body rocked back and forth. He had bleached his hair several weeks ago and some of it had turned an orangish colour hat seemed to glow like embers under the lights. Had his hair been short and curly I might've believed that I'd been dancing the night away with James Holmes.

Anderson stuck out like a sore thumb in a house packed predominantly with jocks, some college kids and even much younger kids, but nobody seemed to notice. Everyone around me was either drinking, doing drugs or having sex. I needed no drugs to get high though sometimes the thought of getting higher seemed attractive. Wanting to remain true to myself and to my values, I decided to wander around the house looking for a safe place to enjoy the rest of the night, away from sin, temptation and debauchery. In the kitchen a game of alcohol and drug-induced strip poker was going on and in the garage it was much of the same story with beer pong.

Anderson followed me as I wandered into the basement and found a mostly sober group of teens playing spin the bottle. We were both repeatedly invited to join but that wasn't exactly the kind of thing I wanted to participate in. I wasn't interested in photos of me kissing random classmates and other students all over social media like had happened to another girl last year. I dragged my feet who had been getting progressively heavier during the night all the way up to the second floor where things were much quieter. Some people were having an orgy across the hall and there were strangers passed out in other rooms but Anderson and I found a vacant bedroom where we could rest peacefully for a little while.

The moonlight coming in through the uncovered bay window illuminated the small room that appeared to be Michael's. Pictures of him and the football team adored the walls along with posters of rock bands and girls in bikinis. A bed big enough for four took up most of the little room and a desk covered in electronics and other junk was crammed in the corner by the window. I flopped down on the leather chair, exhaustion hitting me like a train out of nowhere. Anderson sat on the window sill, a dark figure in the moonlight and a huge shadow on the wall.

"Is it just me or is it chilly in here?" I asked after an extended moment of silence, drowsiness winning me over.

"It is chilly." He replied. "Somebody in another room has the window open but I'm not going over there."

"No, don't go. Stay here with me."

"Here, I'll give you my coat."

I'd left my own coat in the car but didn't want to go out and retrieve it. I didn't want to get even colder by going outside or being pressured into debauchery by going back downstairs.

"No, then you'll be cold too! You've only got a t-shirt underneath!"

"Well, I suppose this coat is big enough for two people."

Anderson and I huddled together in the chair with me sitting on his lap, my head on his shoulder. His body was warm against mine in the cold room. Despite the fact that the door of our room was closed, the cold air was still coming in. Anderson's breath was also warm on my skin, our faces pressed together and his long soft hair tickling me. Our noses rubbed together under the moonlight and after a moment of hesitation he pressed his lips against mine. Anderson's kiss tasted like alcohol but it had a sweetness to it that I'd never previously experienced with any of the other boys I'd ever kissed in middle school.

For the first few kisses I kissed him back, but then my brain got weird. What in the world was I doing? I couldn't be kissing my best friend, someone I didn't have any romantic feelings for, and God forbid I couldn't hook up with him! My body flinched and a worried and shocked expression swept over Anderson's face. He looked into my eyes wondering what he'd done wrong and I didn't know how to explain that it was me, not him, that was the problem. His gentle touch and sweet kisses had felt nice, I couldn't deny that, but they hadn't felt right.

"Are you alright? What's wrong?" Anderson asked me.

"I'm fine," I retorted, "I'm just not sure I can do this."

"I'm, I'm sorry—"

"Don't be sorry Anderson, you've done nothing wrong."

"Here, I'll just give you my coat and I'll go downstairs to have a few more drinks."

"Okay, I'm sorry if I ruined the evening."

"You haven't ruined anything Aly. I just want you to know that I'd never force anything on you and would never do something that you're not on board with."

"I know."

The door closed behind him, leaving me wrapped up in his coat laying on the bed and facing the wall. I wanted, and badly needed, to get some shuteye but an electricity wouldn't stop buzzing throughout my body. I was agitated and somewhat felt guilty about rejecting Anderson's advances because I did love him, just not like *that*, and the last thing I'd wanted to do was hurt the feelings of someone I cared so deeply for. I'd never been one to take my friendships lightly and sometimes I probably loved too strongly which could be both a blessing and a curse for me. A curse when it came to Anderson.

I fidgeted around for a while, tossing and turning until the moonlight had almost completely vanished from the room. Anderson hadn't returned and worry began to consume me. I'd been worried about him for several weeks but that night at the Valentine's Day dance I'd forgotten all about the shroud of darkness that perennially enveloped him. He'd seemed genuinely happy, and I'd been genuinely happy.

I squirmed out of the oilskin duster and wandered into the hallway where I found Tammy involved in a sex act with several members of the football team. I froze for a moment and wanted to turn back but finding Anderson was paramount and my discomfort would have to wait for another day. When Tammy saw me she laughed before opening the door to the room across the hall where the orgy was taking place and dragged the jocks in behind her.

Further down the hall the door to another room was open with wind blowing papers and other things around. It was empty so I walked in and closed the window. It was dark almost everywhere on the second floor but downstairs on the ground floor small groups of people were still living it up. Most of the party had died down however, and the carpet was soaked with urine, vomit and hard liquor.

Many people were passed out here and there, others were semi-conscious, most had left, but a lot were still drinking. I found Anderson slouched over the kitchen counter doing shots of vodka obviously hoping to forget something a lot more than wanting to have a good time. I tiptoed around other people engaged in various debauchery in the kitchen and took the bottle of vodka away from Anderson. He stumbled off the counter and I half-carried him out of the kitchen all the way to the stairwell. He stumbled but managed to drag himself upstairs where he flopped facedown onto the bed. I repositioned him onto his back and covered him with his jacket before flopping down next to him myself.

The sun was almost burning my skin when I woke up again, headache putting pressure inside my skull, the stench of vomit filling the air. I sat up in the bed, Anderson was still next to me, sleeping peacefully in exactly the same position I'd put him in, but somebody else had obviously been in the room. It seemed as though they'd only come to gift us a puddle of vomit before they left because nothing else had been touched. On my phone I saw that it was already almost noon, I'd missed my morning classes at school and I had multiple text messages, many of them angry, from my parents and other friends.

I woke up Anderson who seemed to have recovered well during his sleep considering the amount of liquor he'd ingested, collected my belongings and left the house as fast as I could. I would've loved to have taken a shower, eaten a nice meal and changed clothes but there wasn't any time for that. Anderson and I jumped in his car and raced outta there, not saying a single word the entire drive. At school I mooched some ibuprofen from the nurse and showed up to my next class looking and feeling like crap. It was probably obvious that I'd had a rough night but my headache was the easiest thing about the entire situation.

"Did he drug you and rape you too?" Brandon, Tammy's boyfriend and member of the basketball team, asked me as we crossed paths in the hallway.

"What?" I asked, completely confused, but did not get a response.

What in the world had happened last night? I had neither been drugged nor raped, in fact I'd thoroughly enjoyed myself for the majority of the night. I was not, however, aware of most of what else had gone on. I'd made a point to not focus on the debauchery and not let my eyes wander where they didn't belong the previous night but maybe that had been the wrong thing to do. Maybe a girl would have been spared much pain and horror had I just paid more attention to my surroundings. A lump formed in my throat as I contemplated how close I might have come to a similar fate myself.

During my afternoon break I went to the bathroom in order to clean myself up a little more where I found Tammy and two of her other friends giggling in the wheelchair accessible stall. They weren't aware of my presence as Tammy bragged about her sexcapades of the previous night, and laughing about how somebody was going to have their life ruined. When they opened the door and came face to face with me their joyful and snobby expressions disappeared and were replaced with stoic, almost evil looks. I proceeded to clean myself up a little more before returning to class, one that I shared with Anderson Massey.

"Rapist!" A voice whispered angrily from behind, just loud enough for his entourage to hear it.

I turned around but could not read the expressions on the multitude of faces that surrounded me. But I knew that Anderson was the one being called the rapist. I looked over at him but his face was blank as he worked on his assignment. The comments continued intermittently during the class and I eventually managed to put two and two together; it was Anderson whom Tammy had been laughing about in the bathroom after concocting a story to explain away how she'd been cheating on Brandon at a rave while he was holding his great-aunts hand on her deathbed in the palliative care ward of the hospital. She'd accused Anderson of raping her. I immediately felt like being sick and got up to walk out of the classroom but didn't make it very far.

"He was with me last night." I mustered up the courage to defend my best friend but my voice was shaky and my throat was filled with vomit.

"What?" A boy asked. "Did he do the same thing to you?"

"No. He didn't do any vile and abhorrent thing of the sort to anyone because he spent the night with me."

"Oh, so you voluntarily slept with him? You slut!"

The insults and the name calling continued until the teacher put a stop to it before it got out of hand. The bell rang immediately after and I bolted out of the classroom in a daze similar to a drunken stupor, but one filled with shock, disbelief and rage. I walked into the bathroom and smashed the mirror with one fistful of inhumane anger, mostly at myself because I was the one who'd dragged Anderson to that party. I'd been the one to pester him until he agreed to go just to shut me up, knowing full well that he didn't belong there. Blood dripped all over the sink and I screamed with the wrath of the devil until another girl walked in during my outburst and immediately ran back out.

I wrapped up my bleeding hand with a towel and left before anybody called the police or my parents or God himself on me but my inner turmoil was far from over. I then went straight home and straight into the bathroom to douse myself in cold water before locking myself up in my room for the rest of the evening, ignoring my parents, my friends and Anderson who'd tried to call me multiple times. How would I ever forgive myself for having done that to him? His life was ruined and it had only been a matter of minutes before the rumours and accusations spread like wildfire over social media.

Anderson was a rapist, I was a whore who got what I deserved and Tammy was somewhere in the middle. On one side she had loyal supporters who believed her false claims and on the other she had another group of people who were saying that she was nothing but a slut who just wanted attention. I wanted to break every single bone in her body and then strangle her until her eyes popped out of her head because she'd not only obliterated whatever had been left of Anderson Massey, but she'd also profaned the plight of actual sexual assault survivors and that was the worst part of her false accusations.

There were countless women — and many men too — out there who suffered in silence after suffering the most horrific of violations, some who'd been silenced, vilified, almost crucified, without ever receiving justice while Tammy laughed and bragged about what she'd done. Out on the streets lurked serial rapists looking for their next victim while an innocent young man was being subjected to psychological torture over the internet because one real lying whore wanted to manipulate her stupid boyfriend after he'd also lived through one of the worst nights of his life. The victimization and the witch hunts went both ways, each leaving a devastating trail of suffering.

During my freshman year a another freshman girl nicknamed Lil Amelia had ended up passed out drunk at a party and gang raped by four older boys. They'd taken markers of various colours and drew obscene things all over her body and then posted the photos on the internet. Less than a month later, after suffering not only a brutal assault but also having had to go through hell every single day at school and online at the hands of bullies and trolls, Lil Amelia took her own life. The boys who did that to her didn't even get grounded by their parents for what they'd done to her but those who'd made her life a living hell afterwards were equally to blame. Tammy had been one of those people.

The following day at school neither Anderson nor I were spared hell. The verbal, and sometimes physical, assaults came one after the other and I got a good taste of what my best friend had lived through for most of his time at Belden High. My rage hadn't subsided and seeing Tammy play the victim only added fuel to the fire. She cried to one group of people and then turned around and laughed behind their backs with another. She and I unfortunately had to cross paths in the bathroom yet again later that afternoon. The broken mirror had been boarded up but there were three more panes that I could smash if I felt the need.

Tammy laughed at me with the voice of a demon as I went to the sink and splashed my face with cold water. She knew that I knew the truth but who would believe me now? People might have believed me had it not been about Anderson, but he was the lowest of the low for no good reason. He was shy, socially awkward, not at all athletic, too intelligent and sensitive for his own good and seemed to be content with being a loner for the most part. He was an easy target especially considering that he didn't, and often couldn't, fight back.

"You know I had to protect Brandon," her satanic voice ripped through the air, "he was vulnerable because he'd just watched his great-aunt die. You understand that, right?"

I didn't. I didn't at all. In that moment I wanted so badly to grab her by the hair and smash her zit-infested face into the mirror so it would break into a million pieces and send sparkles flying everywhere into the air but she walked out before I could say or do anything. In a rage, I stomped out myself, unsure of what my next move would be but knowing that I wouldn't go quietly. The only thing that stopped me in my tracks was seeing Anderson walking in the opposite direction towards me in the hallway. Since nobody else was around Tammy didn't feign being terrified of him, in fact she walked defiantly right beside him and disappeared into a classroom.

Once he made it to me I wrapped my arms around his waist and looked up at him, wanting to tell him so many things, but he slipped right out of my hold and kept walking like he'd never known me. I stood immobile and watched him walk away, not turning back to look at me. I knew at that point that my life would never be the same again. It would be the beginning of a long, dark and lonely journey because I'd lost most of my friends in the wake of that scandal, lost my self-respect and self-esteem to a guilt-ridden conscious.

But for Anderson Massey it wasn't just the beginning of the end. It was *the end*.

XIII

OVER AND OVER

I first met Anderson Massey late in my freshman year. It was winter, everything was frozen solid outside and I had managed to fall off a mountain during a skiing misadventure which resulted in a concussion and a fractured pelvis. I'd stayed in the hospital for a few days before they deemed me fit to wheel myself around in a wheelchair and return home. I was 100% sure that it was a curse since I'd been doing so well on skis. What was even worst than a broken head and a pelvis that was as good as broken was the fact that the people whom I thought were my friends didn't even care.

To them it seemed like a temporarily fractured pelvis and a cheap wheelchair made me crippled for life and eternally useless. Apparently I'd never play sports again and I couldn't be a jock anymore. I had never really considered myself a jock, but according to the peer structure at school playing sports and coming from a well-to-do family made me one. But I was a jock no longer. I wasn't even a popular, well-liked girl anymore.

Most of the people I used to hang out with disregarded me like I was trash and it was only the apparent *lesser* students that were considerate of me. Only Elaine and Amanda really stayed by my side. They each took their turn carrying my books while I wheeled myself around the school with my purse on my knees, but they couldn't constantly be there and I was often left alone and mostly helpless during the lunch hour. I did my best to fend for myself since most people except the nobodies actually helped me.

One morning, I was wheeling myself down the east wing on the second floor when I heard some commotion going on in an adjacent hallway. I heard objects, which were probably books, crashing to the floor and the clinging of metal jewelry. I heard boys grunting and fighting so I stayed hidden next to the door of a vacant classroom until the fighting was over because I didn't want to land myself in even more trouble than I was already in. If there was a single unwritten rule in the school that everybody knew, it was that you mind your own business.

The big guys had no mercy for little girls and I knew that if a group of boys were beating up another boy in the hallway, they'd have no problem doing the same thing to me despite the fact that I was already in a wheelchair. They had no mercy for those they perceived as lesser than them, and in my wheelchair I was lesser than everyone it seemed. Luckily, I'd never been physically attacked or beaten up before but I had seen it with my own eyes multiple times. I was also teased on a daily basis by people who were once my entourage. They'd ask me if I could pop a wheelie or if I wanted to race. Even though I ignored them, their words still cut deep.

The fighting in the hallway was becoming louder and eventually ended with a loud bang — I assumed a body slamming into a locker — and one final exasperated grunt. I then saw two members of the football team leave in the opposite direction and laughing at what they'd just done as they left the scene. I quickly wheeled myself into the adjacent hallway where the fight had taken place and saw another boy awkwardly sitting up against a locker and clearly in pain. He had his hand pressed against the right side of his ribcage and his other hand pressed against his mouth and face.

As I got closer he glanced at me and I saw that he was bleeding. I was horrified at such an attach right under the noses of the school administration, but unfortunately I wasn't shocked because that was far from the only violent incident I'd witnessed. I thought that I'd seen the boy around campus before but I didn't know who he was. Maybe I'd overlooked him like I was sure most people did since he obviously wasn't part of the popular crowd. He was a tall young man, well over six feet tall, slim, with some emerald green eyes and sandy hair that was a little longer than most popular men's haircuts.

I opened up my purse, took out some tissue and pressed it against his nose myself so his hands could be freed. He sighed heavily and tilted his head back until his nosebleed stopped. I then wiped his face as he wiped his hands with other tissues I'd given him. I couldn't help him up but I was able to bend down and pick up his backpack and his books while he stumbled up against the lockers, still holding the left side of his ribcage. The boy looked devastated. He looked nothing short of humiliated and ashamed, sad and mortified even.

He muttered out a little *thanks* as I handed him his bag and his notebook. He was a cute boy but he was awkward and shy, seemingly mortified of me too. I wanted to reassure him somehow but I was afraid to make it worst. Doubts crowded my mind and I ended up just wheeling myself away after asking him if he was okay and wishing him the best of luck. I felt bad as soon as I did so because how in the world could he be okay? He had just been brutally attacked! But I left it at that. I left but I thought about him for the rest of the day.

I wondered how he was doing all night after I got back home too, but I didn't tell anyone about what I saw. I didn't know how to feel about what I had seen because it had left me with a certain numbness inside. Part of me felt bad for not having done anything more for him but another part of me didn't want to get involved because I didn't want more trouble in my own life. I knew that was selfish, but part of me was afraid. I already had to deal with depression following my mountain misadventure, not to mention humiliation and lingering low self-esteem. I couldn't help another person if I couldn't first help myself.

So I just did my best to move on with my life and not think about that nameless boy. I never really saw him on campus but he was always somewhere in the back of my mind. Deep inside of me somewhere, what I had seen affected me profoundly. It made me realize how fortunate I was to have people like my few good friends who stood by me even though I didn't deserve it. And he was disliked and harassed for reasons that were completely out of his control. Somewhere in the middle of that we weren't so different from each other.

Eventually the boy was pushed so far back in the back of my mind that I almost forgot about the incident completely. I focused on my schoolwork, and catching up on what I'd missed immediately after my accident, my recovery and nothing else. About a month and a half after that incident I wheeled myself to my locker and opened it when a piece of paper fell out. Somebody else had obviously slipped it in there since it was folded and *Alana* was written on instead instead of *Alyson*. I slipped it into my backpack and read it during the morning break when I had the chance to be alone. I opened up the little piece of paper and read the words.

Dear Alana,

I'm sorry I didn't write this sooner. For a while I just didn't know what to say and then, well, I didn't know your name and I'm too shy to talk to you in person. I just wanted to say thanks for helping me out when you did. Nobody has ever done something like that for me before, so thank you. By the way, if you want to write back my locker is #201 and the combination is 17-05-37.

Anderson

     I smiled as I read the few short lines and decided to write back later on after class. The next morning I got to school early so I could wheel myself to his locker, deposit the letter and put the lock back on before I saw him coming down the hallway in the distance. I wheeled myself away quickly because I wanted my little note to surprise him.

Hey Anderson!

It's Alyson (not Alana) by the way, I just wanted to thank you for the note and check up on you since I haven't forgotten about you. It's good to know that you're okay. I was really worried about you for a while there, and well, I couldn't exactly get a hold of you either. I knew nothing about you up until now. Now I know your name, your locker number and the combination so I can steal your notes and cheat on my math homework! ;)

Just kidding of course, we don't even have any classes together this semester but in the future if we do end up in the same class, there are a handful of subjects that I could use a little help with (and I can return the favour) if you're not in the same boat as I am! I'm not a very outgoing person myself but just know that you have nothing to be shy about around me. I mean, I'm already in a wheelchair, what could I do to intimidate you? The worst I could do is try to run you over! LOL! Well, since you know where my locker is, feel free to drop in notes and math homework anytime you like. I'd like to see you again in person one of these days. Maybe could sit outside for lunch?

Sincerely,
Alyson

I got a reply almost immediately. I was going to sit outside with Anderson that very day! So I met up with Anderson in the little grassy area in front of the school where a bunch of picnic tables were lined up near the trees and a small, currently dormant, garden maintained by students studying environmental sciences and agriculture. It was still quite chilly outside even though there was no more snow but the sun was nice and warm on my face. I wheeled myself across the parking lot and onto the cement path and looked around for a few moments at the other students leaving the building and going out for *outside* food. I was downright useless to all of them since I could no longer smuggle in contraband. None of these people had ever really been my friends after all, they just liked me because I was convenient for them.

"Hi Alyson!"

I turned around and saw that Anderson was walking up behind me with food in his hands.

"Oh! You didn't need to bring me food!" I told told him as he handed me a sandwich with some root beer. "I would've just eaten when I got back inside."

Anderson's emerald green eyes were much brighter, his demeanour less broken and his face much more relaxed. His hair was blowing in the wind and revealed some stitches on the side of his forehead near the temple area. I stretched out my hand to push the rest of his hair out of his face but he didn't allow me to do so.

"It's not from the other day, so don't worry about it." He said, dismissing me.

"I'm so sorry Anderson." I whispered.

"Sorry for what?"

"What they do to you!"

"You don't need to be sorry about anything Aly. I swear I hate them all!"

"I'm starting to feel the same way."

"And just so you know, we should make this quick because I don't you want you to end up in trouble because you're hanging out with me."

"Why would I end up in trouble because of you? I'm useless to them now anyway. I can't smuggle in food and I can't play sports. I'm invisible. You know, I used to be afraid but now I'm just a flower on the wall."

"Well, you weren't useless to me."

I reached out and hugged him. At first he was cautious to wrap his arms around me not to injure me further but afterwards he held me tightly. His hair was soft in between my fingers when I took a few strands of it and placed it over his temple to cover the area where the stitches were. He smiled at me and I couldn't help but smile back. I was relieved to know that he was doing okay, and I wanted him to know that he could be himself around me. I didn't want him to be just another face in the crowd after the circumstances under which we'd met. I smiled at the thought that we'd always have our secret letters which he often adorned with strange drawings as a way to communicate.

"You were an epic player on the girls' basketball team last semester," Anderson told me as he was pushing my wheelchair around the property, "you were really amazing."

"I'll be able to play again," I reassured him, "I'm just not sure I want to."

"Why not?"

"All these people, they are all so superficial. As it turns out, only two of them are actually my real friends."

"I'm sorry, but unfortunately I know how that feels."

"No, don't be sorry. Do you have any friends?"

"Not any real friends."

"What about us? Are we friends?"

"Sure."

Anderson flashed me another beautiful smile that could've lit up the entire neighbourhood if the sun hadn't already been out. He brought me back inside the school lobby where we parted ways just before the bell rang. I then wheeled myself to my next class where I noticed there was a small strip of paper on my chair next to my lap. It said *I want to see you again* in Anderson's handwriting, like it had been ripped out of another letter. I smiled to myself again and wrote to my new friend on another strip of paper saying *I want to see you again too* as well as my phone number and left it in his locker before I left the building for the day.

Being in need of a new friend the way I was, having Anderson come my way was like a blessing in disguise. I smiled as my mom picked me up and drove me home. See didn't seem to have noticed my uplifted mood, but if she had, she kept it to herself. I saw Anderson from time to time in school even though he was adamant that nobody could know we were friends but after school we often hung out. He held my left hand while my dad held the right one when I took my second first steps once I got out of the wheelchair.

My little Anderson loved his new friend Anderson too. Big Anderson, or simply Big Anders, was great with children like he already had that paternal touch built into him even though he was merely a teenager. Even I was never that good with my little brother and I had been there since the very moment he entered the world. I had actually been the first one to hold him after the doctor delivered him! The friendship between Anderson and Anderson was instantaneous, and I couldn't help but smile when I saw the two of them playing. My parents also loved Anderson, and his parents loved me. I'd even introduced him to Elaine and Amanda but as the summer was nearing we had mostly gone our separate ways with our hobbies and educational goals even if we were still friends.

"What are you doing this summer?" Anderson asked me.

"Not much I guess," I replied blandly, "I'm about the only one who isn't going to camp or spending the summer somewhere exotic or whatever. Just gonna take a chill pill because my parents are kinda worried that I'm going to break something again."

We both chuckled but my parents were right deep inside. I'd gotten a little too bold for my own good up on that mountain.

"Well, I can't blame them Aly, you could've killed yourself!"

"You can *always* kill yourself Anderson, no matter what you do! But yeah, it could've been a lot worst I suppose. I mean, I am walking again ain't I? So, what are *you* doing this summer?"

"Takin' pills with you it seems!"

I giggled and took him into a hug. He was the only friend I wanted to spend the summer with.

"You're the best damn friend I could ever ask for!"

"You too Aly!"

Then he put his arms around me and kissed my forehead. I'd never been kissed by a guy like that before and I knew that my parents would flip out if they find out even though Anderson and I were just friends. I was a teen now, my middle school "boyfriends" had really just been cute boys. The love between Anderson and I was purely platonic but it was intense. Anderson was a gentle soul, exceptionally smart, easygoing, savvy and loving. He could be witty and spontaneous and didn't have to try hard to captivate me. His personality was the only drug I needed to uplift my spirit that summer after my injury. It was my time to rediscover myself and the new person I wanted to be, away from the peer pressure, fakery and injustices of high school.

Anderson had also started to come out of his shell and no longer being so shy around strangers. He and my folks had become close but it still took a while for him to warm up to them every time he came over to the house, like he had to get to know them all over again each time. We'd spent the summer having neighbourhood barbecues, boating and swimming in the river and taking day trips with the family. That was just the first summer I spent with him but it was probably the best.

Anderson had changed after that. Once school started again he was different and darkness followed him everywhere. Weeks and months went by and he only withdrew deeper into himself, only giving me glimpses of his true self here and there. He was an outcast that didn't belong anywhere and there came a point where he didn't want to. Although we'd gotten close over the summer months, once school started distance loomed between us. Being in school had a detrimental effect on him, I'd always known it but I'd never seen it up and close like that before.

I wanted so desperately to help him somehow, but what could I do? I was insignificant and nobody seemed to care. I might've been part of a privileged group of people, respected and well-liked but I was just as powerless as if I'd been in Anderson's shoes. The worst part about the situation was that he never wanted to talk about the things that were bothering him and expected me to simply shove what I saw under the rug and never think about it again. But I couldn't. I loved him and I couldn't merely forget about the fact that he was relentlessly bullied every single day, harassed and even assaulted a couple of times.

A group of boys had cornered him in the bathroom during lunch one day, set his hair on fire before extinguishing it by dunking his head in the toilet. I'd never seen him cry before, but that day he ran down the hall and out the door with tears running down his cheeks and falling down like rain. People laughed and poked fun at him as he passed by and further humiliated him on social media. Teachers stood by like they were blind and deaf, not to mention mute. My last chance was going straight to Mr. Pasquale but unfortunately that too went awry.

"Mr. Pasquale will be with you in a minute." Mrs. Phyllis told me as she walked out and closed the door behind her.

I exhaled loudly. I knew Anderson wasn't going to be happy with me. I kept on telling myself that it was the right thing to do, that it was for his safety and wellbeing and everything would be fine afterwards but I couldn't seem to get myself to believe that last part. He had told me repeatedly to leave it alone, to leave him alone, not think about it and just let him be. But I couldn't. He was my friend, I couldn't just let everything go when it was so obvious that he was suffering and I was the only person who seemed to care. At the very least, I was the only person who paid attention.

"Can I help you?" Mr. Pasquale asked as he sat down behind his desk.

"It's about Anderson Massey," I told him in an urgent tone of voice, "he needs help."

It was apparent in his eyes that he was annoyed and didn't want to hear it from the moment I'd said Anderson's name. Anderson hadn't been the kind of guy to get into any serious trouble. His trips to the principal's office had never been for anything serious, but apparently Mr. Pasquale saw it differently.

"What about him? And why do you even bother to mingle with a loser like him in the first place?"

I was appalled that the *principal* had the audacity to tell me something like that! Who was he to judge?! He was supposed to be in charge of the school, the top person to look out for the welfare of his students! That included Anderson Massey whether he liked him or not.

"Mr. Pasquale!" I urged. "He needs help! He cuts himself, he's suicidal, he needs urgent help and I don't know how to get through to him!"

"Alyson, listen to me," he said in an eerie overly diplomatic voice, "stay away from Anderson. He's a delinquent and will only hurt you, damage your reputation and I don't know what else he's capable of. He's dangerous, keep your distance and leave him alone."

And he got up and walked out.

Just like that.

Time after time Mr. Pasquale had adamantly denied that there was ever any kind of bullying or bigotry in the halls of Belden. I found it quite ironic that he'd believe such a thing when he was a bully and a bigot himself. I supposed that maybe you couldn't always see what was going on unless you were in the middle of it, but the truth was that Anderson *was* in the middle of it while Mr. Pasquale sat his overweight rear end behind his desk all day doing God knows what when there were students who needed him on their side. I knew for a fact that he wasn't on mine, and definitely not on Anderson's.

After school I raced to the section of the parking lot that was across the street without any of my winter gear on and jumped on the hood of Anderson's car like a madwoman before he could drive off. My gesture greatly surprised him but I was the one who was most surprised by my own actions. I'd turned into a savage over the last day and a half but in the moment I only cared about Anderson. He unlocked the passenger's side door and let me in. He drove down the street to the nearest Denny's and parked so we could talk without being bothered. Anderson took off his coat and handed it to me once again because February was one of the coldest months and I was shivering. My disgruntled friend shut the engine off and waited for me to speak.

"It's all going to be over soon." I spoke in a low voice, thinking about his upcoming graduation at the end of the semester.

"Oh God, you have no idea!" Anderson's exasperated voice choked out coarsely.

"Just hang on a little longer, in a few months you'll never have to think about these punks again."

"They ruined my life! They finally did it for real this time! How am I just supposed to forget about everything when this rape allegation will follow me forever?"

"Real rape survivors aren't believed Anderson, just give it some time and Tammy's lies will all unravel like they always do."

"And that's a travesty! It's an unforgivable failure of justice and humanity when the real victims suffer in silence. I would never, *ever*, do that to a woman! Anyone guilty of rape deserves nothing less than the death penalty!"

I put my hand on his wrist in a futile hope to console him. Both of his hands gripped the steering wheel to the point that I thought he was going to rip it right out. Anderson was progressively fading away right before my eyes and the most I could do was seemingly watch in horror. The only real thing I could do was comfort him as best as I could because I couldn't change what was going on around us. I'd already gone to the school administration, voiced my concerns to my parents and even his parents had been worried about him, but nothing had changed. Nobody could get through to him.

"They are going to pay for this!" Anderson muttered out in an angry, almost scary voice. "I'm going to make them pay for all of this!"

Not knowing what else to say or do to comfort him, I promised him that they were indeed going to pay someday, that they weren't going to get away with what they had done, though I knew nothing of what that actually entailed.

"I'm gonna kill myself to make everybody pay!" Anderson almost shouted as he smacked the door with his fist. "I wish I was good enough! Then I would know that I'm not in this alone!"

"Anderson!" I yelled at him even though he was sitting right beside me. "What in the world are you talking about?!"

I broke down crying at the thought of him wanting to commit suicide. I couldn't imagine my life without him, not after what just happened. He'd always been so good to me, since day one, and I felt like I'd failed him. I couldn't repay him, couldn't be the rock he needed so desperately and couldn't stop the world from caving in around us. The pain in his voice and the cuts on his arm were proof that no matter what I did, I couldn't reach him. He was a natural disaster in his own right; something you could do nothing to prevent and only pick up the pieces following whatever resulted of the storm.

"Anderson, please talk to me." I begged.

"What you don't know can't hurt you." He retorted sternly.

"What are you getting at?"

"You'll never be able to forgive me after this!"

"After what *Anders?* I won't let you fall into those suicidal ideologies! I don't know what I'm gonna do but you can bet the hell I'm not gonna do nothing!"

"I won't be able to live with myself after this…"

"Anderson, what are you talking about?"

"I don't want to talk about this Alyson, just leave it alone."

He roared the little black Acura's engine back to life and sped out of the parking lot back towards the school. He slammed on the breaks right in front of the main entrance and ordered me out without looking at me. I simply muttered out a barely audible request to call me later in the evening and he said he would so I walked back in to the building that had ruined two lives to retrieve my things and head home. The students who'd been wandering around the premises hadn't been oblivious to the fact that I'd been riding with Anderson Massey.

"What the heck are you doing with a loser like him?" Michael Hazen snapped at me. "You know, I used to have a lot of respect for you

Alyson, but nowadays you can barely respect yourself. Look at you! Look at what you've become!"

"You're going to pay for what you've done!" I growled in response, almost prophetically.

The interesting thing about pain and suffering was that it's *right now* yet nobody ever acknowledges that *right now* aspect of it. People were always quick to dismiss a person's suffering, saying that things would get better with time but it didn't work that way. It's what you did in that time that made the difference, but the real question was what do you do *right now?* Suffering wasn't three months in an abstract future people weren't sure they'd have, or next year or whatever, it was *right now.*

Anderson never told me but I knew that he was afraid and ashamed to ask for help from other people and outside sources. There was this unexplained shyness to him that always kept him locked inside himself, far away from everyone and beyond reach. Even I couldn't seem to reach that place deep inside of him. As for me, I was just as guilty as all of those other people because I'd tell Anderson that it was all going to be over soon, but who really knew that that really meant until *soon* became *now?*

Guilt was a central part of the vortex of emotions I lugged around deep inside. No matter how many times people told me that I was only a teenage girl and that I didn't have the weight of the world on my shoulders, I couldn't help myself. I'd seen Anderson's behaviour change and eventually fall into no other category than downright weird. He'd become odd, strange, sinister somehow. I'd never been able to pinpoint what had been so off about him in the end, but I couldn't blame him for being dark, disheveled and disconnected because I wasn't far behind.

There had always been that sadness to him but somewhere in the middle of that an inhumane rage had surfaced. An eerie, menacing anger that escaped even through his eyes. The sweet boy I'd once known had turned into some Rambo-like troubled young man. His smile had completely vanished and it was almost as though his entity had faded away completely. He was already gone, long gone passed the point of no return. I woul have liked so much to have known what had been going on inside his mind but I had no way of knowing unless he straight up told me. Well, he didn't.

And then he shot up the school.

Anderson had never been violent towards me or anyone else as far I'd been concerned. The only person he'd ever wanted to hurt was himself. For a long time even I blamed myself for being blind to his pain and for the warning signs but I'd never picked up on, or anything else that indicated he was literally going to do a Columbine. Angry teenagers frustrated with school didn't go on murderous rampages every time something went awry, but then again, how much did we actually know what was going on inside? It was erroneous for people to blame the popular media, music, films, video games or his upbringing for his behaviour while at the same time refusing to look at themselves in the mirror and asking the real reasons why.

Anderson Massey wasn't so different than the rest of us. He was just a boy, an ordinary boy with hopes and dreams but who'd made the choice to throw it all away and shatter the lives of everyone he loved and who loved him in the process. There could never be any valid excuse for his actions, but nothing excused what had been done to him by others either. He killed his classmates, not me or his parents or random strangers somewhere else in town. He could've discharged that gun anywhere he'd wanted to but he chose the school for a reason. It was that environment that made him crazy. So much for the *everything's going to be alright* lie constantly fed to us. It would never be again, it could never be again, and I had been in denial about that for a long time.

Back at home I was in for an interrogation as soon as I walked through the door. My parents pressed me about my odd behaviour in the last couple of days but I assured them that it was only drama at school and that I was fine. Maybe it was my ego or my pride, but I couldn't bear the humiliation of telling my parents the truth. I might not have been sexually assaulted at a party, but the people I'd once considered my friends had raped my soul. My parents backed off for the evening but they weren't convinced of my story. I'd always been particularly bad at lying even though I gave it my best shot here and there. Most of us lied and the rest of them tried.

After a supper spent in awkward silence without my brother I retreated to my room feeling numb. I fumbled around my desk trying to find something that would retain my attention for more than a few moments until I ripped my calendar off the wall and noticed that I hadn't yet changed it to February. It was February 16th to be exact and there were precisely four months of school left to the day but that brought me little comfort. Riding out the rest of the year would be agonizing and painful, but maybe I'd ask my parents to send me to a different school. Yeah, I'd bring it up before going to bed.

My train of thought was interrupted by my cellphone ringing and when I saw that it was Anderson on the screen I picked up immediately. I answered but all I heard on the other end were a series of deep, seemingly painful breaths. I could feel a tension through the phone even though he didn't speak. Anderson seemed agitated somehow, anticipating something that I couldn't foresee. I waited for him to speak knowing that sometimes it took him a while to compose himself so he wouldn't cry. A few times he tried to say something but the words didn't come out so finally I decided to make the first move myself.

"Hello? Are you still there? Anderson, speak to me please. I'm right here for you."

"Don't come to school tomorrow."

Click.

Puzzled, I immediately called him back but it went straight to voicemail. I didn't really want to go to school because only a handful of people still respected me but I wanted to see him above all else. My demented thoughts still spiralled around my brain endlessly so I ended up sifting through my yearbook that had been on my desk without having been touched for several weeks. I opened it on a random page, one that just happened to show Lil Amelia's one and only high school photo. I knew very little around her but I almost regretted not having known her. She had seemed like such a sweet person to be around, one who'd never in a million years deserved the hell she had to endure. Nobody deserved to suffer like that.

After her tragic passing, the school had made a small memorial in the hallway that included a guestbook people could sign and write messages in. It quickly filled up with the fictitious condolences of much of the people who'd bullied her to death and as soon as that memorial disappeared so did she and the lessons supposedly learned from that tragedy. Even I ended up forgetting about her entirely after attending my first party.

But Anderson never got such a memorial.

XIV

SECOND CHANCES

Hans drove me back to the Petrov trailer when my parents went off to eat in town since the apartment was in no condition for them to prepare breakfast. I begged him to not let my parents know in any sort of way that I had spent the night at his place. After all we hadn't spent the night *together* but it still wasn't anybody's business and I knew a little too well what rumours could do. Hans had slept in his own bed and I'd slept in the spare bedroom and we were the only two who knew that. I wanted it to stay that way. In other matters, I had slept through the entire night undisturbed by dreams or by any external factors.

Hans looked worried as he drove me down to the radioactive trailer park, seemingly appalled by the environment he was scheduled to clean up. He was probably wondering why I had to go to such a place, or maybe he thought I was some sort of stalker investigating him because I knew that he worked somewhere back there or whatever. He dropped me off on Dmitry's doorstep where he and Sveta came out to greet me. They waved at Hans and he waved back before speeding out of there. I climbed up the stairs and Dmitry hugged me like he usually did.

"There you are!" Dmitry happily greeted me.

"I'm sorry I disappeared like that," I apologized, "but I can explain."

"It won't be necessary dear, Sveta told me everything."

"She did?"

"Yes, your new apartment was ready for you to spend the night in and so you ended your little stay with us early."

I sighed in amazing relief. I knew I could depend on Svetlana no matter what happened.

"Yes, that's right. I'm sorry I didn't get to call you to tell you or anything."

"Oh that's okay, Sveta called and said that she and her sister were going to spend the night at my son's so I didn't expect to see you back. I'm sorry I didn't get to say goodbye either."

Dmitry invited me inside where I found Vera packing some stuff into boxes. I also noticed that most of the interesting wall decorations had vanished. As it turned out, the living room was even dirtier than I'd originally believed.

"What are you doing?" I asked as I walked in.

"Oh, hey there! Welcome back!" Vera greeted as I walked in.

"What's up with all of this?"

"Well, we're going to be auctioning off this junk for money online. Some of it can fetch quite a bit of money and we really need it."

"Believe me, I completely understand."

"Plus seeing Stalin the minute you walk in kinda gets old after a while you know. He looks like Super Mario and I can't stand that game!"

"It's still better than seeing Hitler!"

The room fell silent. I knew that the Petrovs had been unnerved by the recent white supremacist rallies that often became violent and the political situation in the country. I'd also been unnerved by such displays out in the streets but I was blessed with a privilege they didn't have irrespective of the other drama that was happening in my life.

"Is it true that Hitler had syphilis?" Svetlana asked after a moment of silence.

"How the hell am I supposed to know?!" I retorted laughing.

"Some people say that Hitler was actually secretly a Jew." Vera added.

"And some still say that he was a good man…"

Vera finished packing up a box and dragged it into her room. Sveta and I followed her and I did my best to close the broken door behind me but since it wasn't properly hinged it sat in an awkward half-open position. Many posters were missing in the girls' room too but the blank spaces had been replaced with other things. A theatrical poster of *Greetings from the Shore* was the centrepiece, surrounded by a multitude of photos and magazine cuttings. On the other hand, the pile of junk in the closet only seemed to get bigger and bigger every time but I knew that my new room was destined to look like that too.

I chuckled when I heard the doorbell ring because I knew that it was Kaye and the expression on the twins' faces confirmed what I'd speculated. I heard Dmitry answer the door but I couldn't understand what he was grumbling about in Russian. A few seconds later I heard the door slam and Dmitry return to whatever he was doing. I reckoned I'd just learned my first few words of Russian profanity.

"I'm *really* sorry for last night." Sveta apologized in a broken voice.

"Svetlana," I reassured her, "that wasn't your fault and you couldn't have controlled or prevented what happened there anyway."

"I'm still sorry more than I can tell you."

"I'm fine, I promise."

"You don't owe us anything anymore, okay?"

"Are you nuts? I owe all of you *big time* for letting me stay here and everything!"

"Okay, no more arguing. Where'd you stay last night anyway?"

"Hans Wagner's."

Vera seemed to think that I'd slept *with* Hans because she started laughing and Sveta looked incredibly puzzled, especially considering what had gone on at the party before I got up and left. I immediately became angry at myself for telling them the truth because the situation had turned into exactly what I feared it would.

"I didn't sleep *with* him," I grumbled in an exhausted tone of voice, thinking about Anderson, "I only stayed at his place."

"You know, I am *very* sorry." Sveta retorted.

"Long weekend's over tomorrow…" Vera changed the subject although a big evil grin was still plastered across her face.

"Can't believe they gave us a four-day weekend for no particular reason." I commented. "It's the first year they do this."

"They said it was to balance out the rest of the holidays but I think the school board just wants to boost its popularity ratings because they've been in the toilet for a long time."

"I guess it's gonna be time to finish up reading the commandant of Auschwitz…"

"Then I guess we should get on with it!"

I'd almost entirely forgotten about him, but I hadn't forgotten that he sounded exactly like Anderson Massey. When I read the words on the page I felt as though Anderson was reading them to me. His voice resonated at the back of my mind as the commandant lamented his fate while he spoke so casually about the mass extermination of millions of people. Thankfully I hadn't eaten breakfast and nothing could come back up but I certainly felt sickened by everything.

When the twins noticed my discomfort they proposed that we each read aloud a section of the book while putting on a show for each other. I was ready to agree with whatever would lighten the mood because I neither wanted to be sick nor not do my homework and that was something I struggled with ever since my big return to school. Vera was the first to take the makeshift stage that was actually her bed to put on a show for Sveta and I while we waited our turn.

Vera put on some rather comedic antics considering the subject matter and so did Sveta, which made getting through the remainder of the book a much more pleasant experience. My part ended up being the last two chapters of the book so I took the stage and began reading in a deep, creepy voice to amuse the girls. I was doing well up until the very last paragraph of the book. My sickness had come back with a vengeance as my voice cracked and I struggled to get through the last sentence.

"May the general public simply go on seeing me as the bloodthirsty beast, the cruel sadist, the murderer of millions, because the broad masses cannot conceive the commandant of Auschwitz in any other way. They would never be able to understand that he also had a heart and that he wasn't evil."

And then I puked up a pile of bile right then and there on the twins' bare mattress. I got down from the bed, broke the door straight off its hinges and ran into the bathroom, dropping my book somewhere along the way. On my hands and knees I coughed into the toilet bowl but nothing else came out. Dmitry and the twins soon converged around me to see what was wrong with me which only added to my embarrassment even though I knew they meant well.

Dmitry took it upon himself to get a damp cloth and wipe my mouth after I'd vomited like I was a small and helpless child who hadn't digested their chicken nuggets. Vera attempted to clean their bed while Sveta arranged me a spot to lie down on the sofa and brought me some ginger ale once I flopped down on the squishy couch. It didn't appear to matter what I did, I only seemed to dig the trenches deeper down for myself.

"I wish there were more four-day weekends like this." Sveta contemplated as she sat down next to me with a box of crackers.

"Oh me too, believe me! I freaking hate this school." I grumbled through my sips of soda. "Bergen-Belden!"

"You know Aly, I've been thinking about doing virtual school or dropping out altogether and pursing alternative education for a while now." Sveta continued, deep in thought. "That way I could do it at my own pace and the best part of it is that I wouldn't have to deal with ingrate bastards like Mario and Dominic. I'm so darn tired of being harassed constantly!"

Disappearing from Bergen-Belden didn't sound like a bad idea at all. Alternative education options had been offered to me before but there hadn't been any appeal to them in the past. I'd been so determined to conquer Belden that I'd neglected to understand the lingering detrimental effects that place had on me. After the massacre it was as though the past disappeared. I was no longer a whore who slept with the killer nor a well-liked kid. I'd basically stopped existing. Brandon, on the other hand, had *actually* stopped existing.

He'd died of a deliberate drug overdose a few weeks before the first anniversary of the tragedy. The truth about Tammy and Anderson had somehow come to light and combined with unknown things he'd also been going through at the time, it became too much for him. The same week Tammy began dating Brandon's best friend but that hadn't lasted long. Allegations of cheating and abuse flew like sparks before long and the farce of a relationship ended like the Deepwater Horizon almost as soon as it had begun. As for everybody else, their lives had returned to normal. At least they'd adopted a new normal that seemed convenient for them.

"You know Sveta, that doesn't sound half bad."

"I was talking with my sister and we were thinking of leaving school together. You're more than invited to join us. We're all intelligent and dedicated people. We could actually finish school much sooner if we went at our own pace instead of putting up with stories about masturbation in class."

I liked the idea but I would have to give it some serious thought either way. Some part of me had wanted so desperately to press the reset button and start over at Belden, get my old life back in one way or another. I'd only recently begun to understand that problems weren't solved the same way they were created and Belden was part of the problem, not the solution.

"There'd be no more puking in the parking lot," Svetlana attempted to convince me, "or over Rudolf Höss."

"I'll keep that in mind!" I laughed.

Vera disturbed our conversation by asking for help to get the mattress out of her room and throwing it outside. Burdened with guilt, I immediately got up and went over to help her. The three of us dragged the puke-stained mattress outside and and dropped it at the end of the driveway. Vera promised me that she wasn't angry and at me and that she'd hated that bed anyway, and Sveta assured me that somebody would pick it up because the trailer park was a hotspot for dumpster divers.

"I think your sister sold me on the idea of quitting school." I told Vera once we made it back to the living room.

"Sometimes I think of just dropping out completely and getting a job because that's the only future I have." Vera grumbled in response.

"Vera Petrov! Listen to me, you're smart as hell! You could do anything you wanted in life!"

"Maybe, if I had money! I'm not a capitalist pig and in this society you don't get anywhere without money, regardless of how smart you may be. And financial aid doesn't cover a fraction of it. I don't want to ruin myself without any guarantee of seeing any of that money back."

"I can't blame you Vera. I personally don't know anybody who is actually doing what they went to school all those years for. My cousin has a master's degree and flips burgers for a living. Either way, I guess I'm in the same boat as you now."

"Plus, what the hell is being smart good for anyway? What you learn in school is utterly meaningless in matters of real life. They can teach you all about the smallest subatomic particles or refraction or how to get an erection but they teach you nothing about real life! Nothing!"

"I can't argue with you on that! Your performance in school means nothing in terms of your performance in the real world."

"Exactly! And to tell you the truth my dear, I've learned a heck of a lot more on my own than they ever taught me in school."

"I know, school doesn't teach you anything of much value, like accepting and respecting others or helping people like Anderson!"

I regretted it as soon as I said his name. I still hated talking about him and even thinking about him even though I did it all the time. No matter what he was always there, I could never get away from him.

"I taught myself how to knit and crochet from an instruction manual and a VHS tape," Vera proudly continued, "and I learned to have a heart from watching *Greetings from the Shore*. It's my favourite movie."

"And how'd a romantic comedy involving Russian sailors teach you to have a heart?" I asked her, curious. "I've never seen it."

"I have it on DVD if you want to see it, but I don't have a DVD player. I can lend it to you if you want to watch it at home once everything's fixed up nice and dandy."

"I'd prefer to watch it with the two of you, but in the meantime you can still spill the beans."

"So okay, there's this sailor Lars Ramkildestrom who's like the leader of the group."

"Uh-huh."

"And there's a part where he's talking with Jenny Chambers and he's going off about chasing horizons and chasing them forever because it's ultimately impossible to get there. Then she comments about how now she knows why he's the brains of the bunch."

"Uh-huh."

"And he asks her if she thinks he'd really be there right now if he actually had a brain. Then he tells her that he'd much rather have a heart instead, because honestly, what's the use in thinking about something when you have nothing worth thinking about? And really, no reason to think about it in the first place?"

"Wow, that's deep."

"Yeah, he wasn't the star of the show but he star of my show. And my response to what Lars said is that I have a brain but I'm still here. Because I have no damn money!"

"But you have both a heart and a brain, and that's better than money."

Vera laughed at my reply but it was true. Even though it was nearly impossible to get somewhere without money in America, money had no real value to the human heart and certainly did not make life valuable. Some argued that it did buy happiness but it did not buy inner peace. That I knew from experience. And then I went back to thinking about Anderson again. Maybe it was time for me to remove the skeletons from the closet.

"I still write to him sometimes," I changed the topic, "Anderson. We used to send each other these secret letters and even now that he's dead I still write him secret letters sometimes even though he's never going to read them."

"And Aly," Sveta's voice was delicate, "there's nothing wrong with still having tender feelings towards him. He was your friend and what the two of you shared were great times. That hasn't disappeared because of his actions even though it might mess you up inside."

"That's something that I struggle with a lot and it does mess me up inside big time."

"You cope the way you cope with his death and if you feel as if he'd understand what you have to say in those letters, then do it man."

"Sometimes I wonder what it would be like if he actually read them."

"Were you raised Catholic by any chance?"

"No, I don't come from a religious family. What does this have to do with anything?"

"Well, half of this town is Catholic, and just like with Islam, they believe that the dead have some degree of consciousness and can hear you and all."

"So you're implying that Anderson can actually read the letters I still write to him?"

"I believe so. I mean, energy cannot be created nor destroyed, it can only be transferred. Anderson's soul was somewhere before he came here and it's somewhere now that he's gone from this world."

I contemplated that for a moment and it comforted me to know that he wasn't just *gone*. I knew that part of him was always going to live inside my heart, but I still struggled to reconcile one of the greatest friends I'd ever been blessed with and the person who murdered people in cold blood.

"I went to a Catholic church once and it was weird," Vera went on, "but I'm with my sister in believing that the dead aren't gone. They were still here somewhere, somehow. They've gotta be! Otherwise how freaking cheap can life be? Life's a bitch and then you die and there's nothing? I don't think so!"

I still kept thinking about him. The inner conflict raged on. It was like all the perfect moments were gone. Invalid somehow despite what the twins, my parents and my therapist kept on telling me. All of our perfect moments became nothing more than a long list of guilt-invaded notions of a young man I thought I once knew. The entirety of the wonderful times we spent together were wrong because of the way he ended.

But those moments and those memories were still alive within me and I still cherished them just as much. Maybe I cherished them even more because I knew he as never coming back, like he was just some character at the end of a book that we never hear of again without knowing whether he got his happy ending or not, somewhere far away from *here*. My innermost feelings were things society didn't want to hear and couldn't bear to accept but I had no monopoly over any of those things.

"Sometimes I wonder what happens to characters when the stories end..." I commented, mostly to myself.

"If I know one thing from writing stories," Vera replied, also deep in thought, "it's that it's over when it's over. When the story ends, it *ends*. There's no wondering what happened to so and so, it's all over."

"And then I think about Anderson and the fact that he was a real person, not just a character in some book and I can't help but wonder what happened to him, where he is now."

"I'll admit that sometimes I wonder what happened to the characters of *Greetings from the Shore* after the movie ends. Did Lars find his horizon? Did Jenny and Benicio end up together for good? Did Catch meet his son? What about the others? But then again, they aren't real and it ends when the movie ends, that's all."

"Wonder if Lars found his brain."

Both the twins and I cracked up laughing but that did not solve my dilemma. Later on, Vera suggested that I ask Hans if he wanted to watch the movie with us at his place. At first I didn't really want to but Vera made sure to remind me that I should at least try a few dates with a *mature* man so I decided to just do it. And so movie night turned into date night. Did I really have anything to lose? I didn't. So I called up Hans and asked him if he wanted to have a movie night with the twins and I, leaving out any mention of a date, his maturity or anything else for that matter.

I hadn't been expecting much, but to my surprise Hans was actually looking forward to watching a movie with us! He then proceeded to invite the three of us over to his apartment so we could watch the movie there, that very night. Of course Vera was overjoyed about that but I was somewhat apprehensive. Sveta, on the other hand, seemed to be annoyed that she'd have someone else to chaperone but I did not plan on pursuing anything serious with my new neighbour. I had no idea what I was getting into, and much less in what direction my life was supposed to be heading.

After you survive Anderson Massey your life doesn't just pick up where it left of. My own life was an abstract concept to me and I didn't know if I was supposed to try to pick up the pieces and fashion something out of them or burn them all and start anew completely. Both options seemed equally impossible. While I was brooding over my troubles for the billionth time Vera called Mercedes to come and pick us up and drive us over to my new place, leaving out the part about actually going out on a date with the neighbour. God forbid that my parents find out about that! I might've been an adult, but that didn't remove the awkwardness from the situation.

Mercedes showed up in a matter of a few minutes in that old car and parked in the driveway patiently waiting for the three of us to gussy up. Dmitry reminded the twins that tomorrow was a school day and that they weren't to be out too late and properly said goodbye to me since I would not be returning to the trailer after our little outing. He hugged me farewell and I promised him that I'd be back another day before he helped me put my belongings in the trunk of the car. As we did so I managed to notice that somebody had already taken Vera's pukey bed from the side of the road. Once we were all inside Mercedes sped off towards the interstate and played country music on her brand new radio, making the whole vehicle vibrate almost like an earthquake.

"Let me guess," I began, "someone left a brand new radio in your car?"

"Actually, no," she replied, "I found it when I was dumpster diving."

"You seriously rummage through trash bins?"

"Well, yes and no. In town here there's this industrial trash bin where people throw out some amazingly good stuff and from time to time I sneak in there and bring back whatever good stuff I may stumble upon."

"And last time you got a radio."

"That's right! And it sounds damn good too!"

"Awesome! Good for you, your car needed it!"

"You got that right!"

The twins then jumped in and told me about their experiences garbage picking out of the same industrial bin. They were saying that a few people had been caught stealing garbage, which was illegal according to a bylaw in town, so the company who owned the bin installed a metal grid over top of it so people couldn't steal the garbage but Vera was small enough to fit through it so she'd get in and hand the trash over to Sveta who was standing nearby.

The girls went on to say that the company eventually noticed that people could still get into the bin through the grid so they installed a security camera but it didn't have night vision and there were no light near the bin so Vera got a pair of night vision goggles and went rummaging through the bin at night. I couldn't help but laugh at the boldness of the whole thing but when they told me about the kinds of things they picked out of that trash bin I was somewhat compelled to go through it myself. For the moment, however, I kept my thoughts to myself but thought that it might be an interesting adventure.

Mercedes dropped us off at my new place and sped away back to where she came from. I'd instructed her to park on the street, on Hans' side of the building so my parents didn't notice me because they'd probably have questions for me, particularly why I was going to see the neighbour and not them. The twins and I walked in the shadows and knocked discreetly on my new neighbour's door. He answered almost immediately.

"Come on in! Your parents are almost finished with the place. It's been a stressful move for them but they finally delivered the storage container today!"

Under artificial lights Hans' apartment was appallingly small. I hadn't really gotten the chance to take a good look at it in the pitch black darkness before, but as I looked around it I left like I was going to suffocate. The kitchen and the living room were merged together, it was just one little open space with the kitchen table and a few chairs shoved right in the middle. The washer and dryer were right next to the fridge with a bunch of toolboxes and industrial equipment crammed in between everything.

The place looked more like a prison cell than an actual apartment with barely any room to move around in the house in between the furniture and Hans did not have a lot of furniture. The tiny space left for the living room included a dark green couch, a large flatscreen television mounted on the wall and a small coffee table. Vera, Hans and I crammed up the small couch while Sveta sat at the kitchen table, keeping tabs on all of us, as *Greetings from the Shore* came on. Hans smelled good, I had to give him that. His apartment didn't reek of dirty uniforms or environmental contamination either.

I could somewhat understand why Vera would be attracted to someone like him as there was indeed aspects to *mature* men that I was beginning to appreciate too. Despite that, I was distracted from Hans' presence next to me while we watched the movie. The twins had been right, it was a charming film and I'd thoroughly enjoyed it. Hans commented that it was cute and refreshing and that he loved it too. The characters and the storyline left a smile upon my face and that warm and fuzzy feeling inside my heart. After the film ended I couldn't help but wonder if Lars had found his horizon, but most of all, I wondered if I'd ever find mine. After a cup of tea the three of us said goodbye to Hans and loitered around the parking lot, waiting for Mercedes to show up.

"I've made a decision!" I spontaneously told the twins.

"Tell me," Sveta retorted without much interest.

"I'm going to drop out of school with you guys," I said affirmatively, "if that plan is still on of course."

"Of course it's still on!" Vera exclaimed. "I was kind of hoping that you'd tell us that you'd fallen in love with Hans though!"

I knew I'd have plenty of time to do that since we'd be neighbours for an indefinite amount of time. Maybe we'd have fun. Maybe my anxiety and overthinking would gradually subside. Maybe the whole thing was a blessing in disguise. *Maybe*.

"If there's something I learned from Lars and the two of you," I went on, "it's that it's useless to think too much. What did overthinking ever bring me anyway? I mean, aside from anxiety that is... Sometimes I think so much that I think I'm going to think myself to death and the whole time I just end up returning right to where I began in the first place!"

"Just hearing you talk it seems like you've solved every problem you've ever had in your life." Sveta commented, probably not knowing what else to say.

"I've decided that I'd much rather have a heart than a brain too." I affirmed.

Silence.

"I want to go to Lavallette," Vera muttered after a while, "just like in the movie."

"I want to go to Colorado!" Sveta protested. "Like John Denver!"

"Do you know how sick and tired I am of hearing him and his Rocky Mountain High?! Isn't he high enough already?!"

"You're missing the whole darn point!"

The twins bickered back and forth for a while, mostly in Russian, until Mercedes showed up. Mercedes might have temporarily halted the disagreement, but not for long.

"I've always wanted to live by the coast like that." Vera continued.

"Well, you live by the coast of a tar pond if that counts..." I muttered.

The twins and I cracked up laughing until Mercedes honked the horn to get going. It was pitch black outside with only the lights on the building and the garage illuminating our surroundings since the headlights on the old Mercedes stopped working a long time ago. I reckoned it would just be a matter of time before she found replacement headlights in the garbage.

"Why don't you sell your car and some of that fancy stuff you find in the garbage and buy yourself a nicer car?" I asked Mercedes as I walked up to the window. "I mean, one that doesn't sound like that."

"I wouldn't trade this thing for a rocket ship!" She replied fiercely. "This clunker belonged to my granddaddy who raised me. The car's still here but he isn't."

"I'm sorry."

"Hey, don't worry, if I could I'd get a real car too."

"But it's still a Mercedes."

"That's right! It's still better than public transit!"

Our little chat came to and end when my dad came out onto the deck and invited all of us inside. I doubted three more people could comfortably fit into an apartment that probably looked like a game of Tetris gone wrong considering all the stuff we had so I dismissed them and went inside by myself. Much like the unit next door, the living room, kitchen and dining room were a single room along with a narrow hallway with three bedrooms and one bathroom. Boxes and boxes of stuff were piled up all the way to the ceiling and my family's large dining set was noticeably absent.

My room was one of the smallest I'd ever seen and my big bed did not fit in it. It had been left in the storage container and an air mattress replaced it. I didn't know if my mattress would fit in the Petrov trailer, but I knew I owed the twins something for their hospitality. The bathroom was the size of the closet, and my previous closet had actually been bigger than the entire room. Had the apartment building been built exclusively for men? Did they not know that females have tons of cute tops and matching shoes?!

The walls were of a matte light green colour and the floors were made of beautiful real wood but the windows were old and most of them didn't have screens. The place was a major downgrade from what I was accustomed to and it would take a long time before I could properly settle in, but it wasn't nearly as bad as I'd expected. Of course, my constant anxiety and worrying about everything had clouded my brain even though I wasn't thrilled either way. When my father asked what I thought of the place I had to lie and tell him that I was excited so he couldn't have to worry about me even more.

Aside from my missing bed, all of my other possessions were in my room. It looked like a maze in there but nothing else was missing, except order perhaps. On the floor next to the half-deflated air mattress was my box full of special things including all the letters Anderson had sent me and all of my pictures and wall decorations. I clutched my necklace as I rummaged through the box. The memories it brought back were bittersweet; sweet because right up until the end I'd been enjoying everything life had to offer, but the ending was bitter. I could never get passed that. It always came back like bills I couldn't afford to pay. Unfortunately, I couldn't seduce the repo man like a woman on Jerry Springer had done.

Dear Anderson,

Your presence still lingers here. I wonder sometimes if it's really you or if it's just me going crazy, thinking that you're not really gone when indeed you are. The twins say you can still hear me, but I think that you're just gone. Oh, sometimes I wish you could just give me a sign! I wish there was a way for you to tell me... but most of the time I wish that you would just leave. Leave my mind! Leave my life! Get rid of the anxiety you've brought to my soul! Part of me will always regret not loving you the way I should have maybe, and that's why I hold on to you but you're no longer here!

What if I'd just told you that I loved you too and we'd made out in your car down by the river instead of going to that party? Would things have really ended differently? I don't have friends anymore, all the ones I used to have think I'm weird or I think they are weird or at least there's just something weird between us because of Belden now. Gosh, I hate that school now probably just as much as you did.

That's all. I don't know what else to say, or to think for that matter. Maybe I should visit your parents sometime. And you should visit mine.

Aly

XV

REVELATIONS

The least I could do before going to bed was put up my decorations and pictures where they would fit since there wasn't much space left on the walls after all the furniture was crammed into my room. Once I was done I flopped down on the air mattress — that I'd since properly inflated — but I couldn't manage to close my eyes. Not being able to sleep and not knowing what else to do, I did the only thing that came to mind, and that was call the twins who shared a cellphone and see which one would answer. At first I thought that maybe Vera might've been talking to Vladimir, but what the heck, I dialled the number.

"*Allo?*" Vera answered.

"Hi Vera," I whispered so my parents wouldn't hear me through the thin walls, "I'm sorry to call you so late but I just can't sleep. I know that's lame."

"No, that's not lame. What do you want?"

"Just to talk."

"Okay, I want to kill my landlord."

"He's my landlord too now."

"Oh yeah, that's right. How's that working for you?"

"This apartment is seriously claustrophobic but I have yet to meet the man."

"He's a wanker and I'd love to beat his butt! Honestly, I know a duo of hitmen who can take care of this problem!"

"You can't be serious!"

Vera cracked up laughing on the other end of the line for no apparent reason and then I heard Svetlana telling her to cut it out. I could hear the TV playing in the background but could not make out what they might've been watching.

"Nah, I'm just messing with you. They showed *Hitmen For Hire* on the news, you know, Columbine."

"Oh, don't worry Vera, I am painfully aware!"

"Yeah, I figured that."

"What's the news report about? Did somebody go on yet another rampage?"

"No, it's not anything like that. Apparently the popo are releasing some new files about Belden and of course people are talking about Columbine and Parkland, and what was the last one again?"

"I don't remember…"

We spoke for a little while before saying goodbye but the conversation hadn't done me much good. After a few hours of staring at the ceiling and imagining all sorts of things, I finally fell asleep and I had some exceptionally weird dreams of Jihoon Garcia being murdered by the twins and *me*. I woke up in a cold sweat and for a moment I was taken aback by fear because I wasn't used to my new room and it took a moment for reality to hit me. For once I was thankful that reality was on my side!

Since I couldn't fall asleep again I thought of calling the twins a second time but I didn't want to disturb them at four in the morning so I moved on to other things. I talked with myself, debated with myself, contemplated my own existence and the existence of practically everybody else but I still couldn't close my eyes. I tried counting sheep using fractions to wear out my mind and to motivate it to sleep but it did nothing but awaken it even more by forcing it to think. When it all came down to it, I wished I had a heart instead of a brain.

When the daylight finally arrived I looked like the Walking Dead, and believe me, I felt the same way too. Nobody else in the house looked like they'd had a particularly great night's sleep either. My parents were understandably stressed and I felt like a burden to them on top of everything. The two of them had worked hard for twenty years to give me a good life but it had been wiped out from under our feet one day and the blows hadn't stopped. Just like that, life can be gone forever in the blink of an eye. I was still alive, yes, but no matter how many times I told myself that I didn't feel as though I had *a* life. It was time something happened but I was worried about how my parents would react to the news I was going to tell them before I left for school. Well, not really, because I wasn't going back to school again. I had to tell them before I was *supposed* to leave for school, something like that.

"I have something to say…" I began once I had everyone's attention. "I'm not going to school anymore. I'm switching to correspondence."

To my surprise, my parents *weren't* surprised by the words that had just come out of my mouth. It seemed like they'd somehow seen it coming and they were both okay with it. They even encouraged me to take correspondence classes at a different school so I'd never have to deal with Belden again! I loved the idea and decided to call the twins to share the news. Svetlana also wanted to take correspondence while Vera was going to pursue her GED instead because she was convinced that she had no future outside of Wintercrest.

"Vera Petrov!" I told her sternly. "You have a bright future outside of this place! Do you know where all the people with no hearts and no brains are? They are all *here*."

The both of them giggled but Vera wasn't convinced. I could definitely understand, however, because most days I felt the same way. Going to college or university was just an abstract concept in my mind. I didn't see it as a reality.

"When I get enough money from selling all this junk in the house I'm going to Lavallette." Vera replied without emotion.

"I told you I wanted to go to Colorado!" Sveta grumbled in the background.

"Well, hey, it's not Wintercrest either way!"

"Damn right it isn't!"

Vera and I agreed to meet in town at a little pub just before lunch while Sveta took care of other things, like formally withdrawing from school instead of just not going. Since Hans was about to leave in his work truck to replace an absent coworker, I hitched a ride which he was more than happy to give me. I climbed into the big white Ford and rode shotgun like a boss. I told Hans why I wasn't in school when the question popped up and then I told him about the massacre as an explanation for everything because I knew he was wondering why someone like me wasn't going to school anymore.

That conversation ended quickly, but in the very back of my mind lingered Vera's words about a *mature* man. Hans and I were the only ones at an intersection near the downtown area when we hit a red light and I thought about leaning over and kissing him. He'd be taken aback again and would certainly be more confused than anything but the more I thought about it the more I wanted to do it. I fidgeted in my seat for the rest of the awkward trip, ultimately too afraid to screw up my relationship with my brand new neighbour right off the bat.

"Are you okay?" Hans asked me.

"Oh, yes, don't worry about me." I muttered.

Hans dropped me off and I walked into the pub and looked around for Vera. At first I didn't see her and her flamboyant hair but then I noticed somebody sitting at the back of the room that stood out from the rest of the patrons. Upon closer examination, it became apparent that it was her wearing a disguise as though she didn't want anybody to recognize her. Well, I just had. She wore a black wig under a SWAT baseball cap and clothes that weren't her typical attire. I walked across the dimly lit room and sat in front of her at the little brown table.

"What's going on with you?" I asked her.

"Kaye."

"Say no more!"

"When I left I swore she was following me so I went back home and sneaked out as someone else but you found me anyway."

"Well, I'm not gonna harass you so don't worry."

"Not worried."

"So, you taunting with that hat or what?"

"Nah, sorry about that Aly, it's one of the only hats I have and it's *not* meant as a pun or whatever because the real SWAT team didn't do anything at Belden. Oh, and congrats that you finally ditched!"

Finally ditched. *I should have done that a long time ago.* I felt better even though I didn't know where my life was going. That didn't matter, however, because I knew deep inside of myself that I'd made the right decision.

"I guess I ruined your bed for nothing," I continued, "because that essay about the commandant of Auschwitz is going straight to the garbage. But, I have another bed for the two of you, one that will be much more comfortable for you two to share."

"As much as I'd love to explain to you in great detail how unnecessary that is," Vera muttered through her teeth, "right now we need to get out of here."

She got up in a jiffy and grabbed me by the arm before barging out the door onto the street. She looked around for a while, either disoriented or making sure Kaye wasn't on her trail, prior to walking to the parking lot behind the pub where her truck was parked. The two of us got in and she removed her disguise before making the engine roar to life.

"Is everything okay?"

"Yeah, I'll be fine. First it was Kaye and then Murielle walked in. It's been a pretty bad morning to say the least."

"Who is Murielle? Or is it better I don't know?"

"Murielle used to live in the trailer park as well and she is the definition of insane. Probably more so than Kaye, but she'd left town some time ago."

"Oh?"

"Aly, that's too much for me to tell you right here right now but I can make my neighbours tell you."

"I think I'll pass on that one!"

Vera and I laughed even though it wasn't funny. Kaye gave me the creeps and harassed the twins, particularly Svetlana, constantly. That was no laughing matter even though Vera had a way to make everything funny.

"Earlier this year, not long after Murielle left town the weirdest thing happened to me!"

"Tell me."

"So, I was at the drug store using the photo kiosk when it gave me this message that there was no more paper. I told the clerk about it and she changed the roll of paper so I could have the rest of my pictures and do you know what was *inside* the picture machine?"

"What?"

"Naked pictures of Murielle! They had somehow fallen inside of the machine instead of going through the slot."

"Yuck! I bet that was nasty!"

"Yeah, I still get nightmares about that to this day, but the best part is that apparently she gave the rest of those pictures to the kid brother of this Steve guy that was killed at Belden."

"Oh my God! Theodore Hicks!"

I burst out laughing hysterically, I couldn't help myself. Poor guy. Vera drove back to the trailer park to fetch her sister and her uncle because we'd need all the manpower we could find to move my huge mattress in storage since I wasn't about to ask my parents for help and Hans was probably at work or doing something else. Dmitry was in the driver's seat, Sveta was in the middle, I was riding shotgun and Vera was sitting on the floor at my feet when we pulled up into the parking lot of my new apartment.

The four of us managed to get the queen mattress out of the storage container and onto the back of the truck without destroying anything. Half the mattress was sticking out over the side of the lime green truck but it was the best we could do. We drove back to the trailer park hoping and praying that we wouldn't get pulled over by the police, that birds wouldn't poop on the bed and that no other disasters would arise. Thankfully, we made it back to the trailer alright but our problems were just beginning.

The real challenge would be getting the giant mattress into the tiny room. The four of us unloaded it and shoved it through the door, knocking down a bunch of things along the way. With a bit of destruction the mattress made it inside but nobody knew if it would turn the corner and then make it into the bedroom. Picture frames fell and furniture tipped over but the mattress made it across the corner, however, it made it no further. Nobody had any energy left in them anyway.

"Lunch and then destruction," Dmitry muttered, trying to get his breath back, "I'm gonna have to tear down that wall."

An entire box of frozen pirogies and cheese puffs later, Dmitry and Vera took out axes and other tools and started going at it while Sveta and I collected everything that was in the room and moved it in preparation for my former bed's big entrance. Debris out of the way, we pushed the mattress in through the extra-wide door and let it flop on the floor. It took up nearly the entire room and left next to no space for the other furniture now that most of the wall was gone too. I didn't know if I felt better or worst about the situation since my puking episode.

Sveta pulled out a shower pole and shoved it in the enlarged doorway — it fit perfectly — and hung up a blanket so the two of them could have some privacy. The next task would be to fashion some elaborate shelving for the three remaining walls but the girls had a new bed. The girls and I shoved the bedroom door along with the debris onto the curb and let ourselves feel the satisfaction. To relax we then watched TV for a little while while Dmitry went to town and did whatever he had to do.

"This is going to sound a little weird," Sveta began, deep in thought, "but the trailer looks kinds weird without all the decorations."

"I know." I chuckled. "I felt that the moment I walked in. It was like the Petrov signature decor!"

"You're the only person that didn't go running for the hills when you saw that stuff but now it seems too normal."

"Well, ladies, if I had went running for the hills I would've fallen into a tar pond on the other side!"

We began laughing hysterically even though that was another thing that wasn't funny. I felt lighter inside in a way that I couldn't really explain. I was going to be okay. My life was going to be okay. I might've lost my house and by bed, retched on someone else's bed and destroyed a wall but I'd be just fine. For the first time in two years I took a breath and it didn't hurt. On some level I managed to rediscover that inner satisfaction again. Most of all though, I was relieved that I wouldn't be going back to Bergen-Belden.

"No more school…" I liked how that sentence rolled off my tongue.

"No more school, ever!" Vera exclaimed in response.

"No more box-headed teachers and students who prowl around the halls like their friends were never murdered there!"

"That chapter's over and I'm ready to leave Wintercrest forever. If only I could…"

"Now that you've sold most of this vintage stuff, are you still planning to go to Lavallette? Or Colorado? Canada? All three?"

"We're still arguing about what the destination's gonna be but damn right were going!"

If only I could leave Wintercrest forever too… Although I'd never been particularly fond of travelling I was definitely jealous of the twins. I was up for going anywhere and rediscovering life. Life that was outside of the four walls I'd built around myself. It wouldn't hurt me to take an axe and begin tearing down those walls too.

"Can I come to Lavallette too?" I asked on a whim.

"We were actually trying to come up with a scheme to get you to come with us!" Sveta exclaimed. "But considering the financial crisis your family is going through and all the stress you've been under it didn't seem like an appropriate thing to do."

"I know, and I appreciate your concern but I think I'm ready for this and heck, I can always try to get Hans to pay for it!"

"You just keep getting better and better every time Alyson!"

"And it's about time that I live up to Anderson's final wish for me."

"What?"

"Well, last night when I couldn't sleep I rummaged through my things and came across the last letter Anderson wrote to me, in which he wanted me to move on and be happy so badly once he was long gone out of my life."

"He wrote you a letter telling you that he'd die shooting up the school or what?!"

"No, well, indirectly. It didn't really go according to plan."

The twins looked at each other in disbelief and waited for me to continue. I wasn't sure I wanted to but at that point I owed them an explanation.

"The night before the shooting he called me and told me not to come to school the following morning because he didn't want me to witness it all, but he didn't exactly tell me that." I went on. "I didn't understand so I went to school anyway because I was worried about him and as it turned out, he wasn't there. He dropped off a note on my doorstep right before the massacre explaining to me what I was supposed to be seeing on the news."

"But you weren't watching the news…" Vera's voice was nothing but a soft whisper.

"No." I muttered on the verge of tears. "I was holding him in my arms when he took his last breath."

The twins were speechless and dumbfounded. They hadn't been expecting a revelation like that and I'd never told anybody that before, not even the investigators who interviewed me at length about what went on in the library. Not my parents, or the truckload of therapists I had seen over the years, or even Anderson himself in the multiple letters I had written to him since his death. That part of the event had been closed off in my psyche, never to be revisited again, but I hadn't forgotten. I hadn't forgotten the way he held my hand when he was gasping for air, still alive after shooting himself in the head, or the gaping wound and the warm blood on my skin, or how peaceful his face really looked when it was all over.

"I keep holding on to him but I can't bring him back to life!" I choked up through my tears, filled with shame and guilt.

The girls and I held each other and each sobbed uncontrollably in the living room as I recounted for the first time what had really gone on in the library when Jennifer and I were the only two left alive in there. Telling the twins about the massacre was probably the hardest thing I had ever done since surviving the actual thing but I knew it needed to be done. Through the grim details I told them about the good times I'd spent with Anderson and my state of denial somewhere in the middle, but I left out the part about Valentine's Day.

I kept on telling myself that the end never justified the means but even after all the wonderful times I'd shared with Anderson, it was always that last look on his face after he'd just taken his last breath that was etched in my mind. No matter what, that never left me. That was the one thing I could not get over. When my sea of tears dried out though, I felt much better. I felt as though part of the burden I carried had evaporated into thin air.

"Well, I guess that explains why Jennifer went AWOL, eh." Vera told her sister.

"What?" I asked, confused.

"You know, Jennifer's gotten really weird since you came back to school," Vera continued, "and she basically avoids us like we avoid Kaye now."

"I really haven't seen her or spoken to her at all these past few weeks either. I guess I know why now."

"Well, if presiding over Anderson's dead body in the library was the last experience the two of you shared, it's still very frontal in her mind."

"I never meant to hurt her."

"We know you didn't Aly, and what Anderson did isn't your fault either! You didn't do anything!"

"Why didn't I?! Maybe I could've prevented that! Maybe I could've made him see that there was a life after Belden!"

"Don't blame yourself for this! Isn't that what Anderson told you himself?"

He had, in fact, made it clear that it wasn't my fault. But that never stopped me from feeling guilty and having breakdowns exactly as I'd done in the Petrov family living room. I missed Jennifer so much. I missed Elaine so much. I missed Amanda so much. I missed Anderson so much. I missed myself so much.

"Let's stop dwelling over Anderson Massey and think about getting Hans to go on a date with you and then taking his money!" Sveta tried to encourage me while trying not to laugh.

I hugged both the girls and thanked them for listening to me, and apologized about the bed again. They didn't seem to be bothered that their room only had three walls instead of four, but I still felt bad because I was the fortunate one yet I'd also been the one complaining about my living situation. The three of us grabbed some snacks and then headed to my place in the Big Lemon once Dmitry arrived. Vera poked fun at her sister for not being able to drive but I didn't say anything because I couldn't drive either and I was too embarrassed to admit that.

Back at the apartment *he* was there. Jihoon Garcia. I just knew it was him from the vibes he was giving off even from across the parking lot. He was a short hispanic man with a stocky built, a bright yellow suit too tight for him and a haircut exactly like Rudolf Höss had in the photo on the cover of his book. His demeanour was mean, authoritative, and maybe even invasive. There was something about him that immediately repulsed me. Then it hit me in an instant. He reminded me of Mr. Pasquale! Jihoon's world seemed to have come crashing drown when he saw that the twins were with me. I knew that they didn't like him but the feeling appeared to the mutual.

Only my dad was home, playing on his laptop and looking truly bored out of his skull. I greeted my father but didn't really take the time to speak to him. I brought the girls into my room and we goofed off for a while and destroyed my wardrobe trying to find something else to wear since I'd gotten dirty in the wall destruction and mattress moving process. The three of us decided that it would be nice to go out for dinner to unwind but it fell on my shoulders to dig some decent clothes out before Hans came home from from work because we all knew what Vera would try to do. I might've had a little crush on him but I didn't want to go out with him. That was weird.

I ended up going with a pair of black pants, a white tank top and a green plaid blouse to look casual but presentable. We were only going to a little bistro but I still held on to my pride to some degree. The girls picked out some clothes from my closet for themselves after Sveta saw a white jacket that she wanted to wear and Vera fell in love with my brown boots. Vera looked cute with a shiny motorcycle chain for a necklace around her neck but Sveta was the envy of the party. She always looked elegant and beautiful in whatever outfit she picked out.

All dressed up, we didn't wait for Hans to get home, we went straight to the bistro by ourselves. Mercedes and Brad were also there having dinner with some of their friends and I thought of going over to sit with them but it was impolite since we weren't invited, so the girls and I sat on the other side of the room. Vera pointed out an elderly lady a few tables away and told me that it was Jihoon Garcia's mother. She paid no attention to us, and we paid no attention to her. I got a bagel and a smoothie while the girls ordered a whole box of donuts for themselves.

And then Kaye walked in.

She didn't just walk in to the restaurant at the same time we were eating there, she walked in to eat *with* us despite that she wasn't invited! The girls didn't appear to be shocked at all, almost like they knew it was going to happen, but they were visibly disappointed. I, on the other hand, was beside myself. Had she followed us to the bistro?! She seemed to have a reputation of inviting herself to places and into situations in which her nose didn't belong but I wasn't about to let it slide.

"What the hell is she doing?" I apprehensively whispered to the girls as Kaye pulled out a chair to sit at our table.

"I told you," Vera muttered, "she knows *everything*."

"But how?!"

"An alien implant from the weather control and the conspiracies from the industry beyond the tar ponds. That's how."

Kaye constantly had a big evil smile plastered across her face like it was funny to ruin somebody's dinner like that and to make matters worst, without even saying hello, the crazy woman started talking about the newly released Belden files! Before I could even open my mouth to tell her to shut up she went on a tirade about Anderson Massey, Eric Harris, Dylan Klebold, Kip Kinkel, Nikolas Cruz and whoever the hell else that apparently had something to do with Belden but realy didn't. It was always the same story, yet nobody ever thought about what all of those young men were really like as people. Nobody had ever bothered to look at their broken *hearts*, not just their disturbed *minds*.

"SHUT UP!!!" I screamed at the top of my lungs, much to my own surprise.

I stood up and banged my fists on the table as I yelled some more. Everybody in the bistro fell silent, a stereotypical pin drop could've been heard from across the street, then I slapped my smoothie and it splashed all over the floor before I walked out of the restaurant. The girls came running behind me and so did Kaye. I screamed some more until she left but I had a feeling that she wasn't very far away. I sat down on the sidewalk and took a deep breath, both ashamed and impressed by my outburst.

"Seriously?!" I demanded.

"Seriously." Sveta was on the verge of tears herself. "That's Kaye Roberts for you."

"I can't believe that she can just walk in here and start talking to me about the massacre!"

"And I mean, she's really stupid. I didn't know if I wanted to laugh or cry when she was saying that the massacre was the reason why Belden has the lowest graduation rate in the county."

Belden didn't have the best reputation around but definitely not the worst either. The statistics she quoted didn't give the whole story either because after the massacre the students who didn't want to return didn't have to, and it wouldn't count as a failure. Many of the students counted in the report hadn't been enrolled at Belden during the massacre either, so the shooting wasn't the reason they didn't graduate. They hadn't been there, they'd had nothing to be afraid of. The media had been all over that report for the longest time but it wasn't completely erroneous to say that a lot of dumb people went to that school.

"I might've been more understanding if Kaye had blamed stupidity for their failures."

"I hear you, that school was filled with idiots but they still managed to graduate."

"During my freshman year I had a class where the collective average was 36% so yeah, I'd call that stupidity."

"You cannot be serious!"

"Yeah, and my average was 84% which is a typical grade for me."

Belden High might've been filled with a thousand idiots but that did not justify murder. Sure, I hated some of those people, and that hatred hadn't really gone away, but I'd never wanted them dead. If they'd wanted to ruin Anderson's life, on the other hand, they'd gotten their wish tenfold.

"And what is it that all these students really died for?" I asked into the night sky. "Do we really even know?"

"What really makes me sad about the whole thing," Vera interjected, "is that nobody ever considered what it must've been like for Anderson to walk into school with a gun in hand to prove his point, and the fact that even after twenty people died, nothing has changed."

"Yeah," Sveta continued, "I can't imagine he came to that decision easily. Nobody grows up dreaming of shooting up a school. Something very painful undoubtedly happened for him to want to inflict that kind of pain on others."

"Anderson Massey is nothing but scum!" A stranger said as he walked by. "I have no sympathy for him."

"It's people like you that I have no sympathy for," I snapped back, "because it's people like you who make monsters like him!"

While I was at it, I decided to tell the girls about Valentine's Day. It was the last piece of the puzzle, if one could call it that. Our epic fail of an outing couldn't be ruined further so why not just come clean? I didn't see how it would help anything but I knew that I'd have to deal with my unresolved feelings at some point. One day I knew I'd have to acknowledge the guilt I carried, but also let go of it. I regretted so much not saying *I love you too Anderson.* I imagined a thousand different scenarios but it might not have changed anything. I might've only been the killer's girlfriend instead of just somebody who knew him.

"Forgive yourself Aly," Sveta's soft voice pierced through my thoughts, "and start giving yourself the love you wish you'd given him."

"We all see what you're trying to do there Aly, but it seems like you don't." Vera went on. "It's too late to give him the love he wanted, that he'd been hoping for. He's dead Aly, you can't go back and undo what's been done no matter what you do."

"I know that you're right," I muttered after a long moment of silence, "but it's much easier said that done."

"To the two of us, we're always right so you better get used to it my dear."

"And nobody expects you to just be okay overnight Aly, but you can't change what you don't acknowledge and the first step in doing that is accepting what is."

"I badly wished I would've loved him, even just for one night to save everybody, but it's kinda weird now that he's dead. Now it's like I've fallen in love with him and my love will make everything okay and one morning I'll wake up and none of this will be real."

"Look, if your brain needs to be in a relationship with Anderson for a while, that's fine, we each cope differently and I wish society would stop making up rules about love, but you need to put your foot down and not let yourself be victimized anymore. You were legitimately victimized by what happened but this here, this is learned helplessness."

The girls were right about always being right. My brain didn't seem to be as absorbent as it once had been but I could get used to being in good hands. Mercedes and Brad sat down on the sidewalk with us and asked if everything was fine. I assured them that all was well and they didn't press the issue. I had a feeling that they'd had their own encounters with Kaye in the past.

"I know it's not going to make you feel any better," Sveta picked up, "but what you're feeling now is the proof that you truly loved Anderson despite everything. Maybe not in the way he'd hoped, but the fact that it even went that far is proof that there was already a deep underlying love there to begin with. You didn't *not* love him enough Aly, you didn't fail him. You loved him as much as you could, and now you must give yourself that same love so you can begin healing. Part of you will always love him and part of you always should. Everybody here knows what it's like when love is removed from the equation."

That, we sure did.

"If you don't mind me asking, where do you get this clarity and compassion for a mass murder that you've never met?"

"Because I've walked more than a mile in his boots Aly. You might not believe it now but I used to be my own kind of monster."

"And is this the part where you convert me?"

"Nope. This is the part where I tell you that between all of us, you're the one who looks like you've never had any problems in your life."

"Stereotypes are bad!"

I started laughing because that stereotype had been in the media a thousand times. *This doesn't happen in communities like Wintercrest* and the hundreds of others who'd been subjected to the same kind of terror. It didn't matter how high you were, tragedy could strike anybody. Hindsight was always 20/20 as they said, and that was true for me. I'd missed the warning signs but your closest friends are the ones whom you most want to *not* be suspicious when something is wrong, right? I wasn't responsible for Belden. I only had to make that sink in. The conversation was interrupted by the twins' phone playing strange music.

"What's that?" I asked.

"Oh, that's my prayer alarm." Sveta responded, looking embarrassed. "Damn it, I didn't bring my mat. I didn't think we'd be out this long!"

"Well, let's get you home so you can sniff some water and put on your ghost costume." Vera retorted as she got up from the sidewalk.

The three of us got into the Big Lemon and Brad and Mercedes went their separate ways. I hadn't noticed how late it was but I didn't care. The police hadn't showed up at the bistro so nothing else mattered. Vera drove straight to my place and parked. We went inside, the girls gave me my clothes back and I thanked them for taking me out despite everything. Maybe, just maybe, I'd needed that. I only hoped that the girls wouldn't be harassed even more by Kaye because of me.

"I hope I didn't insult you when I — " I began but Sveta cut me off.

"Don't worry, you didn't." She reassured me. "It's happened to me *many* times in my life that people appear to approach me with genuine kindness and warmth only to try to shove Jesus down my throat and then never speak to me again when I refuse their advances to convert me. *Liberate* me, as they call it."

"I guess you should be heading home so you can pray, and put on your ghost costume."

"I might just keep it in the truck next time, and by the way, you became my hero when you screamed at Kaye in public."

I giggled thinking back to that. She'd deserved that, I was convinced of that, but I was the one who'd be the talk of the town in the morning. Since I didn't have to go to school, or anywhere else for that matter, I supposed I could just stay in with my dad and pretend nothing happened because if you ignore your problems long enough they should disappear. Or so I wished!

"You know, it's weird that now that my dad is home all day I'm not even interested in being with him but when he worked I would've killed just to spend an entire day with him like that." I blankly muttered, mostly to myself.

"And I think it's weird that we're so close to Canada yet we're so different." Vera contemplated out loud.

"I don't know much about Canada apart that they have rainbow money and French is really complicated."

"Here schools get locked down because kids with guns roam around the place but up in Canada schools get locked down because moose jump around the playground."

"Seriously, moose?!"

"Yeah, it was on the news the other day, a moose got stuck in a swing set and the school was locked down for hours until somebody could come over and free it."

"Damn, what I would give for the school to have been locked down because of a moose two years ago!"

"And you know, it's funny how a lot of Americans don't know that *moose* is spelled the same whether it's singular or plural. I'm Russian and I know this!"

"I know right? It's not *mooses*, and God forbid, *meese*."

The three of us laughed but looking at the time made us realize that it was time for the girls to head home. My parents and my brother could probably hear us giggling in their rooms and unlike us, they had lives to get back to in the morning.

"One last thing Aly?" Vera asked.

"Yeah?" I asked in return.

"Can I borrow some nice clothes for next weekend?" Her voice was unusually mousy and shy.

"Are you going somewhere next weekend?" Her sister pressed.

"Well," she admitted, "I guess this is the part where I tell you that Vladimir is flying in from Russia on a K-1 visa next weekend."

XVI

A TIME FOR EVERYTHING

In the few days following the shooting, as the full scope of the event was sinking into the minds of everyone in the community, twenty crosses were built in the small park across from the parking lot in front of the school. It was February so nobody was using the area for gardens and environmental projects anyway. Students in shop class had previously built six crosses for an Easter project with the nearby elementary school kids who would eventually transition to Belden High but they'd been repurposed. Turns out those six crosses had never made it to the elementary school, they ended up being erected in front of *my* school, bearing the names of six people that I knew.

KATY HENDERSON
ERIC WEST
ROGER SMITH
NATASHA BLACKBURN
DAVID HOBAN
COREY NICKELS

The fourteen other crosses had been built by a local carpenter that my dad had known well during his youth. I did not personally know the man, but I recognized his truck when he came by the school parking lot to unload the crosses the day after the first six had been erected. That little park across the parking lot and the street was the only place not blocked off by police tape on school grounds.

Windows and doors were boarded up and police officers along with the forensics unit and just about every other law enforcement branches except the army swarmed the place to the point of infestation. Greater swarms of students, mourners and reporters gathered around the crosses in the tiny park, making it impossible to have even a small, private moment of silent mourning.

ELAINE FRECHETTE
AMANDA ANDREWS
FRANCES MASON
STEVEN HICKS
TOBIN DAVIES
LYNNE TAYLOR
MICHAEL HAZEN
TREVOR BRADFORD
GARY LEWIS
ANNIE MICHELLE
DANIEL JONAS
DYLAN CARDWELL
KATHERINE PRICE

The thirteen new crosses stood right next to the six ones the students had made and it turned out that Roger Smith had made the cross bearing his own name. Further down the park, there was another cross, the twentieth cross. It was slightly smaller, made out of different wood and bore a name written in a different font but mourners gathered around it just as much as the nineteen other crosses.

ANDERSON MASSEY

Below the names hung a large colour photo of each person on their respective cross. All of them were smiling, and their cheerful faces were about the only uplifting thing about the whole scene. Their faces made the days less grim and seeing their smile almost made me forget just for a moment that neither one of them would ever see the light of day again. Anderson's smiling face was especially hard to look at because that wasn't what he looked like the last time I'd seen him. The rest of them, on the other hand, were exactly as I remembered them.

I hadn't seen them take their last breath or feel the warmth of their blood on my skin. My memories of them were pure, intact. Steven Hicks' constant smile and that ever-present gentle grin on Elaine's face, but even Anderson's smile appeared somber on the photo. That smile was in no way representative of the expression on his face during the last days of his life.

September 26th 2016

Dear Diary,

I hate this pitiful existence. I miss those days when Jason and I got as high as outer space. I never thought it would all slip away. They say that you don't know what you've got until it's gone but that's not true. You know exactly what you've got, you just never thought you'd lose it. My future has always been filled with so much uncertainty. Never know what's coming next. The scariest thing of all in life is probably the unknown. It's not life or death, joy or sorrow, or any other emotion or circumstance that can hit you when you least expect it, it's uncertainty, the unknown. They say that what you don't know can't hurt you but that's not true either.

There's a part of me that just wishes the loneliness would leave me alone but I don't want to be surrounded by these mindless and superficial crackpots. They are all beneath me. They don't feel, in fact I'm not sure they know how to or are even capable to. Pleasure is all they think about and nothing will ever get in the way of their pursuit of pleasure even if others have to pay the price for their fun.

There's nothing left for me to look forward to in this life because my superficial pursuit of pleasure and instant gratification is over. The hurt I can't handle overflows to a knife but even that doesn't help. I deserve to hurt. I am nothing and no one. No one will miss me when I'm done here. Nobody will ever care to remember me. Nobody will sympathize with me. Nobody will ever love me after it's all over. The world would have been a much better place if I had never been in it. Gotta go now, I have myself to deceive alone again with the razor blade.

-Anders

After the shooting of course people were asking themselves a million and one questions, a million and one that didn't seem to have a proper answer. Many found answers in their faith and their religion, some even going as far as saying that it was somehow God's will that Anderson killed twenty people to *further* some sort of sick abstract cause. And how would that be? Since apparently nineteen innocent children had gone to heaven but the killer was burning in hell! *God doesn't do stuff like that!*

What kind of God would do that? If there was such a thing as God Almighty somewhere out there, I didn't believe that a supreme being described as merciful and compassionate would do something like that. But why hadn't God stopped Anderson either?

Those answers were apparently in mountains of scripture according to some people. I'd never read the Torah, the Bible or the Koran because I never thought that I'd need to. I thought that my life was too good to be needing any of that and somewhere along that same path certain people like Anderson thought they weren't good enough and that if they'd only been better the world wouldn't've been so cruel to them. The worst part of it though, was that nineteen innocent people fell somewhere in between.

October 10th 2016

Dear Diary,

I don't know if I can go through with this. I'm not sure I want to. I know it's gonna hurt a lot of innocent people for absolutely no good reason but I don't see another way to keep going on like this. I keep on screaming but nobody can hear me and I don't want to hurt Aly. I just want her to get as far away from this as possible. I know she's going to be devastated but it won't be as bad if she's far away. If there's one reason I'm not gonna do this it's gonna be her. I just don't see any other way. Is there something for me out there?

I hate it how they all promise you the world when you're young but when you grow up and you actually get there, there isn't anything. There's just pain and sorrow and nothing! Nothing at all. Like I've worked this hard to survive all my life and there's no reward at the end of the line.

I feel so cheated by everyone. All these years that I tried so hard to make it but there's nothing to be made. Nothing to be gained. It's like some cosmic vacuum inside your soul, the world promises you everything but it rips it out from under your feet piece by piece until there's nothing left to lose. And then you die, you're buried and your forgotten. I've been invisible all my life, I don't want to die and have it just be the end.

I tried to be good, I tried to make a positive difference but I keep being shot down time after time after time! I'm going to make them all pay for what they've done. I don't care what it ends up like, I won't let them forget who I am! I'll make sure they remember my name.

-Anders

About a week after the shooting, the authorities had finished gathering evidence at the scene and they let students go back in the school to get their belongs left behind before the extensive repairs were to begin. Most of the community wanted the school to be torn down entirely but it wasn't up to them to decide, and the municipality of Wintercrest was not about to waste a perfectly good building by tearing it to the ground. In the pit of my mental void I wished that Anderson would have bombed the place and blown it right off the face of the earth just so the memories and the pain could have been wiped out completely along with it.

Frankly, it was offensive to think about normalcy but everybody was in some way. I sure wished that things could be normal again, whatever the word *normal* meant after a massacre. I wanted my old life back, but I knew I would never have it back. I would never have my friends back, parents would never have their children back and nobody would ever look at Wintercrest the same way again. On the other hand, some sick part of me *wanted* to hurt and to never forget but another part of me wished to forget and pretend it never happened too.

The last time I'd seen Elaine she had a terrified expression on her face, confused and afraid of the unknown. I hadn't gotten the chance to catch up with Amanda either and it had never occurred to me that moments could just slip on by like that. Then we all huddled under the desk, Anderson's boots walked towards us, and his life ended right in front of my eyes, his blood on my skin. Those images were engraved deep in my mind, never to be purged.

The police officers along with some social workers accompanied small groups of students at a time back into the school so we could pick up our backpacks and other personal items that had been left behind in the fury to get out of there. I knew it was bad, I had been there, but in the middle of the adrenaline and the confusion I hadn't paid much attention to my surroundings and I certainly hadn't been prepared for what I'd see inside the building upon my return.

Not only that, but it was probably too soon for my confused, angry and petrified mind to revisit that place after I'd seen so much blood and bullets flying all around me. The front doors of the school that had once been made of glass were boarded up. There was yellow tape everywhere in the lobby where glass had been shot out and there were bullet holes everywhere in the concrete walls. There were even some ceiling tiles that were shot out.

The main office had a door ravaged by bullets, I could not have possibly imagined what it looked like beyond those doors. In the hallway leading to the library there was blood splattered all over the walls but the floors had been cleaned up already. Almost all of the library windows had been shot out and were boarded up as well. Passed the library doors the carpet hadn't yet been removed and there were bloodstains everywhere. The bullet fragments that littered the place had already been picked up by the forensics team but bullet holes pierced the walls, the furniture and the rows and rows of books. I remembered all the gunfire echoing in my mind, shot after shot.

I walked over to the table I'd been hiding under while other students were collecting their belongings that hadn't been picked up by the authorities. There was a large pool of dried blood where Anderson's body had been. I walked around it and looked underneath the table just to see if there was still something of mine under there but there wasn't. There wasn't anything left of value in the library. Nearly all the books had either bullet holes through them or blood stains on them and the process of throwing them out had already begun. Even the lights had been shot out and not a whole lot remained of the ceiling.

Since I hadn't left anything in the library I went upstairs to the second floor to grab my things out of my locker. Most of the lockers were bullet-ridden as well. Windows shot out, lights shot out, debris everywhere. The blinds covering the windows were torn like shreds of paper and most of the classrooms were pulverized. I didn't go into the auditorium, but according to official reports it was the deadliest scene of the massacre. I couldn't possibly fathom that in my mind after the destruction I'd seen with my own eyes in the library and the hallway.

As soon as I got my stuff from my locker I asked one of the social workers to walk back outside with me where I left and didn't look back at the building. I walked through the crowd of people gathered around the memorial wanting to stop and spend another few moments with whatever was left of the friends I once had but I couldn't be in the middle of such a crowd so I just went home. I couldn't tolerate mourners shouting obscenities at law enforcement on top of the other tense emotions.

I too would've wanted to shout at law enforcement officials but I had no energy left to do such a thing. A million questions still lingered unanswered beyond why another boy brought his gun to school, like why it had taken law enforcement so long to enter the building. It wasn't 1999 anymore. All law enforcement agencies in the country had active shooter protocols which we all knew weren't waiting outside the building until everybody had died. Law enforcement refused to comment on the matter, saying it was under investigation, like everything else.

Interestingly, after the shooting most of the community didn't go hating on Anderson or his family. Most sensible people were supportive of them because they had lost a child too and it probably hurt them the most because they had to live with knowing that *their* son had taken the lives of all the children of these other mourning parents. As if it wasn't bad enough having to live without your one and only child, Anderson's parents had to live with his actions too.

They weren't allowed to go around and brag about how great their son who died at Belden was. I wasn't allowed to tell people who Anderson really was, or how some of the best times of my adolescence were spent with him. Anderson's cross was covered in flowers, teddy bears and sympathy notes just as much as all the other crosses at the makeshift memorial in the park despite everything. The hate only came later. Much, *much* later.

January 8th 2017

Dear Diary,

We live, and we die, but why? What is the purpose of waking up one morning just knowing that you're going to die at the end of the line? Being here right now and knowing that I'll be dead soon and long gone and forgotten makes life seem so trivial. But I might just be seeing it for what it really is for the first time in my life. Just the cold hard facts. No sugar coating pieces of crap. Existence is just a dream, an illusion we create for ourselves and to our lives to add meaning and purpose but what happens when the dream gets taken away? Where are you supposed to go when your dreams are out of reach?

God, I am so tired of dreams that never take flight! I just wish I could get out of here. Just wanna get out of here. But I never will, not alive, not in this life. The struggle alone is just too much. I never pictured my life like this. Once upon a time I had hopes and dreams and I made myself believe that I had a purpose but I'm not sure what that might be anymore.

Eternity is seemingly an endless waiting but I've been waiting long enough. There are no genies that come out of lamps or bottles of Jim Beam, there are no shooting stars to grant your wishes and make your dreams come true. There's reality and then there's perception and somewhere along the way I got caught up in between. So where do I go from here?

We live and we die just the same so what happens when my time here is up? I just know that wherever the hell I go, it'll be a place better than here. If I put my mind to this, there's no turning back. There's no turning back after this. My time here is up after this.

-Anders

During my last visit to the Belden memorial before the beginning of my near-complete seclusion to my house, I had caught a glimpse of Mr. and Mrs. Massey mourning by themselves near Anderson's cross in the morning before anyone else got there to do their snooping around business. The place had turned into a frenzy of superficial meaningless talk about irrelevant subjects instead of a place of mourning. There were so-called experts who went around selling books and newspapers that promised to give answers as to why such a thing could happen in a community like Wintercrest.

Then there were other people who used the shooting as a reason to try to further whatever message they were trying to get out there. This one pastor even had the audacity to come to my house and preach the gospel for my lost and wayward soul that had survived a school shooting. He rambled on about the need for salvation so I would go to heaven if Anderson Massey miraculously came back from the dead and outdid himself at killing kids.

My dad threw him out when he started going back and forth about how Satan had taken a hold of Anderson's soul and was responsible for his actions. What that pastor failed to mention was that God, whether a person really believed in a supreme being or not, loved Anderson as much as he loved me or anyone else. My throat tightened as I thought about love. What if I'd kept on kissing him that night? Would anything have turned out differently? I could only imagine hypothetical scenarios.

Had he, on the other hand, truly loved me the way he said he did he wouldn't have done that. You don't do that to people you love! What hurt the most was thinking that after everything we'd gone through together he decided to blow his brains out right in front of my face. But to be fair, he'd told me to not be there that day. No matter how many scenarios I ran through my brain I never managed to get the answer I was looking for. Then again, that might just have been the story of

Anderson's life. He searched for something he couldn't find because maybe it didn't exist.

One thing that really got under my skin was when people spoke about Anderson like he was nothing but a monster, a zombie or a robot programmed to kill. Nobody ever seemed to acknowledge that he was a person with feelings and emotions too. He didn't grow up wanting to be a mass-murderer and he didn't just decide that it would be fun to bring his gun to school after getting out of bed one morning.

Things had happened to him to make him that way, and that's what nobody wanted to talk about. I couldn't possibly fathom what it must have been like for him to hurt so much and to be so angry that he thought that bringing an arsenal of weapons to school was the only way to solve his problems.

His suffering didn't excuse his actions but had everything been okay within him he never would've gone down that road. A line was crossed in his mind and he came to believe that the only way to be empowered was by doing something that would permanently leave a mark on an entire nation and there was no better way to do that than go on a massacre. Even after the rampage, people's ideologies didn't change. What happened only seemed to reinforce the corrupt mindsets that had made such a tragedy possible in the first place.

February 15th 2017

Dear Diary,

I wonder if these mindless stupid idiots that walk around aimlessly like zombies pretending to have purpose all day are going to run a little faster once I blast the twelve gauge a couple of times. You jerks can't escape the choices you've made. How did it get to this? I don't know but it did and your time to pay for it has arrived. I'm so high on this that I'm never coming down! God, I can't wait to see the looks on their faces when I walk into school with a gun by my side. This is for ruining my life! Congrats, you've done it once and for all! Wishes do come true assholes.

Screw it if it's unforgivable, I never asked to be forgiven. What you did to me is what's UNFORGIVABLE! All I ever did was ask to be loved and accepted but no! I'm just not good enough for anyone. Not even good enough to be freaking loved! LOVED! The most basic human need is to be loved and accepted. I have to do this. There's no turning back now. There's nothing else left for me.

I got my hands on two guns yesterday and I went out in the field out a few miles passed Ridgeway and fired a few rounds to practice. This is going to be too easy. The slugs are gigantic but I kinda wonder what a buckshot would do. Probably wouldn't be lethal though it would do some wicked damage. You idiots should've seen it coming, you are all going to get what you DESERVE!

-Anders

"Hi Alyson." Mrs. Massey spoke in a tender voice at the memorial.

"Hi Mrs. Massey…" I replied not knowing what else to say.

"How are you doing? Are you holding up okay?"

"I don't really know."

"I understand."

"I just want you to know that I'm really sorry."

"Me too Aly, and I want you to know that Anderson loved you deeply."

"I know, he was always very sweet to me."

We hugged each other tightly and when Mr. Massey came back from a few more minutes of private mourning, he hugged me tightly too. I couldn't imagine life without your only child, knowing they'd taken the lives of other children. Mr. and Mrs. Massey had no other children for whom they needed to be strong. There was really nobody else left in their lives. All they'd had was Anderson and he was gone. After they left the memorial I also ended up alone there so I decided to do my own private mourning for the first and the last time, spending a few moments writing on each of the crosses.

I told Elaine and Amanda how much I loved them, how much I missed them. I also told them that I couldn't understand why Anderson would shoot them knowing that they were my closest friends. The investigators had already established that he shot at anything that moved but he had known exactly what the girls meant to me. It had never been a secret. He'd told me repeatedly that he'd never intended to hurt me, but deep inside maybe he wanted to. Maybe the false rape accusation wasn't the last straw. Maybe I'd been the last straw, and maybe he'd wanted to get back at me. If so, then killing Elaine and Amanda had been a good way to do just that.

As I went from cross to cross part of me began to feel guilty for still being alive when twenty people who had bright futures ahead of them weren't. Most of the time I wish I had died along with them so I didn't have to deal with the aftermath. By the time I'd reached Michael Hazen's cross near the middle the numbness had set in and I couldn't write anything more than my name with a heart on the wooden crosses already covered in messages of sympathy and affection. Once I made it to Anderson's cross at the very end I was a complete zombie.

I noticed for the first time that *Anders* and not Anderson was the name written in big bold letters on the cross. He'd insisted that people — everyone except me in fact — call him Anders, saying that he didn't like his name, but I'd never called him like that. It reminded me too much of Anders Behring Breivik and for the first time I wondered if maybe that had been the whole point all along. Had we missed an obvious warning sign? Or did he legitimately just didn't like his name? Was I just being paranoid? Or downright going crazy?

Finding words for Anderson was much harder since there were so many mixed emotions going through my mind. After an extended period of time standing in front of his cross like a zombie I broke down crying and flopped to the ground in the mud and the slush. Everything inside of me was blank. Finally, once my outburst of tears dried up, I got up and signed my name on Anderson's cross before leaving. My dad picked me up by the side of the road and took me home. I knew that he was worried about me but he knew better than to question me. He remained silent and that was the best thing he could've done.

Back at home everyone was awfully silent too. My little brother couldn't understand what was happening. We couldn't shelter him from the tragedy that had permeated every area of our lives but he wasn't old enough to understand. He couldn't understand why Big Anderson wasn't coming back. It pained me so deeply to see my brother going through that as soon as I got home so I just went up to my room, flopped onto my bed, buried my face in a pillow and cried. My life stopped completely after that.

The seasons came and went. The snowflakes fell like the ashes of another life, covering Wintercrest in memories of a life I no longer knew. The more time went on the less anything made sense. We were innocent. Or were we really? There came a time when I realized that we were all responsible one way or another. People often told me that it wasn't my fault, I wasn't responsible, I hadn't done anything. But why hadn't I? Why hadn't I done anything when I had the chance? All I was left with were endless contemplations without endings and whatever my imagination managed to make up during the few hours of sleep I did manage to get.

The sound of the rain on the roof allowed me to float into a peaceful sleep but it was interrupted when a loud pounding noise jolted me awake. Something — or someone — was tapping against my bedroom window. I was frightened since my room was on the second floor of the house, who in the world could have climbed all the way up there just to tap on my window? I looked through it in horror and saw that it was Anderson, completely soaked in rainwater and smiling at me from outside.

I got up immediately and opened the window for him to come in. A massive thunderstorm roared in the skies outside and the rain was pouring down like the ocean was falling from the sky. I let Anderson in and immediately closed back the window since everything was getting wet. Anderson was shaking and shivering since it was so cold out there so I made him strip off his wet clothes and wrapped him up in some extra blankets I had in my closet.

"What in the world are you doing here?" I asked him, dumbfounded and confused.

"Well, I was out late in town and I locked myself out of my car," he said, still shaking, "and it was closer to walk here than back home."

"You know you could've called me and I would have arranged something!"

"Good luck doing that when your phone and your keys are locked inside your car."

"I'm so sorry Anderson, come over here."

I held him against me under the covers to warm up his frigid body while his clothes dried over the heat register underneath the window. Our bodies were tangled up together under the blankets searching for heat, our faces pressed together and his wet hair dripping on me.

Our noses rubbed together as lightning strikes periodically illuminated my room and after a moment of hesitation he pressed his lips against mine. Anderson's kiss tasted like alcohol but it had a sweetness to it that I'd never previously experienced with any of the other boys I'd ever kissed in middle school. I kissed him back and I enjoyed every minute of it. Then my body flinched and a worried and shocked expression swept over Anderson's face. He looked into my eyes wondering what he'd done wrong.

"Are you alright? What's wrong?" Anderson asked me.

"I'm fine," I retorted, "I'm just really cold. *You* are really cold."

"I'm, I'm sorry—"

"Don't be sorry Anderson, you've done nothing wrong."

"Do you want me to stop?"

"No. We won't warm up if you stop."

The sun was shining through the window when I woke up next to Anderson the next morning. The wet clothes on the floor hadn't dried completely but that was about the last thing on my mind. Anderson's eyes seemed to sparkle as I thought that everything was going to be alright. Then I reached out to touch him, his beautiful face and his messy hair but my hand went right through him and I realized that it had been nothing more than a dream.

February 16th 2017

Dear diary,

Got my hands on some more weapons and attack is planned for tomorrow. Call the girl of my dreams and tell her to do a no show, finish gearing up and packing in the morning, leave early and pretend to be at school, show up midway through first period and destroy the place! Ah, maybe she can

212

be my soulmate in another life, one far away from here. We can live eternally in pure bliss just her and me and she can forget about this and I can forget about this too. Part of me just wishes I could make things right for her, just the two of us, but it's too late now. It's just too late. She doesn't love me, and even if she did, my life is ruined either way.

You have no idea how scared I am. My body shakes just thinking about it. I'm gonna be dead in less than a 24hrs and that's it after that. There's no more. The more I think about it the more awful everything gets around me. Ugh, I wish I could stop thinking, period. So when you idiot pigs find this journal DON'T BLAME HER. DON'T BLAME MY FRIENDS AND DON'T BLAME MY PARENTS. None of them were to blame! Blame those who ruined my life. Now gotta write an explanation for this or at least try. If I can just survive the next few hours I'll be dead and everything will be alright. Wherever the hell I go it will be better than here.

-Anders

After the shooting I swear I felt just like Anderson had in those last few days of his life. All of his hopes and dreams had been crushed somewhere along the way, and he had crushed mine with his actions. For a few minutes I understood how it must have been like for him, but then the pain and the confusion swallowed up whatever understanding I may have had at any given time. The pain came and went but it never really left. Somewhere in the back of my mind it was always there just ready to be triggered by something that seemed harmless, like the pain was some sort of evil entity feeding off my misery. If that was the case, then I was ready to surrender to it for good. I was done.

Dear Aly,

You've probably seen it on TV by now. If you haven't just turn it on and it'll be right there for ya. I guess I don't really know where I'm going with this letter, I just wanted to say that I'm sorry. I'm sorry that I couldn't say it to your face. I'm sorry that I couldn't look you in the eye one last time. I'm sorry for my actions and I'm sorry for whatever lies ahead for you because of them. Just know that none of this was your fault. NONE. Don't ever blame yourself for what I've done, there is nothing you could have done. Don't blame yourself for this because you knew nothing, and this has nothing to do with you. It is not about you or because of you. If there was one reason why I wanted to back out of this, it was you.

I know you'll be hurt but I ask that you don't hate me. Well actually it's okay if you do because I hate myself too. I'm sorry. It's gonna be okay Alyson. You're gonna be okay. Your life is going to be so much better without me in it. You might not believe it now as you're probably in shock at what you're seeing but you'll see with time that I'll be just a memory in the back of your mind. Belden will be long gone behind you and the memories of it will be too. So don't blame yourself, don't hate yourself, just go on with the wonderful life I know is ahead of you. That is my one final request from you, live a good life. Don't let me get in the way. I love you Alyson, and I'm so sorry more than words will ever be able to express. There was just no other way.

Like everyone else, you'll be asking yourself why. But don't ask yourself why. Ask THEM why. Ask them why they did what they did to me. That is, of course, assuming that they survive... WHY?! Why did they do that to me? I will never know why. I'll die not knowing why but it doesn't matter anymore. The blame is on them. No one but them.

There are no good answers and no justifications, I know that. I won't try to make excuses but I want you to know that all you ever did for me was positive and that I've always appreciated everything you've ever done for me. But there was no other way. People have treated me like a rat my whole life. They never gave me a chance, and now they're gonna pay. I'm not going to be able to live with myself after this so don't expect to ever see me again. I've had the most awful pitiful life I could have ever imagined. It wasn't no stupid life, it was nothing but an existence. A PITIFUL EXISTENCE.

Wherever the hell I go I know it's gonna be better than here. I know it's gonna be better than this life/existence. Don't worry about me. Don't cry for me. Just be happy and the wonderful person you've always been. I'm sorry for everything. I'm sorry that this letter doesn't say much and is of little value. I just wanted to let you know somehow because I couldn't tell you to your face because I'm just a coward and a bad person. I'm sorry to have put you through all of this. If you don't hate me you can go visit my mom and dad, there is a package for you under the stairs. They don't know it's there so you'll have to point it out but your name is on it. They'll give it to you no problem. I'm sorry about all this crap Aly. Time to die now.

Anderson

Jamila Mikhail

XVII

SLEEPING ANGELS

My cellphone rang and interrupted me reading a book I'd dug out of my closet. It was quite unusual for my cellphone to ring unless it was one of the twins so I didn't ignore it. Sure enough it was their number that popped up on the screen so I answered immediately.

"Alyson! You need to turn on the TV right now!" Svetlana's voice exclaimed urgently. "Put on channel 5, the news."

Without thinking any further, I raced into the living room where my dad was sitting on the sofa watching a movie and immediately tuned in to channel 5. My dad looked alarmed at my behaviour but what was truly alarming were the images that showed up on the screen. A news helicopter was broadcasting live footage of Belden High surrounded by police vehicles and ambulances. *You've probably seen it on TV by now. If you haven't just turn it on and it'll be right there for ya.* I immediately felt like being sick and falling to the floor but I was somewhat reassured by the words of the news anchors, who were also trying to make sense of the situation.

"Police report that no shots have been fired whatsoever and that thus far there's no evidence that any crime has occurred after a distressing call came through from the principal's office."

"That's right Marla, law enforcement believe that this is a mental health call but considering the nature of the information received this is standard police procedure. When I spoke to the sheriff moments ago he confirmed that Mr. Vincent Pasquale, principal of Belden High School since 2006 has been transported to a psychiatric facility following a mental breakdown at around noon today."

"Tony, did the sheriff say anything as to the nature of the breakdown? From the images we're seeing from the helicopter right now it seems as though the situation is extremely serious."

"Yes, in fact Sheriff Medina indicated that in the 911 call Mr. Pasquale reported seeing Anderson Massey's shadow on the wall, pointing a gun at him and indicating that he'd come back to finish what he started. Of course, Anderson Massey murdered 19 students before turning the gun on himself at Belden High School just a little under two years ago."

Mr. Pasquale wasn't just a jerk, he was a possessed jerk apparently. I burst out laughing hysterically even though nothing was funny about being locked up in an insane asylum. I hadn't hung up the phone so the girls could hear everything on the other end and seemed to be puzzled at my laughter since neither one spoke a single word. My dad put his hand on my shoulder but seemed to be equally confused. At the very least nobody else was shooting up Belden. Mental breakdowns seemed to be trivial in the face of mass murder.

"Aly?" Vera asked after I was done laughing, as though she was refraining from laughing herself.

"Yeah?"

"Is everything alright at your end?"

"Everything is fabulous here, I actually just got my driving permit this morning, what about you?"

"Oh, so now you can drive us to Las Vegas after Vladimir arrives!"

"You're eloping?"

"Well, I don't know yet. It depends how the ninety days go."

"In the meantime I guess I could drive you to the bistro for your bachelorette party! I really need to get out of this house."

"Well come here!"

"Can you just get Mercedes to pick me up? My dad actually needs to go out tonight so I won't have a vehicle."

"Sure thing."

Mercedes' Mercedes never sounded any better. New noises seemed to come out of it every time I rode in it. The car was good for the garbage but then again, I never had a clunker like that as the only way to get around town other than my own two feet. I might have gotten my driving permit but I still didn't own a car and while Wintercrest wasn't a very big place, it was spread out across what seemed like endless vacant land. It had a nice little downtown but the outskirts were a mixture of average-looking neighbourhoods and undeveloped plots of land. One could not get to where they were going without a vehicle.

"Tell the girls the fall cleanup started today." Mercedes muttered as she pulled up in front of the Petrov trailer.

"I'm sure that Kaye already told them." I retorted without emotion.

The two of us giggled a little bit before I handed her a few dollars for her taxi service and walked up to the door. It opened before I could knock and I walked in to a trailer that smelled like curry. The girls and their uncle had ordered takeout from an Indian restaurant and offered me a plate. I accepted and after we finished eating the girls just couldn't pass up the opportunity to rummage in the garbage so my bachelorette party would just have to wait. Wintercrest had two major garbage collecting events, one in the fall and one in the spring. People could put just about anything they wanted at the end of their driveways and the city would pick it up for free.

I'd never gone on a garbage run as they called it but what the heck, I had nothing to lose. Dmitry and Vera got in the Big Lemon while Svetlana and I jumped in with Mercedes who'd been lurking in the area, knowing full well that the Petrovs couldn't say no. As it turned out, picking up garbage was far more interesting than I could ever have imagined. It was incredible to see the kind of things people were ready to throw away without a second thought. Sveta and I awkwardly shoved two bicycles into the trunk of the Mercedes, one missing a wheel but Sveta insisted that her uncle could fix it.

On the other side of town Mercedes made me pick up two big bags of brand new shoes that were right there by the side of the road, ready to be thrown away into a landfill site. I dragged them onto the backseat with me and we drove off to another neighbourhood. It was beginning to get late and the sky was becoming dark but the girls had some flashlights and some newly installed headlights on the car to illuminate the endless treasures just waiting to be found. Sveta picked up multiple computers and bogus computer parts and shoved them all in the backseat with me to the point that I barely had any room to move back there.

The run was fun and I picked up a brand new purple purse for myself with *money* in it! It was just a few coins at the bottom, but it was still quite awesome to pick up a handbag out of the trash and have it have money in it! I put it on my lap and grinned to myself as the girls filled up the front of the car with more junk. When it got too dark to properly see what we were doing, even with the flashlights, we decided to call it quits and head back to the trailer park. That meant passing through a police barricade on the main road as they looked for drunk drivers.

I was somewhat embarrassed considering we were riding in a clunker full of junk but the girls seemed to be finding it amusing. A young officer checked us out when Mercedes stopped the car. Mercedes rolled down the window and the young cop stuck his head inside the vehicle as standard police procedure.

"Did you ladies have anything to drink tonight?" He asked Mercedes and Svetlana.

"Well, I had some Pepsi," Mercedes replied in a serious tone of voice, "and ice cubes, which is water."

The cop didn't look impressed.

"Did you have any *alcohol* to drink?" He pressed.

"No, I don't drink." Mercedes replied.

"Where are you headed tonight?" The cop probed on.

"No, I don't drink." Svetlana repeated Mercedes' statement even though that wasn't the answer to what the officer asked.

I started giggling in the backseat but the officer never seemed to notice that I was back there buried in between the junk.

"Where are you ladies headed tonight?" The police officer asked again.

"I don't know," Mercedes muttered, "we're just picking up garbage."

"Yeah!" Sveta exclaimed in annoyance. "We're picking up computers to see if we can watch some porn tonight!"

The officer's face turned so red that I thought his head was going to detonate. I burst out laughing like a madman in the backseat and the cop started flashing his light in my face. Nearly half his body was entered through the window of the car to look at me behind the junk. His neck was right in Mercedes' face and it was apparent that she wasn't very fond of that.

"No pigs in my car!" She said as she pushed him back out through the window.

Mercedes then sped off as the three of us laughed to the point that we could barely breathe. When we got to the trailer park Dmitry and Vera were unloading their massive load of junk so we were on our own to unload the car and let Mercedes go home. We brought the junk into the basement so we could better examine it since it was the only available space in the trailer. Most of the plants that had once been down there had been sold off for money so there was no shortage of space to sort out everything.

Most of the computers were junk, which was the reason they ended up in the trash in the first place, but some of them were indeed salvageable. Two of them had only been thrown out because they were too old it seemed but to Vera and Sveta an old computer was like winning a million dollars. We spent a good part of the evening playing a retro version of Spider Solitaire and having fun on the Windows 95. Back in the day it must have been a really nice machine but Windows 95s weren't exactly the *it* thing of 2018. And no, no pornography was found on any of the computers.

"I guess we're going to have to start our correspondence classes soon," I muttered, "or at least pretend to."

"Pasquale's in the nuthouse now so it ought to be safe to go back." Vera muttered in response.

"Y'all be my guests but I'm not going back." Sveta grumbled.

"I ain't either!" I affirmed.

The girls and I watched the late evening news but there were no further updates on what the hell had gone on at Belden for the principal to completely lose it but I had to accept the fact that I might never know. After that I couldn't sleep and I didn't wanna go back to my place so I asked the girls if they wanted to go to the bistro for that bachelorette party after all. It was still open for another hour and a half or so. That was enough time to have some lighthearted fun.

"I'm not sure if I'm up for going back to town at this hour," Sveta replied, "but the two of you can go right ahead."

"How about we go watch the midnight train?" Vera proposed instead. "It's not far and we could watch the stars. I think I'm all funned out for tonight."

"You? All funned out?" I laughed. "But I'd sure like to see the train and watch the stars."

Sveta dug out some old baggy clothes to wear for the hike so we could stay warm and not get dirty while Vera packed flashlights, blankets, snacks and other little things into a duffel bag for our little outing. The girls and I then creeped out of the kitchen window since the front door was way too noisy and we didn't want to wake up Dmitry, if he was actually sleeping in the first place.

Outside, the late October air was cool but not too chilly, just right for a midnight hike. We each took our turn carrying the duffel bag since it was heavy and when my turn came I fell behind the girls who were much more accustomed to hiking up the hill behind their trailer than I was. I was about halfway up the mountain when I slipped in the mud and went tumbling back down noisily all the way to the bottom and eventually crashed into a bunch of metal trashcans near a trailer right at the edge of the hill. The lights of the trailer came on and I saw the girls quickly running up the rest of the way and hiding down on the other side.

"The bears must be in the garbage again!" Somebody shouted out from inside the trailer whose trash I'd landed in.

I stayed crouched behind the trash bins not to be seen by the tenants. I was uninjured but a little banged up and dizzy from a wicked tumble. I could imagine the girls laughing their heads off up on the hill at my fall and I began to giggle too at the thought of it. I did my best to be quiet until the lights of the trailer went out again. Then I tried to get away as fast and as quietly as I could and started climbing up the hill again.

I went at it a little slower and periodically looked over my shoulder just in case there weren't any actual bears in the area or people pointing guns at me thinking I was a bear. The girls helped me up once I got to the top of the hill but they weren't laughing. I promised them that I was fine, that I was unharmed and that I was ready to continue but they both insisted that I should no longer get my turn with the duffel bag because it was *too dangerous*.

Safely on the other side of the hill, far away from all civilization we took out the flashlights so we could actually see where we were going. The tar ponds were gigantic, a lot bigger than I'd originally thought they were. They probably only seemed bigger because I had to hike around them in the middle of the night and the hike was an exhausting one too. It took about half an hour before we heard the train coming in the distance. The girls decided that it was the perfect place to camp out to watch the train and later the stars.

The three of us sat on the blankets and huddled together for warmth. On top of the toxic hill the wind was chillier but the night sky was breathtaking. I looked around me only to find that we were incredibly far away from everything and there was only the moonlight and our flashlights illuminating our surroundings. On one side of the hill there were multiple toxic ponds of gunk and nothing but a railroad, and on the other some trees and the distance the interstate leading away from where we were. The darkness around me enveloped me and comforted me.

It was something truly spectacular to watch the midnight train from the top of the toxic hill. Only the sound of screeching steel and old boxcars pierced through the night with the humming of the locomotive engine in the backdrop. The stars shined bright in the midnight sky over the railroad making it for a spectacular night. The twins and I sat side by side over the hill and watched the train until the very last car was out of our sight. It had been nothing short of a beautiful experience. My soul had been lifted and my heart rejuvenated.

"You really picked a good night not to sleep!" Vera teased me.

"Sleeping is useless," I muttered, "we spend so much time sleeping and so little time living. Vera, I want to live again. Plus, the trailer park is very noisy anyway."

"Well," Sveta continued, "I hope you enjoy the nightlife because this night is far from over! Now that y'all dragged me out of the house I don't want to go back!"

After a while of talking, laughing and contemplating the universe under the stars we decided to keep going and hopefully warm up along the way. We hiked along the top of the toxic hill since there was no longer anything but gunk and trees surrounding us until we arrived to a mostly destroyed factory or power plant of some sort. Nothing but the wreckage was left on the lot much to Vera's disappointment. There were no such things as aliens, clones or weather control much to my own displeasure as well.

"Well, this sucks." Sveta grumbled.

"You got that right!" Vera added.

"Look over there!" I shouted anxiously. "Alien spacecraft coming our way!"

The girls cracked up laughing and went running into the remnants of the structure. I ran behind them making alien spaceship noises and laughing uncontrollably afterwards. The three of us ran around the abandoned building only to find that were was no more roof and the moonlight illuminated the rusted structure, giving it an eerie alien glow. Only the sound of three pairs of stomping feet could be heard, making the old metal resonate throughout the night. Some pieces of the floor were missing on some levels of the mostly destroyed building and my leg went through a couple of times but thankfully I didn't fall to my death in the basement.

I was having too much fun to think about health and safety hazards, me who was usually a very cautious person. The place was probably blocked off because the environment was contaminated irrespective of the remnants of the building, but for the moment that didn't matter. Once we were out of breath after an extended game of alien tag we laid out the blankets and slouched down on the rusted metal floor. We had some snacks and some drinks before laying down and looking at the stars. The entire galaxy lit up before my eyes, reminding me of how small I really was.

"Look at that one there," Vera said as she pointed to the right side of the sky, "the stars form what looks like an angel."

"A constellation of angels." I muttered in contemplation. "Do you really think they are among us?"

"Absolutely." Sveta answered authoritatively. "Some you see, and some you don't."

"And what about the kids from Belden? Are they out there too?"

"They are right here Aly. They can see us, hear us. It seems to us like they are long gone to somewhere unattainable but I promise you that they're right here."

Along with the cold air an inner sense of peace came over me. I closed my eyes and for a moment I felt like I was floating. I finally understood what people of all faiths had been talking about when they spoke of God's grandness and power. The universe, with all of its flaws and disasters, was so beautifully and intricately crafted. I couldn't believe that it was just an accident or a chemical reaction to something random and spontaneous. It was much too grand for that, but I was much too small to understand.

"What time is it now?" I asked after many long moments of private contemplation.

"Oh, time for Svetlana to pray for me to pee!" Vera exclaimed as she got up.

"Almost five in the morning. Wanna go back to town?"

"Yeah, it would be kinda funny to show up at my place right before Hans leaves for work. He'd be so weirded out."

"I like the new you Aly. Whatever change happened inside of you did you good."

XVIII

WHEN SHADOWS FADE

Vera came back from her bathroom break with some news that she could see lights in the distance further down the hill. It seemed as though it would be quicker to walk there, whatever was actually down there, than hike back to the trailer park. By that point I could feel sleep fighting to consume me but I did not regret for a moment my little outing. We couldn't waste any time because if Dmitry woke up and discovered that the girls were nowhere to be found we'd have a big problem on our hands.

As we reached the other side of the patch of trees I could see several work trailers with their lights on in a clearing and several trucks arriving on a dirt road beyond the trees. As we got closer I noticed a sign that read *Red Deer Environmental Cleanup* and workers had just begun showing up for the six o'clock shift. The only option left at that point was to walk up to the front door and hope that one of the twins was more creative than me and could make up a story on the spot to explain everything.

"I guess you won't have to weird out Hans outside his apartment," Sveta giggled, "you can totally creep him out right outside his workplace!"

We loitered around the parking lot for a while until we saw Hans' truck arrive. We darted across the lot and waited for him by the front door of the building so he absolutely couldn't miss seeing us. Vera and I leaned against the building while Sveta sat on the duffel bag when Hans came walking towards us. Mixed emotions swept across his face, shock, fear, horror, confusion but in the middle of that, delight. We probably all looked like zombies but Hans managed to smile joyfully at us anyway.

"What are you ladies doing here?" He asked in a cautious, confused voice. "How did you get passed the security checkpoint?"

The security checkpoint? The girls and I tried our best to resist the urge to burst out laughing as we looked at each other, wondering how to respond. I didn't even know myself what in the world I was doing there so I didn't say anything. Our little escape out to his job site had definitely stopped him in his tracks.

"We were out garbage picking." Sveta retorted, dismissing the question. "You find the best stuff during the fall cleanup."

Hans looked confused but didn't make any further comments or ask any other questions on the subject. I hadn't expected him to actually accept that answer, not that I thought he actually believed it, but I had no choice but to hold out hope that he wouldn't tell my parents about my little adventure.

"Do you want a ride home?" Hans asked.

"Yes please," I replied, "I'm exhausted."

The girls and I climbed into Hans' work truck and he went speeding down the dirt road, passed *two* security checkpoints and onto the interstate. I was riding shotgun while the twins sat in the backseat with the duffel bag. The truck was dirty and muddy even on the inside but I didn't mind since I wasn't exactly clean either after my night of exploring. Nobody spoke a work during the drive all the way back to my apartment. Hans looked angry since his face was tense and he drove unusually fast but he didn't say anything.

I somewhat felt bad that he'd have to come into work late because he had to drive us back to my place but above all, I was extremely grateful that he did so. I didn't know what would have become of us if we hadn't stumbled upon him or the company headquarters. The three of us thanked him from the bottom of our hearts before getting out, and then bursting out in laughter to the point where I was on the ground holding my stomach once he drove off. Once we composed ourselves we took off our baggy clothes only to reveal that our clothes underneath were dirty too. We shoved everything into the duffel bag and I unlocked the door to my apartment.

My folks had just gotten up and were getting ready for breakfast. Anderson and my parents pretty much had the same expression Hans did upon stumbling upon us at work earlier. The three of us greeted my parents on the way to the living room where I flopped down on the sofa and passed out almost instantaneously right then and there. I awoke sometime in the afternoon still slouched in exactly the same position with aches and pains from my prior fall down the toxic hill. My body was paying the price, but it had all been worth it.

Both the twins were already awake next to me on the couch and the lazy chair, drinking water. My dad was sitting nearby at the kitchen table, looking into the living room. He didn't look too happy with us but I was eighteen, almost nineteen years old, he couldn't do anything. My head was sore but thankfully not pounding like a bomb about to blow as I sat up and slouched over the armrest.

"Looks like the three of you had a wild night," my dad muttered in a neutral tone of voice, "what did you do for the bachelorette party?"

"Actually, it hasn't happened yet." I responded, only half-awake.

Both my dad and I looked over at the twins, expecting one of them to say something. I wasn't accustomed to lying to my parents and wasn't nearly as creative as they were.

"That was just a little warm up," Vera jumped in like she always did, "I have some guests coming from out of town for the real thing."

"Yeah," Svetlana continued, "we just wanted to have fun just the three of us before the big night."

My dad didn't make too much of a big deal out of it after all. He trusted me and he trusted my judgment. He knew Dmitry Petrov very well and he trusted that he took care of me when I was over there with the girls. When my father left the room the girls and I had to refrain from laughing again.

"You're so lucky to have him as your dad," Vera whispered to me, "my uncle Dmitry is going to kill me if he finds this out."

I silently prayed that nobody would ask Dmitry to corroborate any of the lies we'd told but just like a bad scene out of a cheesy movie, the phone rang as soon as I thought about that and I had a gut feeling that it was him calling.

"Yes, they're here." My dad confirmed my suspicions.

He handed the phone over to Sveta who apprehensively pressed it against her ear, bracing for the worst.

"*Allo.*" She spoke cautiously.

Dmitry grumbled something in Russian but he didn't seem to be angry.

"*Kak?*" She went on. "*Kogda?*"

Dmitry muttered something else much to Sveta's dismay because a horrified expression swept across her face.

"Da," she continued in a distressed tone of voice, *"spaciba. Ya tebya tozhe, paka."*

Everyone looked at her, waiting for herto say something.

"Brad's dead."

I was taken aback more than words could describe when I heard those two little words come out of her mouth. My relief at not being asked about my outing was short-lived because that phone call was even worst.

"He overdosed sometime early this morning," Sveta continued blandly, "they're treating it as suspicious considering the circumstances."

"If there's anything we can do for you and your uncle please let us know," my dad told her, "I'll get you some more water."

The news of Brad's death had a strange effect on me. It struck something deep inside of me that I had buried and hoped that nobody would ever dig up again. It rubbed me the wrong way and reminded me that I owed Mr. and Mrs. Massey a visit. I had only visited them two or three times after the shooting and had subsequently cut all contact with them. As much as I still loved them deep inside my heart, it was easier and probably better for everyone to not get together.

I'd felt guilty for a long time for cutting them out but I'd kept on making myself believe that it was better that way. Back then I'd stopped living, but things had changed since then. After Brad's death I felt like I owed it to them to visit them. The following day, once I'd gotten the opportunity to sleep well and clean myself up properly I called Anderson's parents and asked them if I could stop by sometime and asked them if it was okay if I brought the twins with me, for moral support. They were overjoyed and requested that I show up at their door as soon as possible.

Later that afternoon the girls and I showed up at Mr. and Mrs, Massey's for some coffee and a chat. Anderson's parents looked exactly like they had the last time I'd seen them, almost two years prior. The house had been renovated since the last time I'd went in there though, and there were few traces that a disorganized teenage boy had once lived there. The first thing I noticed was the beautiful stone fireplace that was adorned with family photos, mementos and the green marble urn holding Anderson's ashes.

Bittersweet memories came flooding over me as I sat on the large leather couch facing the window adjacent to the fireplace. I'd spent many afternoons in that living room. Not only that, but it awfully reminded me of my old house. I didn't feel sad though. In fact, I felt glad. I felt relief. Mr. and Mrs. Massey had a beautiful house but they'd lost their son, I had a nice family but lived in what wasn't the greatest apartment ever. It was erroneous to compare my life to others but I knew deep down inside that I was one of the lucky ones.

I sat in between the twins and looked around the room. Sveta wore a shiny berry-coloured headscarf that sparkled in the sunlight. She was distracted because she was obviously thinking about Brad's funeral later in the evening. I'd decided not to attend but I'd still agreed to drive them to the chapel immediately after our visit. Mr. Massey handed each of us a cup of boiling hot coffee in a fancy brown mug before he sat down next to us. Neither of the twins drank their coffee but I gulped down my cup very quickly because my throat was so dry. It burned as it went down but still made me feel better.

"Thank you for letting the three of us come over today." I spoke softly, hoping my voice wouldn't crack.

"You know that you can always come here whenever you want," Mrs. Massey replied in a gentle voice, "you were basically like our daughter when Anderson was alive."

I only seemed to be able to ramble on about a million different things except the real reason why I had come back to visit Mr. and Mrs. Massey after two years. How are you supposed to talk about death to a family whose son died? It didn't seem right to me. Not after everything. Both the twins remained unusually silent throughout the whole thing like their tongues had been cut right out of their mouth. Unfortunately, I couldn't look to them to do the talking for me like I usually did.

"My friend Brad recently passed away," I finally blurted out after a while, "and, well, I couldn't help but think about the two of you. I really didn't know Brad very well but it did something unexplainable to me when I heard the news that he was gone."

"I understand," Mrs. Massey spoke softly as she tried hard to hold back tears, "did you know him too, Vera, Svetlana?"

"Yeah, we were pretty close..." Vera spoke for the first time as she looked into her cup of coffee like it was the most interesting thing on earth.

She didn't say anything else after that. I explained to Mr. and Mrs. Massey why I hadn't visited them in forever and they reassured me that they understood and that they'd never felt any anger or disappointment towards me. They made sure to tell me many times that they loved having me around and that I was a great source of comfort for them. After the crying and the hugging and the sorrow was over, we shared laughs as we reminisced about old times.

I felt way too young to reminisce about what was commonly referred to as *the good old days* but then again, they were all over never to return again. The afternoon sunshine came in at an angle through the living room window so it would shine directly onto Anderson's urn on the fireplace mantle. Guilt struck me as I looked on blankly. Guilt that I'd failed him. Guilt that I'd failed the rest of them. I knew that it wasn't my fault, but I couldn't help it. Twenty people should've still been alive.

"We're both very glad to have you around Alyson," Mr. Massey told me, "you know, we can't talk about Anderson to just anyone. To most people he's nothing more than a child killer."

And I felt his pain. I couldn't talk about Anderson to just anybody either because they simply didn't understand. Many people were sympathetic, particularly if they'd been bullied or had felt the wrath of Belden's elite, but neither one of them had known him like I had. They'd never known Anderson the person, Anderson the dude you could always count on, Anderson the guy who always had your back. And those who had nothing but hatred for him didn't understand that it was precisely that kind of attitude and mentality that led to his downfall in the first place.

"If there's one thing I've learned through this grief and this pain it's that I can't force myself to hate Anderson because of the way his life ended or because it's taboo to do otherwise," I replied, "because I don't. There was enough hate going around when he was alive without me continuing to hate now that he's dead."

Everyone looked at me expectantly but I wasn't sure if I could say more. I didn't even know what I wanted to say.

"If my parents or my little brother went to prison for murder I wouldn't love them any less, so why should it be different when it comes to my best friend? Yeah, you bet I'm angry and hurt and everything else that goes with the aftermath of a tragedy but that's not how I choose to remember him. I don't think anybody should. After all, the first year there was a cross built for him too, and people covered it in flowers and messages of sympathy just as much as the other ones."

I grabbed Sveta's cup of coffee and gulped it down like a pig because I felt my throat becoming dry and tight again. It was cold and not very good but it made me feel better. I also knew that Svetlana didn't want to drink it anyway.

"And I chose to remember Michael Hazen for the great athlete he was, and for his great taste in fashion. Not for the clique he belonged to and the awful way they treated others. Not for his behaviour after the party. Not for his last words to me."

A deafening silence fell over the room but that had needed to come out. If the entire German population was guilty of Nazi war crimes then the entire Belden student body was guilty of murdering twenty students. There weren't isolated incidents that went unnoticed in those halls. The school administration wasn't blind to what was going on. The only person who'd chosen to do something about it had been Anderson. Had anyone else lifted a finger for him, for Lil Amelia, and for the other individuals who'd been reduced to a mere statistic, there might not've been twenty crosses in the park after Valentine's Day.

"It's time that the entire social construct at school changes because their hatred and bigotry for guys like Anderson are precisely what led him to walk down that road," I continued aimlessly as I looked up at the clock on the wall, "and oh my God! We're going to miss Brad's funeral!"

I promised Mr. and Mrs. Massey that I'd be back as I bolted out the door like a leaping llama on meth and by the time the three of us made it to the car I'd decided that I was going to attend Brad's funeral after all.

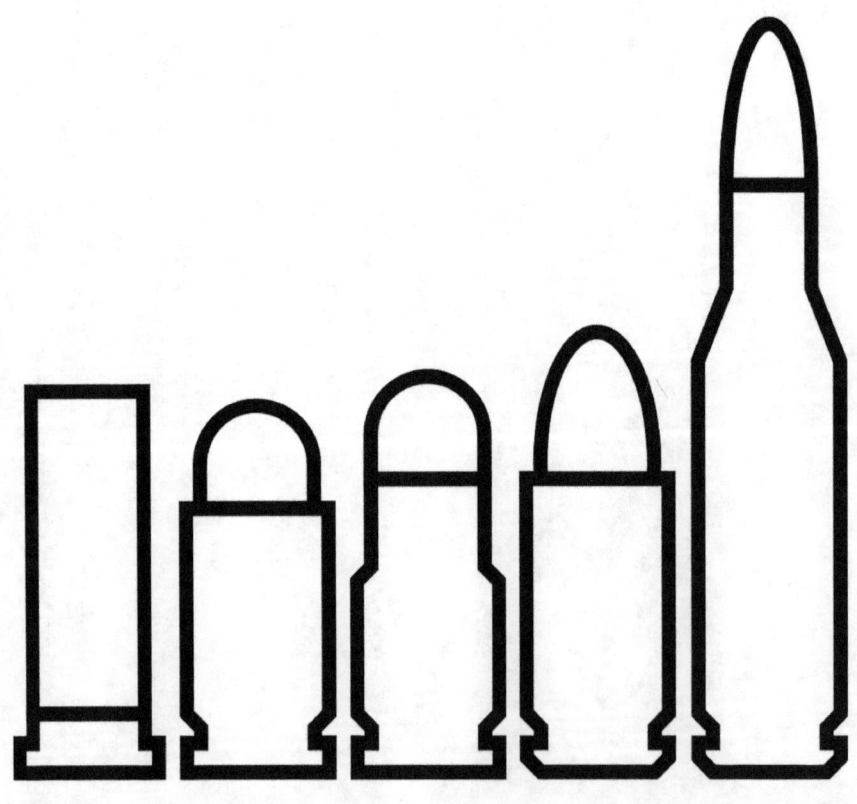

XIX

IN GOD'S HANDS

Goodbyes were only for those who loved with their eyes, because there was no such thing as separation for those who loved with their hearts. At least that was what Jalāl ad-Dīn Muhammad Rūmī wrote, and what Svetlana Petrov believed. I admired that kind of belief and devotion, and the inner peace that accompanied it. For me goodbyes were still too permanent and there certainly wasn't anything good about them.

Dear Anderson,

What is it like out there, wherever you are now? Have you been released of your pain, or do you still carry it around? Is there really serenity in death? Because it's been nothing but the opposite for those of us left behind. It was Brad's funeral today and the coroner ended up ruling it an accidental overdose, but it didn't hurt any less. Sveta read a beautiful eulogy and a beautiful poem for the occasion. She's been teaching me a lot of things and I always find comfort in her words but I don't have the rock solid faith that she does. I haven't been able to find that one thing to believe in and hold on to since you left me out in the cold.

I sound a lot like you right now, don't I? Whatever I used to believe or understand about life and death, I don't anymore. But I guess sometimes it's like what Mercedes said, sometimes there isn't a straight or logical explanation for what happens. The world just wants to say a great big hello in some evil wicked way. Whether I try to find the reasons why or I don't it doesn't seem to make a difference. It's not like you can help me anyway. You're dead. Gosh, sometimes I wish you could still he here to tell me everything to my face.

What I can tell you, however, is that these invisible atoms all around us aren't empty and devoid of potency. They are active and powerful. They are mighty and they interact with us. What we're looking for is also looking for us. Have you found what you're looking for in death? You should be here. Nineteen other people should also be here. I'm sorry that this world has failed you, and I hope that one day you can forgive me for not doing more.

Aly

The day following the funeral and the day before Vladimir was set to arrive on his K-1 fiancé visa — the two of them deciding not to participate in the show — I decided that it was time for me to take Vera out for a real teenager-appropriate bachelorette party. I'd gotten Dmitry's blessing to take the girls out to the state's capital for a night of going out to the movies, the arcade and a list of shopping destinations and tourist attractions. Following Brad's funeral Vera had come clean to him about her fiance and although he'd been furious, his anger had dissipated quickly. Deep inside he was probably looking forward to having someone to spend the days with since the girls were rarely at home.

My mother had given me permission to borrow the car for the trip so the girls and I filled up the trunk with our luggage and made sure that Vera had plenty of snacks and other stuff to be entertained during the two hours it would take to get to Concord. Sveta rode shotgun while I drove, still not entirely accustomed to the experience of being behind the wheel. Nonetheless, it was beautiful to see nothing but the headlights of the other cars coming from the opposite direction on the road. I was taking the trip for myself as much as I was doing it for Vera. I knew it would do me good to get out of Wintercrest, even just for a night.

"So, what would the two of you like to listen to?" I asked the girls.

"John Denver!" Sveta replied even before I was done speaking.

"No!" Vera grumbled. "You listen to him 24/7 at home! This is my bachelorette party, I want to listen to Slipknot for once!"

"Too bad for you because I'm the one riding shotgun!"

"This is the only time I swear I hate you!"

I flipped through the radio station in the meantime and eventually ended up on one playing U2's cover of Johnny Cash's *Don't Take Your Guns To Town*. Sveta changed it immediately and tuned in to one of the region's French stations instead.

"Somebody needs to rewrite that song and call it *Don't Take Your Guns To School*. It would be more appropriate for today's reality." I grumbled.

"You're not wrong about that." Sveta muttered in response.

"Y'all are being too serious on what's supposed to be a fun day!" Vera protested.

"You don't take anything seriously enough!" Sveta snapped back.

The two bickered back and forth in Russian for a while as I drove, following the instructions on the GPS I had borrowed from Mercedes for the adventure. In a way it was weird to be riding in a car that didn't make scary noises at every turn. As I drove on the sky grew progressively darker as my worries became farther and farther behind me. The present moment seemed surreal, like I was living someone else's life, driving into another world. Unfortunately for me, the realm of my daydreams didn't turn the road into a straight line and make the traffic signs disappear!

"Roundabout! Roundabout!" Sveta shouted. "Aly! There's a roundabout!"

I'd only encountered one of those roadway time warps circling round and round like water going down the drain once in my life before and I was thankful that there were no cops around because I probably would've had my driving permit revoked on the spot! First I didn't stop for any of the other cars — they were the ones who thankfully stopped for me — and then I took the wrong exit without using any turn signals.

"Recalculating…" The lady trapped inside the GPS spoke robotically. "Make a U-turn."

The girls wouldn't stop laughing and eventually I started laughing too. I ended up having to pull over on the road's nice freshly-paved shoulder because I wasn't about to attempt a U-turn after completely blowing a roundabout. One of the girls would have to drive or Concord would just have to wait.

"And they say that roundabouts are supposed to make our roads safer!" Sveta choked up through her laughter, running out of air because she was laughing so much.

"Look's like Concord's a failure," I muttered as I fidgeted with the GPS, "but according to this thing the city of Inverness is right up ahead. We can be there in half an hour and still go to the movies and whatnot."

"Fine by us!" Vera and Sveta both said in unison.

And off to Inverness we went.

We began by renting a hotel room for the night and unloading our luggage into the little room. Our quaint little motel was by the river so the three of us decided to take an evening stroll along the boardwalk to decompress from the last few days. The very first person we encountered during our walk was a drunk man who introduced himself as James Stewart. He was drunk so nobody really knew if *actual* name was James Stewart or if he only *thought* his name was James Stewart, but he rambled on about someone named Brad Stewart.

James was an older man with no particular features, perhaps except the stench of alcohol. He had on a plaid shirt and some jeans, everything was average. In between his incoherent rambles he took my hand and kissed it before giving me a hug like I was an old friend he hadn't seen in twenty years. He then proceeded to do the same thing with the girls before going off about more incoherent things, one of them being Brad Stewart. The man made no sense so neither one of us could figure out what exactly he wanted to say, but it always came back to Brad.

"Are you talking about Brad Stewart from Wintercrest?" Vera asked him.

James said something incoherent.

"If you're talking about him," Vera went on, "he died a few days ago of a opioid overdose. It was ruled an accident."

He didn't seem to understand what we were telling him. He was one of those happy drunks who were overjoyed like they were on cloud nine after having a drink. It was quite amusing to see someone enjoying life so much — or perhaps he'd forgotten about life in his state of intoxication — and wanted to share that happiness with others.

"So, what are you doing around here?" Sveta asked him. "Are you a tourist too?"

"I came here to see you!" James Stewart replied as he jumped into her arms again.

He kept on talking incoherently until he said that it was time for him to go see someone else. He grabbed a green backpack on the boardwalk — probably his alcohol or God forbid his entire home — and went back to where he came from. The three of us then continued walking, mostly in silence, listening to the subtle noises the river made and looking up at a mixture of stars and satellites. A light breeze blew through my hair and even though it was a little chilly outside I did not feel the cold.

The freedom was the only thing I felt and I wasn't even the one getting married in the next three months. My constellation of angels was looking down on me from above as I stared aimlessly into the distance. Only through the heart can one touch the sky, Rūmī had also written. And my heart was with them wherever they were. Per Svetlana they were with *me*, wherever I was. I closed my eyes as my phone started vibrating in my pocket but were quickly reopened after I heard Anderson's ringtone playing. I yanked it out of my pocket faster than the speed of light and sure enough, Anderson's name showed up on the screen.

"Anderson! Anderson please talk to me!" I pleaded as I answered the phone. "Please just say something!"

There was nothing but silence on the other end of the line but it wasn't a deafening eerie silence. In fact I felt connected to something bigger than me, like eternity was calling or God Himself was on the other end of the line. In that moment I felt as though my heart had literally touched the sky and had landed among the angels. I fell to my knees and held on to the boardwalk's railing to not fall flat on my face.

"I told you that they were right here Aly," Sveta spoke softly as she took my phone from my hand, "God is faithful. God sent you an angel."

God had indeed sent me an angel and if that wasn't a sign of God's grandness I didn't know was. I got back up and stumbled a little bit, all the energy drained from by body and grabbed a hold of my phone. I pressed it to my ear and listened some more. There were a million things I wanted to say but I understood at that point that the universe already knew and understood them so I simply hung up. I clutched my phone in one hand the railing in the other for a few moments as I tried to get myself grounded. I knew that everything was going to be alright so I threw my phone into the river below.

"That move you're probably going to regret."

"It doesn't matter anymore. I'm not a hostage anymore. It's in God's hands now."

The twins each put an arm around me as we walked back to our room in silence. I didn't bother to take a shower, have any snacks or watch TV, I went straight to bed and all the activities I promised Vera went straight out the window. We still had another day ahead of us so I'd make up for it somehow. I drifted into a dreamless sleep as I thought about going to the mall or something. When my eyes opened up again the sun was shining through the dirty hotel room window and the dust particles danced in the air.

The girls were already awake and watching TV. The news channel showed that the west coast had just been blasted with several inches of snow, causing delays, crashes and general chaos. Thankfully the pavement had been bare when I encountered the roundabout! I got up took a shower and got dressed before taking the girls out to breakfast at a restaurant right across the street. Walking through the parking lot to get back to the motel after our meal, we encountered James Stewart, still drunk, stumbling around.

"Well hello there!" James greeted us happily in his drunken stupor.

"Hey James!" Vera greeted him in return. "What brings you here this morning?"

"I came here to see you!"

"Well, that's very sweet of you. Where are you from?"

"Niagara Falls."

"New York or Canada?"

"I don't remember."

The twins and I tried hard to refrain from laughing but a few giggles escaped anyway. James Stewart sounded neither like a Canadian nor a New Yorker. He began laughing too and muttered something about swimming before taking a bottle of vodka out of his backpack. He then dropped his backpack to the ground and took out a second bottle of vodka which he handed to me. I politely thanked him before saying we had to get somewhere. I went back in the hotel room and shoved the bottle under the bed and hoped that nobody would discover it because we were all too young to drink.

At last I took the girls to the mall and made sure that Vera had a great time. The three of us all had a good time window shopping, buying a few things from the thrift store and grabbing some overpriced real fruit smoothies. It was early afternoon by the time all was said and done and I was starting to get hungry. My poached eggs were long gone by the time we got back in the car and headed back for the hotel room. As I drove I spotted a Chinese restaurant and asked the girls if they cared for something there.

"I'm not really up for Chinese food," Vera retorted, "not after what happened last time."

"And what was that?" I asked her.

"We were out with Brad at the Chinese cafe that used to be on Blair street, you know the one that burned down four months ago?"

"Yeah."

"Brad was drunk, and although he wasn't a racist person, he started teasing the Chinese guy. He asked for some *coonyounyanyang* and just some derogatory stuff like that and the cook came out from the back with a knife and chased us out."

"You cannot be serious!"

"That was the first and the last time we had Chinese food."

"Damn, I wish I could've known Brad longer. I liked him from the very first time I met him."

"I know, he was one of those people that you don't meet twice in your lifetime."

I thought about a parallel universe as I drove. We simply couldn't be alone in the entire cosmos. Impossible. There *had* to be more to life than what I could see and touch. I dared to believe that there was something more. I dared to believe that God had great plans for my life and that there was a new beginning for me out there. One for me right *here* in a continuum of endless time and space. Back at the hotel room we collected our belonging and got ready to head back to Wintercrest, and to the airport to pick up Vera's fiance. The bottle of vodka hadn't been discovered by the cleaning staff and the girls hadn't fallen victim to their phobia of peeing in the bed. James Stewart was nowhere to be found. I would have liked to say goodbye but after everything that happened I couldn't help but wonder if he wasn't really a drunken angel with broken wings who had crashed on earth from another realm.

At the airport the girls and I sat in the waiting area, trying to be as patient as we possibly could, waiting for Vladimir to arrive. Vera stared impatiently at the set of doors under the *Arrivals* sign while I aimlessly looked around the place when I swore I caught a glimpse of Anderson from the corner of my eye. I swore it was him from a distance, his emerald green eyes and his unruly hair, everything. I got up and raced towards him amidst the crowded airport. People everywhere blocked my way and prevented me from being able to see him but I didn't want to lose sight of him. I only wanted to find him again, to speak to him one last time and say goodbye. As I was arriving near the exit I felt a pair of hands grabbing me from behind and pulling me back to the real world.

"It wasn't him!" Sveta shouted a couple of times before it finally sank in to my skull.

She basically had to drag me back to the waiting area because I kept on glancing back over my shoulder to see if I could just catch another glimpse of him. Was he looking back at me to see if I was looking back at him? Had he been looking for me all along?

"Look," Sveta tried to be gentle with me, "I know that a heck of a lot has happened recently and your brain must be declaring a state of emergency right now but he's dead Alyson. Anderson isn't coming back."

"But you saw him!" I blurted out.

"Yeah, I saw a young man with bleached hair glancing back over his shoulder for whatever reason it was before he walked out the door."

"Svetlana, I *swear* it was him! I know it's crazy but you have to believe me!"

"I believe that it was real to you Aly, but Anderson is dead."

Nonetheless, I kept on scanning my surroundings looking for him as I followed Sveta back to the waiting area. Vera shot a worried glance at me but she was far too focused on meeting her fiance for the first time to pay much attention to me. I sat down next to her and it wasn't long before the moment of truth arrived.

"That's him!" Vera got up like a rocket when she saw her lover walk through the gate.

I couldn't say I was surprised when I saw him. He looked a lot like Jonas the car salesman from *Ulykken,* one of her favourite Norwegian films. Vladimir had some wide dark green eyes underneath long hair that fell over his face. He was big and athletic and that was rather intimidating but he was very polite and mild-mannered with us. He tried to speak to me in broken English but I couldn't understand a whole lot. Driving back to the Petrov trailer he and the girls couldn't stop talking in Russian. Vladimir seemed to be a decent guy considering that he'd just flown in from Russia and nobody really knew much about him.

He could've been a scammer, a killer, a rapist, a woman even! But it was him. He was the voice over the phone and the man in the pictures Vera had received in the mail. Back at the trailer Dmitry wasn't there, much to our disappointment, so it was just the four of us in the house. Of course Kaye stopped by again but nobody answered the door. Being the nosy person that she was, she stuck her face in the picture window where she could clearly see all of us sitting on the couch in the living room having some snacks and drinks. Sveta taunted her by waving and smiling like it was nothing but after the stunt she'd pulled on me last time, I was furious.

I grabbed my glass of root beer and threw it at the window, aiming straight for her face. Kaye was taken aback by my sudden assault and left immediately after the soda splattered all over the window, the wall and the floor. A pin drop could've been heard in the room after the glass stopped rolling around but Vladimir and the girls looked at me with admiration when I got up to clean up my mess. The three of them helped me and I apologized to the girls for constantly destroying their belongings and dirtying the trailer but they assured me that Kaye had deserved every drop of that root beer.

As I cleaned up the soda that had splashed in the window I looked across the street and noticed that some new tenants had moved in to the previously vacant trailer and the children in there were obviously unsupervised. The two of them, a boy and a girl, were dancing around on the coffee table completely naked pretending they were rockstars. I finished cleaning up quickly and closed the curtains to cover up the child pornography going on on the other side of the road. Shortly thereafter Dmitry arrived and I drove back home, completely exhausted from everything.

"You're home early," my mom exclaimed as I walked through the door, "considering the times you've been coming home lately."

"I'm sorry mom," I apologized, "it's so easy to get carried away in life. I completely forgot what it was like to live for two years."

My parents understood that and that was part of the reason they let me do almost whatever I wanted, like dropping out of school, not getting a job and not paying rent. They treated me as normally as they could and they always had following the massacre, but I could see right through them. On the other hand, as bad as the Belden shooting had been, it was a good excuse for rebellious behaviour. *What was that for Alyson? I survived Belden, cut me some slack.* End of story.

Dear Anderson,

This is the last time I'm writing to you. I've started visiting your parents again lately. You have no idea how much they miss you. I know that visiting them is something you'd like me to do, and I really enjoyed it actually. I'm planning to pay a visit to Elaine and Amanda's graves to talk to them too. Their families have moved out of town and I don't know where they are now so I can't exactly go see them but I owe it to my two other friends to honour them. I imagine myself being there with them at the cemetery on a cloudy day and a single ray of sunlight beaming down on us. Or maybe their names will show up on my caller ID.

It's been so long since I've revisited all these parts of my life that were ripped right out from under my feet when I was least expecting it. And I thought that something like that could never happen to me. It's amazing how your life can change in the blink of an eye like that. You never think it's really true until it happens to you. It taught me so many things though, and I pray that it made me a better person somehow, as cliche as that sounds, even though I may never understand all the reasons why.

I wish I was stronger so that I could make a real difference in the world. Maybe I'll never change the entire world but I hope I can change one person's world because I failed miserably to change yours. Sometimes I wonder what things would be like if you had lived. Would you have been given the death penalty? Would the government have executed you? Would they have let you speak, for the first time in your life? What would you have told the world? I guess that's a rhetorical question because you said what you had to say with a gun in hand.

After Anderson

It's all over now. You can no longer keep me hostage. I forgive you for what you've done and I'm letting you go. Finally I've understood that forgiveness is for me and not necessarily for you. Whether or not you deserve forgiveness or asked for it isn't the issue, but I do. I deserve to be okay. But if you ask me, you do deserve to be forgiven. You deserved a million good things in life. I'm always going to be sorry that you never found what you were looking for but it's time for me to allow myself to live and start seeking what I'm looking for.

May we see each other again someday, even if it's just for a moment.

Alyson

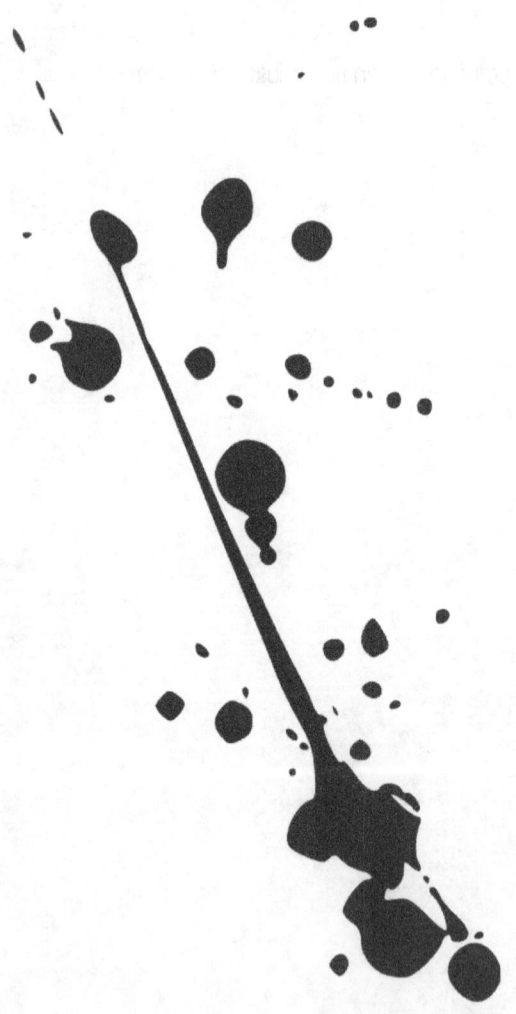

XX

SAID AND DONE

Svetlana ended up with a high school diploma before the New Year rolled around but Vera and I dragged our feet. Vera was much too busy enjoying her new husband to worry about school and I decided to attend an adult learning centre twice a week and volunteer at the animal shelter two more days a week. My dad got a minimum wage job and I began rebuilding my relationship with my little brother. I made new friends and began having a mostly typical social life again. Step by step the pieces were falling into place.

"Are you going to the memorial this time around?" Sveta asked me as the two of us drove back to the trailer after an outing.

"I ought to," I replied with a sigh, "I didn't attend last year because I couldn't handle to see nineteen crosses instead of twenty."

Last year I hadn't attended the ceremony but I had watched an interview that Mr. Pasquale had subsequently given and I couldn't have been more insulted upon hearing him say that he'd done nothing wrong in his usual overly self-righteous diplomatic voice. Had he forgotten what he'd told me after I'd gone to see him, concerned about Anderson? He could've prevented the deaths of twenty people, I was certain of that. At least Anderson's parents had tried to help him, but the school principal had practically turned us into lambs and sent us to be slaughtered.

"Yeah, I understand that. I also understand why there wasn't a twentieth cross at the memorial last year."

"Me too."

"But my uncle knows a carpenter, Perry Barrymore."

"What are you getting at?"

"Well, Perry could build a cross for Anderson."

"You think? I mean, I'm sure he could build one but nobody is going to want it at the memorial."

"Says who? They didn't destroy the cross that was made for him when it was put up there the first time!"

"Maybe not, but he never got another one either after the makeshift memorial was removed."

"Did it ever occur to you that maybe no one dared to build him a cross for last year's memorial because the job was left for you?"

"You're just as crazy as your sister, you know that right?"

"We have the same DNA, remember? So what do you say?"

"Well, I guess we'll have to ask Perry."

"Oh, you don't ask Perry Barrymore anything. You have to *tell* him."

"Then let's have a little chat with him, shall we?"

Svetlana called Perry Barrymore from my phone and told him she needed a cross for the Belden memorial in two days and he immediately agreed to build one but we had to go over there and tell him exactly how we wanted it. Perry lived in Woodpine Township some twenty minutes east of Wintercrest where he was a self-employed carpenter but he owned a motorcycle shop up in New York City where he used to live. He had moved back to Woodpine, where he'd grown up, after his father passed away and left him the house. Rolland Barrymore had been a real estate agent his whole life and he had actually been the one who'd sold my former house to my parents.

Rolland Barrymore had passed away shortly before the Belden massacre. It was such a shame that the old man wasn't around anymore considering that my old house wasn't either. My parents had said that Mr. Barrymore was a very kind man who passionately loved real estate.

He wasn't in it just for the money or the high profile, he was in it because he genuinely cared about the quality of the home and life for all of his clients. He sure had matched my folks with the perfect house, but it was all gone. The house was gone, and he was gone too. And the Petrov sisters were another piece of the puzzle linking my old life to the new one.

"Do you want to go over to Perry's right away, if he's available?" I asked Sveta. "Or do you need to be back at the trailer?"

"Nah, I have no commitments," she responded, "and Perry is also available."

"Just give me directions and I'll get you there. I'll do my best to avoid roundabouts!"

About half an hour later we arrived in front of the large industrial garage door behind Perry's house. I killed the engine and waited for him to come out, open the door and let us in. I was looking forward to getting it over with and not think about Belden again for a very long time. After a few moments a woman came out of the house, got into a vehicle and drove off without paying any attention to us.

"I don't know if he's having trouble with women again," Sveta muttered, "poor guy, he's such a good man but he's been really unlucky with his girlfriends."

"Oh?" I asked.

"Yeah, when his last relationship ended he washed up on our doorstep and my uncle had to console him. The two met at a bar several months prior, where Perry had also washed up to drink away his sorrows after the worst relationship of them all."

"Ouch."

"I don't know why all the nice guys end up with nasty women, and vice versa. His ex-wife sounded like an incarnation of the devil. He spilled the beans to my uncle Dmitry the last time he came over. He said that it was right after New Year's and he was sitting at home all by himself when he got a phone call from his ex-wife. "

"Uh-huh…"

"She told him that she was coming over the following evening. Poor guy didn't know what to do when the time came so he went to the bar just to clear his head, not to get drunk or anything, but he ended up having so many drinks that the bartender refused to sell him anymore alcohol."

"Wow."

"And do you know what the worst part is? He had to call his ex-wife to come pick him up and take him home!"

Just as I burst out laughing the large garage door opened up and Perry signalled me to drive right in. There were four expensive motorcycles parked next to one of the walls in the garage while the other wall was hidden behind industrial equipment and woodworking machines. A large stack of multiple kinds of wood was piled up at the back along with blueprints to build various structures with it. Perry had his own miniature industrial operation going on in his garage and I was impressed with what I saw.

"Alright ladies," Perry spoke in a scratchy voice as we both got out of the vehicle, "it is to my understanding that you want me to build you a cross."

"Yes," I answered, "but right now my main concern is how the hell we're going to bring that thing from here to the memorial site. That cross is gonna be huge!"

"First, let's start off with an approximation of the height and width and then we'll see what we can do for the transportation."

"Alright, let's get to it!"

Perry and I worked out measurements and specifications as best as we could for Anderson's cross considering that I didn't know the specifics of the other ones. The cross wasn't going to be anything fancy, just a big wooden cross with Anderson's name on it that people could write messages on, just like the ones that had been built after the massacre initially occurred. Perry worked his magic right before our eyes and the final product was nothing short of beautiful. The wood was flawless and so was the craftsmanship that had gone into it. The cross could also be easily taken apart and put back together to facilitate transportation, which was still my primary worry.

Svetlana and I made plans for us, Vera and Vladimir to come and pick it up from Perry's place in the middle of the night and erect it along with the other crosses across from the school early the morning of the memorial and then return to bed and pretend that nothing happened. Once the ceremony started at eight thirty, Anderson's cross would be there and we'd just show up at the event like everybody else.

The plan was prone to more than a few hiccups but nobody had a better idea. I then drove Sveta back to the trailer where she would brief Vera and Vladimir about the specifics of our little plan and I would return home and tell my parents that I was planning to attend the memorial without further details. There were thankfully no roundabouts on the way back to the apartment!

"Mom, dad," I hesitantly began because I knew their reactions would be mixed, "I want to attend the Belden memorial this year and I want the two of you to come with me."

Yep, they were shocked.

"Are you sure?" My mom's voice was filled with worry.

"I'm sure mom," I tried to reassure her, "I owe it to all of them to attend, at least this year."

"Okay, we'll be there with you. You know that we're always there for you and that we both love you very much Aly."

"I know, thank you. Oh, and actually we're going to have to meet there because I want to spend the night at Vera and Sveta's place, you know, for moral support."

The moral support the twins gave me was always appreciated, but the real reason I was going to spend yet another night with them was so I didn't have to sneak out in the middle of the night and then try to reenter my own apartment without anybody noticing. Back at the trailer Dmitry Petrov had agreed to keep our secret and cover for us if anything arose unexpectedly. The evening before the memorial he hugged me much tighter than he usually did and told me that I was doing the right thing. Everything was set for us to leave at four in the morning, but then Kaye showed up.

"Buzz off!" Vladimir shouted before grumbling something in Russian that I figured was profanity.

Vladimir turned out to be a very intelligent man, and he and Vera made a great match. Once Kaye left the two of them camped out in Sergey's former room that they'd since converted into their own private sanctuary while Sveta and I slept on my old mattress in her room that she'd since redecorated. Her islamic decor was much more inviting than that big picture of Stalin that had fetched a decent amount of money on an eBay auction. One of the obese cats climbed into bed with us and slouched at my feet.

"I'm real glad you're here Aly," Sveta told me after Dmitry turned off the remainder of the lights inside the trailer, "it's been pretty lonely in this room without my sister."

"I'm glad to be here too, I don't think I would've been feeling this confident alone in my own room," I answered, "and my old mattress is way better than the new one."

The two of us talked about everything under the moon for a while until sleep got the best of me. The noise outside faded in the background and I drifted into a deep, dreamless sleep. The morning came fast, too fast. First it was Sveta's prayer alarm that woke me up and merely a few minutes later Vera came barging in, ripping the shower curtain from the doorframe and shouting at everyone to get up and get ready.

"Five minutes!" I begged.

"More like five seconds!" Vera snapped back.

"Okay, five seconds."

"We've gotta head down to Woodpine Township and get the cross loaded up in the Big Lemon. We're running late so we've got no time to waste!"

I forcefully pulled myself out of bed and got dressed before climbing into the truck only half-awake. Vladimir was behind the wheel while Sveta sat in the middle, I rode shotgun, and Vera sat at my feet. A bigger truck certainly would've been helpful now that three seats weren't enough for the Petrov family but we all did what we could. Perry opened the garage door as soon as the Big Lemon pulled up and helped us load the cross into the back of the truck. Once it was secured in place and we had everything we needed to erect it, we went speeding back down the interstate towards the school.

Thankfully, we only encountered a few tractor trailers, next to no cars and certainly no law enforcement patrol vehicles. Once we arrived at the school most of the things for the ceremony had already been set up. A stage has been built in the sports field behind the school and nineteen crosses had been lined up at the other end of the field. It had rained overnight so the ground was muddy and disgusting but at that point there was no turning back or backing out. Vladimir started digging the hole for the cross while the twins and I unloaded it from the truck and started putting everything together.

By the time everything was said and done everyone was covered in mud but the cross was in place. It stood at a somewhat crooked angle but we'd done the best we could under the circumstances. We then hopped back into the truck and drove back to the trailer park hoping that everything would go according to plan once we returned for the actual ceremony. The whole thing had taken approximately an hour and a half and I was profoundly satisfied with myself. No matter what happened, I was at peace with what I had done.

Back at the trailer Sveta was the first one that jumped in the shower and put on some warn, clean clothes. I went last since I helped Dmitry clean out the truck of mud and dirt before heading back out to the school, not even getting an extra five minutes of sleep. My breakfast had gone down sideways as the anxiety came creeping back in. I had buried Belden so far into the back of my mind and hoped that nobody would ever dig it up again but I had dug it all up myself and was finally ready to put it to rest once and for all no matter how nervous I was in the moment.

By the time we got to the high school there were already plenty of mourners and nosy people there. Most of the people there genuinely wanted to pay their respects to the victims but others only wanted the inside scoop on the lives of other people in the community. The twins and I met up with my parents while Vladimir drove back to the trailer park to pick up Dmitry, and, of course, we saw Kaye. As we walked around I caught a glimpse of Anderson's cross. It was still there, still standing next to the other crosses. People loitered around it just as much as they loitered around the other ones.

"Good morning everyone!"

I did not recognize the voice of the man who was speaking over the airways. It wasn't Pasquale's, which was a big relief. Everyone turned to face the stage where an unknown man who introduced himself as Lloyd Brown — Pasquale's replacement — continued the ceremony's introduction.

"It's great to see such a turnout for this kind of occasion. All of your support is very meaningful to this school and everyone who has been affected by this tragedy. Right off the bat I want to take a few moments of silence to remember the students who were murdered here on this day, two years ago."

The twins and I kept on walking around the crosses as Mr. Brown kept on speaking. I spotted Tammy, Mario and Dominic in the crowd along with a bunch of freshman holding candles. Part of me wanted to show them the finger but I knew that it wasn't an appropriate thing to do. In between two of the crosses I noticed that somebody had erected a little something of their own.

A large photo of Mr. Pasquale was mounted to a decorated cardboard frame with the words *Pray 4 Pasquale* written on top. People were gossiping that he still wasn't doing very well, and I was convinced that his conscience had finally begun haunting him.

Seeing the messages of sympathy that the monster had gotten on his picture frame angered me to the point that I spit in his face and kicked that Pray 4 Pasquale farce into the mud. I knew that he had never really cared about any of those students and had entertained a circus of fake sorrow last year only because they had died in *his* school. But it wasn't his school anymore. Part of me couldn't help but wonder if Mr. Pasquale would have been more lovable if he had perished in the massacre too.

The twins didn't say anything as they followed me. I continued walking along the memorial looking at the crosses adorned with flowers, teddy bears and messages of sympathy. Anderson's cross was covered in as many flowers, stuffed animals and signatures as all the other ones. The community had reacted well to having a cross for him at the memorial. Just as the girls and I stood in front of it Mr. Brown began reading the names of the deceased students.

Elaine Frechette

Frances Mason

Steven Hicks

Tobin Davies

Amanda Andrews

Roger Smith

Katy Henderson

Lynne Taylor

Michael Hazen

Trevor Bradford

Corey Nickels

Eric West

Gary Lewis

Natasha Blackburn

Annie Michelle

Daniel Jonas

Dylan Cardwell

Katherine Price

David Hoban

But not **Anderson Massey.**

I heard a few echoes of people whispering Anderson's name behind me but nobody seemed to be brave enough to shout it. *Please forgive me* I wrote on Anderson's cross. A few moments later the sun came out of the otherwise overcast sky and illuminated the entire memorial grounds. The three of us huddled around the beautiful cross Perry had built just crying and praying. Random strangers joined us and hugged us as they mourned with us. Afterwards I felt compelled to write something else on Anderson's cross.

You are the reason I will never turn a blind eye to anyone else ever again. I want you to know that I deeply cherished our friendship and that one day I will see you again my friend. I know I will. I hope that you are finally gone to a place where you belong.

"Let the rain wash away the pain to a place where it can't be found." Sveta whispered to me as it began to rain again.

I stretched out my arms and felt the tiny raindrops in between my fingers. They were cold but so pure. The heavens above cleansed my soul as the girls and I went back around the memorial grounds a second time, spending a few moments at each cross and writing a few words for each person. Pasquale's picture had seemingly disappeared too, but Sveta found out the hard way that it had only been covered by a thin layer of mud when she slipped on it and landed on the ground, sending mud flying everywhere in the process

"*Molodets*," I told her as Vera and I helped her up, "you smashed Pasquale's face with your butt!"

"I told that school to kiss my ass months ago," her sister continued, "but you're the one who took my *Belden my ass* comment literally!"

The moment was perfect. Pray 4 Pasquale had been reduced to a warped piece of cardboard covered in mud. A teacher walked over to us after she'd seen Sveta in the mud and asked her if she was okay before picking up the piece of cardboard and discarding it in the trash. The three of us laughed before moving on to the other crosses.

"Guard your modesty!" I teased Sveta as we walked forth through the mud.

After the ceremony was over Vladimir brought the twins and I back to my place for lunch and he returned to get Dmitry to go back to the trailer. It had still drizzled a little bit on our way back to the apartment but as soon as we crossed the bridge the sun had come out again. My atmosphere became overcast again, however, when I saw Hans and Jihoon arguing in the parking lot. My parents hadn't made it back from their quick trip to the grocery store yet, and it seemed like it was only us on the lot.

"You're the one who's unreasonable!" Hans shouted at Jihoon.

"What in the world is going on here?" I asked my neighbour as I inserted the key into the lock of my respective apartment's door.

"He came into my apartment unauthorized," Hans grumbled angrily, "and I caught him in the act!"

Why didn't that surprise me? The Petrovs had told me stories of similar incidents in the past. As for Jihoon, he didn't speak, he only gave all of us some dirty looks. I then entered my apartment and found my little brother hiding in the closet, looking frightened, when I opened the door to store my jacket. He then recounted to the twins and I how he hid from Jihoon when he barged into the place and started snooping around. Nothing seemed to be missing from our unit, but Jihoon had nearly scared my brother to death.

Not only that, but it was illegal to enter a rented apartment without permission or without a pressing immediate need, even if you owned the building. As angry and violated as I felt, it unfortunately did not surprise me one bit that Jihoon Garcia had pulled a stunt like that on my folks considering what I knew about him. I could still hear him and Hans shouting at each other outside so I went back out and joined in the screaming match. To my surprise Hans, a usually soft-spoken and gentle man, seemed to be just about ready to brawl with Jihoon.

"He entered our apartment too!" I grumbled. "Nearly made my little brother have a heart attack!"

Shouting in multiple different languages erupted and the next thing I knew fists were swinging and mud was flying. Jihoon had Hans in a chokehold, Vera jumped on Jihoon and I was frantically trying to separate all of them while Svetlana called the police. I elbowed Jihoon so he let go of Hans but in the process I fell in the mud. That did, however, give me an awesome vantage point for what happened next. Sveta leaped like a llama and slugged Jihoon right in the face! He was taken aback and that gave us the opportunity to tackle him and restrain him.

Just at that moment my parents pulled up and my dad leaped out of the vehicle and ran towards us. Hans and I managed to pin down Jihoon while the twins tied his hands behind his back with Sveta's headscarf until the police arrived, which they did approximately thirty seconds later. Two police cars with the sirens on and their tires spinning in the mud of the dirt parking lot pulled up and broke up the brawl. The girls, Hans, Jihoon and I were unrecognizable covered in mud from head to toe. Sveta went digging around looking for her phone that she'd dropped when she came across a pocket watch on the ground.

"You stole that from me you wanker!" Hans shouted at Jihoon as he reclaimed his watch from Sveta.

"Look at what he did to my daughter," my dad muttered out in disbelief, "and her friends! This guy is our landlord!"

The police officers briefly questioned us before taking both Hans and Jihoon to the hospital in an ambulance because they both complained of aches and pains. Hans appeared to have a muscle sprain while Jihoon had a bloody nose and a bloody lip. The fight had broken out because Hans alleged that Jihoon had stolen from him that time he found him in his apartment and said that over time several things had mysteriously disappeared. My little brother testified to what he'd seen and both my parents ranted and raved about how they'd seen Jihoon assaulting the four of us when they arrived.

My parents ended up cooking us a nice little lunch after all while the twins and I took our turns taking a shower and overloading the washing machine with our disgusting dirty clothes. It was nice to sit around the dining room table after the events of the day. It no longer mattered that it was crowded and crammed in the kitchen because we were all in one piece, all safe, and things weren't looking good for Jihoon and his illegal shenanigans. I ate my sandwich and my pasta in silence, secretly thanking God that at the end of the day peace and quiet had at last been restored.

My folks ended up buying a modest little house on the outskirts of town after Jihoon Garcia was banned from owning any rental properties in the municipality of Wintercrest and my dad got a job working for Red Deer Environmental Cleanup. I had nicely settled in and was enjoying life by the time the summer rolled around. Vera and Vladimir had moved out of Wintercrest and shacked up in upstate New York instead. Svetlana was enjoying her last few weeks of freedom with her uncle before she was set to attend university all the way over in Kuwait for a year.

As for me I ended up taking classes at night and working as a part-time postal clerk during the day. Hans had left town as well, and I'd never asked him out on a real date after all. I wasn't particularly interested in things like that at the moment, I was more focused on finishing school and maybe making a few more friends since I wasn't going to see the last one I had for at least a year, if ever. I knew that Sveta didn't like Wintercrest and after graduation I had my own plans to leave too.

"I don't know what I'm gonna do without you here for the next eight or nine months…" I told Svetlana as we both sat in my room after work.

"You could write a book," she proposed casually, "or perhaps two."

I sat at my desk in front of my new laptop and she sat on the desk slouched against the wall, her burgundy headscarf only showing a few flyaway hairs that I'd helped her dye blue the previous evening. A framed picture of the girls and I on the beach in Lavallette hung above her head and another one of Anderson and I adorned the other wall of my cozy little room.

"About what?"

I wasn't much of a writer, I had never really been but perhaps a new hobby would be something positive in my life. I'd only rediscovered life, and part of that came with the realization that I didn't still enjoy many of the things I used to. Discovering my new likes was fun, but everything was still in its early stages.

"Belden? Your life perhaps?"

"Aren't there enough books about school shootings already?"

"But those books don't contain a story like yours. Their authors didn't know Anderson Massey, or any of the shooters the overwhelming majority of the time, but you did."

Several books had been written about Belden by survivors, journalists, psychologists, law enforcement and a bunch of other people I didn't know about. Anderson's psychological profile had also been drawn up and dissected by an endless number of people who thought they could figure everything out, as if the answers weren't plain enough.

"And what would I have to add? Everything's already been said I'm afraid."

"Well, what does the world need to know about Anderson?"

The world could know everything they wanted *about* Anderson Massey, but they'd never *know* him. Perhaps I'd never truly known him either, but do we really know anyone? Only God knows our hearts, but I'd been blessed enough to know a little part of Anderson's.

"That he also had a heart and that he wasn't evil."

IF YOU ENJOYED THIS BOOK PLEASE LEAVE A GOOD REVIEW ON GOODREADS, YOUR BLOG OR AN ONLINE RETAILER OF YOUR CHOICE!

COMMENTARY

This story was originally written in 2014 not long after I walked out of my high school for the last time, after an incident that reminded me a little too much of Columbine for me to feel safe ever returning there. Thankfully no shots were fired, but police cars and armoured vehicles swarmed the place and arrested a 14-year-old boy for plotting to carry out a school shooting.

The previous evening a janitor had found a very detailed hit list that had fallen to the floor — or perhaps dropped on purpose as some would argue — and called the police. Unfortunately, that wasn't the last time gun violence at school would make its way into the community I lived in at the time.

In 2018 it happened again at the local high school I'd once attended as a student doing correspondence classes. A 15-year-old boy walked into school armed with a silver pistol and pointed it straight into another student's face in the hallway after class. Once again, no shots were fired but this time the school's personnel miserably failed to properly address the situation. Instead of calling the police or putting the school on lockdown, the principal covered up the incident.

The student in question was never suspended and several weeks after that incident he brought his gun to school again. This time the police were called but didn't arrest him until later that day at his home. The principal ended up being caught with a black plastic toy gun in his office, saying that that was the weapon the kid had brought to school. Not only was the gun the wrong colour, but why would the principal have kept it in his office even if it had been the actual weapon?!

Unfortunately, students and their parents never got clear answers from law enforcement or the school board as to what really went down that day but one thing is sure: those two incidents left a profound mark on me. I'd never known any of the two kids who felt compelled to take their guns to school but one things stood out to me: I did not feel any hatred or anger towards them.

Au contraire, I felt profound sadness for them, and I might even had feelings of compassion. What had happened in those halls that had been so bad? What had pushed the two of them to that point? Why didn't anyone do anything about it? Bullying is far from the only factor that plays into situations like this, and in this book I never promised answers or a way to miraculously stop the next massacre, but I hope that it will force people to look at things differently. Obviously the current discourse on gun violence at school fails miserably to address the underlying issues. Politicians and lawmakers would much rather push agendas than push real change, in whatever form that change might be.

Nothing can ever excuse or justify mass murder in the classroom but what I noticed in the aftermath was that serious incidents did not bring people together longer than it took for TV camera crews to get enough footage for a news report. After that things went right back to what they'd been before, and often being even worst. The violence had only strengthened the corrupt mentality that had brought us all to that point to begin with.

To be honest, however, I was not surprised that things had gotten to that point at that school in that community after the bullying and other violence involving assaults, stabbings and contraband I'd seen with my own eyes in those same halls while I was a student there myself. My one attempt to express my concerns to the principal left me feeling like the bad guy. Humiliated and in disbelief at the fact that the principal had twisted things around and did not take me seriously, writing this book was how I coped with the crazy things that went on inside my head in the aftermath.

The original story had never gotten far and after the Parkland massacre and the upcoming 20th anniversary of the Columbine massacre I felt that it was an important story to share for reasons that are obvious to anyone who's ever turned on the evening news and seen the chaos and the destruction time after time as school shootings only seem to become deadlier and more common. It's gotten to the point that it's almost normal — and if that doesn't bother you there's something wrong — and at this point it's not that we don't know what to do, it's that we refuse to do it. So what are *you* going to do about it?

I literally grew up in the "age of Columbine" since that happened the year I started school and basically my entire schooling took place under the shadow of that tragedy. All of the new policies, lockdown procedures, changes to the dress code and whatnot that happened over the last twenty years began there. On the other hand, though, I have found security and peace of mind at the academic institution I currently attend here in Ottawa and I am profoundly grateful for that.

I could go on and on and on about these issues but I won't because I highly doubt that I have anything to add that hasn't already been said before, if only we listened. The lessons to be learned are also there, we must only pay attention.

This was the story of what could've been but thankfully, by the grace of God, never was. Unfortunately, we all know that others haven't been so lucky.

Jamila Mikhail
Ottawa, Canada

ABOUT THE AUTHOR

Jamila Mikhail — or simply Mila for short — is an indie author based out of Ottawa, Ontario. She lives a quiet yet always interesting life with her cats Carling and Squeaker in the nation's capital. In 2018 she received the title of *Top Writer* on Quora and various awards and delightful editorial reviews for her previous writings.

A polyglot and a fierce defender of human rights, Mila can often be found protesting on Parliament Hill or eating shawarma and Beavertails in the ByWard Market when she's not sitting in a classroom or a lecture hall being taught things she already knows. She has a good sense of humour and likes to write snail mail letters because she tends to be paranoid of the spam and scams of social media.

To contact Mila you can log on to www.jamilamikhail.com or ride the new O-Train long enough to find her in her olive green headscarf.

GET IN TOUCH

Visit www.jamilamikhail.com for a list of mental health resources, more books, bonus stories, cat videos and all links to social media and how to get in touch with the author. Don't forget to sign up for the newsletter to receive exclusive deals and a bunch of free stuff!

Instagram: https://www.instagram.com/keepyourgoodheart/

Twitter: https://twitter.com/keepurgoodheart

Facebook: https://www.facebook.com/JamilaMikhail42375/

Patreon: https://www.patreon.com/jamilamikhail

Author Central: https://www.amazon.com/-/e/B078TQD7K6

COPYRIGHT INFORMATION

Front cover image, "Hallway Abandoned Damaged Deserted" by user Free-Photos on Pixabay <https://pixabay.com/en/hallway-abandoned-damaged-deserted-1245845/> available under a CC0 1.0 Universal Public Domain Dedication license <https://creativecommons.org/publicdomain/zero/1.0/> Used with permission.

Back cover image, "Glass Broken Fragmented Hole Crack" by user kiragraphie on Pixabay <https://pixabay.com/en/glass-broken-fragmented-hole-crack-1497229/> available under a CC0 1.0 Universal Public Domain Dedication license <https://creativecommons.org/publicdomain/zero/1.0/> Used with permission.

Bullet holes vector graphics, "Bullet Holes Target Shooting Gunshot" by user Clker-Free-Vector-Images on Pixabay <https://pixabay.com/en/bullet-holes-target-shooting-gunshot-36943/> available under a CC0 1.0 Universal Public Domain Dedication license <https://creativecommons.org/publicdomain/zero/1.0/> Used with permission.

Image on page 218, "Desperate Stress Stressed Problem" by user BedexpStock on Pixabay <https://pixabay.com/en/desperate-stress-stressed-problem-2676556/> available under a CC0 1.0 Universal Public Domain Dedication license <https://creativecommons.org/publicdomain/zero/1.0/> Used with permission.

Image on page 234, "Ammunition Munitions Ammo Bullets" by user OpenClipart-Vectors on Pixabay <https://pixabay.com/en/ammunition-munitions-ammo-bullets-147588/> available under a CC0 1.0 Universal Public Domain Dedication license <https://creativecommons.org/publicdomain/zero/1.0/> Used with permission.

Image on page 244, "Splatter Blood Drops Paint Color" by user Clker-Free-Vector-Images on Pixabay <https://pixabay.com/vectors/splatter-blood-drops-paint-color-303569/> available under a CC0 1.0 Universal Public Domain Dedication license <https://creativecommons.org/publicdomain/zero/1.0/> Used with permission.

Vector graphic on spine, "Gun Pistol Weapon Handgun Military" by user BedexpStock on Pixabay <https://pixabay.com/en/gun-pistol-weapon-handgun-military-2864368/> available under a CC0 1.0 Universal Public Domain Dedication license <https://creativecommons.org/publicdomain/zero/1.0/> Used with permission.